AMPED

Douglas E. Richards

Paragon Press

ISBN: 978-0-9853503-1-4

First Edition

Printed in the United States of America

ALSO BY DOUGLAS E. RICHARDS

WIRED

THE CURE

Middle Grade/YA
(for ages 9-adult)

The Prometheus Project: Trapped (Book 1)

The Prometheus Project: Captured (Book 2)

The Prometheus Project: Stranded (Book 3)

The Devil's Sword

Ethan Pritcher, Body Switcher

Out of This World

ABOUT THE AUTHOR

Douglas E. Richards is the *New York Times* & *USA Today* bestselling author of *WIRED*, its sequel, *AMPED*, and *THE CURE*. He has also written six middle grade/young adult novels widely acclaimed for their appeal to boys, girls, and adults alike. In 2010, in recognition of his work, he was selected to be a "special guest" at San Diego Comic-Con International, along with such icons as Stan Lee, Ray Bradbury, and Rick Riordan. Douglas has a master's degree in molecular biology (aka "genetic engineering"), was a biotechnology executive for many years, and has authored a wide variety of popular science pieces for *National Geographic*, the *BBC*, the *Australian Broadcasting Corporation*, *Earth and Sky*, *Today's Parent*, and many others. Douglas currently lives in San Diego, California, with his wife, two children, and two dogs.

To my insanely talented sister, Pamela Richards Saeks, for her undying encouragement, support, and assistance, which have all meant the world to me.

AMPED

Douglas E. Richards

Paragon Press

PROLOGUE

Kira Miller approached the bulky contraption in the center of an isolated lab in the nuclear physics complex and couldn't help but smile. It was about the size of a small car and looked like a Rube Goldberg device constructed by a plumber, or an abstract sculpture that had escaped from a museum of modern art.

But it was neither of these things.

Instead, it was the holy grail of energy production. A cold fusion reactor. A generator that would basically run on water and produce clean energy at a fraction of the current cost. Something that would revolutionize the world if it could be perfected. And if they *let* it.

David Desh, standing beside Kira, extended his right arm toward one section of the device and ran his hand along several of its many surfaces. Desh was technically Kira's husband, although they only had a small wedding with a few friends in attendance, and no marriage certificate had ever been filed. In the eyes of the United States they were not husband and wife. On the other hand, in the eyes of the United States they were also both dead, buried in separate cemeteries, and long since decayed, so this wasn't surprising.

It was well after hours and Kira, Desh, and their friend and close colleague, Ross Metzger, were alone in the expansive facility—one with a state-of-the-art electronic security system set to ensure they remained that way. The company, *Advanced Physics International*, had been purchased from its founder a year earlier by a broker, keeping the deep-pocketed financiers behind the transaction anonymous. Ross Metzger had been installed as CEO, and he immediately hired a president to run day-to-day operations while he worked on projects of his own.

Metzger walked over and stood by the reactor he had built in what was essentially his private lab. A lab designed to lock up tighter than Fort Knox when he wasn't inside with just a scan of his thumbprint.

"This version is putting out about two percent more power than I'm putting in," he explained. "Which isn't enough to get excited about, by itself. But it proves the concept. And my smarter half is convinced he can improve this a hundred fold."

Desh whistled.

"Congratulations," said Kira warmly, leaning over and giving him a hug and then a peck on the cheek.

"Thanks," said Metzger. "But we have your therapy to thank." He grinned sheepishly. "Let's face it, I don't have a clue how it works. *Or* how to improve it."

Kira Miller was a genetic engineer who had developed a gene therapy treatment that for short periods of time could dramatically increase human intelligence. Metzger had only gotten as far as he did because of it.

Like the rest of them, only eighteen months earlier Ross Metzger had lived a far different life. He had been a special operations major, an officer and pilot with a keen technical mind who was well schooled in aeronautics and avionics. He enjoyed math and electrical engineering in the same way that others enjoyed chess, and he had continued to learn exotic mathematics, electronics, and even cutting edge robotics as a hobby.

Now he was completely off the grid and on the core council of a team with grander capabilities and ambitions than any group in history. But a team woefully short of physicists.

So when Kira had learned of his hobby, she had pressed him into service, and he had spent months reading everything he could about nuclear physics, quantum mechanics, and chemistry. He had spent hour after endless hour carefully reading texts that were largely incomprehensible to him, knowing that during the short periods in which he was enhanced his soaring mind would find the memory traces of these thousands of pages of complex reading and grasp it all, and much more, in mere minutes. While nothing could take the place of an enhanced world-class physicist who had spent a lifetime acquiring knowledge of the field, Kira had been convinced that for a very focused problem like cold fusion, Metzger's aptitudes and background, combined with the mother of all cram sessions, could work. The proof that she was right was now an unsightly jumble of hardware in front of them.

Metzger suggested the group adjourn to a nearby conference room so Desh could fill him in on the new facilities they were building, which were nearing completion. Before accompanying the two men, Kira took one last look at the reactor and ran her hand along some of its surfaces as had her husband. Doing so would never have occurred to her if not for him, but perhaps his boyish impulse to experience things tactilely really did allow him to better appreciate the essence of the device more fully. And if Metzger could improve it the way he thought he could—or at least the way his alter ego, with an IQ amped to the stratosphere, thought he could—this would be historic stuff.

Or maybe not. Kira couldn't help but caution herself. Whether it would be released or not was still unclear.

Kira Miller had written the book on the science of unintended consequences. She had found a way to double the span of human life only to find upon further analysis that releasing this discovery to the world would end in disaster. That such a profound increase in human longevity would cause devastating overpopulation, economic collapse, and the inevitable self-destruction of the human race. Now she insisted that the implications of even the most breathtaking discoveries be analyzed, ad nauseam, before releasing them into the wild.

Energy this cheap and abundant would power homes, businesses, cars, and factories. It would drive an unprecedented explosion of growth in world economies, changing the face of civilization overnight. But would it be *too* revolutionary? Would the tectonic shift it would cause be *too* dramatic and disruptive? And what would oil based economies—often in the world's most volatile regions and in the hands of the most ruthless regimes—do when the rug was pulled out from under them and their ocean of money was about to run dry? Go to war? Unleash weapons of mass destruction?

Assuming the device was perfected, the final analysis would be done by the core council when their minds were amplified, but even so these questions would be brutally difficult to answer.

Kira quickly caught up to her husband and Ross Metzger, who led them from his lab, past the recessed thumbprint scanner just outside the door, and into a short hall. Just beyond this was another lab, about half a football field in length, with a high ceiling. It was packed with monitors, lasers, and exotic physics equipment of every kind. Even so, it was so spacious and well laid out that it was anything but crowded.

Just past the lab they arrived at one of the company's four conference rooms. Black, high-back swivel chairs surrounded a long conference table whose cherry wood veneer was so polished it had become reflective. They settled in and began a lively discussion.

Twenty minutes later they were interrupted by a grinding sound coming from Ross Metzger's pocket. He glanced down suspiciously and pulled out his vibrating phone. "Sorry," he said. "Wasn't expecting any messages." He tapped the screen a few times with his index finger and frowned.

Desh raised his eyebrows. "Problem?"

"I'm sure it's nothing," he replied. "But I should check it out anyway. Wait here. I'll be back in five minutes." He walked to the door, but turned back before he exited. "Five minutes," he repeated with a sly grin. "Don't let me catch the two of you in any compromising positions when I return."

Desh smiled back. "Come on Major, give us *some* credit. We're not hormone gushing high school kids," he said in mock indignation. "I think we can manage to keep our hands off of each other for *five minutes.*" He stared at Kira lecherously and raised his eyebrows. "On the other hand, since you brought it up and all . . ."

Metzger shook his head and exited, making a show of leaving the conference room door open as he did so.

Desh pulled Kira up from her chair and gathered her in his arms. "I've always liked the way Ross thinks," he said, and then brushed his lips gently against hers. She responded by moving even closer and kissing him with a tender, unhurried passion. Thirty seconds later their lips parted and they opened their eyes.

And they were blind.

Their faces were almost touching, but they couldn't see each other at all.

The entire facility had become an impenetrable cave.

Desh carefully extricated himself from the embrace, and as he did so the backup generator on premises took over and the lights snapped on with a loud *thunk*—and then back off, plunging them once again into absolute darkness.

Kira surged to a heightened level of alertness. A power outage could have been accidental, but one followed immediately by an outage of the backup generator *had to be deliberate.*

"We've got trouble," whispered Desh unnecessarily. He reached out clumsily until he found Kira's hand and took it in his.

Kira fished in her pocket with her other hand until she felt the metal LED penlight attached to her key ring. It was a red cylinder about the size of a double-A battery. Small but surprisingly powerful. She unclipped it from the ring, turned it on, and pressed it into Desh's free hand. He shielded the light in his palm so that it provided just enough illumination for them to find the open door, and peered cautiously into the hall.

Kira jumped as a burst of gunfire filled the air, coming from the direction of Metzger's lab. The all pervading darkness amplified her startle reflex and her heart accelerated wildly.

Desh had seen considerable action in the special forces and the gunfire threw his mind and body into a heightened state of alertness that few could match. He swept the tiny penlight in an arc through the lab until he discovered the base of a bulky, high-energy laser. Without power it was nothing more than a large paperweight—but it could still serve as a fortified hiding place. He rushed to it, almost dragging Kira behind him in his haste. "Wait here," he whispered. "I'll be back soon."

"I'm coming with you," she whispered back. "You know I can fend for myself."

"I know you can. But wait here anyway," he replied firmly, rushing off in the direction of the gunfire with the penlight as he did so, leaving Kira once again in total darkness and with no way to follow.

She crouched low behind the heavy steel base of the laser and strained her hearing to its limits. She was tempted to activate her cell phone for the light it would give off, but knew this would only serve to give her position away.

Shit, she thought angrily. They had become too complacent. Too sure they were completely off the grid and that their hacking skills were too accomplished for them to ever be discovered. Too sure that their breakthrough advances in electronics and optics, which they used to transmit false images to street cameras and otherwise hide their existence, were foolproof.

After a few torturously long minutes of absolute silence she heard someone enter the far end of the large lab. Was it David? If not, her only chance was to remain as quiet as possible and hope she wasn't spotted.

Blood pounded in her ears. Not being able to see an inch in front of her was unnerving on a primal level. She had been in any number of deadly situations against incredible odds, but she couldn't remember ever feeling as helpless, or afraid, as she did now.

A faint light source accompanied the person into the lab—*a partially covered penlight.* Her heart swelled with relief. It had to be David.

The form was moving quickly in her direction, slamming into small obstacles as it did so. But as it neared she could vaguely make out a bulky, monstrous shape; a shape that couldn't possibly be David. A shape that couldn't even be *human.*

She opened her mouth to gasp when what she was seeing finally registered. It was David, all right. But he was running with a large body draped perpendicularly over his neck and shoulders, in a classic fireman's carry.

An instant later she realized that the man he was wearing like a two hundred pound scarf was Ross Metzger.

He was unconscious. And quite possibly even dead.

***

Desh thrust the tiny flashlight into Kira's hand as he reached her location. "Lead us to an office," he whispered, his movement remarkably steady given the dead weight draped around his shoulders and neck. "Hurry."

Kira began picking her way between the equipment, with Desh behind her.

"Ross?" she asked simply.

"Gunshot to the stomach. I applied a makeshift bandage, but he doesn't have much time."

Less than a minute later they arrived at a row of large offices. Kira chose the fourth one down and threw open the door. Desh carefully lowered Metzger to the floor just outside. He searched his friend's pockets, hoping for matches or a lighter, but came away with only a cell phone. He handed this to Kira and followed her into the office.

"A large group of Commandoes breached the facility," whispered Desh. "A few dismantling the cold fusion reactor. Ross was able to draw the others into his lab as well. He was shot, but he managed to crawl out and scan his thumb to seal up the room."

The battery-powered steel outer walls of the lab had just finished sliding into place, taking the men inside by surprise, when Desh had arrived.

"Before Ross lost consciousness he told me there were at least six of them, all in black," continued Desh grimly. "And all with night vision equipment. He said he could tell from their equipment and weaponry that they weren't affiliated with the U.S. military or black-ops, but were high priced mercenaries. The cream of the crop."

"Mercenaries hired by whom?" whispered Kira.

Desh shook his head helplessly. He had no idea. And he had no idea how they had managed to pull it off, either. What they had done should have been *impossible*. No team was *that* good. They had breached a facility protected by electronic security second to none—without setting off a single alarm. They had killed main and backup power using timing a Swiss watch would envy.

Desh guessed they had only made one mistake. One of them must have tripped a sensor in Ross's lab when they had begun to dismantle the reactor, which had alerted him. Since breaching the company after hours without an alarm going off was impossible, Metzger must have thought the sensor had malfunctioned.

A deeply troubled expression marred Kira's flawless complexion. "How long before they break out of Ross's lab?" she whispered.

"Five minutes—ten minutes tops."

"Five or ten *minutes*? I've seen the specs. It should take them hours—at best. You think they're *that* good?"

"Better," replied Desh simply. "But they'll have to be cautious while they're pulling their Houdini, just to be sure I'm not waiting to pick them off as they exit. So maybe ten to fifteen."

Desh fell silent as he thought through their options. These men were sure to be running this op by the numbers, which meant they'd have at least one man watching the exit and one watching the parking lot, each with night vision equipment of their own. A blind man going up against a sighted adversary had about as much chance as a naked man going up against a tank.

Desh knew he only had one hope: he had to even the playing field.

If only they had brought a gellcap, the ultimate in emergency protection, things would be different. But they had become convinced they were safely off the radar. And they had decided that amplifying their intelligence outside of a secure facility, invoking their brilliant but often sociopathic alter egos, wasn't worth the risk.

Kira lit up both cell phones in her possession and handed Desh the penlight. He began rifling through desk drawers. He stopped when he found a pocket-sized packet of facial tissue. He carefully removed all of the remaining tissue and cracked open the door, shining the penlight down the hall in both directions. The coast appeared to be clear.

"Stay by the door," he instructed Kira. "I'm gonna torch the place. It'll nullify their night vision advantage and set off alarms."

The facility conducted ultra-high temperature experiments on a regular basis, so while powerful hoses were located in each lab, an automatic sprinkler system had not been installed.

"Good thinking," said Kira.

"If we're lucky they'll decide to take their reactor and call it a night."

Desh glanced at Kira's worried but dazzling face and could tell her mind was racing. "Hold on a second," she said. She tapped the screen of Ross's phone three times and held it to her ear.

The call was quickly answered and a young woman's voice came over the phone. "9-1-1. What is your emergency?"

"There's a huge fire at Advanced Physics International on Industrial Parkway!" she blurted hysterically. *"Send fire trucks right away! And an ambulance. There's a man here with a gunshot wound to the stomach. Hurry!"* she finished, ending the connection.

Desh nodded in admiration. "Well done," he said, stacking a loose pile of facial tissue on the floor near the desk. He didn't have matches, but he had been trained to improvise with whatever was at hand. He removed the cover from the back of his cell phone, popped out its thin, wafer sized battery, and scraped the plastic away from the positive and negative leads on one edge with his pocket knife. He then laid the blade across both leads, creating a short that shot sparks into the stack of tissue. An ember was born almost immediately, and seconds later he had nursed it into a flame. He carefully fed it sheets of loose paper and in less than a minute the flames were licking up the sides of the wooden desk.

Finally, Desh tossed the cell phone battery into the adolescent fire and retreated to the door. The outer part of the battery quickly melted away to unleash the lithium inside, which was violently combustible and erupted the fire to double its size.

The light from this office bonfire was more than welcome, but the heat was already becoming intense. Even so, within five minutes he needed this entire section of offices to become a raging blaze; a wall of fire reaching up to the ceiling.

Desh used the penlight to verify the hall was still clear and then hefted Metzger back into position slumped across his neck and shoulders.

"We need to help it spread," he said to Kira, and then rolled up some paper and held it against the edge of the fire. When it took, he moved rapidly to an office two doors down, seemingly oblivious to the weight he was carrying, and tossed the makeshift torch onto a pile of stapled papers on the desk. Kira took his lead and did the same to an office two doors down in the opposite direction.

They waited almost five minutes as the fire leaped from one office to another, growing exponentially at a staggering rate.

"Let's go," said Desh finally, heading toward the building's entrance. "We'll stay close to the fire and keep it at our backs. Night vision will be useless and we won't have to worry about attacks from behind. But stay alert to everything in front of us," he cautioned.

The building was becoming ever hotter as the blaze continued to double in size every minute or so. The bigger it got the faster it spread, and they found they had to keep farther and farther ahead of the invisible wall of unbearable heat that extended outward from the raging wall of flames. Worse, air quality was quickly deteriorating, and every lungful of air seemed to have a lower oxygen content, and a higher smoke and soot content, than the one before. They began coughing.

Desh made a command decision. The fire was giving off enough light now that they could leave it a much greater distance behind them. It was time to go for broke. He communicated his thoughts to Kira and covered the remaining thirty-five yards to the main lobby at a slow jog.

They arrived about twelve minutes after they had started the fire and took cover behind an oversized marble reception desk, crouching low to avoid being seen. Desh lowered Metzger to the floor and considered their options.

If a merc or two were still manning the entrance, their night vision would now be useless, but that didn't mean they couldn't spot Desh and Kira the old fashioned way. It just meant that both sides would now be able to see, taking away a huge advantage from the mercs but still leaving them with superior weaponry and a far superior tactical position.

Desh's eyes swept the periphery of the lobby, calculating possible approaches. Finally he peered cautiously around the reception desk, wondering if he would be greeted by immediate gunfire.

His eyes widened in excitement. Firemen were streaming into the building, pulling on oxygen masks as they did so. And there was no sign of armed mercenaries. If any had been guarding the door, they appeared to be gone. Tension poured from Desh's body.

He shot Kira an expression of relief and motioned for her to take a look. She did so and blew out a long, grateful breath, while Desh pressed two fingers against the carotid artery in Metzger's neck.

A horrified look came over his face.

Metzger hadn't made it. They had been just a few minutes away from getting him to an ambulance. But they had been too late.

As hardened as Desh was, he reeled from the loss. For a few seconds he couldn't breathe, as though he had been sucker punched in the gut. His reaction told Kira everything she needed to know. A tear escaped from her eye and rolled down her face.

Desh forced his mind back from the depths of despair. They weren't out of the woods yet. He would have to mourn the loss of his friend another time. He and Kira had a long night ahead of them. They couldn't afford to be questioned and would need to slip away while everyone was distracted.

Desh lifted his friend so the fire wouldn't take his body, and he and Kira headed toward the entrance. While it was possible the assault team was still in Metzger's lab surrounded by flame, Desh was nearly certain that they had escaped.

But who were they? Where had they gotten their information? And what was their ultimate objective? He had absolutely no idea.

All he knew for sure was that Kira and their group were no longer off the grid. That they had been caught with their pants down by a lethal and exceedingly capable adversary. And that this unknown adversary was almost certain to strike at them again.

PART ONE

"Internet servers worldwide would fill a small city, and the K (the world's most powerful supercomputer) sucks up enough electricity to power 10,000 homes. The incredibly efficient brain sucks up less electricity than a dim lightbulb and fits nicely inside our head. The human genome, which grows our body and directs us through years of complex life, requires less data than a laptop operating system."

—Mark Fischetti, Computers vs. Brains
Scientific American, November, 2011

1

Seth Rosenblatt paused on his way to the parking lot to take in his surroundings. No matter how many visits he made to this place, how many times he walked the tranquil, idyllic wooded grounds, he always felt awestruck and privileged to be here, where giants had stood on the shoulders of other giants to see ever farther into the previously impenetrable secrets of nature. Here was a cloistered retreat that had welcomed and financed the likes of Albert Einstein, John von Neumann, Kurt Godel, Alan Turing, J. Robert Oppenheimer, and Freeman Dyson. For a physicist there was no more hallowed ground.

He soaked in the ambience of Princeton's fabled *Institute for Advanced Study* one last time before walking to his rental car, wanting to put off leaving the grounds for as long as he could manage, especially since he was going straight to the airport for a brutal flight to Tokyo. He hated flying. He hated lines and pat downs and cramped seats with too little legroom for his lanky body. He hated stale, recycled, dehydrating airplane air. A trip from the East Coast to Japan, with a stop in California, seemed never-ending.

Just as he entered the nearly deserted lot where he had parked, a white minivan appeared out of nowhere and began hurtling toward him. Rosenblatt froze, waiting for the driver to see him and take corrective action. Precious seconds passed before he was finally able to comprehend the incomprehensible: the driver hadn't just failed to see him for a brief moment; the driver had seen him and was intent on turning him into *road kill*.

His muscles tensed for action but he knew at a visceral level that it was too late: he couldn't possibly remove himself from the vehicle's path in time. He closed his eyes and braced for the bone crushing impact.

Mercifully, the impact never came. At the last instant the minivan swerved sharply and screeched to a halt in front of him, its side doors only two feet from his face.

Rosenblatt's profound terror transformed into pure rage, directed squarely at the asshole who had dared to scare him so intensely. *"What in the hell are you doing?"* he bellowed. *"Are you crazy?"*

While he was shouting the minivan's side door began to glide open. As the sight of this pierced through his fog of rage, alarm bells blared in his head. Panicked, he began to spin around to face what he now guessed was there.

Before he could turn, his arm was seized in an iron grip. As Rosenblatt's instincts had warned him, someone had stealthily—almost magically—maneuvered behind him. The man twisted Rosenblatt's arm painfully behind his back and used the limb to propel him through the now open minivan door, where a partner was waiting to catch him as he spun inside.

As Rosenblatt struggled to grasp what was happening he felt the bite of a syringe as it was plunged into his leg, straight through his pants. He tried to make sense of the pain message coming from his thigh, but his thoughts were strangely disjointed, and by the time he realized he had been stabbed, and with what, his body went totally limp and a blanket of darkness rushed up to greet him.

"Well done," the driver said to his two associates. And with that, he pulled out of the lot and drove calmly through the streets of Princeton, as though he were a senior citizen intent on nothing more than enjoying the scenery.

2

Seth Rosenblatt's return to consciousness was sudden, but his eyes were still heavy and he only managed to open them halfway. Seated across a small metal table from him was the driver of the minivan, holding an empty syringe, which no doubt had been used to revive him. The man had the patient look of someone who was happy to give his prisoner time to fully regain his faculties and take stock of his situation and surroundings.

Both of Rosenblatt's hands were cuffed to a steel chair that was affixed to the floor, and he was inside a small, windowless steel shed, a portable structure you might buy at Home Depot to put in your yard and store your rakes and lawnmowers. But this one was pristine. For all he knew it, and he, were still *in* a Home Depot.

He realized with a start that his watch and clothes had been removed, and he was now wearing a zippered one-piece gray jumpsuit. He tried to ignore his drug-induced lethargy and growing panic and focus. *He had to concentrate.*

A large dose of adrenaline hit his bloodstream and blasted the last bit of grogginess from his system, but he retained his slumped posture and nearly closed eyes to buy more time.

What was going on? He was the last person anyone would want to kidnap. Unless these men *knew.* But how? *It couldn't be.* But even as he thought this he realized there was no other explanation for his abduction and the care, speed, and precision of his abductors.

How long had he been out? He had no way to tell for sure, but he didn't think it had been long. The makeshift nature of the shed lent support to the thesis that whoever had grabbed him was in a hurry. The fact that they suspected or knew he had advanced technology imbedded in his clothing that could be used to send a distress signal was highly troubling. He had to also assume they knew he would be missed if he was out of touch for too long, which added further support to his hypothesis that little time had elapsed and he wasn't very far from the Institute. They had also snatched him right before his long flight overseas, when he would be expected to be out of touch for as long as twenty-four hours. Coincidence? He doubted it.

He felt an odd throbbing in both ears and had an eerie suspicion that his every orifice had been probed, and every inch of his body, from his scalp to between his toes, had been checked and rechecked—for what, only his attackers knew.

Rosenblatt fought to steady his still racing pulse. He was terrified to a depth he had never before experienced. He studied his abductor, the only other inhabitant of the shed, from the corner of one heavily lidded eye as the man continued to wait patiently for him to become fully alert. The steel structure was illuminated by two tall patio lamps that had been set up inside. The man seated across the table had a calm but intense air about him, a head of short black hair, and a lean, athletic build. Rosenblatt estimated he was in his late thirties.

Rosenblatt guessed his chances were less than even money to live out the day. These men were too professional. And they had let him see their faces.

He took a deep breath and opened his eyes all the way for the first time. He shook his head as if to clear it. "What the hell is going on here?" he demanded.

The driver tilted his head but did not respond.

"Look," continued Rosenblatt anxiously, knowing he needed to pretend that he didn't know what this was about. "You can have anything you want. I'll give you my ATM code. *Whatever you want,*" he pleaded. "Just let me go and I promise to forget this ever happened."

The slightest of smiles played out on the driver's face. "That's a very generous offer, Dr. Rosenblatt," he said. "But I'm afraid I'll have to pass."

"How do you know my name?" demanded Rosenblatt, feigning surprise. "Who *are* you?"

The driver studied him dispassionately, as though he were an insect under a magnifying glass. "Call me Jake," he replied at last. "I'm with the government—the military." He shrugged. "Well, more like *outside* of the government. Congress and the president vaguely know of our existence, but they don't want to know more. They can't. Plausible deniability. I run a black-ops unit responsible for keeping our country safe from weapons of mass destruction. From threats so great I have a free hand to do whatever I have to do to stop them."

"Weapons of mass destruction?" repeated Rosenblatt in disbelief. "*Are you mad?* You're making a *horrible* mistake. Whoever you're looking for, I'm not it."

"I agree with you," said the man who called himself Jake. "But you're the key to *finding* who I'm looking for." He paused. "Look, Dr. Rosenblatt, I'm a reasonable man. And I happen to think you're an innocent caught up in something way over his head. So as long as you're completely honest with me, we're going to be good friends." He spread his hands out in front of him, palms up. "But if you aren't totally forthcoming, things can get uglier than I suspect you're capable of even comprehending. Do we understand each other?"

"Yes. You're threatening to torture me."

Jake sighed. "Not at all. I wouldn't *think* of using physical torture. What I have in mind is worse. *Far* worse. Trust me, if you don't tell me what I want to know you'll wish in every fiber of your being that I *had* tortured you." He shook his head and looked sincerely troubled. "Please don't give me any reason to elaborate further. There's already more than enough unpleasantness in the world."

"This is crazy. The reason we have laws is to prevent mistakes like this from happening. To prevent innocent people from being terrorized by their own governments. Groups like yours, not answerable to anyone, abuse their power every time. It's inevitable."

"Don't believe everything you see in the movies, Dr. Rosenblatt. Military units like mine have become the go-to villain in Hollywood, but we *are* answerable, just like every other agency. Someone has to watch the watchers, after all."

"Like who?"

"Other black-ops groups review our actions on a routine basis. In the heat of battle, soldiers have to be able to make life and death decisions. They have a license to kill, and tragically, sometimes innocents become collateral damage. But their actions are reviewed, and if they exceed the rules of engagement, abuse their power, they are brought up on charges. The same goes for us. If I go off the reservation, if I kill innocents who aren't clearly collateral damage, I'll be judged and put in a military prison—or even executed."

"And what happens when— "

"Enough!" said the black-ops agent in a clipped whisper that, while low in volume, was off the charts in intensity and so commanding it was impossible to ignore. "We're not here to talk about me, or for me to justify my existence. I've told you more than I should have already."

Jake reached down into his lap and revealed a sleek tablet computer. He used its outer case to prop it up on the table facing Rosenblatt. He slid his finger across the screen and a document appeared, the pages turning automatically every few seconds. Each page was crammed with exotic, multicolored geometric shapes that could only be generated by a computer and dense equations that to the layman looked like nothing more than Sanskrit written by pigeons.

The black-ops agent rubbed the back of his head absently as he studied his prisoner. "Recognize this?"

Rosenblatt shook his head.

"Really?" said Jake skeptically, raising his eyebrows. "Well, let me help you out. I'm told it's a stunning advance in the mathematics and physics of the Calabi-Yau manifold. I had no idea what this was. But my science people tell me it's a six-dimensional space that results when the ten dimensions of superstring theory are rolled up. This means nothing to me, of course, but I know it does to you. You sure you don't recognize it?"

"Positive."

"That's interesting. Because we got this from your computer."

Rosenblatt's eyes widened in disbelief. "What?"

"You're a far better physicist than you are actor," said Jake, shaking his head in disappointment. "Now I wouldn't know a Calabi-Yau manifold if one bit me in the ass. But the three world-renowned physicists we gave this to were salivating over it so much I'm surprised they didn't collapse from dehydration. They're stunned by it. They seem to believe this leapfrogs everything known about the mathematics and physics of this area. That it contains numerous breakthroughs—at least the stuff they're capable of grasping, which is only the tip of the iceberg. I'm told they feel like primitives trying to grasp calculus." He leaned closer to Rosenblatt. "What I'd really like to know, professor, is how you were able to do work this advanced." His voice was soft but with a razor edge of intensity and menace. "I'm all ears."

"You actually think *I* did this?" said Rosenblatt, an incredulous expression on his face. "Look, if you say you found this on my computer, I have no choice but to believe you. But *I* didn't put in there. Yes, I've dabbled a bit in this area, but that's it. You said yourself that this is far beyond even the top people in the field—and I'm not even one of these."

"Okay. I'll humor you for a moment. If *you* didn't put this on your computer, then why don't you tell me who did."

"I have no idea," responded Rosenblatt with a shrug. His eyes narrowed in thought. "The only possibility I can see is that it was done by a modern day Ramanujan."

"Ramanujan?"

"Yes. Srinivasa Ramanujan. He was a math prodigy who grew up in India with virtually no formal training. Out of the blue he sent a sample of his work to a world class mathematician at Cambridge named Hardy. Hardy recognized his brilliance right away." He paused. "You ever see the movie *Good Will Hunting?*"

The black-ops agent shook his head no.

"Well, that's not important. My point is that this Ramanujan was unknown to the world, but was in a class all his own. A guy like that must be responsible for this. What else could it be? I bet he designed a worm and sent it to the computers of thousands of scientists. Don't know why he'd do it anonymously, but that's probably what happened."

A slow smile crept over Jake's face. "Very creative, doctor. I'm impressed. But I'm afraid this work was done by an intellect that couldn't have arisen naturally."

"Do you even hear what you're *saying?* What does that even mean, *couldn't have arisen naturally?*"

"You know what it means. It means the work required an IQ in the thousands."

"In the *thousands?*" echoed Rosenblatt, rolling his eyes. "I guess that leaves out humans, doesn't it. So are you suggesting this is the work of *aliens?*" he finished in amusement.

Jake stared intently at the physicist for several long seconds, but didn't respond.

"I'm sure you've overestimated the work," insisted Rosenblatt, his smile now gone. "Einstein was a low-level patent clerk when he helped usher in multiple revolutions in physics; revolutions that stunned the greatest minds of the day. Or was he an alien too?" He shook his head. "Every year breakthroughs are made that seem beyond the capabilities of human intellect."

Jake steepled his fingers and considered the man in front of him. "The difference, as you well know," he responded finally, "is that even though these breakthroughs seemed beyond human capabilities, other humans could understand them once they'd been made. At least a few." Jake sighed. "But I'm done humoring you," he said, his tone both weary and disappointed. "We both know the truth of what I'm saying."

The black-ops agent slowly rubbed the back of his head and stared off into space in thought. Several seconds ticked by in total silence. "I'll be back in a minute," he said at last.

As the door opened daylight streamed into the structure, further evidence that Rosenblatt hadn't been unconscious for long. The black-ops agent returned only a few minutes later, holding two plastic bottles of ice-cold water. He uncuffed Rosenblatt's right hand, screwed the cap off one of the bottles, and set it in front of the tall, wiry physicist.

The man called Jake sat down across from his prisoner once again, took a sip from his own bottle, and considered the physicist carefully. "You've been lying to me, Dr. Rosenblatt," he began disapprovingly. "I know that. But I'm willing to overlook the past in the interest of remaining friends. But trust me, actions have consequences. Lie again and you'll be in a realm of misery few have ever experienced."

Jake paused to be sure this had time to sink in.

"As a measure of my good will, I'm going to tell you a story. I have no doubt you're familiar with it, but I want you to appreciate that I already know so much, it makes little sense for you to continue trying to be evasive. But I'm not telling you *everything* I know. Remember that the next time you consider lying to me." He paused. "Okay then. This is a story about a remarkable woman named Kira Miller."

Jake watched Rosenblatt's face carefully, but the physicist showed no outward reaction upon hearing this name.

"Kira was a brilliant genetic engineer who found a way to alter the wiring of her own brain—for about an hour at a time. Pop a cocktail of genetically engineered viruses housed inside a gellcap and, presto, in the mother of all chain reactions her brain is rewired, and she has an IQ that's beyond measure."

Rosenblatt frowned in disbelief. "When you said you would tell me a story," he said evenly, "I didn't expect it to be science fiction."

Jake's upper lip curled into a snarl. "I've been more than patient with you, doctor," he said icily. "But my patience isn't endless. Don't test my good nature any further." He paused and then picked up as though Rosenblatt hadn't spoken. "So after developing this capability, Kira Miller murdered several people and fell off the grid. Disappeared. She was known to be behind a lot of bad shit, like working with jihadists to wipe out millions of people. That sort of thing. A lot of people were sent looking for her, but none were successful. Then an ex-special forces operative by the name of David Desh was sent after her. Tough and smart and patriotic. And he found her. But as patriotic as he was, she turned him somehow. With an immeasurable IQ, we can only assume she knew which buttons to push."

Jake stopped and took a deep drink from the water bottle he had been holding. Reminded that he had his own bottle in front of him, Rosenblatt did the same.

"Interestingly, every classified military computer in the land contains a report from unimpeachable sources showing that what I just told you is all wrong. That the evidence and accusations against her were totally false, and that she was never anything more than a misunderstood girl scout. That she was framed for it all. Desh too. Worse still, she and Desh were killed before this came to light." Jake stopped and locked his eyes on Rosenblatt with an air of expectation, as though he refused to continue until his prisoner made some kind of utterance for him to gauge. "But you don't believe these records are accurate," said Rosenblatt on cue.

Jake studied his shackled prisoner for a few seconds longer. "Correct," he said finally. "In fact, I *know* these records aren't accurate. Kira Miller and David Desh are still very much alive. Even without her IQ cocktail they would make a formidable pair. But *with* the ability to give themselves an insanely high intelligence the world is at their mercy. They could turn entire countries and governments into their playthings. We also know they've been recruiting a select group of others for unknown reasons. We suspect most of them are just dupes, unaware of Miller and Desh's endgame—whatever that might be. Impossible to predict with mere human intelligence."

Jake paused. "But despite our knowledge, we've never been able to identify any of their recruits." He gestured suggestively toward the wiry physicist. "Until now, that is."

"*Me?*" spat Rosenblatt incredulously. "*That's* what this is about? You think *I'm* involved with these two people? I've never heard of either one of them before. *Or* of this magical elixir of yours."

Jake ignored him. "They've done a remarkable job of covering their tracks," he continued, almost in admiration. "Even more impressive when you consider they had no reason to believe anyone even knew they were alive. We finally realized our best hope was to find work that was being kept anonymous and that was too advanced to be done without Kira Miller's IQ boost. We hacked into hundreds-of-thousands of computers, including those belonging to scientists and mathematicians who were tops in their fields, like you, and those used by employees of science-based companies and institutes. And we analyzed the contents of these computers. We used our most advanced supercomputers and expert systems."

Jake paused and brought the plastic bottle of water to his lips once again. "I can't begin to understand the techniques that were used to sort through it all," he continued, "to determine if any of it represented a transcendent advance. But we succeeded." He paused. "True, the system mostly generated false alarms, but your work was the real deal. A breakthrough of inhuman proportions."

Jake raised a single eyebrow. "You may be interested to know the computer pointed us to one other man, in addition to you. Responsible for bits and pieces of work that didn't really lead anywhere, but that were very advanced. The CEO of a private physics lab named *Advanced Physics International* in Davis, California."

He watched Rosenblatt carefully for any reaction, but his prisoner remained poker faced. An almost imperceptible look of disappointment flashed across Jake's features, but only for an instant.

"Is he the next innocent man you're planning to abuse?" said Rosenblatt.

"I think we both know the answer to that," replied Jake, ignoring his prisoner's pointed barb. "I would have liked to have a little chat with him, yes. But he died from a gunshot wound to the stomach, apparently after surprising an arsonist who had torched his lab. Eleven months ago, in fact. As I'm sure you're aware. When we tried to trace his background further, we hit an absolute brick wall. Which even makes us more sure he was involved with Miller and Desh." He raised his eyebrows. "But no matter. I have every confidence that, among other things, you can tell us all about his history. Help clear things up."

Rosenblatt opened his mouth to reply but then thought better of it and remained silent.

Jake leaned forward and his eyes bored into those of his prisoner. "We've come to the moment of truth, Dr. Rosenblatt. I need you to tell me everything. This is your last chance. I can't stress this enough. I won't tolerate anything less than a hundred and fifty percent cooperation from here on out."

"I *am* cooperating," insisted Rosenblatt. "You've got the wrong guy. I have no idea how this work ended up on my computer. All I know is that *I* didn't put it there."

Jake frowned deeply. "To say I'm disappointed doesn't begin to cover it," he growled. He snatched his tablet computer from the table and his fingers slid over its surface. When he set it back down, the manuscript was gone. In its place was a live image of Rosenblatt's living room back in Omaha, Nebraska. Two of Jake's men, heavily armed, were sitting on his maroon leather sofa, looking bored but very dangerous.

And sprawled on the floor, on their backs, were Rosenblatt's wife and three young children.

3

Rosenblatt gasped and color drained from his face. *"What have you done to my family?"* he screamed, pulling away from the chair so hard he nearly broke his left wrist still handcuffed to the chair. The pain didn't even register.

"I tried to warn you that I wasn't playing games," whispered the black-ops agent. "I tried to tell you that you'd prefer physical torture." He shook his head almost sadly. "The good news is that nothing has happened to them." He paused for several seconds and then added, "Yet."

The black-ops agent removed a cell phone from his pocket and placed it on the table in front of him. "How long this continues to be true is up to you."

The camera began to pan around the room, beaming the picture to Jake's tablet. One of Jake's men was standing on Rosenblatt's beige carpeting, in front of his mahogany bookshelves and baby grand piano. The camera settled on a picture of the physicist and his family. Rosenblatt, tall and thin with curly brown hair, cut close, holding his five and seven-year-old daughters, one in each arm. His wife, short and on the plump side, standing behind their eight-year-old son Max. All wore contented smiles.

Jake raised the silver cell phone to his mouth. "Show him they're okay," he ordered.

Seconds later the faces of Rosenblatt's family returned, and the camera zoomed in close on one of them at a time. Long enough for Rosenblatt to see their chests rise and fall in each case, ever so slightly.

"They're only unconscious," said Jake. "Sleeping peacefully. We entered this morning before they awoke and administered a knockout drug. I'm trying to do this as compassionately as humanly possible. If you cooperate, they'll never know what happened, never know they were in any danger. No psychological scars to bear for the rest of their lives." His expression hardened. "But I'm all done with warnings. The next time you lie or don't cooperate one of them dies. Period. Fail to cooperate after that and a second one dies. And so on. Starting with the youngest." He paused and leaned in closer. "Jessica, isn't it?"

"*You bastard!*" screamed Rosenblatt hysterically. "*You fucking bastard! You lay a finger on them and I'll see you rot in hell.*"

"Do you think I *want* to threaten your family?" said Jake softly. "Did you think I get some kind of twisted joy out of hurting helpless kids? It's the last thing I want to do. But I will do what I have to do. Make no mistake. And yes, I have no doubt that I will rot in hell, but I can't afford to be squeamish. Kira Miller represents the single greatest threat to humanity the world has ever seen."

"*Kira Miller represents humanity's greatest hope!*" shouted Rosenblatt.

There was absolute silence in the steel shed for several long seconds.

"I'm relieved that you've decided to admit your involvement and cooperate," said Jake.

Rosenblatt gestured bitterly toward the tablet computer. "It's not like I have a choice."

"Still, I'm relieved that you recognize that. Please understand that regardless of whatever lies they've told you, Miller and Desh have to be stopped. Miller called off her planned bioterror attack, yes, but she's got bigger things brewing."

"Kira Miller is the most brilliant, generous, compassionate woman I have ever met."

"She's brilliant, all right. No denying that. But she's also a fraud. A serial killer who comes across as a saint. It's a remarkable talent."

"I don't know where you get your information, but it's all wrong."

"Is it? Kira Miller is a pure sociopath to begin with. But did you know that her therapy has a side effect? It turns even model citizens into megalomaniacs. Into the kind of power mad, unbridled monster you think I am."

"Of course I know that! I've used it myself. You know that's the only way I could possibly do the Calabi-Yau manifold work you found." Rosenblatt shook his head. "But I'll say it again—you have her all wrong. She enhances herself—that's what we call it—far less often than she could. Why? Because she knows better than any of us that it leads to sociopathic tendencies and is terrified of letting that Genie out of the bottle too often. And do you know why the group is so small? Because the core counsel sets a higher bar than you can imagine before allowing a new member in. The personalities and ethics of those considered for membership are rigorously tested in ways that only an enhanced intelligence could devise. Only those predicted with near one hundred percent certainty of being able to withstand the effect without turning into a monster are recruited—no matter how promising they seem. She's careful to the point of absurdity," finished Rosenblatt.

And this was true. The purpose of Rosenblatt's visit to the Institute had been in the hope of adding at least one additional world-class mathematician or physicist to the team, but the trip had been a total failure. They had identified three brilliant men at the Institute who had passed their first level screens and he had come to Princeton to test them further, without their knowledge. All of them had failed. At least by Kira's standards. He had thought for sure van Hutten, from Stanford, had passed a few weeks earlier, but Kira had given him a thumbs down. They had not added a new recruit in several months now, and he was becoming convinced that they wouldn't. Kira and Desh had grown too afraid. The more the core council underwent enhancement, the more they realized the dangers of near absolute power and the stakes they were playing for, both positive and negative, the more paranoid they became about making a single wrong choice.

They had been extremely lucky with the five founding members of the group: Miller, Desh, Griffin, Connelly, and Metzger—the core council, now down to four after Metzger's tragic death. Each of them had been extremely stable, moral, and compassionate before they had been enhanced. Even so, none of them would have met the current standard. Knowing this, they didn't even trust *themselves* while enhanced. They insisted that all members of the group, themselves most of all, only take a gellcap while inside a specially built room, that was locked from the *outside*.

But Jake was correct. A single loose cannon, a single mistake that got away, could threaten the entire world. Kira's own brother, Alan, had been the prime example of this. If he hadn't been stopped, there was no telling the damage he could have inflicted.

"She has you fooled," said Jake simply. "Did she promise you extended life? Is that why you're so loyal?"

"I'm loyal because I believe in what she's doing: what *they're* doing. You've seen the advances I was able to make while enhanced. In five hours! Imagine the improvements we could make to the human condition."

"You're being naive. First, the extended life thing is phony. The injection doesn't do a thing. It's just the ultimate lure to snare anyone gullible enough to believe it. Do you know what she and Desh have been up to during the past year? They've been responsible for several major terrorist attacks around the world. And I have incontrovertible evidence that they're planning worse."

"If it's so incontrovertible, why don't you show it to me?" snapped Rosenblatt skeptically.

"Because it would take too long for you to convince yourself of its veracity. And I would lose the element of surprise."

"Very convenient," said Rosenblatt.

Jake's demeanor darkened. "This conversation is now at an end," he said through clenched teeth. "I need you to tell me where I can find Miller and Desh. And after that, the names of everyone who is a part of their little cabal."

"I'll tell you everything I know," said Rosenblatt. He glanced at the computer once again. At his helpless family, and the armed men looming nearby. "But I *can't* tell you how to find them," he added, panic creeping into his voice. "They and the other two members of the core council are more careful than you can imagine. They move around all the time, and even they don't know each other's whereabouts unless they have to. And I'm just a junior member."

Jake's expression could not have been grimmer. "I warned you, doctor," he said evenly. He spoke into his cell phone once more and on the tablet computer one of Jake's men pulled out a high-caliber weapon and a small red circle appeared on the forehead of Rosenblatt's sleeping five-year-old daughter. She was wearing a bright yellow sun dress and had the serene look of an angel.

Rosenblatt shook his head in absolute terror, his eyes bulging from their sockets. It was impossible to love anyone or anything more than he loved this beautiful little girl; a girl whose inner spirit and zest for life were infectious and a never-ending joy to be around. He choked back bile.

"You have thirty seconds to tell me how to find Kira Miller, Dr. Rosenblatt. And don't make up a fake location to buy time. If Miller isn't where you tell me, I'll wipe out more than just your daughter. I hope to hell you believe me."

Rosenblatt forced himself to turn away from the tablet computer and think. Would they really kill a five-year-old child in cold blood? He refused to believe it. But how could he possibly take that chance?

But how could he give up Kira Miller? He knew what she and the group were trying to accomplish. What was at stake for the entire human race, including vastly extended life for billions, and possible immortality within a generation. His captor had told him this was a lie, but he had seen the evidence himself. And he knew Jake's other accusations were fabrications as well. Desh and Miller and the entire group were being framed somehow. He didn't know by whom, but he knew it was happening.

Kira Miller was the key to unimaginable improvements in the human condition. The key to the next step in human evolution—directed evolution. She was the harbinger of an eventual galaxy or universe spanning intellect. Rosenblatt had been enhanced himself, and was well aware of the dangers, but he was also intimately aware of the breathtaking potential.

Far too much was at stake for him to betray Kira. *But he had to protect his baby girl.* He would sacrifice the entire universe if this is what it took to save his daughter.

But *did* he have to? Jake had to be bluffing. He *had* to be. He couldn't be certain that Rosenblatt wasn't telling the truth. This was simply a test. If Rosenblatt stuck to his guns and didn't waver, even in the face of an impossible threat, Jake would *have* to believe him. No father would lie when up against this kind of compulsion.

"I'm waiting, Dr. Rosenblatt. You have ten seconds left."

Tears began streaming down the physicist's face. "*I really don't know,*" he said, his voice distilled panic. "*Really,*" he pleaded. "*I would tell you if I did. Oh God, I would tell you. I'll do anything. Don't do this.*"

Rosenblatt wasn't near the edge of hysteria, he was *over* the edge. He was betting his daughter's life he could convince Jake he was telling the truth, so his terror at the prospect of losing her forever—worse, of miscalculating and being *responsible* for her death—couldn't have been more real. "*Miller and Desh are insanely paranoid,*" he babbled on. "*I'll tell you anything you want. But I can't tell you what I don't know!*"

Although his vision was distorted by tears, Rosenblatt saw a deeply troubled look come over Jake's face. What did this mean? Was he convinced that Rosenblatt didn't know Kira's location? How could he *not be* convinced? No father on earth would hold this information back in these circumstances. That's all Jake was after. He had produced the ultimate threat to be absolutely certain he had gotten all the information there was to get. And now he could be sure.

Jake whispered into the phone, and on the computer screen the man aiming the gun at Rosenblatt's lovely daughter pulled the trigger. Jessica's small head exploded like a melon dropped from a skyscraper, scattering blood and brain matter across the room and spraying the other unconscious members of Rosenblatt's family.

"*Nooooo!*" screamed the wiry physicist, almost losing consciousness—his mind unable to cope with a blow to his psyche this great. "*Noooo!*"

"Should we move on to your next oldest daughter, or are you beginning to remember where I can find David Desh and Kira Miller?"

An expression of pure, thrilling hatred wrapped around Rosenblatt's face, even as the tears continued to pour down his cheeks, but only for a moment. He was too shattered to maintain any emotion other than profound guilt, and bottomless grief. "I'll tell you what you want," he tried to say through sobs and the heaving of his body, but the words were unintelligible.

Jake nodded anyway. "Good," he said, having easily guessed their meaning. "But you need to compose yourself first. I'll be back in five minutes."

Jake exited the steel shed, never glancing back at the emptied husk of a man behind him, who was sobbing into the one arm that wasn't handcuffed to a steel chair.

***

The moment the door of the shed swung shut, Jake steadied himself against the trunk of a nearby maple tree. He was shaking and fought to stop the moisture accumulating in the corners of his eyes from sliding down his face.

He closed his eyes and took several deep, cleansing breaths. Finally, regaining some semblance of control over his emotions, he walked the twenty or so yards to where the white minivan was parked. One of his men was monitoring the area for trespassers, but this was possibly the most secluded spot in Princeton and they hadn't expected to have to turn anyone away.

He opened the door to the minivan and slid inside. His second in command, Major John Kolke, who had been monitoring the interrogation on a video monitor, was waiting inside, along with a lieutenant.

Jake turned to the lieutenant, his eyes still wet. "Please excuse us," he barely managed to get out. "I need to be alone with Major Kolke."

The moment the man left, the major caught his commander's eye. "Are you okay, sir?" he asked softly, concern written all over his face.

Jake didn't answer the question, but looked deathly ill. "What kind of hold does Kira Miller have on these people?" he whispered, his eyes wide with horror. "*How could he have been willing to risk his daughter's life?*"

Kolke shook his head solemnly but did not reply.

"I can't do this anymore," muttered Jake, his eyes becoming moist once again. "I've been in firefights against overwhelming odds, and I've never complained. But this is too much to ask of *anyone.*"

"Colonel, I know the scene was devastatingly realistic. And I know you had to commit to the bit a thousand percent. But you've immersed yourself too deeply into method acting. Pull yourself back. You know it was only a special effect. That little girl is probably scribbling in a coloring book at her preschool even as we speak."

Jake shook his head. "I know that. But what I did to that man's soul wasn't a special effect. I tortured him far worse than if I would have pulled out his fingernails. It was beyond cruel." He looked away. "If you could have seen the look on his face." He shuddered. "I have a little girl myself. I can't even imagine . . . "

Jake lowered his eyes and fought once again to compose himself.

"You had to learn if he was holding a bluff all the way to the end," said Kolke. "And now you know. He was. The important thing is that we're within twenty-four hours of bringing down the most dangerous person on the planet. You'll be saving *millions* of lives."

Jake nodded but didn't look any better.

"Colonel, you've just proven once again that you're the right man for this job," continued Kolke. "Rosenblatt wasn't the only one being tested. If killing a single innocent girl to save millions—or even just *pretending* to do so—eats at your soul, you're the right man. If you can do something like this and it doesn't tear you apart, then you're the last person who should wield the kind of power that comes with this job."

Jake looked away, alone with his thoughts for almost a minute. Finally, he took a deep breath, put his hand on the arm of his second in command, and said, "Thanks, John. This helps." In reality it hadn't helped much, but Jake knew it would have to be enough. He had a job to do.

"Now that you've cracked Rosenblatt," said Kolke, "do you still want four men surveiling his family?"

"No. That's overkill. Recall Perez and Ferguson. Tell the other two we don't expect trouble, but to be cautious since there won't be any backup for them to call in. And that if anything suspicious happens, don't hesitate to use the satellites."

"I'll tell them."

Jake nodded and turned to the small monitor. Rosenblatt had sobbed himself dry. His head was still down on the table and he was whimpering softly. "He's shattered," said Jake. "But I think he's reached the point where he can make himself understood. I'd better go back in and get the information we need."

"What's the plan once you do?"

"He's just an innocent pawn. Once we kill Miller and imprison Desh and the others in the core council, we just have to make sure none of the peripheral players have access to her treatment. She's the only one capable of developing it from scratch. Once she's dead the threat is over. We'll hold him until we've taken her out, and then we can let him and the others go back to their lives. We can keep them under surveillance for a few years, just to be sure. . ."

He stepped out of the minivan, but turned back to face John Kolke before he left. "I'd love to tell him the truth the moment he gives Kira Miller up. Tell him his little girl is fine. That it was all just a computer generated illusion." He sighed. "But I can't, of course. Not until we're sure we've got Miller. Just in case we still need leverage on him." A pained look crossed his face.

"Keep in mind how many lives you're about to save," said Kolke once again. "The country needs you."

"Yeah," said Jake in disgust. "I'm a fucking hero."

He moved away from the minivan as its door slid quietly shut behind him. When he reached the steel shed, he took a deep breath, gathered himself, put a stern expression on his face, and opened the door.

Where are you, Kira Miller?

He was just seconds away from—finally—finding out.

4

Dr. Anton van Hutten, full professor in Stanford's department of applied mathematics and theoretical physics, stepped lightly onto the steep escalator, moving to one side of the grooved silver steps to let those in more of a hurry rush down unobstructed. He had a broad cherubic face, thinning hair that was turning white, and black-framed Harry Potter glasses that contrasted with his hair and light complexion. Several men and one woman formed a rough semicircle fifteen feet from the bottom, each holding up a sign with a name on it. He walked over to one of them, a man wearing tan slacks and an Oxford knit shirt who had an air of self-assurance and competence.

"Dr. van Hutten?" asked the man as he approached, lowering the sign on which van Hutten's name was written.

The professor nodded.

"Welcome to Denver. Did you check a bag?"

Van Hutten shook his head. "I've only brought myself, I'm afraid."

The driver nodded and motioned for him to follow. Van Hutten knew they were proceeding to the vehicle that would transport him to the somewhat mysterious *Center for Research Excellence*, abbreviated CREX, a think tank nearby.

Van Hutten had received a call two weeks earlier from a woman who introduced herself as Devon—no last name given. She was affiliated with CREX, a think tank near Denver, she explained, and wanted to sign him up as a consultant. Was he available for a full day in two weeks time?

He wasn't sure, he had told her. He had several important meetings in the morning and early afternoon on the day she had suggested

But Devon had assured him they'd be happy to host him from five in the afternoon until nine at night. While normally they would ask him to fly commercial, in this case they would schedule a chartered flight so he could return home that night. And when she described the pay—one thousand dollars an hour—van Hutten quickly decided that her proposal would work just fine.

One thousand dollars an hour.

And if he would spend the late afternoon and evening at their facility, they would guarantee a minimum of *ten thousand dollars.*

A limo would pick him up from his home and drive him to the airport for his flight to Denver International. All they asked was that he sign an ironclad confidentiality agreement, which included a provision that he not disclose how much he was being paid.

He wasn't sure if he could believe it, but the next day he received an express package with a five thousand dollar advance.

Intellectual rewards appealed to him far more than financial ones, but ten thousand dollars for a day was ten thousand dollars for a day. Besides, he was intrigued. What could they possibly want from him that would warrant that kind of money? It wasn't as if he kept any of his research confidential. If they wanted access to his work they could read his scholarly papers in one of several journals.

He had tried to get the woman to tell him what the consulting engagement would entail, but she had only assured him he wouldn't need to prepare and he was the right man for the job. When he had asked for the center's address, he had been told not to worry: that a driver would meet him at the airport and make sure he was taken the rest of the way to the facility in comfort.

A quick Internet search revealed a very professional webpage that spoke of the think tank's mission—to extend the boundaries of human knowledge—and the large endowment it had received from anonymous donors. Other than this, there was not a single mention of CREX anywhere else online. Hard to imagine a think tank with such a professional website and money to burn wasn't mentioned *somewhere*. If he'd Googled the name of the kid who bagged his groceries he'd probably get a dozen hits. In addition, the website didn't have a "contact us" page, nor could an address be found anywhere.

Curioser and curioser.

He had considered backing out, but decided this would be an overreaction. It was no crime if a think tank backed by anonymous donors wanted to keep a low profile, and he was certain there were any number of perfectly legitimate reasons for wanting to do so.

His mind returned to the present, where the driver was leading him through a busy parking lot. The man stopped beside a silver industrial van, with no windows on the sides or back and no descriptors of any kind stenciled on. Van Hutten might have expected their facility to be depicted on the van, or at the very least the words, "Center for Research Excellence," but once again they had decided to keep a low profile. At least they were consistent.

The driver opened the side doors. "Do you need a hand up, sir?" he asked.

Van Hutten hesitated. He liked the idea of being able to see where he was going, and the back of the van was a self-contained compartment that offered no means to do so. He opened his mouth to ask if he could sit in the passenger seat in front when he noticed it was unavailable—several large computer monitors had been carefully placed on the seat and floor. He frowned. "No, I can make it," he said. "I'm not that old yet," he added with a forced smile as he stepped into the van.

It was beautifully appointed, as luxurious and elegant as the inside of a high-end limousine, except more spacious. The ride was smooth and remarkably noiseless. Thirty minutes later the van wound up inside a small, underground parking lot and the driver led him through a door into what looked to be a newly built and very modern office building.

As he entered he was immediately met by a three person welcoming party. The first of these was a bear of a man who towered over all the others. He had long wavy hair and a bushy brown beard, and must have weighed three hundred pounds—although he was far from obese, just a land mass of his own. "Matt Griffin," he said, sticking out a massive paw that looked capable of grinding van Hutten's hand to paste, but which was soft and gentle as they shook. "It is a rare privilege and honor, sir," added the human mountain, his voice as erudite and proper as the stodgiest Harvard professor.

"Thank you," replied van Hutten as the man next to Griffin stuck out his hand. He was the oldest of the welcoming committee. His features were angular, his hair and mustache neatly trimmed, and he had a distinct military bearing about him, much like the driver.

"Jim Connelly," said the older man as they shook hands. "Welcome to our facility."

"Glad to be here."

For the first time van Hutten turned his attention to the lone woman in the group, who had been partially hidden behind the gentle giant calling himself Matt Griffin, and his breath caught in his throat. She was absolutely *stunning*. She flashed him a dazzling, sincere smile that added even further to her appeal. Just standing there, doing nothing, she had a force of personality, a radiance, that was magnetic. His eyes decided they were quite content to rest on her for long periods of time and would not be easily coaxed to move on.

"Thank you so much for coming, Dr. van Hutten," she said as she shook his hand, her hand and wrist delicate but strong.

"Please . . . everyone. Anton is fine."

"Anton it is," said the woman for them all. "Welcome to The Center for Research Excellence. I assume you recognize my voice."

"Yes. You were the one who contacted me by phone. Devon, I believe."

She winced in such a way that it was both devilish and apologetic at the same time. "Well, yes. But I have to say I mislead you about my name. Just in case you weren't interested, I thought it better to go by Devon. Sorry about that. But no need for any subterfuge now. My name is really Kira. Kira Miller."

He was already suspicious of this outfit, and this revelation only made him more so. He almost wanted to flee back home now, but a sinking feeling in his gut told him he was past the point of no return. And this woman, who had unabashedly admitted to giving him a false name, wore an expression so open and sincere, and was so clearly enthusiastic about meeting him, that he found himself strangely at ease.

His eyes refused to leave her face until he felt a gentle nudge from behind. The man who had driven him here was still present, and now his hand was outstretched. "I'm part of CREX as well," he said. "I thought I'd wait until you met the others and then introduce myself properly."

Van Hutten took the offered hand. He had suspected there was more to this man than met the eye.

"David Desh," he said.

"Nice to meet you, David."

Matt Griffin could barely contain his excitement. "You're *undoubtedly* wondering why you're here," he said.

Van Hutten stifled a smile. For some reason he wanted to say, "*undoubtedly*," in reply, but resisted the urge. "No question about it," he replied instead.

"Good. We'll get right to it then," said Griffin, leading van Hutten and the others toward a conference room at the center of the building.

Kira Miller strode beside the physicist and said, "Just to warn you, some of what we'll be telling you will seem a little outrageous. We fully expect you to be skeptical at first. All we ask is that you keep an open mind and give us the chance to convince you."

The queasy feeling in the pit of van Hutten's stomach returned with a vengeance. "You'll have my full attention," he replied.

He had no idea what he was getting into, but if worst came to worst, if they revealed themselves as some kind of quasi-scientific cult—the church of the quantum cosmological spirit or something equally lunatic—he was prepared to humor them: at least until he could remove himself from their company.

"You have me intrigued," he said, deciding to begin humoring them now, just in case. "It sounds as if today may be more interesting than I thought."

Kira glanced up at him without replying, but an amused bearing came over the affable giant lumbering next to her. "You have no idea," he said, raising his eyebrows. "You really have no idea."

5

Colonel Morris "Jake" Jacobson exited the F14 Tomcat that had rocketed him to Peterson Air Force Base in Colorado Springs, and boarded a car that was waiting to take him to a civilian helicopter waiting nearby. Landing a civilian helicopter on a street or field in Denver would attract far more attention than he would like, but not nearly as much as a *military* chopper would attract. The night sky was crystal clear and dense with stars, but this was the last thing on Jake's mind.

"Give me a situation report, Captain," he said into his cell phone.

"We found the glass building precisely where you told us it would be, Colonel," said the special forces captain who had been on scene for some time now. "And the warehouse eighty yards to the east as well. Our teams have established a hundred-yard perimeter around them both. We arrived in civilian vehicles and used maximum discretion during our deployment. We have twenty-four men who are dug in, including four snipers. We're in an industrial area, poorly lighted, and it's well after work hours, so our confidence is high we weren't observed by anyone in the vicinity."

"And you can confirm that Kira Miller and David Desh are in the building?"

"Yes, sir. I saw them enter with my own eyes. They matched the photos you provided exactly. There's always the chance one or more of them has a body double, or has altered their appearance as a decoy. But if so, they did a masterful job."

Jake considered. While *masterful* was well within the capabilities of these two, he believed the chance they were not who they seemed to be was virtually zero in this case. He had broken Rosenblatt, of that he was certain. The physicist had given Jake this location less than seven hours earlier, breaking into tears periodically as he did so and begging him not to hurt his remaining children.

It had been heart wrenching, but Rosenblatt had been beyond the possibility of deceit. And if the captain had seen only one of them, perhaps it was a case of mistaken identity, but both Desh and Miller together entering the building Rosenblatt insisted was their working headquarters was too much of a stretch.

"You're certain no one has left since they entered?"

"Positive. They're still in the center of the glass building. Judging from the spacing, it may be a kitchen area, but we believe it's a conference room. We've been reading the heat signatures of five humans for hours."

Jake searched his mind for anything he might be missing, but came up empty.

He had them, he thought triumphantly, but the sober part of his nature returned almost immediately to restrain his enthusiasm. From what he understood, they had been in situations just as hopeless before and had slipped the noose. He couldn't allow himself to be overconfident.

"Thank you Captain Ruiz. I'll be coming in by civilian helo, with an ETA of about twenty minutes. I'm going to have the pilot land in as secluded a spot as possible about three miles out, just to be certain the sound of the chopper blades doesn't alert them."

"Three miles, Colonel? Civilian helos are quieter than military ones."

Ruiz was correct, but he hadn't been briefed on the exact nature of what they were dealing with. Who knew what kind of technology Miller and Desh had up their sleeves? Who knew what kind of automated listening devices they might have invented for sniffing out incoming choppers? The more he thought about the capabilities of a group who could amplify their intelligence to levels that made the brightest humans seem like gorillas, the more nervous he became.

"Very true, Captain, but I'd like you to spread the word to the team. While on this op, assume we're facing hostiles with capabilities and skills even greater than our own. It's critical that they not be underestimated."

"Roger that, sir."

Jake inhaled deeply. It was time. He needed to make several critical decisions, and he needed to make them quickly. The current tactical situation could not be more ideal. But if Miller and the others entered the tunnel to their warehouse the situation would grow more complex and uncertainties would make the op more difficult.

He vowed that whatever it took, he would see to it that Miller and Desh would not slip the noose again.

6

Van Hutten and his four escorts arrived at the conference room, which was large and bright and packed with life. Kira loved plants, believing they were both good for the human soul as well as the quality of indoor air, and there were more plants within the facility than could be found in many outdoor gardens. The conference room itself was home to three Chinese fan palms, each of which reached the ceiling, and two amstel-king-braid ficus trees, all potted in round, one-hundred-gallon brushed silver containers that fit with the conference room's theme of contemporary simplicity.

They took seats around an elegant glass conference table that was shaped like a giant's surfboard, pointed at a fifty inch monitor on the wall.

Kira studied van Hutten with barely concealed enthusiasm. A physicist of his caliber who had made it through all of their screens was potentially huge for the project. They had told Seth Rosenblatt that van Hutten wasn't acceptable, but this was part of their security plan to compartmentalize information, especially personnel information, whenever possible. What Rosenblatt didn't know couldn't hurt him—or others.

"Anton," she began. "We really are honored that you could join us. But I'd like to get right to the point. And once again, I'll ask for your patience and open mindedness. I promise you everything we tell you is completely accurate. And we'll prove it to you before we're through."

Van Hutten's face tightened, and he looked understandably uneasy, but he just nodded and said nothing.

Kira had always been the type who liked to tear band-aids off swiftly. "I'm a molecular biologist," she said. "Several years ago I developed a gene therapy. For about an hour at a time, this therapy can boost human intelligence to . . . well, there's no other way to say it: to immeasurable levels."

Van Hutten blinked several times as if he had no idea what these words meant. A quizzical expression came over his face. "Immeasurable levels?" he repeated, as if his ears hadn't been working properly.

Kira nodded. "That's right."

She could tell van Hutten was trying hard to remain expressionless, but even so the slightest sneer of disbelief flashed over his face. He glanced at the three men at the table, as if looking for an expression that would confirm that this was an elaborate joke, that he was being put on. She could only imagine what must be going through his head. Was he wondering if this was an initiation rite? If he was being tested to see how he would react? More likely, Kira knew, he probably thought he was in the company of a group of dangerous, delusional zealots.

"The human brain has nearly unlimited potential," she continued. "But it's wired for survival rather than pure intelligence. Autistic savants give us a small window into the possibilities. There are autistic savants who can memorize entire phone books in one reading and can multiply ten digit numbers faster than a calculator. What if you could unleash capabilities even greater than these across all areas of thought and creativity?"

Van Hutten's eyes narrowed as he considered this argument. He tilted his head and his expression became slightly less skeptical; slightly more thoughtful. "Go on," he said.

Connelly and Desh excused themselves from the room as Kira forged ahead. She described how she had experimented on animals before eventually turning herself into a human guinea pig. She described the enormous plasticity of the human brain, which allowed for a ten-fold range of human intelligence, from an IQ of twenty-five to above two hundred, even without being engineered to optimize the potential of what was basically an infinite number of neuronal connections. She explained how she had ultimately developed a cocktail of engineered viruses contained within gellcaps, which delivered a genetic payload that rewired the brain in minutes—in a chain reaction that ordered neurons in a way that random evolution never could. And she explained that they were telling him all this because they wanted to recruit him to their cause, which they would elaborate upon later.

Along the way van Hutten began asking questions and making comments, seemingly unable to avoid becoming intellectually engaged by the discussion, despite himself.

Finally, Kira presented video footage of early experiments she had done on lab rats, who unlike the repulsive sewer rats of horror movie fame, were gray faced and had pink, Mickey Mouse ears that made them look almost cute and cuddly. The footage showed the rodents learning a classical water maze, swimming in a panic inside what looked like a rat hot tub, the water made opaque with powdered milk, until they found the quadrant with a submerged platform. While natural swimmers, the rats always looked to be on the verge of drowning. Many repetitions were required before the test subjects spent most of their time searching for the platform in the correct quadrant.

The video then showed a rat that had just arrived at the facility, one that had never been trained. This rat was injected with Kira's virus cocktail and twenty minutes later placed in a cage overlooking the water maze, able to observe an untreated cousin flail around in the water until it finally, randomly, found the platform.

The moment the cocktail treated rat was placed in the water maze it swam straight as an arrow for the platform.

Kira explained how stunned she had been the first time this had happened. The rat had learned how to beat the test just by *watching* a single one of its brethren. A single time. It was unheard of.

Toward the middle of the video, Desh and Connelly had returned to the meeting carrying water, soft drinks, and a tray of heaping roast beef, chicken club, and tuna salad sandwiches, which had undoubtedly been prepared ahead of time and stored in a nearby refrigerator. By the time the video ended and Kira had finished her narration, the men had eaten their fill.

Kira clicked off the screen with a small black remote and turned her attention to van Hutten. He was deep in thought. She sensed from his questions and reactions that he wanted to believe, but her claims were so fantastic, so audacious, that he couldn't get beyond his last shred of skepticism. She was no stranger to this reaction.

"Now we all know that everything I just told you could be an elaborate hoax," said Kira. "And the rat footage could have been faked." She paused. "I could also go on to show you discoveries and inventions that are clearly beyond the current state of the art. We've done this before as well, with mixed results. Some who've been where you are, Anton, believe us and let down their guard, while some continue to be skeptical. Once you've seen a few Vegas magic acts, you believe that anything can be faked in close quarters. Inventions, videos, what have you."

Van Hutten allowed himself a shallow smile. "True. But at least I'm convinced you're a molecular biologist. Your knowledge of the brain and genetic engineering is impressive. And I have to say your arguments make the impossible seem almost reasonable." He paused. "But you're right. I still can't help but think this might be nothing more than a magic act—although admittedly a dazzling one."

The room was totally silent for several long seconds. Kira removed a roast beef sandwich from the tray and caught Griffin's eye, giving him an almost imperceptible nod. Her part of the show was now over. Desh had insisted long before that she not be involved in the part of the discussion that could often get unpleasant. Not because she was a woman and they were men, but because she was the unanimously acknowledged leader of the group and they all thought it important that she stay above the fray.

The giant blew out a long breath. "The only way you'll believe us the proverbial one hundred and ten percent," he said, "Is if you take a gellcap and see for yourself." He paused to give van Hutten time to digest this statement. "I promise you that the effects are not dangerous. And they only last for about an hour. You'll be famished afterwards, but we'll supply you with plenty of high-glycemic-index food." Griffin smiled. "For those of us who experimented a little in college with cannabis sativa," he added, "these are better known as *munchies.*"

Desh fixed an intense gaze on van Hutten. "Are you willing to try it?" he asked.

The physicist removed his black framed glasses, rubbed his eyes, and placed them back on his face. "And if I'm not?" he said finally.

"We can respect that," replied Desh. "I was reluctant myself. It's as if you're being pushed to take LSD. We're telling you it's harmless, and there are no after effects, but this requires you to trust us implicitly. And it *is* mind altering. No one could blame you for not wanting to rush into something like this."

"Then you're okay if I pass?"

Desh grimaced. "Actually no," he said. "I'm afraid we'd have to insist. We know that forcing this on you couldn't be more unethical. We try to make ourselves feel better by using the ends justify the means argument, but we know this argument is the last refuge of the incompetent. But I also know you'll be thanking me when this is all over."

"For forcing me into something I don't want to do?"

Desh nodded. "Unlike you, *we* know it won't have after effects." He tilted his head. "Suppose you come across a man from a primitive culture dying from a bacterial infection and you have penicillin. Suppose this person believes he can get better and refuses to take the penicillin, knowing nothing about it and not certain he can trust you. But *you* know this antibiotic will cure him, and he'll die otherwise. Do you force him to take it?"

"Yes," replied van Hutten with only a moment of thought. "Some wouldn't, I suppose, but I would." He shook his head. "But this is the most strained analogy I've ever heard. I'm not a primitive dying of a bacterial infection. This is far from life and death. The comparison you're trying to draw couldn't be more flawed."

Desh grinned. "Quit beating around the bush, Professor, and tell me what you really think."

Griffin smiled as well. "Can't say you don't have a point, Dr van Hut . . . um, Anton," he added. "The problem with recruiting brilliant people is that they're so damn . . . well, brilliant. Not easy to persuade."

"Look," said Desh, "we're asking you to do this voluntarily. But again, we're prepared to make this happen by force if necessary. Even knowing we have no ethical ground to stand on. We're not proud of it. But we can't let you leave until you've been what we call *enhanced*."

"Why? Why is this so important?"

"Because no one who has been enhanced even a single time has not joined our efforts," said Connelly, who had remained largely quiet throughout the proceedings. "If you don't experience this for yourself, realize that everything we've told you is true, the security risk is too high. You know too much about us."

"Will you volunteer?" pressed Desh.

"I'm not sure we have the same definition of *volunteer*," responded van Hutten. "Basically, my *voluntary* choices are to take the gellcap myself, or be manhandled and have the pill forced down my throat. Is that about right?"

Desh frowned. "I'm really very sorry about this. You're a good man and a brilliant scientist. We've studied you closely, and we've all come to admire you. The thing is,

I'm certain you'll forgive me once you've experienced what *we've* all experienced. And you'll understand the tradeoffs we felt we were forced to make."

Van Hutten sighed and then nodded. "Okay," he said in surrender. "Let's do this thing. Since it's clear I'm getting a dose of this no matter what I say or do, I might as well take it, um . . . voluntarily. I do have to admit to being intrigued. And if you *are* a group of dangerous lunatics, you have to be the most reluctant and respectful group of dangerous lunatics I've ever seen."

"Thanks," said Desh with a wry smile. "I think."

Desh and Connelly remained in the conference room while Kira and Griffin led their visitor to a spacious room nearby, completely transparent, with a single steel chair bolted to the ground in front of a mouse and a laser generated virtual keyboard. Four computer monitors were hung just outside the room, but all were easily visible from the chair through the thick Plexiglas walls.

"This is our enhancement room," explained Kira. "Once you're locked in it's escape proof. Even for someone as brilliant as you're about to become."

Kira waited while van Hutten surveyed the room.

"The keyboard and mouse are connected to a supercomputer outside of the room," she continued. "Which is connected to the Internet. But only in such a way that you can access the web for informational purposes. An even *more* powerful supercomputer monitors your activities, and if it detects any attempt to hack into a site, or affect outside computers in any way—unless these activities are preapproved—it will block them. You'd be smart enough to get around any firewall built by a normal programmer, but Matt put this in place while his IQ was amped."

Kira paused for breath. "When you make breakthroughs, you should enter them into the computer as fast as you can. The good news is that you'll be able to type at many times your normal speed with perfect accuracy."

Kira was working on a brain/computer interface, and after a few more sessions with a gellcap she was confident she could come up with a system that could send human thoughts directly to a computer, eliminating the need for typing and facilitating the transfer of gellcap induced breakthroughs a hundred fold.

"We'll be monitoring you," she told him, "but we won't try to communicate. For your first time, we want you to be able to soar without having to divert even a fraction of your attention to converse with dullards like us."

"Very considerate of you," said van Hutten drily.

"Are you ready?" asked Griffin.

Van Hutten nodded.

Kira handed him a gellcap and a bottle of water, and after taking a deep breath, the Stanford physicist downed the pill without ceremony.

Kira recovered the bottle and she and her colleagues retreated to the thick door, which they would lock behind them tighter than a vault.

"It will take a few minutes for the effect to kick in," said Kira. "But when it does. . . Well, let's just say that you'll know it right away."

7

Jake weighed possibilities from within the cocoon of the helicopter as it darted northward. The cleanest and most obvious choice, he knew, would be to breach the facility with overwhelming numbers and take them out at point blank range, bin Laden style. It was the surest, most direct route.

But it was far riskier in this case than it would have been if this were any other group. If one of them could elude his men long enough for a gellcap to take effect, the odds could well turn in their favor. Their minds would then work too quickly—their reaction times would be too fast. He had seen footage of this in action, and it was truly impressive.

There was far too much at stake for him to take any risk at all. He could leave nothing to chance. He lifted the right side of the heavy black headphones he was wearing just long enough to slide an earpiece into his right ear, connected by a thin cord to his cell phone. A small microphone attached to the cord hung near his mouth.

"Captain Ruiz," he said into the mike, "what have they been doing in there?"

"It's impossible to know for sure just from heat signatures, but they're mostly seated. Over several hours they've gotten up to move around, separated for brief periods, and fidgeted. In my experience this looks like a very long meeting, with occasional bathroom and drink breaks."

Jake nodded. "Are they together now?"

"They are, sir."

Desperate times called for desperate measures, thought Jake. This was why his group existed in the first place.

Sure, he would get second guessed by those judging his actions. The threat wasn't a nice tidy nuke wrapped up in a bow. Unlike a nuke, it could be argued that the threat presented by Miller and crew was overblown. If he wasn't steeped in knowledge of their activities and their potential for destruction, he might think so himself. But there was no turning back. He knew what had to be done.

"Okay then, Captain," he said. "Here's the plan. I'm going to scramble a bomber to fly overhead at an undetectable altitude and drop a five hundred pound JDAM down their throats." This would vaporize every living thing inside the building, right down to the cockroaches.

"A JDAM, sir?" said the captain in disbelief.

Jake couldn't blame him for reacting this way. It didn't get more unlawful than dropping a smart bomb on a civilian building sitting on U.S. soil. But the situation was perfect for it. Their target was a building not too close to any others. And there was little traffic in the neighborhood.

"You heard me, Captain," responded Jake. "We'll set it so it doesn't explode until it's entered the building. Miller and Desh won't have any warning, and there won't be any chance it will be seen by anyone in the vicinity."

This would reduce the building to rubble with such accuracy that there should be no collateral damage—not unless someone was within fifty yards of the building. But even so, he wanted to be absolutely certain. "Have some of your team set up unmanned roadblocks at major points of ingress to the target. Make sure no friendlies get inside your current perimeter. I'll want you patched through to the bomber pilot so you can give him the *all clear* when the time comes."

"Roger that. How will you explain the explosion, sir?"

"Gas leak? Grease fire? I don't know. We have some very creative people who can handle that end. I'm confident we can pull this off."

"Sir, are you certain all of this is necessary? Even if they're *all* better than we are, we have superior numbers and tactical position. We can capture them or take them out without the need of a JDAM. I'm sure of it."

A scene from a movie materialized in Jake's head. It involved several policemen breaching a building to apprehend a lone woman. The police were certain they had the situation well in hand. *I think we can handle one little girl* the lieutenant in charge had said. Jake put on the deadpan voice of one of the characters in the film, an agent named Smith, and whispered his memorable reply: "No, Lieutenant—your men are already dead."

A confused voice came through Jake's earpiece. "I'm sorry, Colonel, but I didn't quite make that out."

Jake cleared his throat. "I said, proceed as ordered, Captain. Proceed as ordered."

8

Van Hutten sat in the room's only chair and closed his eyes, waiting for . . . he had no idea. The pill could have been nothing more than a placebo, but he suspected it was either a strong hallucinogen or worse. It could well be lethal.

There was nothing he could do about it now, in any case, regardless of its effect. Whatever was inside that gellcap was coursing through his bloodstream, and no power of will or sleight of hand could remove it now.

He turned his thoughts to the group he had just left. They seemed genuine and caring people. Not that a psychotic who had been told by a humming bird to kill his wife for the good of mankind couldn't be genuine and caring as well.

One thing was certain, though: Kira Miller was a force of nature. She had a potent combination of physical and intellectual appeal that he had never seen matched. A persuasiveness, a charisma, and a winning personality that were off the charts. If he were a younger man he could see himself falling in love with that one in a hurry.

His mind exploded.

A hundred billion neurons rewired themselves in a chain reaction that was almost instantaneous.

He gasped.

His thoughts had been traveling at pedestrian speeds, but they had suddenly been punched into warp drive—and then some. His mind experienced the equivalent of a starfield rushing toward it; a starfield that elongated and blurred as his mind made the impossible leap into hyperspace.

Everything they had told him was true! Everything.

He diverted a tiny portion of his mind to ponder the implications of this while the rest explored its newfound power.

Somehow he knew that only 1.37 seconds had elapsed since the effect had hit him—exactly 1.37 seconds. He wasn't sure how, but his mind was now as accurate as a stopwatch.

An hour—a period of time that once seemed stingy—suddenly seemed generous beyond measure.

He turned his attention to problems in theoretical physics that had proven to be insurmountable and epiphanies presented themselves almost as quickly as he could focus on them.

His fingers began flying over the keyboard, faster than he had thought they were capable of moving.

He hadn't wanted the effect brought on by the mysterious gellcap to begin. Now he wished fervently that it would never end.

***

The Stanford physicist shoved yet another glazed devil's food cake donut into his mouth and washed it down with his second sixteen-ounce bottle of apple juice.

"That was unbelievable! Extraordinary," he said to Kira and Griffin for the third time, not realizing he had settled into a verbal feedback loop.

"Even if I had believed you completely, *nothing* could have prepared me for that! I could have never come close to even *imagining* it."

"Sorry we had to force it on you," said Desh with a sly smile, just having entered the room with Connelly.

"No you're not," said van Hutten happily as Desh took a seat. "And I'm not either. Thank you. I couldn't be more grateful. Maybe that penicillin analogy wasn't so bad after all. Although penicillin is like an incantation from a medicine man compared to that gellcap of yours, Kira."

"Make some astonishing breakthroughs in our work, did we?" said Griffin.

"Absolutely," replied van Hutten, as this part of the experience came rushing back to him. "I had a perfect memory of everything I've ever seen, heard, or read; and every thought I've ever had. And I could access all of this *instantly. Incredible.* I contemplated problems I've spent my entire career trying to solve. I just had to focus on one for a few seconds and an answer revealed itself like . . ." He paused, searching for the right metaphor. "Like an exhibitionist in a peep show," he finished

"Wow," said Griffin. "Well said. Linking the powers of an amplified intellect to live pornography is truly inspired."

"I don't suppose you'd let me rephrase that?"

"Why would you want to?" said Griffin.

Van Hutten smiled and turned to Kira. "Okay, then. Consider me a true believer. Can you bring me fully up to speed?"

A delighted smile lit up her face. "I thought you'd never ask," she said.

"You and David are in love, aren't you?" he said out of the blue.

"One of the things you picked up during your hour?" responded Kira in amusement.

He nodded. "You just seemed like close colleagues to me. But to my improved mind, you both might as well have been holding billboards advertising the fact that you're madly in love."

"An unexpected bonus to heightened intelligence," explained Kira. "Body language and other subtle clues to human behavior become so clear you can almost read minds."

"I assume you also discovered your ability to direct every cell and enzyme in your body?" said Matt Griffin. "And to change your vital signs at will?"

The physicist grinned. "Oh yeah," he replied giddily. "That too. All in all, it was the ultimate ride."

The group spent the next hour sharing their history with van Hutten. They covered Kira's early days after her first batch of gellcaps were stolen. How she was framed for a bioterror plot and hunted by the government. How David Desh was recruited to find her, and how lurking in the shadows, orchestrating it all, was her brother Alan, whom she had thought was dead.

They explained how the therapy altered personality in a dangerous way—creating megalomania at best and sociopathy at worst.

"Did you notice this kind of change in your personality?" asked Desh.

"Not really. I was having too much fun solving problems."

Desh nodded. "These effects start mild for most, but seem to build," he explained.

"And you've been vetted far more than you know," said Griffin. He grinned and added, "or as David might say in that more direct vernacular of his favored by the military, *we screened the living crap out of you.*"

"You'll be happy to know you're at the very top of the scale when it comes to ethics," said Kira, "as well as the innate stability of your mind and personality."

"How do you screen for something like that?"

"In ways that only someone using Kira's therapy could devise," replied Desh, clearly not wanting to sidetrack the conversation with any details. "Given the stability of your personality and the fact that, as Kira once put it, the first time you're enhanced you feel like Alice in Wonderland, it isn't all that surprising that this effect didn't hit you yet."

"Just for the record," said Griffin. "I never went through the *Alice* stage. The treatment seems to have hit me the most negatively of anyone. Along with everything else, I become the most outwardly arrogant."

"The team has come up with a more technical term to describe good old lovable Matt when he's enhanced," said Desh with a broad smile. "He's what we call a *total asshole.*"

Van Hutten laughed, now completely at ease.

"Okay, okay," said Griffin. "I'll admit it. I turn into an asshole. But a prodigiously productive asshole," he added proudly—the word prodigious long since having become an inside joke among the group.

"That's the only kind of asshole we allow," said Desh.

Kira didn't want to spoil the mood, but there was still a lot of ground to cover. "Colonel, do you want to walk Anton through the logistics of the operation," she said.

"Colonel?" repeated van Hutten.

Connelly nodded. "In a past life."

"Why am I not surprised?"

"I'll take that as a compliment," said Connelly, taking the small remote from Kira. "So given our history, and some troubling events that occurred early this year that we'll brief you on later," he began, "our security is tighter than ever. The building you're in is our headquarters, so to speak. The four of us are the leadership. Not because we're more intelligent or capable than any other recruit—well, other than Kira here, of course—but because we were the founders. Grandfathered in."

For many months Kira had objected to the steady stream of flattery from the rest of the core council, which she considered greatly exaggerated, but had finally given up. Desh had explained that anyone who created a tool that led to breakthrough after breakthrough, and that was certain to alter the course of human history as profoundly as fire or the wheel, deserved to be put on a pedestal.

"The think tank and this building are fronts, of course," continued Connelly. "It's not a place of business—basically it's our home. It has bedrooms, kitchens, etc. Maybe a better way to think of it is an apartment complex. We're not zoned for it, but then again . . ." Connelly shrugged. "That's the least of our worries."

Connelly pressed the remote and an image of a long corridor came up on the monitor, about as wide as a two-lane highway, its concrete floors and walls painted white. "At the far south end of this building is a corridor—a concrete tunnel—about twenty feet below ground level and eighty yards in length. It leads to a hundred-thousand-square-foot warehouse."

An aerial image of a windowless warehouse, which looked to be abandoned, flashed up on the monitor. Connelly explained that it had been sealed up tight and the only entrance was now through the corridor linking it with the headquarters building they were in. They had purchased the warehouse first and then built the headquarters and tunnel, using a number of different groups of contractors and carefully disguising, erasing, or confusing all records of the work.

Connelly then showed images of a row of standard golf carts in the tunnel that were used to cross back and forth between buildings.

Images of the inside of the warehouse came next. Each photo showed different views of a number of state-of-the art labs. The first to be shown was the biotech lab, within which Kira produced additional gellcaps and her longevity therapy. Then additional labs were shown in quick succession; high-energy physics, chemistry, electronics, optics, and others. Each was pristine, and no expense had been spared on equipment.

"Hopefully, we'll have time to take you over there and give you a tour before you leave," said Kira. "Showing you photos is a bit, well . . . lame, but we still have a lot to cover. Besides, being enhanced is physically taxing, so we'll let you relax and eat donuts for a while longer."

"Very thoughtful of you," said van Hutten, realizing that he hadn't yet consumed the last of the dozen dense black donuts and reaching for it as though he hadn't eaten in a day. "Impressive set-up," he added.

Only the core council knew that there was a second facility, nearly identical, in Kentucky, also connected by tunnel to a distant warehouse filled with labs, and also housing a room in which Kira's therapy could be given securely.

The group recruited from across the country and the world, although they had focused primarily on the U.S. to begin with for logistical reasons. All recruits were signed up as consultants, which gave them an excuse to visit their respective facilities frequently, although they kept as low a profile as they possibly could about this.

Both facilities were within a thirty minute drive of a major airport, and had been located so that no one in the contiguous United States would be more than two or three hours flight away. They had taken a map of the United States, split it into equal east and west halves, and then tried to pick international airports in approximately the middle of each half that could be reached by direct flight from surrounding states. Denver International was the winner in the western half, and the Cincinnati/Northern Kentucky International airport held this honor to the east. The core counsel split their time between both facilities about equally, even though they considered the Denver facility to be their true headquarters.

"Thanks," said Desh. "We've put a lot of thought into this. Not to mention a mountain of money. The good news is that enhanced Matt is basically able to create money at will."

"Really?" said van Hutten, raising an eyebrow.

Matt shrugged. "Just change a few pixels and bytes in computer systems around the world and your bank account never runs dry. There are safeguards and checks against doing this, but by removing relatively modest sums from thousands of the largest banks and businesses in the world, and overcoming the cross checks, it can be done. I also make sure all the accounting is fixed to show that those pixels and bytes never existed in the first place. So the money is never missed."

"Nice trick," said van Hutten.

"We try not to abuse it," said Kira. "But we do go through, um . . ." she glanced at Griffin mischievously, "*prodigious* amounts of money. We contract out a lot of manufacturing and other work, which tends to be expensive, especially since we're not the patient type. And doing things in a way to maximize security and cover our tracks takes even more money."

"What's nice," added Desh, "is that if you need something, or think an item might be of use to you, even in the slightest, all you have to do is ask." He pulled out his cell phone. "Jim and I, for example, wanted phones that could survive a war, but that look like normal phones anyone would have. This is a ten thousand dollar phone, but it's as rugged as it gets: military grade and fully submersible. I could use it to pound a steel spike into concrete and then check my messages." He paused. "So don't be shy. If you want something, we'll get it for you."

Van Hutten nodded slowly. "I'll keep that in mind," he replied thoughtfully.

"But back to the briefing," said Connelly. "Recruits are organized in groups of six." Individuals were placed in groups based on their collective proximity to one of the two facilities, but since they all thought only one facility existed, they were unaware of this. "You could think of these groups as *cells*. But since this word is usually used in connection with terrorists, we decided not to use it. We call them *hexads*."

"I see," said van Hutten. "Like a *triad*. Except for six."

"Exactly," said Kira. "On most days the members of a given hexad congregate here and take turns being enhanced. I dole out the gellcaps, which are meticulously accounted for. And there's a scheduling program that ensures the hexads are always kept separate."

"We're a bit on the paranoid side," added Griffin.

"Yeah, just a bit," said van Hutten with a smile. "So however many recruits you have—which I'm sure you won't disclose—each one only knows you four and the five other members of their hexad?"

"Exactly," replied Jim Connelly. "We ask recruits not to use their real names and not to attempt to identify each other."

"We also try to get single people like you with few attachments," added Desh. "Just in case. If they *are* married, we prefer those without children. Or with grown kids who are on their own. We've mostly adhered to this, although we've had to make an exception in a few cases. If a hexad is compromised, this policy helps make it easier for them to go to ground. If this were to happen, anyone with a wife and kids would have it pretty tough. They'd have to join our equivalent of a witness protection program. For everyone else, given a worst case scenario, it would just be a simple matter of faking their deaths and then keeping them off the grid."

"Faking a death doesn't sound like a simple matter to me," said van Hutten.

Desh smiled. "Well, we've gotten pretty good at it," he said. "It's our best trick."

There was a long silence in the conference room as the team let van Hutten digest what he had been told up to that point. Jim Connelly took the opportunity to politely excuse himself from the proceedings once again.

Kira thought the aging physicist was holding up surprisingly well. They had escorted him on a few bathroom breaks during this marathon session, and they had taken a few themselves, but other than this they had plowed ahead relentlessly.

Kira gestured at the pink faced physicist. "How are you feeling?" she asked. "We can take a twenty minute break if you'd like. We're throwing a lot at you all at once. It must be like drinking from a fire hose."

Van Hutten laughed good naturedly. "I'm fine," he assured her. "These are all once in a lifetime revelations, so I think I can keep my mind from wandering for a few more hours. What you have going here is truly remarkable. You're like a well-oiled machine. With these kind of facilities, funding, and the kind of brilliance you can unlock with your therapy, utopia might not be a pipe dream after all."

Kira frowned. Van Hutten had hit a nerve. Utopia was a far more difficult concept to pin down than she had ever realized. Even if she could wave a magic wand to accomplish anything she wanted to, the issues just got thornier and thornier.

What if you could magically invent ways to totally free up humanity, to mechanize all labor, to make the world so affluent there would be no need for anyone to work to make a living? Would this be utopia? Her study of the science of happiness indicated that this might actually be a *disaster*.

Humans were worriers by nature. If a person's mind wasn't fully occupied they would find endless things to stress about. This trait allowed early humans to anticipate unseen and far future dangers, helping physically unimpressive hominids survive to become the dominant species on the planet. So while leisure and pleasure in moderation were good things, humans needed to be engaged in challenging activities, during which their attention was so utterly absorbed that there was no room for fear or worry or self-consciousness.

Kira knew that contrary to popular belief, humans were happiest, not during lengthy periods of leisure, but when they were growing as people. When they were achieving. When they were striving to overcome difficult and worthwhile challenges, and then overcoming them. When they were feeding a sense of accomplishment and self-esteem through effort. Even the accomplishments of menial labor brought a sense of personal satisfaction far greater than most realized.

Make your utopia *too* utopian and boredom would set in. And malaise. Some would continue to work hard and challenge themselves at every turn—even if all of their physical and financial needs were taken care of. But many more would fall into the trap of being lulled into a low energy state of endless leisure—and little true happiness. A state of dependence without any real sense of progress, or growth, or accomplishment. A slow poisoning of the soul of the species.

Kira had become convinced that a true utopia was impossible for humans in their current state—no matter what the conditions.

Desh threw her a glance, with an expression that told her he knew exactly what she was thinking and that he was about to take the reins of the conversation for a moment. They had discussed the human condition and utopian dreams at length, and were on the same page, although she didn't expect him to get into any of this with van Hutten. He didn't. Instead, he took the opportunity to bring the understandably euphoric physicist back to earth, a place he would need to be for the rest of their discussion.

"Not to burst your bubble," said Desh, "but while we have some pretty grandiose goals, things are not going nearly as well as we had hoped." His expression darkened. "On a number of fronts," he finished grimly.

9

Jake was minutes away from landing, but he wasn't about to delay the operation just so he could have a ringside seat. Every minute was precious. Between one instant and the next he could lose the element of surprise. Miller and Desh could decide to leave. Anything could happen.

And failing at this point would be *unthinkable*. To finally have found and cornered them and then squandered the opportunity would be the ultimate tease, far worse than never having found them at all.

From the intel Rosenblatt had delivered, their organization was structured as brilliantly as he had expected. Six member cells, with each member discouraged from learning the identities of the others. Even so, from the descriptions and other clues Rosenblatt had given them, Jake was confident they would identify the other five members of the physicist's cell—eventually.

The structure of Miller's group had the advantage that no cell had any knowledge of any other cell. But it had a critical flaw. While the cells had no connections to each other, each was connected to the hub. Which meant that each member knew the identities of the core leadership. Jake was surprised they had allowed this, but then again, given they were all legally dead and thought that no one knew of their existence, this arrangement should have been more than sufficient.

And they had continued to exercise as much caution as they could. They had taken care to make sure that none of their recruits ever learned the address of their facility. Rosenblatt had described how each member of the group was always driven to the facility in the back of a van, with no way to see outside. More polite than asking guests to wear a blindfold, but with the same net effect. But Rosenblatt had known enough to lead them to the right place anyway. Miller had made one mistake. During one of the many updates she presented to Rosenblatt's cell, which they called a hexad, she had thrown the wrong presentation up on the screen. It had only remained there for a few seconds before she caught her error, but it had been long enough. The slide had been entitled, *Headquarters Building—Artist's Rendering*. An Icon of Denver International was shown at the bottom of the slide and their headquarters was depicted to the northeast. Its perimeter was nothing but large panels of mirrored glass, reflecting its surroundings. The structure was a perfect rectangle two stories tall, and judging from several trees drawn nearby, it wasn't all that big; perhaps confining fifteen or twenty thousand square feet of space.

They had been lucky. Without seeing this particular slide, Rosenblatt would never have known the approximate dimensions of the building or that the outer perimeter was mirrored, having no way to tell this from inside. Nor would he have known its position with respect to the airport.

Once Jake knew the size and style of building they were looking for; one northeast of the airport and eighty yards from a massive warehouse, he had more than enough to go on. Marshalling the vast resources at his disposal, computer, satellite, and otherwise, his black-ops group had found it almost immediately, and Desh and Miller's presence there had confirmed it.

And now he was just minutes away from ending a threat unlike any other in history.

Jake put in a call to his second in command. "The strike on Miller is now imminent. What's the status of your search, Major?"

"We've been working the computer guys hard," replied Kolke. "We're confident we've identified two members of Rosenblatt's cell: the two who were the most physically distinctive."

"How confident?"

"Extremely. Both are accomplished scientists. Not tops in their fields, but solid. One is at a university and one at a company. Beginning about six months ago, both began flying to Denver on a regular basis, something they had never done previously. Bank records indicate that both cashed five thousand dollar checks just prior to their first flight, which fit with what Rosenblatt said of the group's MO." The major paused. "While you were in route to Peterson, I alerted teams near their locations to ready themselves and await instructions."

"Good work, Major. Have them raid the homes and offices of these two as soon after we take out Miller as possible, placing a premium on stealth and discretion. At this time of the night your teams should be able to slip in quietly and not attract any attention. And I want the scientists treated as gently as humanly possible. No lethal force under *any* circumstances. Bring them back for questioning, and everything else you can get your hands on, with computers being the highest priority."

"Roger that," said Kolke.

10

"Given the miraculous effects of Kira's therapy," said the Stanford physicist, "it's not surprising you'd have some pretty far-reaching goals. So what do you have in mind?"

"We're thinking big picture," replied Desh. "*Very* big picture. Immortality. A galaxy or universe spanning civilization. And ultimately, perhaps, a galaxy or universe spanning intellect."

"Wow, it's too bad none of you are ambitious, or this could be an interesting group to join."

"Which is why inventing a killer shoot-em-up video game isn't on the agenda," complained Griffin. "In some parallel universe somewhere, the goals of this group aren't quite so soaring, and I'm a superstar in the gaming industry. With beautiful women flocking all over me, I might add."

Van Hutten shook his head in amusement and then turned to Kira. "David mentioned immortality. I'm not a biologist, but do you really think this is possible?"

"Yes. With enhanced intelligence, probably in the next fifty to one hundred years," she replied. "While enhanced, I've managed to design a therapy that can double the span of human life. But biology and medicine alone won't get us much farther than this. There's a limit to how much you can do with the human organism. Along with neurologists, immortality will require enhanced physicists, roboticists, and computer scientists to find a way to transfer the precise quantum state of a given human mind to a more stable artificial matrix, in an artificial body. A mind that will be indistinguishable from the original down to the last spin of the last electron. Then all you'd need is to have your personality matrix automatically backed-up each night.

The same way you do with your computer's hard drive. So if your artificial body is destroyed, your mind can be automatically reinstalled in another one."

"Not a big believer in the soul, I take it?" said van Hutten.

"Let's just say I hope the soul is inherent in the complexity of the infinitely grand workings of the human brain. And that no matter where the mind is housed, the soul will follow."

"Poetically said," acknowledged the physicist. "But issues of the soul are just the beginning. Do you know how many other thorny religious, ethical, and philosophical cans of worms this would open up?"

Kira nodded. "So many it boggles the mind. Even the enhanced one. What is the meaning of life? How much are emotions a function of our neuronal circuitry and how much are they a function of hormones? Without an endocrine system, can we experience love? Can we experience *any* emotions? And if not, will we lose all drive and purpose? Will we still even be *human*?" She paused. "For those who believe in an afterlife, would this process rob us of this? Or would our original, organic selves, upon death, still go on to the afterlife, and look on in horror at the pale imitations of themselves running around the cosmos. And what would stop someone from loading thousands of copies of their mind into thousands of artificial bodies? And even if an identical copy of your mind was reborn the instant you died, the original you would still cease to exist. So is this even immortality?" She sighed. "And these questions only scratch the surface. I could go on all night."

"You obviously haven't done any thinking about this," said van Hutten with a broad grin.

Kira laughed. "None at all."

The smile stayed on van Hutten's face for several seconds before finally fading. "Growing up," he said, "my favorite author was Isaac Asimov, the science fiction writer. Have any of you ever read the short story *The Last Answer*?"

There were blank stares all around, except for Kira, who nodded appreciatively. "I have to admit to being a science fiction geek," she said. "Asimov was a bit dated when I grew up, but he was still a favorite. And this might have been his most thought provoking piece of all."

"I couldn't agree more," said van Hutten, obviously delighted to have found a fellow fan. "But for the benefit of those who haven't read it, let me tell you a simpler story that makes a similar point, although not quite as interesting and thought provoking as Asimov's."

Van Hutten gathered his thoughts for a few seconds and then began. "A guy dies and finds himself welcomed to the afterlife by a brilliant, all encompassing light; by an almighty being who tells him that he can now pursue his wildest dreams for all eternity. There are no rules. He can do whatever he wants. And he can travel anywhere in the universe in an instant. For the first ten thousand years or so the guy is having the time of his life. But after a *million years*, he's got the *been there, done that* syndrome. He's bored out of his mind and weary of the burden of consciousness. So he finds the almighty being and asks that his existence be ended. But he's told that this is the one thing that isn't possible. So he goes off for another *billion years*. Finally, he's so fatigued, so bored, that he *begs* for his existence to be ended. And once again he's told this isn't possible. 'Well if that's the case,' he says angrily, 'then I'd rather be in hell.' To which the almighty being, from deep within the all-encompassing light, replies, '*Where do you think you are?*'"

There was silence around the conference room for several seconds.

Kira finally nodded and said, "It's a fascinating point. Seems like there is no perfect world. All I can say is that at least future immortals will be able to end their own existence if they choose to. And maybe boredom and weariness from the drudgery of existence is only a factor of our limited intellect and perspective. Or our endocrine system. It's possible the enhanced mind won't have any problem with eternity."

"Maybe," allowed van Hutten, but he still seemed unconvinced. "And sorry to be diverting the conversation," he added. "I've just always been fascinated by the philosophical implications of immortality."

Matt Griffin rolled his eyes. "you're really gonna fit right in here, aren't you?"

"I have to admit, I enjoy kicking around big ideas. And since this group has the chance to turn just about any big idea into reality someday, it's even more intriguing." He motioned to Kira. "But let me circle back to something you said earlier, if I may. You've really found a way to double the span of human life? Why haven't I heard about this?"

Kira described her longevity treatment further, and then the subsequent analysis that convinced her its release would lead to disaster. "Since this time, we've been careful to examine any major breakthrough we come up with to see what impact it might have if unleashed. Unintended consequences. As you pointed out, even immortality has them." She sighed. "But I have to say we've been rethinking this position."

"Why? It seems like a reasonable one."

"Centralized planning doesn't work," replied Desh. "History has demonstrated this over and over, although many refuse to accept the evidence. Besides, in any advance there are winners and losers. If we had invented the car in the nineteenth century, would we have released it? Or would we have concluded it would be too big a blow to the thriving horse industry? Too radical a change for society to digest?"

"Think *The End of Eternity*," said Kira, raising her eyebrows. "By your favorite author."

In *The End of Eternity*, Asimov envisioned a huge bureaucracy existing outside of time, which could make changes to the time stream wherever it wanted. The group was genuinely devoted to ensuring the best outcome for the most people, and so would change history away from wars and other disasters. It would eliminate risky discoveries and innovations. It opted for the status quo, for not upsetting the apple cart. But this benevolent intent ended in disaster. Progress and evolution, by their very nature, could be painful and cause upheaval. A sober, safe analysis would often steer civilization away from dramatic advances. Yet sometimes the birthing pains of a revolutionary advance were the price of survival and advancement of the species.

Van Hutten rubbed his chin thoughtfully. "Interesting. Haven't thought of this book in ages. But I understand what you're saying."

"We're smart enough while enhanced to realize we're not smart enough to be central planners," explained Desh. "Still, we're clinging to our paranoia just a little longer. And as far as doubling the span of human life, this is too far beyond the normal progression to be absorbed, even in a traumatic way. Doing this in one fell swoop will break civilization's back."

"That's why you're so important to our efforts," said Kira. "You could be the key that allows us to disclose this discovery—and all others as well."

Van Hutten tilted his head in confusion. "I'm not sure I understand."

"The bottom line is this," said Kira. "Inexpensive and efficient faster-than-light travel makes all of these problems go away. Right now, humanity has all of its eggs in one basket. As a species, we're exceedingly vulnerable to catastrophe. If Earth gets hit by a meteor—we're done. If we blow ourselves up—we're done. But if we colonize the cosmos," she said, her voice becoming passionate and her eyes more alive than ever, "even if the Earth is destroyed, humanity lives on. We can extend our lives as long as we can manage without fear of overpopulation. No invention would ever have to be withheld. Humanity's place in the universe and continued growth would be assured." She paused. "But it all hinges on our ability to rise from our planetary cradle and put our eggs in many other baskets."

Van Hutten nodded vigorously, dazzled by the vision Kira had laid out in her typical, mesmerizing fashion. "It's obvious once you point it out," he said. "Truly a cause worth believing in. It goes without saying that I'm at your disposal."

"You're not making that offer just to Kira, personally, are you?" asked Griffin playfully.

Van Hutten chuckled. "I meant the entire group, of course," he replied innocently. "I'm at the disposal of the Center for Research Excellence."

"Actually," said Griffin, "there is no such thing. We make up a different name for our fictitious think tank for every recruit."

"The true name of our organization is Icarus," said Kira.

" Icarus?"

"Yeah," said Desh with a grin. "We figured every good radical, covert organization should have a name. And Al-Qaeda was already taken."

Van Hutten laughed.

"Jim Connelly and I wanted to go with something less symbolic, less comic-booky," continued Desh. "But the geeks are in the majority here, so we were outvoted."

"I see," said van Hutten. "I have to admit, it is a geeky name. But once you think about it for a second, it's a good one. Icarus. The Greek who flew too close to the sun. A cautionary tale of the dangers of hubris."

Kira nodded. "We thought it was appropriate," she said. "A reminder not to get carried away with ourselves. And given that hubris becomes overwhelming when we're enhanced, not a bad thought to keep in the back of our minds."

"So welcome to Icarus," said Griffin. "It's great to have someone of your caliber join our efforts."

The other three members of the group nodded their agreement.

"Thanks," replied van Hutten.

The physicist turned to David Desh with a more sober expression. "You said earlier things weren't going so well. What did you mean by that?"

Desh paused for a moment as though deciding where to begin. "Recruitment has gone slower than we anticipated," he replied. "Finding accomplished scientists who can pass our screens has proven more difficult than we had thought. We could lower our standards—after all, the four of *us* couldn't have passed—but the danger of a single mistake is greater than you might imagine."

"And cheap, efficient faster-than-light travel is proving far more intractable of a problem than we had guessed," added Griffin.

"Yeah," said Desh in amusement, "even *expensive, inefficient* FTL travel is proving impossible."

"We naively thought that if we enhanced any good physicist a few times," said Kira, "they'd come up with revolutionary solutions. But this hasn't been the case. The few physicists who've joined us have made remarkable advances in many areas. But as far as FTL is concerned . . . not so much." She frowned deeply. "And everything—everything—depends on us solving this problem."

"What makes you so sure I can do it?"

"We're not. But in this area, you're in a league of your own. So we *are* hopeful."

"Thanks for the compliment. But what if I strike out as well?"

Kira sighed. "There is one other possibility I've been working on," she replied. A pained expression crossed her face and she looked as though she wasn't eager to elaborate further.

Van Hutten waited patiently for her to continue.

"There is a higher level of enhancement," she said finally. "Far higher."

"*Far higher?*" repeated van Hutten dubiously. "I don't believe it. Hard to imagine how what I just experienced could possibly be surpassed."

"Not just surpassed. Blown away. The first level is impossible to imagine, also, unless you've been there. But the second level . . ." Kira's eyes widened and she shook her head in awe. "I was there for five minutes. But my mind was moving so fast it felt like *five days*. I can't recall most of the thoughts I had, but I do know this: this level was as far beyond what you just experienced as this level is beyond normal. And it came with the greatest bonus of all: it was so transcendent that the pull of sociopathy and megalomania was totally gone."

"That's fantastic," said van Hutten.

Kira's eyes fell and she turned away.

"Something went wrong, didn't it?" said van Hutten softly.

Kira nodded and she wore a pained expression. "I barely survived it," she replied. "The first minute or two afterwards I felt great, but my body crashed almost immediately after that. At this level your mind burns too brightly. You saw how starved you were for glucose after being enhanced. This was worse. It was complete depletion of, well . . . just about everything."

"We rushed her to the hospital," said Desh. "Just after we arrived she lapsed into a coma. It lasted for almost two weeks." He looked deeply troubled, as though it were happening right then. "She pulled through at the end, but it could have easily gone the other way."

There was more to the story, but it was something that only she and David Desh would ever know. While at this transcendent level of intelligence, when she had perfect knowledge of every cell in her body, she had discovered that she was newly pregnant, long before this would have shown up on any diagnostic test. But the drain on her body had been too much for this new life to continue. And afterwards, she and David had reluctantly come to realize they should wait to have children. It had been a painful decision, but she knew it was the right one. With all due modesty, she and David would likely play a pivotal role in human history. No matter how badly they wanted to be parents, their responsibilities were too great to allow themselves the luxury.

"What if someone was preloaded with nutrition and anything else that might get depleted?" asked van Hutten. "You know, hooked up to an IV for a few days before undergoing this second level of enhancement. Isn't it possible that this would make it feasible?"

"We had the same thought," said Griffin. "And given the importance of FTL propulsion, and the lack of real progress, a physicist on our team volunteered." He paused. "We did our best to talk him out of it, just to make sure he was absolutely certain. But he insisted that having the chance to glimpse the mind of God, as he put it, was worth the risk." He shook his head somberly. "He didn't make it. Despite intravenous preloading. Despite the advanced medical equipment on site. When he returned to normal, his eyes went wide, he whispered, 'the answer is obvious,' and then he lapsed into a coma from which he never recovered."

The incandescence left Kira's eyes and her expression left no room for doubt that she blamed herself for what happened.

"I'm so sorry," said van Hutten. "But it wasn't your fault, Kira. He knew the risks. And after having been at the first level, it's easy to see why he was willing to volunteer. His death couldn't be more tragic, but during the last five minutes of his life . . ." He shook his head. "I can't even imagine the insights into the nature of reality he must have had."

"That's at least some consolation," agreed Kira, but she was clearly unconvinced. She visibly gathered herself and continued. "I've been working to understand what happened and perfect the therapy. I've also been trying to modulate it. If the first level is ten and the second is one hundred, maybe I can engineer a setting of fifty or sixty. Something transcendent, yet survivable. This is what I've been spending most of my time on."

"Any progress?

"Some, but not enough. It's a neuronal chain reaction. A crystallization process that has discrete endpoints. There doesn't seem to be an intermediate setting."

Desh glanced at his watch. "I hate to say it, but I'm afraid we need to start wrapping things up." He gestured to the Stanford physicist. "We wouldn't want you to be late for your flight."

A delighted smile slowly spread across van Hutten's pink, cherubic face. "At this point I'm so euphoric I could probably *float* home. This has been the most remarkable day of my life."

"Well, there's a lot more going on," said Kira, "but we can bring you more fully up to speed next time. The good news is that we've managed to hit all of the highlights."

Desh shot the physicist a troubled look. "Well, almost all," he said.

Van Hutten raised his eyebrows.

"We can't let you leave without making you aware that there are dangers associated with joining Icarus."

Desh recounted what had happened with Ross Metzger. How they had purchased a private physics company, *Advanced Physics International,* about two years earlier while the current facilities were being built, and how the lab was raided by mercenaries, with Ross being killed. Someone out there knew of their existence. Someone who was lethally competent.

Van Hutten rubbed his chin in thought. "I take it the cold fusion reactor hasn't turned up, or it would have been all over the news."

"That's right," confirmed Kira. "But this isn't surprising. The energy it produced was barely above break-even. Enhanced Ross was convinced it could be dramatically improved, but whoever took it would have no idea how to do this." She shook her head and a grim expression settled over her face. "To be honest, I think the raid was more about sending a signal to us than about stealing this particular invention."

"Do you have any leads?"

"None," replied Desh. "And the only suspect we came up with was Ross Metzger himself. But we quickly ruled him out."

"The guy who was killed?"

Desh nodded. "The raid was nearly flawless. So good I can't help but think it was the product of an enhanced mind or an insider," he explained. "In either case this would point to Ross. But Ross was the most stable among us. The one who handled the therapy's ill effects on his personality the best. He was enhanced over and over and his personality was largely unchanged, unlike the rest of us. He'd be the *last* of us to go rogue."

"And *this* was what ruled him out?" said van Hutten. "Not the fact that he was *killed* during the attack?"

Kira smiled. "You've experienced how easy it would be to fake your own death while enhanced. You have absolute control of your autonomic nervous system. You can see to it you don't have a pulse whenever someone is checking for it. If Jim Connelly was in the room he could tell you all about it."

"Like we mentioned earlier," said Griffin, "it's our best trick. Everyone you've met today is thought to be dead. If Ross had decided to go rogue and remove himself from the board, it's the first idea he'd have."

"But in this case, Anton, you're right," said Kira. "His death did rule him out, because he couldn't have faked it. He would have needed a gellcap, and he didn't have one. I produce them and keep meticulous inventory. They couldn't be more secure, and there's never been one that was unaccounted for."

"So the short answer," said Desh, "is that we have no leads or ideas whatsoever."

Van Hutten paused to digest this. "So you have an unknown but powerful enemy out there gunning for you. Have you ever considered coming out of the closet? Maybe not to the public at large, but at least to the government?"

Griffin laughed and then immediately looked guilty about it. "Sorry," he said. "I don't mean to make light of your idea. And it's not as though we haven't discussed it now and then ourselves. But Kira's therapy offers absolute, unlimited power to whoever controls it. Along with a side effect that can gradually turn even a Gandhi into a selfish, power starved dictator. Would you really want our government and military to have knowledge of this particular golden egg, and with apologies to Kira, the goose who lays them? Can you even imagine?"

"Yeah," said van Hutten sheepishly. "I clearly hadn't thought this through. But after hearing your argument, the image that comes to my mind is a huge bloody carcass in a steel cage being lowered into the world's most shark-infested waters. It would be the feeding frenzy to end all feeding frenzies."

"*Now* we're on the same page," said Griffin in amusement. "Take away the steel cage and I think you've got the picture exactly."

11

"Arm the JDAM, Lieutenant," ordered Jake as the chopper he was in settled down for a landing several miles from the target. A car would be picking him up momentarily to drive him to the site.

"Roger that," came the response from the bomber pilot. "JDAM is armed and ready."

"Captain Ruiz, how is the perimeter looking?"

"The perimeter is clear, Colonel. I repeat, the perimeter is clear. You are good to go."

Jake took a deep breath and held it. "Engage target, Lieutenant," he said.

"Target engaged," came the reply.

And six miles above Colonel Morris Jacobson, a five hundred pound bomb streaked angrily away from the jet that had restrained it, like a rodeo bull when its gate was pulled open. The munition hovered for just a moment as its onboard computer got its bearings from the continuous stream of GPS data being fed to it. Then, satisfied that it could achieve its mission parameters and arrive within ten feet of dead center of the mirrored glass building, and only then deliver its devastating payload, it made a slight turn and accelerated downward.

12

Madison Russo finished making love to her boyfriend of four months, Greg Davis, and a warm sense of both physical and emotional contentment settled over her. Only two days earlier he had said "I love you," to her for the first time, and given that this same sentiment had been threatening to burst from her for weeks, this was a very good thing.

Her life couldn't be going any better, she decided. And falling in love was only partly the reason.

In high school she had been socially awkward, and while her figure and looks were slightly above average, her confidence was well below. And winning the state science fair hadn't exactly cemented her reputation as one of the cool kids. Given that her intelligence was already intimidating to almost every guy her age, she could have bottled her science fair victory and sold it as *male* repellent. Upon graduation from high school she had yet to be kissed.

But this situation changed quickly in college. As a physics major she was around other bright people who shared her passion: other bright people who were predominantly men. And the further she went forward in her major the greater the men outnumbered the women. The incoming class for the physics graduate program at the University of Arizona consisted of eighteen men, her, and one other woman who was now her closest friend. While many red-blooded males in physics departments around the world welcomed relationships with women who could understand their work, most had to seek relationships outside of the field. It was either that or get used to being very, very lonely. But as for Madison and her friend, they tended to get their pick of the litter.

But she still hadn't been happy during her first three years in graduate school. There was more to life than dating, and she had struggled to find a thesis project. Everything in cosmology these days was string theory. It was the cool kids' table from high school translated into academia. If string theory wasn't your thing—and it was definitely *not* hers—then you were a second class citizen. She found herself foundering, and there were times when she contemplated dropping out of the program with a master's degree and going into industry.

But then, just this year, new developments in the emerging field of gravitational wave astronomy had come along—just when she needed a new direction the most. Gravitational wave detectors had previously cost hundreds of millions of dollars, had required oscillation of the mass being detected, and their sensitivity—if one could call it that—had been laughable. But a new breed of detector had emerged. A breed that took advantage of novel theoretical principles, could be built for just a few million dollars, and had off-the-charts sensitivity.

In fact, if anything the new technology was *too* sensitive, generating the equivalent of a library of congress full of data each day. If not for supercomputers capable of many trillions of operations each second nothing meaningful could have ever be extracted from the morass, unless one was looking for the Sun, which Madison was pretty sure had already been found.

She had leaped onto this new bandwagon immediately. This powerful tool was sure to launch careers like so many bottle rockets on the 4th of July, and catapult gravitational wave astronomy to an unforeseen level of prominence in the cosmological quiver. And she was perfectly positioned to be in on the ground floor. Given the ocean of data a single detector could generate, if she used the most powerful tool of all, the one between her ears, she was confident she could find a way to make a major breakthrough.

The U.S. physics community, having been denied the Supercoliding Superconductor—ensuring Geneva's Large Hadron Collider would become the particle physics capital of the world—was hungry to take a leadership position in this emerging field. Centers around the country had embraced the new technology, even before all the bugs had been worked out, and once perfected, additional waves of adoption had occurred overnight. Now almost seventy percent of all detectors in operation were located in America. While this advantage wouldn't last long, U.S. physicists couldn't have asked for a better head start. And The University of Arizona had been in the very first wave. Madison had truly been in the right place at the right time.

As she basked in the knowledge that her life had come together more perfectly than she could have dared to hope, her computer monitor on a desk ten feet away began blinking. The light from the full screen was vivid in the darkened room. Greg Davis groaned beside her. "You're not going to check that, are you?"

She smiled. "Yeah. Pretty much."

"I think we need a new rule. We turn off our cell phones during sex. I think we should turn off computer monitors also."

"But this isn't during sex," she pointed out. "It's *after* sex."

"Well, given how often that false-alarm generator of yours goes off, a case of *false-alarm-us interuptus* is only a matter of time."

"And you'd like to make sure that doesn't ever happen?"

"Right. I mean, you wouldn't interrupt Da Vinci while he was painting a masterpiece would you?"

"So you're suggesting you're the Da Vinci of sex? Wow, *really?*" She rolled her eyes. "So what are you worried about Leonardo—that your brush might go limp?"

Davis laughed. "Not at all. You just don't want to interrupt a master at work."

Madison kissed him briefly and then grinned. "We could always stop having sex," she said. "Then you'd have nothing to worry about."

"As great as that sounds," he responded wryly, "I'm going to have to pass." He shook his head and gestured toward the computer. "Go ahead. I know it's killing you not to check it out."

He glanced at the clock on the end table nearest him. "We can probably catch the late movie if you're still interested, but we'd better drag ourselves out of bed and get ready. How about if I take the first shower while you take a quick look at your data."

Madison had her robe on and was seated at her computer almost before he got the sentence out. Davis just shook his head and wandered into the bathroom.

Madison's desktop was tied into the university's supercomputer, which sifted through the billions and billions of pages of data generated by the physics department's detector at incomprehensible speed. For months now she had been perfecting a program that would alert her if it spotted anything truly out of the ordinary. And Davis had been right. She received several alerts each day, and each time they were false alarms. But even so, these false alarms pointed out flaws in her programming. With each one her program got a little bit tighter, her filters a little better.

She looked at the data from a few angles, wanting to determine as quickly as possible the ordinary occurrence she had failed to take into account *this* time. But after several minutes of thought and study, her jaw dropped as low as it could go.

Nothing about this occurrence looked ordinary. *In fact, the data were impossible.*

"Nah," she mumbled out loud. "Must be a glitch in the detector."

She ran a quick diagnostic. The detector was working perfectly. But how could that be?

Madison Russo was checking her calculations for the third time when Greg Davis emerged from the bathroom, clean, fully clothed, and ready for a late night on the town.

She frantically began to run other crosschecks on her data, her eyes so wide they looked unnatural.

Davis watched her in fascination, knowing better than to interrupt—if this were even possible. He suspected he could have played a trumpet in her ear and she wouldn't have noticed.

After several minutes she finally turned away from the screen for just a moment and he said, "You found something big, didn't you?"

Madison nodded, her stunned face communicating awe—but also more than a hint of fear.

"What is it?" he asked breathlessly.

"Something that will change *everything*," she whispered. Then, exhaling loudly, she added, "Forever."

13

The JDAM penetrated the two story structure and erupted into an orange-yellow fireball nearly twice the size of the building before collapsing into a raging firestorm. Every inch of the mirrored glass perimeter shattered and the inside of the building was vaporized in an instant.

Over a mile away the explosion shook the car Jake was in and the resultant fireball was impossible to miss against the night sky, even at this distance, and even if his eyes had been closed at the time.

The moment it hit, Jake felt as though the weight of the world had been lifted from his shoulders. There was no end to possible threats from WMD, but none were like this one. Given Miller's ability to dole out superhuman intelligence and Desh's training and skills, he had eliminated what he was convinced were the two most formidable people on the planet.

This was a rare moment to savor. The execution of the entire operation had been flawless.

Jake arrived, congratulated Ruiz and his team, and waited patiently while a dozen firefighters arrived in three large trucks to battle the resultant blaze. He had contacted the Denver Fire Chief using an alias—one with considerable authority that could quickly be verified—and insisted that the firefighters on the scene leave immediately once they had conquered the blaze, after which Jake, Ruiz, and a select group of his men would move in, scrub the scene as best they could, and look for remains that would prove that Kira Miller's short time on earth had come to an end. Given that ground zero was basically at a point halfway down her throat, this would likely prove quite challenging.

A call came in on Jake's cell phone from his second in command, thousands of miles away. "How'd it go?" he asked Kolke, his tone upbeat.

"Not well, I'm afraid, Colonel. The assault teams went in, but came up empty in both cases. Neither scientist was in his home or office."

"Any chance this was just coincidental?"

"No, sir. They'd been *warned*. Their computers were either gone or wiped. They knew we were coming."

Jake's expression hardened. He didn't care about missing the two scientists. Now that he had cut off the head of the snake, they had become nothing more than harmless bit players he needed to interrogate for the sake of thoroughness. But the fact that they were warned introduced just the slightest uncertainty into the results of the operation he had just conducted. *Shit.* "How long after I gave you the signal did your men arrive?"

"The soonest twenty minutes. The latest forty-five."

"Any evidence of disarray or hasty packing?"

"None."

Jake frowned. This was getting more troubling by the second. Still, if the destruction of Miller's headquarters had set off a warning signal the two scientist's had received immediately, they would still have had time to disappear. They could have kept a suitcase packed and money on hand as a precaution. Given Miller and Desh's paranoia, each cell member was almost certainly prepared to disappear at a moment's notice.

Even so, the possibility that they'd been warned *before* the JDAM hit couldn't be ruled out either. And if this were the case, it could only mean that Miller and Desh had known he was coming.

Jake walked the short distance to where Captain Ruiz was watching the firefighters at work through a pair of high-powered binoculars. "Captain, I want to go through this entire op from start to finish. I need to be sure there's no chance they slipped the noose somehow."

"Slipped the noose, sir?" said the captain dubiously. "We recorded their heat signatures the entire time, right up until the instant the building was turned into slag. They couldn't have escaped. And they couldn't have survived."

"I appreciate your assessment, Captain, but let's do this anyway. You saw both of them enter the building. And the physical match was unmistakable, correct?"

"Correct."

Jake stared off into space for several seconds in thought. "Okay, I assume this was before you were fully in position. Any chance they saw you as well?"

"None at all, sir. I was five miles away at the time. We had just identified this facility as the likely target and wanted eyes on the scene as soon as possible. While in route, we discovered there was a street camera close enough to get clear images of the facility's entrance. So we commandeered it."

Jake reeled as though from a physical blow. His eyes widened in horror, and for a moment he looked to be in danger of exploding into a bigger fireball than had the building behind them.

It was impossible for the captain not to notice his superior's reaction and he swallowed hard. "Colonel, it was *real-time video*," he said defensively. "And it was Miller and Desh. Their images couldn't have been any clearer."

Jake nodded and walked quickly away, knowing that this was the only way to prevent his mounting fury from escaping and lashing out unfairly at the young captain.

Their quarry had escaped. He was sure of it.

But it wasn't the captain's fault. He hadn't been briefed on the Rosenblatt intel. It was *Jake's* fault, and his blood almost boiled from a mixture of frustration, anger, and self-recrimination.

He had been duped. Miller had been on to him even *before* the captain and his team were in place around the facility. But how?

Even as he posed this question, one possible answer presented itself. This group—Icarus according to Rosenblatt could have hacked into defense computers and placed watchdog programs that would warn them if anyone was using satellites and pulling records looking for specific real estate northeast of the airport. He should have been more cautious. He should have located their facility without using satellites or computers.

And he should have considered this possibility earlier. He hadn't because things had been going so well. *Too* well. He should have known an op against a team as formidable as this couldn't have been as easy as this one had seemed to be.

Rosenblatt had told him the Icarus team had invented technology that could prevent street cameras and satellites from getting a clean image of them. The core council carried this technology in a tiny device on their key rings and kept it with them at all times. While the scientific expert listening in on the interrogation had said this was flat out impossible, and that Rosenblatt was lying to him, Jake knew otherwise. Rosenblatt's psyche was truly shattered. He was well beyond the ability for elaborate deception. And Jake thought this scientific expert was a narrow-minded idiot. Electricity had once been flat out impossible. The microwave oven as well. *And* the cell phone. The word *impossible* had little meaning where Kira Miller was involved.

The fact that the captain had seen a clean image from a street camera—especially one they had allowed to point at their headquarters—was a dead giveaway. This could only have happened if Miller and Desh *wanted* it to happen. The images had been faked. And the heat signatures must have been faked as well. No known technology could do either of these things as effectively as they had been done, but this was hardly noteworthy. Being able to interfere with cameras was just the beginning of Icarus's capabilities. Rosenblatt had told him Miller's group had perfected any number of breakthroughs in the fields of optics, electronics, and holographics over the past several years.

Yes, he had destroyed their headquarters, set them back, but that was all. They had managed to disappear again without sustaining so much as a scratch, and had done so in a way that seemed effortless. And the remaining members of Rosenblatt's cell had gone to ground as well— at least for now.

He had held all the cards. He had wrung their location out of Rosenblatt in record time and then hadn't hesitated in the slightest before mounting an attack.

Yet still he had failed.

He had been so sure that he would find and eliminate Kira Miller—eventually. But his confidence was now badly shaken.

And for the first time, he was beginning to wonder if he and his unit might have finally met their match.

14

The entire group drove van Hutten to the airport. Kira, Desh, and Connelly kept him company in the back of the van while Griffin drove. Seven hours earlier van Hutten was a total stranger and now, because of the shared experience of enhancement and a shared vision to better humankind—he was now family. He shook the men's hands warmly and hugged Kira as he exited the back of the van, both exhausted and exhilarated.

As soon as the door was closed, Griffin hit a switch that threw his image on the screen in the back of the van, and video of his three colleagues appeared on a small monitor next to him. "Where to, gentlemen?" he said somberly to his two special forces colleagues. "Or will you be leaving us here to take a flight?"

"Drive to the trailer park," said Connelly. "We'll fill you in on the way."

"Will do," acknowledged Griffin, moving back into traffic.

"They bombed the shit out of the decoy facility," reported Desh grimly. "Just like we thought."

"Under the circumstances," said Kira, "you and Jim did an impressive job of keeping your focus on our meeting."

When Kira had kidnapped David Desh almost three and a half years earlier, she had stripped him totally naked. At the time he had said something on the order of, "What are you worried about? Do you think I've imbedded some kind of subtle tracking device in my *underwear*?" At the time she had laughed and admitted this was pretty unlikely, but always liked to err on the side of caution. But Desh had given her an idea.

Once Icarus was up and running, she turned her attention to creating undergarments more technologically advanced than cell phones. She had already invented a powerful but tiny bug and transmitter combination; one easily hidden, which worked on principles so unlike those in use that it was undetectable even by the most advanced equipment. Desh had been at the wrong end of this technology once, having been sure that he was clean, while all the while Kira had listened to his every word.

Kira had simply combined this advance with technology capable of non-invasive monitoring of certain vital signs, which was already available. She had married the two technologies, seamlessly, in elastic waistbands, and while this was never discussed during a first recruiting meeting, each member of Icarus was issued a set of custom made undergarments to wear at all times with this technology imbedded. She made sure the components were nearly microscopic and able to withstand the immersion and thrashing they received in a washing machine.

If an Icarus member was in trouble, they could press the section of waistband below their navels and the bug/transmitter would activate. If their vital signs indicated they were having a heart attack, stroke, or had been rendered unconscious in any way other than sleep, the bug/transmitter would activate automatically. In this way the core council would be alerted to any attack, whether the member remained conscious or not, and would also be alerted to medical emergencies—very useful functions for a pair of underwear to have.

While Jake had taken the precaution of removing all of Rosenblatt's clothing, including his underwear, and scanning it for bugs—not finding any, of course—he had left the clothing near his second in command, Kolke, who had listened in to the entire interrogation.

But he hadn't been the only one listening in.

The Icarus core council had been totally blindsided by the emergence of this black-ops colonel, this Jake, and the threat he posed could not be overstated. But there hadn't been time to cancel with van Hutten, so Desh and Connelly had done their best to multitask. They had told their guest about the attack that had killed Metzger, but not about the one they knew was ongoing even while they spoke. What would they have said? "No hexad has ever been compromised—well, until today that is." Not exactly something to inspire confidence in the newbie.

Desh and his old commander, Connelly, were in charge of security and operations, which were more than full time jobs. While enhanced, both men had come up with numerous security related inventions and innovations.

They hadn't built just one headquarters set-up in Denver and Kentucky. They had built two. Not identical, but very similar. A real facility and a decoy facility in each city. Both of the Denver facilities had mirrored exteriors, were the same approximate size, and were in proximity to similar warehouses, outfitted in the same way. Kira made sure each recruit was *accidentally* shown a slide pointing them in the direction of the decoy rather than the actual facility being used—just in case.

"Isn't the fact that they bombed it rather than raiding it a good thing?" asked Griffin from the front seat. "With a raid they'd know they'd been tricked. This way, the colonel will be convinced we're all dead."

"He will be for a few days, at least," replied Jim Connelly. "But when he doesn't find even a hint of physical evidence he'll eventually conclude that we're not. The good news is that he'll never guess he hit a decoy building. He found the structure he was looking for, and he'll find labs in the warehouse that we've cluttered up to look like they were in use. He'll decide we figured out he was coming and used advanced technology to plant false heat signatures. He'll know we're alive and well, but he won't doubt for a moment he took out our headquarters."

"Are you positive?" pressed Griffin. "Seems like if he gave it some thought, it would be pretty obvious."

"All magic tricks seem obvious once you know their secret," said Desh.

Kira turned to Connelly with a pensive expression. "How are the rest of Rosenblatt's hexad doing?" she asked.

"They've all checked in," he replied. "And they all followed the evacuation plan perfectly. After I gave them the signal they had plenty of time to get to an airport before this colonel was anywhere near them. I'd like to visit with each of them personally, make sure the transition to ghost is going well, but we don't have that luxury."

"Let me guess," said Kira. "You're going after Rosenblatt's family?"

Desh nodded. "Good guess. This Jake will continue to keep them under surveillance. We need to get them started on our version of the witness protection program." His expression darkened. "We're going to have to uproot a family with three young children. It's going to be a nightmare for them."

Kira met his eyes and nodded sadly. "Omaha is three or four hundred miles from here," she said softly. "Why not fly?"

"The colonel and I discussed this while van Hutten was being enhanced," replied Desh. "We have some weapons and other equipment we'd like to have with us that makes flying, uh . . . *problematic*. Also an RV is kid friendly. The Rosenblatts can live inside until we spring Seth and come up with a more permanent arrangement."

Kira Miller had made great use of RVs to help her stay off the grid before she had met Desh. They were mobile, and yet when they were parked inside a trailer park they could offer a stable address. And while authorities would leave no stone unturned when it came to residences and hotels, trailer parks would fly beneath their radar, having been stigmatized as bastions of ignorance and poverty. The idea of Ph.D. scientists living in trailer parks was something not likely to ever occur to them. So Icarus maintained a number of these vehicles around the country, with several near their headquarters buildings in Denver and Kentucky.

"Won't it be dawn when you arrive?" said Griffin "Wouldn't it be better to go at night? To avoid satellites?"

"It wouldn't help much," replied Connelly. "The NRO has launched several IR and radar satellites that can see in the dark."

"They're supposed to be secret," added Desh, "but the NRO purposely leaks their existence. After one supposedly *secret* launch they passed out patches with the slogan, *we own the night*, written on them. Raised a lot of eyebrows in the press at the time."

Griffin parked next to one of Icarus's RVs and announced they had arrived. He slid open the side doors of the van and peered inside as his colleagues rose from their seats.

Desh caught the eye of the brilliant hacker and said, "Matt, I need you to take a gellcap. I need you to get as much intelligence on this black-ops colonel and his unit as you can, including this Major Kolke. And we'll need to find a way to free Seth Rosenblatt. So anything you can learn that would help in this effort would be great. You know the drill. But wait a few hours. I'll call you beforehand with further instructions."

"Why wait?"

"While we're driving, I'll put myself in this colonel's shoes and think about how he'll try to find us. Now that we've been compromised he knows our MO. Hiring recruits as consultants, paying them an advance before they fly out, etc. Before now, it wasn't critical to totally cover our tracks. But now I'll need you to hack into banks, change the records of Icarus members, that sort of thing. To more properly erase any trails."

"Makes sense," acknowledged Griffin.

Kira stared into Desh's eyes worriedly, and then shifted her gaze to encompass both her husband and Jim Connelly. "Don't forget about your key rings," she said.

"We shouldn't need them," said Desh. "But we won't be shy about it if we run into trouble."

After the raid that had killed Ross Metzger, the core counsel decided they should each carry a single gellcap with them at all times, after all, as a measure of last resort. Kira had devised a gumball-sized container for the pills that attached to their key rings. The container would detect the fingerprints of whoever tried to open it, and if it wasn't the owner, would dissolve the gellcap inside.

Kira sighed, and lines of worry continued to mar her delicate forehead. "Good luck, gentlemen," she said. "And be careful."

15

Desh and Connelly arrived in Omaha, Nebraska just after five in the morning. They had switched off driving duties during the long trip and had each managed a few hours sleep. During the time they were both awake, they had performed a virtual recon of Omaha via computer and had planned out their mission.

They had two objectives: extract Rosenblatt's family and capture one of Jake's men to interrogate. They couldn't waste any opportunity to learn what they were up against. They had come up with an elaborate plan to accomplish these objectives—probably *too* elaborate—but they had always erred on the side of paranoia and overplanning and it had served them well.

They parked the RV at a campground deep within an Omaha woods and jogged the quarter mile to where they had instructed a cab to meet them. Fifteen minutes later the cab deposited them at a twenty-four hour rental car company where their vehicles were waiting for them, which they rented using false identities.

Desh drove to Rosenblatt's house in a blue, family-friendly Toyota SUV, with three rented children's car seats strapped in, amused at himself. It seemed like all he ever drove anymore were RVs, vans, and minivans. Why didn't any of his missions ever call for expensive sports cars?

When Desh arrived at the professor's small Tudor home just outside the University of Nebraska grounds, he drove around the neighborhood in ever larger circles to recon the area for physical surveillance, but found none, as expected. Rosenblatt's family was harmless and would never suspect they were under surveillance. And Jake had no reason to believe anyone would be trying to extract them just now, so a physical stakeout was a waste of effort and manpower.

Even so, the colonel's men had certainly hacked into the Rosenblatt family's computers. And they must have been inside their home to gather the video footage that, with special effects added, had been used to break the lanky physicist. While inside, they were sure to have hidden bugs, cameras, and intruder alerts. Seth Rosenblatt was Jake's only current lead to Icarus, and even though the black-ops colonel thought their leadership was now dead, he would make certain that any communication to or from the physicist's family was intercepted and recorded.

Desh and Connelly could have devised a cleaner extraction, especially with some of the technology they could access, but in this case flawless execution wouldn't serve their needs. They needed Jake's men to come after them, so they could capture one for interrogation.

Desh returned to Rosenblatt's residence and pulled the SUV quietly into his flagstone driveway. He disabled the alarm and broke silently into the house. He guessed he had from ten to fifteen minutes before the two men responsible for surveillance were alerted to his breach and arrived on the scene. If they arrived while he was still there this would put the Rosenblatts in greater danger, which he didn't want, but he was confident he could take care of a few men at the low end of Jake's field hierarchy who had been assigned this tedious job.

It was just after six when he slipped into the master bedroom and leaned over Lauren Rosenblatt, who was sleeping peacefully. These would be the last few seconds of peace this poor woman would have for a long time to come—and she had done nothing to deserve this. He frowned and shook his head. This was *his* fault. Rosenblatt had been compromised only because he had failed in his security responsibilities.

Desh reached down and put his hand over Lauren Rosenblatt's mouth as firmly but as gently as possible, and held her head steady with his other hand.

She bolted awake instantly and began screaming. The sound was muffled by his palm.

"Seth sent me," said Desh quickly as her muted screaming continued. "Lauren, listen to me. I'm not here to hurt you."

Recovering from her initial shock, she stopped fighting and trying to scream and her eyes almost returned to their sockets. Desh loosened his hold, but didn't remove his hand from over her mouth. "I'm with the think tank Seth consults for in Denver. There are some very bad people who want to get their hands on something he invented," he added, knowing this wasn't true, but needing to give her a simple explanation she could grasp instantly to justify his actions. "Your husband *isn't* in Japan. He's in trouble and so are you."

Desh could tell she was fighting to get her panic under control and concentrate on what he was saying, which was a good sign. "Your phones and computers are tapped, so I couldn't warn you," he continued. "But I'll do everything I can to protect you and your children. I'm going to remove my hand now. You can scream, but you'll only panic your kids and make it harder for me to help you." As he finished he released his hand from her mouth and took a few steps back.

She flipped on a dim lamp by the end table. "Where is my husband?" she blurted out in a tone that was just shy of hysterical.

"He's in danger," said Desh. "But he's being looked after and he should be fine." This last was a stretch, but he knew it was necessary.

"Why should I trust you?"

"Seth told you not to mention his consulting to anyone, correct?"

She nodded.

"So how would I know about it? Or that he wanted you to keep it secret? If I wanted to hurt you or your family, I could have done so already. The men I told you about are monitoring this house. The second I broke in I put myself in as much danger as you're in. If we don't work together, we don't have a chance."

She looked scared and unconvinced, and Desh sensed she was seconds away from either becoming paralyzed with indecision or breaking down. He made a decision instantly. "Look," he continued, "we have to trust each other. So I'll go first."

He removed a taser from his pocket and tossed it gently beside her on the bed. "I'm guessing you're not comfortable with a gun, but this will give you some protection." He turned his back to her and sat on the floor by the side of her bed, facing away.

Lauren pressed the button on the black device, which looked like a smooth, extra-wide TV remote, and tiny bolts of brilliant white light arced between the electrodes at its business end, emitting a crackling, buzzing sound that was unmistakable. The device was only inches away from Desh's neck, but he made no effort to move away or protect himself.

After a few seconds, she removed her finger from the button and the mini lightning bolt and the buzzing sound disappeared.

"We have to get moving," urged Desh, lifting himself from the floor. "Get your kids and tell them we're going on a surprise trip. No school today. Try to keep them groggy so they'll fall back asleep when they're in the car. I'm parked in the driveway. I'll be in the car waiting. Every minute counts."

Lauren stared at him uncertainly.

Desh gestured to the taser, still in her hand. "Look, there's nothing else I can do right now to gain your trust. Either you're with me or you're not."

Lauren Rosenblatt considered him for several additional seconds and then slipped the taser into one of her pajama pockets. She blinked as though fighting back tears. Given what he had thrown at her all at once, that she and her family were in jeopardy, and that her life was about to take a dramatic change in course, she was handling this well.

She wiped away a few tears that managed to escape, despite her best efforts. "Have the car doors open," she said, her features hardening in determination. "I'll be with you in two minutes."

Desh returned to the driver's seat of the SUV. True to her word, the garage door opened almost immediately and she walked out to his car. She carried one little girl on each hip, and her eight-year-old son Max trailed behind her like a baby duck, dressed in Iron Man pajamas and clinging to a small stuffed lion. All three kids looked at least half asleep.

Lauren's eyes bored into Desh's face. "You'd better not be some kind of psychopath," she whispered to him as she began placing children in car seats in the back of the hulking Toyota.

Desh began driving the moment the door was closed, while Lauren continued to seatbelt her kids.

"Mommy," said tiny Jessica sleepily from inside her pink, heart covered pajamas. "I have to go potty."

"I know, Honey, and we'll stop soon. Just hold it for a little longer."

"I'll try, Mommy," she mumbled, closing her eyes once again. Her brother and sister had already fallen back asleep.

Lauren Rosenblatt leaned forward toward the front seat. "Where are we going?" she said in low tones.

"To just before an on-ramp near the intersection of the I80 and 480," he whispered back. "Where several intersecting overpasses will screen us from satellites."

"What?" she said in disbelief. "You're not saying there are satellites watching us, are you?"

"Maybe not this second, but there will be soon enough."

Lauren digested this for several seconds. "This is totally insane, you know."

Desh sighed. "I know. And I couldn't be sorrier."

There was silence in the car for the next ten minutes. Desh checked his mirrors often, but saw no evidence they were being followed, although he was confident that this was now the case. Once a satellite was locked on, their pursuers could follow at a leisurely distance and not have to risk discovery.

Desh called Jim Connelly.

"Everything on track?" asked the colonel upon answering.

"So far. Our ETA is approximately five minutes."

"Copy that," said Connelly. "I'll be ready," he finished, breaking the connection.

"What's going on?" asked Lauren from the back. "Who was that?"

"We're about to arrive at our destination. There's a traffic signal there. We'll stop at it, whether it's red or not, and conduct a bit of a fire drill. My partner, who is a very nice man, by the way, will be in a Chrysler minivan pointing the other way, with his hazards blinking."

"What do you mean by a fire drill?"

"The instant we stop, you and your kids are going to switch to the minivan. As quickly as possible. I'll continue on, taking the eyes of the satellites and any followers with me. No one will have any idea you're in the minivan."

"And then what?"

"We have a large RV parked at a campground nearby, close to the Missouri River. With plenty of trees to block the view of satellites. You'll leave Omaha in that."

"I thought you said no one would know we were in the minivan. So why are you still worried about satellites?"

"Just paranoid. Two switches out of sight of prying eyes are better than one. And the RV is very nice. Big. With a bedroom, bathroom, living room, kitchen—the works. Have your kids ever been in one?"

"Never."

Desh nodded. "Well, this is a horrible situation, but being driven to your next destination in an RV will at least be more fun for the kids than being strapped in a car." He paused. "We're almost there. If you'll carry the two girls into the minivan, my friend can carry Max. I need to stay in the driver's seat so I can pull away the moment the light turns green."

Lauren took a deep breath and nodded. She reached over and shook her son gently. "Max, honey. Wake up."

"Huh?" he said sleepily.

"Wake up, Honey. In a minute we're going to do something kind of silly. We're going to switch from this car to another one—in the middle of the road. But it's a little dangerous, so I'm going to have an old friend of mine carry you. Okay, Max?"

Max stretched as best he could in the car seat he was in and tilted his head. "Okay," he said, not understanding this new game but willing to play along. He was still at an age where he often didn't understand why adults did some of the crazy things they did.

A snarl of crisscrossing overpasses loomed only a few blocks away. As Desh approached the light was green, but he slowed considerably, which elicited an angry honk from the driver behind him. The light turned red and Desh stopped the SUV under the concrete overpasses, making it invisible to prying eyes gazing down from space. A white Chrysler minivan, its hazards blinking and its side door open, was facing the opposite direction one lane over, just as Desh had said it would be. Jim Connelly pretended to inspect the front tire on the passenger's side.

"*Go*," barked Desh the second the car came to a rest.

Lauren threw open the door and jumped out of the vehicle while Connelly appeared magically beside her. She leaned in and removed her two girls while Max stood and let Jim Connelly carry him across the space between vehicles.

The colonel and Lauren Rosenblatt were still depositing kids in the back of the minivan when the light turned green and Desh accelerated through the intersection and onto the highway on-ramp, heading north. Less than a minute later, Jim Connelly turned off his hazards and drove calmly out from under the overpasses, heading south, with his hidden cargo safely belted in back.

Desh felt more relieved than he would care to admit. Part one of the operation could not have gone better. Lauren Rosenblatt had cooperated and had marshaled her children like a champ. The gamble he had taken to earn Lauren's trust had worked great, which was a good thing, since if he had miscalculated he could have easily found himself incapacitated by his own taser.

Now it was time for part two. And while this part of the operation was more dangerous, with the innocent civilians now out of the picture, Desh was confident it would end successfully.

16

Desh drove for another fifteen minutes, secure in the knowledge that the two men Jake had left in Omaha were following him, and because satellites couldn't see in the back of an SUV, were still convinced the Rosenblatt family was along for the ride.

He arrived at his destination, a road that ran beside the tree line of another thick woods. When he saw a section in which the spacing between trees was greater than average he drove off the pavement and slowly into the woods, maneuvering the large SUV between trees, the Toyota's oversized tires, built for off-roading, having no trouble climbing large, fallen branches, high underbrush, and thick cords of roots protruding aboveground.

He picked his way forward for almost thirty yards, stopped the car, and began rooting through a duffel bag that had been on the floor of the passenger's seat, gathering the equipment he needed.

Desh stepped out of the vehicle and onto the floor of the woods, where he could not have felt more comfortable. He was surrounded by elms and tall cottonwoods. It was spring and the woods were vibrant and alive, producing a clean, outdoor scent that he had always loved. Birds trilled repetitively high up in unseen branches.

Desh had a gift for operating in the woods. Traversing terrain such as this without making the slightest sound, without causing the faintest rustle of leaves or crunch of a twig, required balance, athleticism, and experience, as well as uncanny instincts. Desh could move through the densest forest more silently than another man could walk across a plush carpet, and he could do this so cleanly that nothing short of a bloodhound could track him.

But on this occasion he *wanted* to be tracked. He did a sloppy job of moving away from the SUV, leaving faint but obvious footprints in his wake. This would ensure he was followed—and underestimated.

He travelled north for twenty yards, still in sight of the SUV, and then walked dead center between two cottonwoods that were twelve yards apart, like a human football splitting two goal posts. He continued north for several minutes with reckless abandon and then circled back, this time with feline grace, and carefully strung a tripwire between the two cottonwood goal posts, eight inches off the ground. He settled in to watch the SUV.

He didn't have to wait long. Off in the distance a small gray sedan was approaching the bulky Toyota, having followed its tracks from the road. Since this vehicle was low to the ground and not built for off-roading, it had been scratched and dinged and was littered with brush and leaves and dirt. The car stopped a good distance from the SUV and two men exited cautiously, their guns drawn. Both were dressed in casual civilian clothing, one in tan slacks and a black t-shirt and one in blue jeans and a thin gray sweatshirt.

They approached Desh's rental from either side, crouching low, with their eyes never leaving its windows in case someone popped up from the seat or floor and began shooting. When they were ten feet away they both rushed forward and hazarded a look inside the vehicle, making sure their guns shifted along with their eyes, ready to fire at any hidden danger.

When the two men were satisfied the vehicle was empty they scanned the woods in all directions and then had a quick, whispered conversation, before spreading out and moving at a slow jog through the trees.

Desh knew what they were thinking, because it was what he *wanted* them to think. They were now panicked that

Desh and the Rosenblatt family were getting away, and could emerge from the woods at any one of thousands of places. They might get lucky with the satellites and find them once again, but on the other hand, they might not. So they needed to hustle and catch up to the young family, counting on the three children Desh and Lauren had in tow to slow them down. Desh was certain it would never occur to these men that they were chasing a highly skilled operative not weighed down with any civilian baggage, who had no intention of running away.

As the two men moved forward, Desh took a wide angle around their perimeter and maneuvered behind them. His timing was perfect. Just as he got into place, the gunman to the west hit Desh's tripwire and did a face-plant into the dirt with a loud grunt.

The fallen man rolled and jumped to his feet in alarm, gun at the ready, but he was too late. As he was turning Desh shot him in the neck with a tranquilizer dart, and he fell once again into the undergrowth, unconscious before he even hit the ground.

One down, one to go, thought Desh.

The unconscious man's partner rushed to his comrade's aid while Desh sprinted off through the trees as fast as many men could have run on a track.

The remaining gunman watched Desh's retreat and kneeled by his fallen partner, shoving two fingers into his carotid artery. His face registered surprise when he detected a steady pulse. He had clearly thought his colleague was dead, or at best, fighting to cling to a life that was ebbing away. He found the tranquilizer dart protruding from his partner's neck a moment later and pulled it out to examine.

Desh's retreat had been noisy, but when he circled back to his original position he was whisper quiet, and the remaining soldier, still in a crouch by his partner, had no idea Desh was behind him until a tranquilizer dart buried itself in his thigh and injected its fast acting drug.

The man collapsed beside his colleague, as neatly as two slabs of meat arranged side by side at a butcher shop.

That was relatively straightforward, thought Desh. Now all he had to do was lift one of these men in a fireman's carry and meet Connelly and his minivan at the designated coordinates.

He contacted Connelly. "Mission accomplished," he reported.

"What took you so long?" said Connelly wryly.

"I guess I'm losing my touch," replied Desh with a smile. "How are the Rosenblatts?"

"They're doing as well as can be expected under the circumstances. I'll tell them to sit tight for a minute while I pick you up. Do you want to drive a family to Denver in an RV, or a prisoner to Denver in a minivan? Your choice."

"Definitely the family," said Desh. "I should reach you in about fifteen minutes."

"Roger that. See you in fifteen."

Desh hung up the phone and approached the two unconscious men. Hopefully the one he chose could provide useful information about Jake and his operation.

Desh saw movement in the corner of his eye.

He dove to the ground before his conscious mind fully registered what he had seen, just as a bullet drove through the air where his head had been a moment earlier and imbedded itself deep in an elm.

He rolled to his feet and darted off through the trees. As he ran bits of bark exploded near his head as his assailant continued shooting. Hitting a moving target in a heavy woods was not easy, and Desh knew it would take a lucky shot. Even so, being shot at did wonders for one's speed and concentration.

When Desh had put some distance between himself and his pursuit, and he was no longer being shot at for fifteen full seconds, he risked a quick look around.

There were four men working their way cautiously but rapidly through the woods behind him, each dressed from head to toe in black. *Four of them?* And everything about their movements and style shouted special ops.

So much for Jake's men not having access to any backups. What was going on?

Desh resumed his sprint through the woods, but this time he took a course that was at a right angle to his initial one. He knew the strategy that was surely being used against him—it was one he had used himself. They had organized their forces both behind and ahead of him before revealing themselves. Had he remained on course, he would have been stampeded straight into an ambush.

As he ran he tried to put the pieces together. Jake had told his second in command, Kolke, there would only be two of his men in Omaha, and to warn them that backup wouldn't be a possibility. So Desh had set a trap for these two men.

But Jake had used Desh's own trap *against* him. He had been a step ahead. How? Somehow this colonel had figured out the core Icarus team had escaped the bombing of their headquarters. Somehow this man had figured out they were on to him. The speed with which he had come to this conclusion, and had acted upon it, was impressive.

Jake must have reasoned that the only way they could have been warned of his attack was if they knew Rosenblatt had been captured. Which meant they probably knew his family was under surveillance. From there it was a simple, logical step for Jake to predict that Icarus would try to extract them.

Jake's team must have arrived in Omaha hours before he and Connelly had, and had waited patiently until they could spring a trap of their own. And Desh had made it easy for them.

Desh put on the brakes, removed a flashbang grenade from a pocket, and threw it in a long arc behind him, into the vicinity of the men on his left flank. It hit a tree and exploded with a deafening blast that could be heard for miles, and a flash that was so bright it could temporarily blind anyone who got an eyeful, even during the day.

He hastily strung a trip wire between two trees. This one would be ineffective against men as good as these, but the flashbang and tripwire would give them something to think about. Slow them down a little. Keep them the tiniest bit off balance.

Desh considered taking the gellcap he had with him. Skilled as he was, he had very little chance of surviving with normal human faculties. But this wasn't a decision to be taken lightly. Being judicious in the use of force wasn't the strong suit of an enhanced mind. Once Desh was enhanced, he would be looking out for number one, with zero regard for life—other than his own. It would be difficult for him to prevent his alter ego from mowing through these men without mercy or remorse.

And this was a big problem. He had served in units just like these, and he considered these men the good guys. They were soldiers risking their lives to stop those trying to kill millions of helpless civilians. Children. The innocent. They had been led astray with respect to Kira, but he and these men were on the same side.

Several more bullets whistled by him and he knew he had no choice. He had to boost his capabilities and he had to do so *now*. He just prayed that he could somehow find the force of will to deflect his enhanced self, that his alter ego would retain enough of his values to get to safety without slaughtering these good men. He pulled the key ring from his pocket, put on an extra burst of speed, and then dove behind the wide trunk of an ancient cottonwood tree. He put his thumb over the small silver container attached to the ring and the top slid open.

As he reached for the gellcap, bark flew up around him as shots came in from another direction. He dove to the underbrush and rolled, sending the gellcap flying. He searched for the small pill frantically, but a wall of gunfire prevented him from trying to recover it, even if he was able to spot where it had landed.

He spun around and everywhere he looked, black-clad men were moving in on him, slowly and inexorably. He was in the center of a slowly collapsing net with no gaps, and he now had no means to improve his mind and reflexes.

"*I surrender!*" he shouted at the top of his lungs, knowing he was seconds away from being turned into hamburger. "Cease firing! I surrender!" he screamed again, emerging from behind a clump of trees with his hands held high over his head.

The gunfire halted as he came out in the open, but well over a dozen guns were trained on him as he stood there. A colonel emerged from the pack of elite soldiers.

"David Desh," he said in amazement. "I'll be damned."

And then without another word, he raised a gun in one smooth motion and fired.

Desh had just enough time to realize he had been hit with a tranquilizer dart before he sank to the dirt, unconscious.

17

Kira Miller paced across her bedroom inside Icarus's industrial headquarters once again, continuing to feel sick to her stomach. A framed picture of her and the man she loved mocked her from the end table. It wasn't her bedroom—it was *their* bedroom. She saw David's smiling face in her mind's eye. His strength. His compassion. His intelligence. His sense of humor. She loved him with all of her might. If she lived an eternity, she knew she would never meet his equal.

Knowing he was alive was the only thing holding her together. The bug and vital signs monitor in the waistband of his underwear had been activated and had transmitted data. Desh had been rendered unconscious, and the bug had transmitted numerous military voices before he had been stripped. At least the last vital signs reading she had received had been strong.

And *she* needed to be strong. As strong as she had ever been.

She checked her watch. It was noon. Connelly was driving back with the Rosenblatts and would arrive in an hour or so. He would deposit the RV and the family in a nearby trailer park and come immediately back to headquarters.

She picked up her cell phone and dialed a number Griffin had given her. It was answered after the fourth ring.

"*Hello?*" said a deep voice questioningly, clearly confused as to why his phone had failed to identify the caller.

"Admiral Hansen, this is very important. Don't hang up."

"Who is this?" he demanded. "How did you get this number?"

It was one thing for a stranger to dial the closely guarded private cell phone number of the Chairman of the Joint Chiefs of Staff by mistake. It was another for a stranger to call it and *know* who was at the other end. He would attempt to trace the call, but it would be a waste of time.

Kira ignored his questions. "I need you to deliver a message to a Colonel Morris Jacobson. It's a national security matter of extreme importance." Jake's first and last name had never been spoken while their bug was in range, but since the bug had revealed he was working with a major named John Kolke, Griffin was able to use his amplified intellect to learn the colonel's true identity almost immediately.

"I'm not a messenger and I've never heard of this colonel. Contact him yourself. If you can find my number, you can find his."

"You'd think so, but no," said Kira. "He's in charge of a group that carries out black operations. You're the high profile Chairman of the Joint Chiefs. Your information may be heavily protected, but at least you're a public figure. He isn't."

"Black-Ops are performed independently. I don't know this colonel of yours, this . . ." The admiral paused, obviously having forgotten the name Kira had given him already.

"Morris Jacobson."

"Right. Morris Jacobson. I have no idea who he is."

"Maybe so, but if you expect me to believe you can't find out, you must think I'm a fool. How many people have managed to hack your private number, Admiral? Don't you think you should be taking me a little more seriously?"

"If I wasn't taking you seriously, we wouldn't still be talking."

"It's a matter of national security, Admiral. And it's a simple message."

There was a long pause. "What's the message?"

"Tell him to call Kira Miller. That's a code name," she lied. "But he'll know who it is."

"That's the entire message?"

"Yes, and he has to make a computer to computer connection. The call has to be video as well as audio. I'll text you with the exact time and instructions for making contact." She paused. "I can't possibly overstate the importance of this. Even you can't be in the loop on everything, Admiral, but trust me, this is big."

"Okay," said the admiral. "Send your text."

"Thank you, sir," said Kira. "It should be there any second."

***

Colonel "Jake" Jacobson appeared on Kira's large computer monitor precisely at the time she specified. She had expected nothing less. She studied his lean face, black hair, and dark five o'clock shadow that looked as though it was perpetual, burning details of his appearance into her memory.

He looked a little wary, but mostly intrigued.

"Thanks for calling, Colonel," she began.

He nodded slowly. "Well, you did extend an invitation I couldn't refuse. The great Kira Miller. Since I consider you to be the most remarkable woman who ever lived, having the chance to speak with you in person is impossible to pass up under any circumstances."

"Remarkable for my accomplishments? Or remarkable for what you think is the blackness in my soul?"

"Both," admitted Jake without hesitation. "By the way, how did you discover my name?"

"Lucky guess," said Kira.

The corners of Jake's mouth turned up into the hint of a smile, which quickly vanished. "Look," he said, knowing that pressing this question further wouldn't get him anywhere, "I'm on camera like you asked. How about letting me see who *I'm* talking to? It seems only fair."

Kira shook her head. "Didn't your mother ever tell you that life isn't always fair?"

Jake frowned, but she could tell he wasn't surprised by her response. "Nice trick getting Admiral Hansen to contact me," he said. "But for someone of your capabilities, far less surprising to me than it was to him."

"Did you tell him what this is about?"

"Of course," replied Jake immediately.

On the bottom of Kira's screen two words appeared. *He's lying.*

She glanced at Jim Connelly inside the enhancement room, who was watching Jake and monitoring the conversation on his own screen, and nodded her thanks. They had timed things so Connelly would be enhanced throughout the call, diverting a tiny portion of his amplified focus to act as a human lie detector.

Those who were enhanced learned immediately that they could read the combination of facial expressions, body language cues, and vocal intonation in normals so well they could predict what they would say next with an accuracy that bordered on mind reading. And as far as determining the truth or falsehood of anything a normal actually *vocalized*, their accuracy was absolute.

Kira welcomed learning Jake's statement was a lie. The last thing she wanted was for the Admiral to be brought up to speed and enter the game.

"So let's cut to the chase," said Jake. "What can I do for you?"

"I believe you're holding a few friends of mine."

"*Friends?* Plural? My understanding from the one *friend* I'm holding is that the other one is *more* than just a friend. Word is you're in love with him."

Kira's heart ached just thinking about David Desh, but she couldn't afford the slightest sentimentality. "Really?" she said. "Can a person with a soul as black as you think mine is fall in love?"

"In their own fashion, maybe. I understand that even Adolf Hitler had a girlfriend."

Kira sighed in frustration. "I trust both Seth and David are in good health?"

"Desh is still unconscious and hasn't been touched. Rosenblatt couldn't be healthier."

A message scrolled onto her screen faster than she could read, put there by someone with superhuman typing skills.

He's hedging. Rosenblatt is fine physically, but Jake is worried about his psychological state after the stunt with this daughter. He continues to feel quite guilty about that, and regrets the damage he felt forced to inflict on someone he believes is an innocent man.

How fucking pathetic, added Connelly coldly, an editorial sentiment that his normal self would never have shared.

Jake's eyes narrowed and he checked his connection, no doubt wondering why Kira was taking so long to respond.

"The reason I wanted you to contact me," continued Kira finally, having finished reading Connelly's note, "is to propose a trade."

"A trade?"

"That's right. Me for the two of them."

As good a poker player as Jake was, he couldn't hide his surprise.

He expected you might bribe or threaten him to attempt to get them back, but he never expected this, wrote Connelly unnecessarily. *His mind is racing, weighing the offer, weighing possibilities, with a high level of excitement.*

"I give up two prisoners and I only get one in return?" said Jake, sounding almost bored. "Doesn't sound like a fair trade to me."

Kira laughed out loud. "Come off it, Colonel. Either we deal with each other honestly or I'm rescinding the offer and hanging up."

The corners of Jake's mouth turned up once again into the slightest of smiles. "Okay," he said. "I won't deny it.

I'm interested." He raised his eyebrows. "I'm just having trouble believing you'd really put yourself in my custody."

"Believe it," said Kira. "But I need something from you. I need your absolute assurance on a few matters. Your word of honor."

Jake looked at the screen in disbelief. "You can't be serious. *My word of honor?* Why would you possibly believe anything I told you?"

"I'm a good judge of character, Colonel. If you give me your word, that's good enough for me."

He doesn't believe this for an instant, but sees no point in arguing further.

"Okay," said Jake. "I'm listening."

"First, I want your assurances that you'll let me live once I'm in your custody. Don't answer immediately. Think it through. Be absolutely sure you're willing and able to honor your commitments before giving your word."

Jake pursed his lips in thought for an extended period. "I won't kill you," he said finally. "You have my word. But I won't promise anything else. And if you resist or try to escape, all bets are off."

He's telling the truth, typed Connelly. *His plan was always to kill you—just to be sure the threat he thinks you pose is nullified—but he'll honor his word now that he's given it. His new plan is to interrogate you thoroughly and then lock you away in a high-security cell for the rest of your life.*

"That's acceptable," said Kira Miller to the colonel. "Second. I need your word that you won't interrogate Desh when he regains consciousness and that no harm will come to either prisoner."

Jake considered again and then finally nodded. "You have my word," he said.

He's telling the truth.

"Finally," said Kira, "I want your word that you'll hold up your end of the bargain. That if I give myself up, you'll let Desh and Rosenblatt go, in perfect health, and not try to follow them. And neither will any of your men. Or your satellites. Think very carefully about this one, Colonel."

Jake paused, and rubbed the back of his head, as though this would help in the thinking process. "Okay," he responded finally. "You have my word. *If* you give yourself up—which I'm still not convinced you'll do—I'll release them in perfect health. And I won't have them followed."

He's telling the truth, but he's trying to deceive you in his own way. Good for him. I didn't think this giant pussy had it in him, wrote enhanced Connelly callously. *He'll let them get away, but he'll use what he gets out of you to do everything in his power to recapture them as soon as possible.*

Kira caught Connelly's eye and nodded. This was good enough for her.

"I'm counting on you to be a man of honor, Colonel, and not decide later to go back on your word."

"I won't," said Jake.

He won't, typed Connelly. *But he still doesn't believe you really trust his word. He's convinced he's missed something. So he'll be exceedingly cautious and prepared for anything.*

"While we're at it," added Jake. "How about giving me your word that you'll hold up *your* end of the bargain."

"What prompted *that?*" asked Kira. "My word means *nothing* to you, and we both know it."

Jake smiled. "You have a point. Even if I thought I could trust you, I'm a firm believer in the trust-but-verify process anyway."

"Don't worry," said Kira. "I won't jeopardize my friends. You'll have me on a platter." She paused. "But I do have one other condition before I agree to the trade. Once this is met, you can call back in thirty minutes and we can hash out the details of the, um . . . personnel exchange."

Jake's expression was easy for Kira to read, even without Connelly's help. He had been thinking this was too easy, and he expected this final condition to be an unpleasant surprise that would mean she had no intention of giving herself up, and that this had been an elaborate tease for unknown reasons. "Go on," he said guardedly.

"I need you to tell Seth Rosenblatt that little Jessica is alive and well. That what he saw was concocted by your special effects wizards."

Jake's eyes widened.

He's wondering how you have any fucking idea that this happened. There was a pause. Now he's putting it all together. He's figured out you must have been listening in, although he can't imagine how you pulled it off.

"Gladly," said Jake at last.

"Then we have an agreement," said Kira. "Go talk to Seth."

Jake nodded. "I'll call you back in thirty minutes."

18

Madison Russo could barely breathe. She had never suffered from stage fright before and was comfortable in front of large crowds, but in addition to the many hundreds of reporters in the massive convention center ballroom, well over a hundred million more were watching on TV.

She had sent her findings out to the gravitational wave astronomy community at the speed of the Internet. This was too important to wait, even until morning. Within hours her findings had been confirmed at a dozen centers around the world.

The governments of almost every nation instinctively tried to suppress the data. After all, information this explosive needed to be analyzed endlessly before a determination could be made if the hapless citizenry could handle it. But governments quickly realized that the genie was out of the bottle and there was no way to cram it back in. They'd have better luck trying to stop the eruption of an active volcano with their bare hands.

As it was, Madison's discovery caused sleepless nights around the world and a flurry of activity the likes of which had never been seen. If the entire Earth were an anthill, her findings had just kicked it like a planetary-sized boot, and seething masses of its inhabitants were scurrying every which way.

Dr. Eugene Tobias, the head of NASA, was at the podium first. Across the world similar press conferences were taking place, headed by government officials and scientific luminaries. In the United States, dozens of politicians and scientists had jockeyed all night to be the featured speaker, but since one of their own scientists had taken the shot heard 'round the world—which wasn't surprising since the majority of work in this field was being done in America—Madison Russo was the obvious, and fair, choice. Also because she was still a grad student, it would make the press conference less formal and intimidating, and enhance the human interest angle.

Most of the untold millions tuning in already knew of her discovery, of course, at least the punch line, but this was the first formal announcement. Panicked speculation and rumors had gone viral almost as quickly as had the discovery.

Eugene Tobias stood at the microphone until the audience chatter gradually ceased. When the room was silent, he began. "As many of you are now aware, at 10:23 Pacific Standard Time last night, a graduate student at the University of Arizona named Madison Russo made a discovery that has shaken the foundation of science, cosmology, and religion. Indisputable evidence of not just extraterrestrial life, but of *intelligent* extraterrestrial life. This discovery has now been repeatedly confirmed." A thirty foot image of Tobias also appeared on a screen behind him, so those in the back could detect his every facial expression.

"I will now ask Miss Russo to make a brief, prepared statement. She will be followed by Dr. Timothy Benari, an expert in something called *zero point energy*. He will make a prepared statement as well. Then we will introduce our full panel and open up the floor for questions." He gestured to Madison. "The microphone is all yours."

Madison approached the lectern in flats and a dark suit, consisting of a pencil skirt and matching jacket. She hated formal wear and found the outfit restricting and uncomfortable. But if there was ever a time to dress formally, headlining a press conference in front of most of America was probably it. She adjusted the microphone and cleared her throat.

"Hello," she croaked, and to her own ears her voice sounded tiny and meek. "As Dr. Tobias said," she continued, managing to increase her volume despite the trouble she was having taking in oxygen, "my name is Madison Russo. Before I describe my findings, I thought it was important to give a quick—and I hope painless—review of Einstein's theory of relativity."

She half expected to hear a unanimous groan from the crowd of reporters. She hadn't slept in thirty-six hours, so didn't entirely trust her judgment, but while everyone had heard of relativity, she guessed that few non-scientists fully understood its implications. Or how profoundly it had turned mankind's intuitive sense of how the universe worked upside down.

She smiled nervously. "Naturally, this will be a huge oversimplification. But relativity is critical to understanding the discovery that Dr. Tobias spoke of.

"So here is a three minute course. Suppose I threw a ball twenty miles per hour at a boy racing away from me on a bike, also going twenty miles per hour. How fast would the ball gain on him? The answer is, it wouldn't. Relative to the boy, the ball would be going at zero miles per hour. If he was racing *toward* me at twenty miles per hour, the ball I threw would be closing the gap at *forty* miles per hour."

Madison looked out over the audience to see how the reporters were reacting, but they might as well have been made of stone. "So relative velocities are just a matter of addition and subtraction," she continued. "Pretty simple, and true for every object ever measured." She paused. "But then light came along. It travels at an incomprehensible speed of *670 million miles an hour.* And as impossible as it seems, it doesn't obey this simple rule. The speed of light measured by an observer is exactly the same, no matter how fast he or she is moving toward it or away from it. If you were traveling at ninety-nine percent the speed of light, and chasing a beam of light, it would still be moving away from you *at the full speed of light.*"

She turned a page of notes and continued. "This would be like being in car going fifty-nine, chasing a car going sixty, and the car you're chasing is still gaining on you at *sixty miles an hour*. Just as fast as it would if you were *standing still*. Seems impossible, and defies common sense. Newtonian physics couldn't explain it. Fortunately, Albert Einstein developed a physics that could."

Madison paused for just a moment and looked out at the sea of reporters. They still could have been made of wood for all the interest they were showing. *Oh my God*, she thought. *I'm boring an entire nation to death.* Her throat tightened, and breathing became even more difficult. But there was no turning back now.

"Einstein devised a theory and set of mathematics to account for light's strange behavior," she continued, forcing the words out. "According to him, speed changes *everything*. As objects get faster, to an unmoving observer, they shrink in length and increase in mass. At just a hair away from light speed, an object's length would be very near zero. And its mass would approach *infinity*. And time would slow down for it as well. If you traveled very near the speed of light for just a few minutes—at least for you—a million years could have passed for your sister on Earth."

Madison could tell from the body language of the room that interest in the subject matter was growing.

"Pretty mind-blowing stuff. And it seems totally crazy. But Einstein's predictions have now been proven over and over again. Particles that decay at one rate when they're slow, take far longer to decay when traveling near the speed of light. Precisely as the equations of relativity predict. Even GPS satellites are corrected for relativistic effects using Einstein's equations. The reason these effects seem so ridiculous to our intuition is that they only take place at insane speeds, far faster than anything on earth can travel.

"Einstein also provided a new take on gravity. He realized spacetime is like a trampoline, which is dented by any object with mass. Put a bowling ball in the center of a trampoline and it causes an indentation, so that anything else you put on it wants to roll downhill toward the ball. This is gravity. When a mass indents spacetime it sends out gravitational waves at the speed of light. Until very recently, these were all but impossible to detect. But a new theory has arisen which has allowed for super sensitive detection of these waves.

"My research gives me access to such a detector. I designed software to sift through billions of pages of gravitational wave data from endless masses, big and small. From asteroids to planets to suns. My software crunches this data and alerts me if it detects anything unusual." She paused for effect. "And last night it did. It detected a mass the size of our moon in interstellar space, in the plane of the ecliptic, hurtling towards us from the direction of galactic center. Dr. Tobias has provided the exact coordinates in your information package."

She paused and took a sip of water from a glass on the lectern. "Now a moon sized mass by itself isn't all that interesting. *But the mass of this object was falling precipitously as it went.* First it was the mass of the moon. Then this moving object was only half as massive. Then only a fifth. Then a tenth. And so on.

"This made no sense at first. But then I remembered relativity. Remember that an object's mass increases as it gets closer and closer to the speed of light. If an object were traveling very near the speed of light, and then began to decelerate, one would observe exactly what I had observed.

"But objects in interstellar space don't travel anywhere *near* the speed of light. So I was sure I was mistaken. But when I drove this data through Einstein's equations, it fit *perfectly*. Crosschecking its apparent mass at different time points and at different locations gives a precisely consistent picture mathematically. I'll spare you the math, but the picture that emerged from the equations is as follows: a spherical object that, when not moving, would be roughly the size and weight of a small car, was traveling at greater than 99.99999 % of light speed. It then began braking smoothly. At its initial speed its apparent mass was huge, but as its speed fell its mass decreased dramatically.

"As most of you now know, further gravitational readings and further math indicate that this object is headed directly toward Earth. As of an hour ago, it was travelling just over a million miles per hour, and it is still slowing. If it continues to decelerate smoothly, it will intersect our planet in exactly twenty-two days time."

19

John Kolke waited patiently for his commander to return to his office, one of several the colonel maintained at military bases across the country.

Colonel Morris Jacobson entered and took the chair at his desk, facing his second in command, and he didn't look good.

Kolke was confused by his demeanor. "You did tell Rosenblatt about his daughter, right?" he asked.

Jake sighed. "Yeah, I told him."

"Then why do you look so miserable?"

"It didn't go the way I thought it would. I might have made things worse."

"What? How is that possible?"

"Part of him is desperate to believe me. But part of him thinks this is some kind of cruel mind fuck. That I'm giving him hope, just so I can snatch it away later to destroy him even more. So he's afraid to believe me, just in case it isn't true. If he believed me, and then it turned out I was lying, it would be like losing his daughter twice."

"I see what you're saying," said Kolke.

Jake checked his watch. He had about twenty minutes before he called Miller a second time. His people had gotten nowhere tracing the call or finding Miller's IP address, as expected.

"So what did you think of Kira Miller?" asked Jake. Kolke had listened in on his call, but Jake had wanted to delay any postgame discussion until after he had spoken with Rosenblatt.

"She's impressive," replied the major. "Her reputation is well earned. Her charisma comes through, even when you can't see her. And from her pictures, I can only imagine how much seeing her in person adds to the effect." He paused. "You can't possibly believe she's sincere about this trade, though."

"No," agreed Jake. "Not for a second. But we need to figure out what her angle is. She didn't go through this charade for her health."

"It has to be a rescue attempt."

"I agree that's the most likely explanation. She'll set up the handoff so she'll know where we'll be with her people. Then she'll attack. Or members of her group will. She'll count on those pills of hers giving them the advantage, no matter how we protect ourselves."

"So how do you want to play it?"

Jake didn't answer for almost a full minute. Kolke waited patiently while the colonel weighed options in his head. "We restrain Desh and Rosenblatt at a location far away from where we acquire Miller. Metal handcuffs, plastic handcuffs, leg irons, the works—we bind and gag them so thoroughly we can walk away without any worry they'll escape. In an apartment, maybe. Or a hotel room."

"What about in a self storage facility? In one of those little steel rooms you can rent out?"

"Perfect," said Jake. "When Miller is safely in our custody, we tell her people where to find Desh and Rosenblatt. This way, ambushing us does them no good. Not if they want their people back."

"I like it. But she'll never agree to it."

"If you're right, I'll have at least forced her to show her hand. She'll still be intent on outsmarting us, so the discussion won't end there. The ball will be in her court, and you'd better believe she'll hit it back." He paused. "But for some reason, I think she'll agree to just about anything I propose."

Kolke's face wrinkled in confusion. "Why?"

"Because she's a lot smarter than we are. Even without her magic pills. We're just thinking a move or two deep and congratulating ourselves. She's playing a different game. I think she already factored this play into her equation."

"If that's true, then you should refuse to deal. Period."

Jake smiled. "Yeah. Probably. But if I do that she'll have won forever. She already has me second guessing myself, jousting at shadows. But if I believe no matter what I do, she's a few steps ahead, then I'm paralyzed and may as well pack it in now."

"So what else do you think she might have up her sleeve?"

Jake rubbed his head. "There is one flaw in my plan. Even if she can't directly free her friends, she could try to capture me and force me to give up their location."

Kolke considered. "Not if you don't know it," he said.

"Good thought, Major. Very good thought." Jake paused for several long seconds. "So we can play it like this. You and I separate. You leave Desh and Rosenblatt bound somewhere, but you don't tell me their location. But now it should be in an apartment. Far more of these than there are storage facilities. If she really does give herself up, you tell her people where to find our two guests. If she kills or captures me and our team while we're trying to take her into custody, you just re-gather the prisoners and she's no better off."

"Not to rain on this parade or anything," said Kolke wryly, "but under this scenario, she might not get her people back, but you're still captured or dead. Doesn't seem like much fun on your end."

Jake laughed. "Well, I'll do my best to see that this doesn't happen. It's just a worst case. We can have her rent an SUV and give her driving instructions as she goes, so we can't be ambushed. We'll find a stretch of low ground between two cliff walls—like a shallow canyon," he said, his head tilted back as he thought it through and tried to envision the handoff in his mind's eye. "One she can get to quickly by off-roading. We can have helos overhead making sure she isn't followed and snipers on both cliffs. Most with live ammo—but a few with tranquilizer rifles, just on the off chance she doesn't try anything."

"That seems like . . . adequate . . . protection," said Kolke, and Jake could tell his second in command was convinced this was overkill. Maybe so, but this woman's capabilities had him spooked.

Kolke was about to continue when Jake said, "hold that thought," and picked up the phone on his desk. He described the kind of terrain he was looking for in the Colorado area to the woman who answered, and that he needed the GPS coordinates of such a place communicated to him as soon as possible. He hung up and gestured to the major. "Go on," he said.

"I was just going to say, if she agrees to this—a huge *if* in my book—she'll have zero chance. Even if she takes one of her pills when you encounter her."

"Don't forget that she and her Icarus friends can come up with breakthrough technology every time they're enhanced. Very little is beyond the reach of their minds. And even without a technology advantage, if she's able to take a gellcap, you don't want any part of her. That's where the tranquilizer comes in. We use one to put her to sleep. When she's down, we maintain our positions—snipers and helos—for ninety minutes. Even if she enhanced herself just prior to the encounter, the effect only lasts about an hour. After ninety minutes, we tape her mouth shut so she can't surprise us and take a pill, strip her naked to eliminate the possibility of hidden technology, and take her in."

"Easy as pie," said Kolke dryly. "What are we waiting for?" He paused and shook his head. "It's a good plan, Colonel. But I'm still afraid she'll never agree to it," he added.

"That's funny," said Jake grimly. "I'm more afraid that she will."

20

Madison Russo finished her prepared statement, took a seat on the podium, and Dr. Timothy Benari replaced her at the lectern. He glanced down at his notes.

"I'm going to keep this short and simple," he began. "As Dr. Tobias mentioned, my work is in the field of zero point energy. I'm glad Miss Russo described relativity to you. The other major breakthrough that occurred around this time, which Einstein also had a big hand in helping to launch, was quantum physics. I'm not going to explain this to you now, simply because it's *so* strange that it makes relativity seem intuitive. Even Einstein could never bring himself to really believe the implications of this theory. This being said, modern electronics wouldn't be possible without it, and it is arguably the most successful theory of all time."

He paused. "But it *is* unbelievably bizarre. What it says is that particles can be in two places at once, can be linked over unlimited distance, and can pop into and out of existence. Oh, and it suggests something else: that there is a nearly infinite amount of energy in every square centimeter of vacuum. That the vacuum really isn't a vacuum. That as close to a free lunch as this universe will ever offer is just waiting to be harvested. Zero point energy.

"This was confirmed in 1997, an event the *The New York Times* described particularly well in an article entitled, *Physicists Confirm Power of Nothing, Measuring Force of Universal Flux.* I'll read a few excerpts from it now:

"For half a century, physicists have known that there is no such thing as absolute nothingness, and that the vacuum of space, devoid of even a single atom of matter, seethes with subtle activity. Now, with the help of a pair of metal plates and

a fine wire, a scientist has directly measured the force exerted by fleeting fluctuations in the vacuum that pace the universal pulse of existence . . . Dr. Lumoreaux's experiment was the first direct and conclusive demonstration of . . . the Casimir Effect, which has been posited as a force produced solely by activity in the "empty" vacuum. His results came as no surprise to anyone familiar with quantum electrodynamics, but they served as material confirmation of a bizarre theoretical prediction.

Quantum electrodynamics holds that the all-pervading vacuum continuously spawns particles and waves that spontaneously pop into and out of existence on an almost unimaginably short time scale.

This churning quantum 'foam,' as some physicists call it, is believed to extend throughout the universe. It fills empty space within the atoms in human bodies, and reaches the emptiest and most remote regions of the cosmos."

Dr. Benari stopped reading. "So why is any of this relevant?" he said. "Because speeding up an object the size of a car to near light speed takes some *serious* energy: more than the total output of our sun over a fifty year period. With current human understanding, the only way this could be done is if a civilization found a way to tap this zero point energy. Even taming antimatter wouldn't provide enough power. I've spent my entire career trying to find some way to tap this infinite free lunch, and so have my colleagues. We haven't gotten very far, to say the least. Many of us believed it couldn't be done." He nodded his head slowly. "Well, now we know otherwise."

He paused for several seconds. "I've theorized that if this zero point energy, or ZPE, were tapped," he continued, "it would change something called the Planck constant. I'd be happy to explain what this is later on. The bottom line is that an object harvesting this energy would change some fundamental properties of the universe around it, including light, and result in a telltale spectroscopic pattern that I've called *Casimir Radiation*."

Dr. Benari smiled broadly, unable to help himself. His theory had been attacked without mercy, and until yesterday, his prediction had been considered to be untestable. What a difference a day made. Einstein had predicted that light from a distant star coming close to the Sun would be bent, but it was years before an eclipse occurred and proper equipment was in place to measure it. Once it was, the deflection of the light turned out to be 1.7 arc seconds, matching Einstein's prediction exactly, proving his vision of gravity and spacetime and making him the most famous scientist on the planet. Now it was Benari's turn.

"Turns out my theory isn't just a theory anymore," he continued. "We've discovered this Casimir Radiation coming from the object, precisely as my theory predicted. Whatever is coming towards us is not only alien life, and *intelligent* alien life, it's from a highly advanced civilization that has conquered the ultimate energy source."

He raised his eyebrows. "And assuming it doesn't veer off course, I, for one, am dying to get a peek under the hood."

21

Jake trained a pair of binoculars on the red SUV that had just entered the center of the wide ravine. Hundred-foot cliff walls rose sharply on both sides.

"Nice choice," noted a self-assured voice from the earpiece in his left ear, coming in clearly despite the whipping sound made by the blades of three helos circling overhead, maintaining a three mile surveillance perimeter. "How many men do you have on each cliff?"

"One or two," replied Jake noncommittally.

"More like five or ten, I'm guessing," said Kira Miller. "And helicopters to boot. Looks like someone was paying attention the day they taught how to take the high ground in military school."

"Just a sign of how much respect I have for you," said Jake.

"Lucky me," she mumbled wryly. "I'm getting out now," she added. "How about reminding your men of our little agreement. No killing the helpless girl."

"They know," said Jake.

A moment later the front door of the car sprung open and a lithe woman stepped out wearing faded blue jeans and a teal, v-neck blouse. He could see her well enough but he used the binoculars to zoom in on her face. His heart picked up speed. It was Kira Miller in the flesh. At least it seemed to be. With this woman you could never be sure of *anything*.

"Walk ten or fifteen yards away from your car with your hands in plain sight," he instructed.

She was wearing a headset as he had asked, so her hands were completely free. She raised them above her head and began walking. "As you can see, it really is me," she said into the microphone extending toward her mouth. "I've done everything you asked for. I'm in your control. Now how about living up to your end and texting my associates where to find your prisoners?"

"Don't worry. I'll stick to our agreement. But I'm not quite satisfied. Not yet."

"Another sign of respect?"

"I'm afraid so. I'm going to add someone to the call. She's going to ask you a few questions."

He manipulated his phone and a second later a woman joined them on the line. "Tell me the properties of a Type III restriction enzyme?" she said, her voice low and scratchy.

A wide, unselfconscious grin came over Kira Miller's face, which Jake saw clearly through his binoculars. "Okay, *now* I'm impressed," she said. "You take caution to whole new levels, Colonel. If this isn't really me in the middle of nowhere, who do you think it is? You think I found a perfect double and convinced her to give herself up in my place?"

"Probably not. But I thought you were in the building I destroyed, and I was wrong about that. You can never be too careful. I promised to give up Desh and Rosenblatt for Kira Miller. Not a stand in."

"A fair point," allowed Kira. "Okay. A Type III restriction enzyme cuts DNA about twenty to thirty base pairs from its recognition site, which consists of two, inversely oriented, non palindromic sequences. They have more than one subunit, require AdoMet for DNA methylation, and need ATP as a cofactor. They methylate only one strand of DNA, at the N-6 position of adenosyl residues." She paused. "Are we done?"

"Not quite yet," said the woman. She went on to ask four additional questions, each of them more difficult, and several which could only be answered by someone with a practical knowledge of genetic engineering, rather than just book knowledge.

When Kira had answered the last question, Jake's expert told him that in her professional opinion the woman on the phone was a top flight molecular biologist, and left the call.

"Satisfied?" asked the stunning woman in the gorge below.

Jake signaled to a sniper nearby, and seconds later Kira Miller crumpled to the ground, unconscious.

"Completely," replied Jake to no one in particular.

***

Jim Connelly broke the lock on the door labeled 47J in the *Pinewood Knolls* apartment complex east of Denver and carefully stepped inside, although he knew this wasn't an ambush. He had complete confidence in the assessment his altered self had made of Jake's veracity, and would have bet his life the man would not go back on his word. In fact, he realized, he *was* betting his life.

As he entered the unit, Connelly found David Desh and Seth Rosenblatt bound together in the center of the living room in multiple ways, with layers of gray duct tape firmly affixed to their mouths. Connelly found the keys to multiple pairs of handcuffs and leg irons in a potted plant in the corner, as he had been told he would. He quickly removed these devices from both men and used his freshly sharpened combat knife on Desh's bonds first, sawing through the tough plastic handcuffs and other fasteners that continued to immobilize him.

While he was doing this he pulled the tape from his friend's mouth in one quick motion.

"*How could you let her do this?*" demanded Desh the instant his mouth was free. "*She's more important than all of us combined!*"

Connelly continued cutting through his bonds. "When Kira Miller is intent on doing something," he responded calmly, in marked contrast to his friend's rage. "No power on earth is going to stop her." He gestured toward Rosenblatt. "But let's talk about this later."

Seconds later Desh was free, and within another minute they had both managed to free the tall physicist. Desh was still fuming, but he remained silent.

"David, you're with me," said Connelly. "Dr. Rosenblatt, I'm going to ask you to stay here for just a few minutes."

Rosenblatt looked confused but nodded his acquiescence.

Shortly after Desh and Connelly left there was a knock at the door. The physicist eyed it warily and then opened it.

His wife was standing at the entrance, tears welling up in the corners of her eyes.

Below her, a tiny figure looked up at him.

"*Daddy!*" squealed little Jessica excitedly, her voice tiny and endearing.

Seth Rosenblatt fell to his knees, and his daughter ran forward and launched herself into his arms.

He drew her close, hugging her as though he might never let go, drawing sustenance from this tiny, precious, perfect little girl—one he had been sure he had lost forever.

Quiet tears poured down his face. *Jake had not lied about her, after all.*

"I love you, Honey," he said. "I love you *so* much." He continued to cling to her as desperately as if she were a life preserver in a roiling sea.

"Daddy, are you okay?" asked Jessica, pulling away and looking at his face uncertainly. She had never seen her father shed a single tear, yet multiple streams continued to roll down his cheeks.

He nodded. "I'm more than okay, Sweetie."

Jessica's mother knelt down beside her. "Sometimes grown-ups cry when they're happy," she explained.

The little girl looked up at her daddy, who was smiling through his tears, but she still wasn't entirely convinced. "Are you happy, Daddy?"

Seth Rosenblatt pulled his daughter close once again and squeezed, his tears continuing to fall. "Oh yes," he said euphorically. "Happier than you can even imagine."

22

Kira's eyes finally fluttered open as the last of the tranquilizer was reversed by the agent Colonel Jacobson had administered several minutes previously. She was dressed in a gray, zippered jumpsuit, and every means of ingress into her body—ears, nostrils, throat, anus, and vagina—throbbed slightly, or in some other way advertised that they had been thoroughly probed. Her hands were bound together with tough plastic cuffs and had been placed in her lap.

She shook herself fully awake and took in her surroundings. She was in a large office, although it was non-descript and hadn't been personalized in any way. She was sitting before a large desk, facing the man who had appeared on her computer screen to arrange the swap, this Colonel Jacobson. Behind him, an eight-by-ten picture frame was lying face down on a credenza.

The colonel studied her calmly, in no apparent hurry to get the proceedings started.

She gestured to her surroundings with her head. "What, no interrogation room? No leg irons? No spotlight shining in my face and a team of experts behind a two-way mirror?"

"I like to start on the civilized side when I can. And in these days of video cameras, two-way mirrors are only useful in bad spy movies."

"Good point," she admitted. "I must still be a little groggy from your knockout drug." She raised her eyebrows. "Although I can't say I'm sorry I was unconscious for my proctology and gynecology exams."

"Sorry about that," said Jake, with enough sincerity that Kira believed he really was. "If it makes you feel any better, we had a woman conduct the examination below the waist."

"How gallant of you," she said, rolling her eyes. "Find anything interesting?"

Jake shook his head. "Not for lack of trying. On the other hand, after my experience with Seth Rosenblatt, we've taken your clothing—including your panties and bra—to a lab where everything will all be taken apart atom by atom. And we'll assume we're being listened to when we do. We made a mistake with Rosenblatt's clothing. When our scans indicated no activity, we didn't examine it further. Now we have, and we've found some advanced electronics in the waistband of his jockeys, very nearly microscopic. Desh's too. I'm looking forward to finding out what's inside *your* panties."

"I bet you say that to all the girls," said Kira with a wry smile.

Jake couldn't help but return the smile, but this quickly faded. "We've already begun reverse engineering the technology. We should know how you've managed it soon."

"Good luck with that," said Kira, unconcerned. "But before we go any further," she added, "can I assume you held up your end of the deal? That David and Seth are free and unmolested?"

"I held up my end of the deal, yes. Which means I have no idea if they're free. All I know is that I texted their location to the e-mail address you gave me."

Kira studied him. "I don't suppose you'd be willing to tell me where we are and how long I was out for?"

"I don't suppose you'd be willing to tell me about your work on WMD and interactions with terrorist leaders and dictators? And details of your husband's activities?"

"Since I've been framed—yet again—and none of this is true, I'd be more than happy to tell you everything I know." She paused. "But you first. Where are we? And how long was I out?"

Jake studied her with a renewed intensity, perhaps seeing if she would begin to squirm. She waited patiently, her cuffed hands folded in her lap, the scrutiny not appearing to intimidate her or make her uncomfortable in the least.

"It's funny," he said. "My instinct is not to tell you. You're cuffed and have no weapons—or gellcaps. No technology, period. You've been stripped and probed extensively. Even if you had an invisible bug and transmitter—which this time I'm sure you don't—your friends couldn't rescue you. You're going to tell me what you know, one way or another, and be a prisoner for the rest of your life. So I have no reason not to answer your questions."

Jake stared at her once more for several seconds. "But you're so damned *relaxed*," he continued. "You're not playing the captured terrorist about to rot in prison. You're playing the carefree, affable young woman, chatting with a friend. Almost as if you arranged this just to size *me* up." He paused. "What have I failed to take into account? Is there another shoe about to drop? Tell me, Kira Miller, what am I missing?"

"Not a thing. I'm not nearly as dangerous as you seem to think I am. You're as thorough as they come. I did have a few rabbits up my sleeves," she added with a grin. "But then you took away my sleeves."

Jake raised his eyebrows. "Your charisma is remarkable. They say Steve Jobs was so charismatic, he projected something that came to be known as a *reality distortion field*. But I've never experienced something like this in person. Until now. And Jobs didn't have your looks."

"Thank you, Colonel. To be honest, I had expected to be beaten around the head with a bag of doorknobs, not to be given compliments." She frowned. "But for all of my supposed charisma, I can't even get you to tell me where we are or how long I was out."

"You were out for seven hours. And we're at Peterson Air Force Base in Colorado Springs."

Kira digested this information. Given Icarus was headquartered in nearby Denver, she knew Peterson well. It housed NORAD, as well as the air force and army space commands. And it was within a hundred miles of where she had been captured. "Isn't Peterson a bit obvious?"

"Maybe. But your colleagues won't expect someone as careful as I am to do the obvious. And since you could be anywhere, they'd have to be absolutely positive you were here to risk a raid to extract you. And even if they did they wouldn't succeed. Not from a base this secure."

"Impressive reasoning," said Kira. She leaned forward. "By the way, is this conversation private, or do you have those video cameras you spoke of sending it out to a bunch of your friends?"

"Why do you care?"

"Maybe I'm not the exhibitionist type," she replied dryly. "If I'm going to bare my soul, I prefer to know who I'm baring it to."

"We're being videotaped, but just for my own use. No one else knows about that. For this session only, our discussion will be private. But just so you don't get any ideas," he added, "there are three guards outside of this room. While you're here, they're checking in every ten minutes with my second in command. If they fail to check in, special forces teams will descend on this area like locusts."

Kira lifted her hands and nodded toward the plastic cuffs locked around her wrists. "Are you sure three guards and handcuffs are enough? I mean, if you think it'd be safer to use leg irons attached to a cannonball, I'll wait while you get them."

"Don't test me," he warned. "My instincts tell me you're still dangerous. Maybe I *should* restrain you further."

Kira realized she had miscalculated and decided it was time to change the subject. "So tell me, Colonel," she said, as if the prior exchange had never taken place. "How did you figure out I was alive? And learn about my ability to boost IQs? And most importantly, where did you get your misinformation as to my intentions?"

"Not misinformation. Unimpeachable evidence."

"So you've said. How about showing me some of it then?"

Jake nodded slowly. "Okay," he said. "Why not?" His eyes narrowed in thought. "We'll start with your, um . . . good friend, David Desh."

He worked the touchscreen on a thin laptop on his desk connected wirelessly to a monitor on the table behind him. A video appeared on the screen.

Kira saw herself and David Desh sitting on the floor, their backs against a concrete wall in a gray, dimly lit basement. Heavy steel rungs had been bolted into the wall, and both prisoners had their wrists bound together behind their backs and through one of the rungs with plastic strips.

The scene came rushing back to her with a dizzying intensity. Her brother's puppet—who they had first known as Smith, but who had later turned out to be a man named Sam Putnam—had captured them and moved them to the basement of a safe house.

The events of that night were seared into her mind. Putnam had taunted her, and had convinced her he had implanted an explosive in her skull that could liquefy her brain.

She hadn't thought about this for a long time. Watching this footage brought back too many bad memories, but she couldn't look away. Desh had managed to take a gellcap, and had faked illness. On the screen, sweat began pouring out of him in the cool basement, forced through his pores by the conscious application of his amplified intellect, which gave him exquisite control over his every cell and bodily system, autonomic or not.

Kira watched the video in horror and fascination. There was no doubt in her mind that this footage was real.

Three armed men now entered the frame. Desh had convinced them the contents of his stomach were about to erupt onto the floor, and that they needed to let this happen in the bathroom rather than suffer the mess and smell for an entire night.

One of the men freed him from the steel ring and began to lead him to the bathroom. A few steps later Desh doubled over and pretended to vomit. In the instant the guards looked away in disgust, he snatched a knife from the man beside him and buried it in the chest of one of the other guards. The moment Desh released the knife, he spun the man who had freed him to his left, just in time for him to take a tranquilizer dart meant for Desh.

The third guard was highly trained in several forms of martial arts, but Desh dismantled him as if the guard were moving in slow motion.

Desh had taken out the three men like an over-the-top hero in a martial arts film, with timing and fighting skills impossible in the real world. His actions were effortless. And just like in a highly choreographed stunt fight, Desh had known every move the men would make, almost before they did.

After having disabled the three armed men, he ducked behind the wooden staircase. A fourth man came rushing down to check on his comrades, and Desh calmly buried a dart in his leg through the opening between stairs. The man rolled down the last few stairs, unconscious.

Desh then freed Kira, and they both rushed up the stairs.

The footage continued, but the basement was now still.

"Okay," said Kira. "This did happen. I'll admit it. But so what? We were obviously justified in escaping. And David used non-lethal force when he could. Hardly evidence that he's an enemy of the state."

Jake shook his head grimly. "Nice try. But you can't really think we don't have the rest of the footage."

"What are you talking about?" she said.

Jake touched his laptop and the video jumped ahead. David Desh was now bounding down the stairs. Kira had forgotten he had returned to the basement briefly, while she had waited upstairs, to see if any of the guards had carried wallets or ID.

The guard with the knife protruding from his chest was dead. The other three were unconscious, but in good health. Desh made no move to check their pockets. Instead, he calmly took a knife and surgically slit each man's throat, one by one, using great care so he wouldn't get blood on himself. Like a butcher slaughtering cattle.

Kira's eyes widened in horror and she choked back vomit.

It was his total lack of expression, his clinical detachment, that was the most frightening of all.

"Good acting, Miss Miller—or Mrs. Desh—whatever you're calling yourself these days," said Jake as the video stopped. "You do shocked and horrified about as well as I've ever seen."

"This footage was doctored," croaked Kira weakly, still not recovered. "It had to have been." But she looked even less sure than she sounded.

Jake frowned and shook his head. "Sure it was," he said sarcastically. "You do realize we've analyzed the hell out of this footage. Not a single frame has been altered in any way. It's one continuous shot. If the first part you saw is accurate—and you admitted as much—then the last part is also."

Kira turned away with a look of revulsion. David Desh was the most compassionate man she knew. Yes, he had killed in battle, but never helpless men. Not like this. True, her therapy brought out the worst in human nature, and it could be brutally difficult to control this Mr. Hyde personality. But a loss of control this great was shocking. And worse, he had never told her about it after he had returned to normal.

This would have been important information for her to have. At the time, they had little experience with the effects of enhancement. And she would have expected him to be horrified by the actions of his alter ego, to be beating himself up for not finding a way to prevent them. Yet he hadn't said a single word, nor had he appeared the least bit remorseful.

They had been through so much together. But what she had just seen made her question everything she *thought* she knew. Could she trust David Desh? She would never have believed this possible of him, even enhanced. How could she possibly have misjudged him so greatly? And if he could keep this from her, what other secrets might he be keeping?

But as she turned her thoughts back to the video she had just seen, she had a startling realization, one just as disturbing as her husband's betrayal of her trust.

23

The object continued to hurtle toward Earth, its speed now below a million miles per hour. Nearly every gravitational wave detector on Earth, and every space and ground-based telescope, tracked every inch of its arrival. It continued to decelerate with smooth and steady perfection, never deviating one iota from its direct course to the birthplace of humanity.

The world kept revolving. People still needed to work and feed their families. Planes still flew and buses still ran.

But alien visitation was the topic on everyone's mind, spurring endless debate and endless speculation. It filled up all news and entertainment forums almost absolutely. And rightly so.

It was a seminal moment in history. Perhaps *the* seminal moment in history. Humanity was no longer alone in the universe. A stunning development. Nothing would ever be the same.

Everyone had an opinion on the subject. Religions took the news in a variety of ways. Some clergy embraced the idea of intelligent alien life. Others saw it all as a ruse, the work of the devil, to test the faith of true believers. God had made man in his image. If intelligent aliens existed, why hadn't God, or Allah, or Christ, not made mention of this important fact?

And of course the crazies came out in droves. The nutcases. The conspiracy theorists. The end-of-the-worlders. Only this time they had almost as much chance of being right about events to come as were the most sober and rational scientists.

Science fiction had speculated about aliens and first contact for decades, but with every last one of Earth's billions now engaged in their own speculations, all ideas ever considered by this burgeoning genre were touched upon in a matter of hours by someone around the globe, along with scores of ideas that had never been previously contemplated.

The object was small. Was it filled with aliens the size of ants? If so, was there a minimum brain size necessary to support intelligent thought? Was it simply a hot rodding robot? A computerized probe? Would it send out a signal to awaken huge colony ships buried under miles of ice in the arctic, or under the ocean floor? Was it coming to bring the final enlightenment? To welcome humanity into a vast intergalactic community? Or was it coming to destroy humanity? Was it a modern day flood sent by a vengeful God to punish the race for turning the entire planet into a den of iniquity that would make the residents of Sodom and Gomorrah sick to their stomachs and flush in embarrassment? Or was it just a scout? Would it simply fly by, record activity, and then never be seen again? Was it randomly sampling planets, or was it aware of the presence of humanity and actively seeking it out? Had it been sent by an alien army corps of engineers to puncture a hole in spacetime and create a stargate for the good people of Earth to use? Was it pure good? Pure evil? Pure indifference?

The conjecture never ended. Peaceful prayer meetings sprang up across the globe, conducted by a number of different religions. Riots broke out. Con artists, crazies, and spotlight seekers arose who insisted they were in contact with the incoming craft, and who declared themselves prophets.

But the majority of the world's inhabitants continued going through the motions of living their lives. Billions upon billions adopted a wait-and-see fatalism.

Oblivious to the commotion it was causing on its target world, the small craft effortlessly tapped into the near infinite amount of energy available in every square centimeter of vacuum, and hurtled onward.

The people of Earth watched. And waited.

24

Kira had been so intent on watching the video Jake showed her, she had failed to consider the implications of its very existence.

The footage had come from Sam Putnam's basement. From the safe house they had been in. But her brother, Alan, had never seen it. In the last minutes of his life, he had wanted to know how they had managed to escape from Putnam's concrete dungeon.

So Putnam hadn't been fully forthcoming to Alan. He had been playing a game of his own.

And why not? He was an intelligent, highly placed operative in the NSA, who had amassed power that was unequaled. And he was a true psychopath. Alan was an even bigger psychopath, true, and was behind Putnam's meteoric rise through the NSA, but it would hardly be surprising to learn Putnam hadn't been the loyal puppet he had appeared to be.

But both Putnam and her brother were dead. So how had Jake ended up with this footage? The most likely explanation was that it was recovered by someone who had been working closely with Putnam or her brother. And if this were the case, all bets were off.

"Before you showed this video," said Kira, "I had asked you for your source of information about me. The existence of this footage has raised some disturbing possibilities. So the answer to this question is more important than ever."

"What possibilities?"

"I'll tell you, but it's better if you start. Really."

He considered. "Why do I continue to feel that you're interrogating *me?*"

Kira didn't respond.

"I received an e-mail from someone I consider a mentor," said Jake. "The most patriotic, heroic man I've ever known. A man of Islamic heritage who has spent years deep undercover, infiltrating the highest levels of Hezbollah."

"Born in America?"

"Yes, but able to speak unaccented Arabic. Anyway, the message had a large file attached that detailed everything about you. Your history. How you were hunted because of your involvement in a bioterror plot. Your IQ cocktail. How David Desh was sent to stop you. Your longevity treatment, along with proof that it was a hoax. Everything."

"Any mention of my brother, Alan?"

"Only that you had burned him alive. Again, you were later cleared of this, but my mentor knew otherwise." He paused. "In addition, there was unimpeachable evidence of you meeting with terrorist leaders—that's how he knew about you—working on WMD, both nuclear and biological. And also of your involvement in major terrorist attacks around the world."

"And where did he say he got this evidence? Did he claim all of this activity was somehow tied up with Hezbollah?"

"I don't know. He's in very, very deep. I can't contact him. He only risked contacting me once before. With information that was instrumental in stopping a plan to sabotage the San Onofre nuclear reactor in Orange County—which would have turned Southern California into Chernobyl. The fact that he risked another communication shows how important of a threat he thinks you are."

"But if you never followed up with him, how can you be sure he sent you the message?"

"It was him. The e-mail and IP address matched up. He referenced history that only he would know about."

Kira considered. She had no reason to doubt Jake that the evidence against her was airtight, and had been vetted repeatedly for authenticity. So what did this mean? Either she really was an evil terrorist set out to destroy the world, or . . . or all of this had been set up by someone with access to her therapy. It was the only way this could have been handled so flawlessly. But none of the gellcaps she had produced had been involved. She was certain of that.

Which meant that somewhere out there, there was someone who could make active gellcaps. Putnam had blackmailed a molecular biologist, a man they later learned was named Eric Frey. Kira's brother had stolen a number of gellcaps from her, and he had fed some of these to this blackmailed biologist, pushing him to recreate her work. When Putnam and her brother were killed, this Frey had been close to succeeding. But without access to several more doses of Kira's therapy, he was sure to fail.

But maybe not. Maybe he had been playing a double game as well. Maybe he had made more progress than he had let on. He may have been in league with Putnam to cross her brother. If so, this Eric Frey could well have access to the video footage she had just seen.

And if there were others, unknown to her, who could amplify their intelligence, they could have easily managed to fabricate airtight evidence against her. And could have hacked into the right computers to get the IP address and background information necessary to convince Jake the evidence had come from a trusted friend, conveniently deep undercover so this couldn't be checked further. It all fit together perfectly.

And then another piece of the puzzle suddenly slid into place.

"Colonel, there's something you're not telling me," she said. "When you read your friend's message, you should have thought he had gone off the deep end. You should have never believed in IQ enhancement. It's too fantastic. I know how improbable it is, and *I* developed it. Even with my genetic engineering abilities and study of autistic savants, it's astonishing that nature allows for it."

"My friend saved my life more than once. I trust him implicitly. If he's convinced of the power of your therapy, that's good enough for me."

She shook her head. "I think you're lying. Even if you believed in enhancement, you'd still never be able to imagine the transcendent capabilities of an enhanced mind. No way. But your actions suggest you *can* imagine it. I've seen your paranoia in action when you're dealing with me. You've been ridiculously careful. *Too* careful."

"What's your point?"

"Your friend didn't just send you an e-mail. He sent you a small package as well, didn't he?"

Jake gazed at her and sighed. "Very perceptive. I have to remember you're one of the few people in this world who are off-the-charts brilliant, even without any artificial help."

"So you admit it?"

He nodded. "Yes. You're right, of course. He sent me a package. With a single gellcap inside. He said the only way I could truly understand the threat, truly understand what I was up against, was to try it myself. If it had been anyone else I wouldn't have done it. But it was him. And the evidence was compelling."

"Only one?"

"Only one."

"So you learned firsthand just how amplified your intelligence becomes, and the spectacular capabilities that come with it." She paused in thought. "And the sociopathic tendencies must have hit you hard. Very hard. That's why you're so overzealous when it comes to the threat you think we pose."

A faraway look came to Jake's eyes. "That's right. The information I was sent detailed the side effects—the changes in personality. I thought I was prepared for it, but not by a long shot. I became ruthless. Savage. I had access to a computer and the Internet, and in that single hour, I doctored files, removed funds, and destroyed the careers and finances of two rivals of mine. *Friendly* rivals. I'm not a computer expert, and to this day I have no idea how I did it." He made no attempt to hide his self loathing. "I tried to undo the damage later, but got nowhere. I've been helping get them back on their feet anonymously, but they'll never be where they were."

"Does anyone know you were behind it?"

"No. I would have admitted it, but I couldn't recall how I had done it. And I couldn't even find evidence against myself. A confession would have raised too many questions I couldn't answer. I tried to undo the damage, but I couldn't."

"Now it all makes sense. Why you have so much respect for what my therapy can do. And why you believe I'm more dangerous than the devil. You've experienced the awesome power of an enhanced mind, and know this can turn even a saint into a tyrant. And you've been given evidence that I was a psychopath even before any therapy. So killing me, stopping me, became your crusade, your obsession."

He nodded. "I'm the only one outside of Icarus who knows how truly dangerous you can be. How truly creative and brilliant you become. Einstein and Edison times a hundred."

"You're being played, Colonel," said Kira evenly. "I'm not saying my therapy isn't dangerous in the wrong hands. Or even in the right hands if not enough precautions are taken. But the e-mail you received wasn't sent by your friend."

"And what do you base that on?"

"Did your friend tell you where he got the gellcap he sent?"

Jake shook his head no.

"Well he didn't get it from me. I know where every last one of them has gone. So whoever sent this message has their own source. Which means they have gellcaps for themselves. How hard do you think it would be for an enhanced mind to hack your buddy's IP address and history to fool you into thinking the message was from him? No matter how deeply buried it was. How hard would it be for an amplified intelligence to fabricate evidence to frame me? Evidence that could pass your every test for authenticity."

"Not hard, I'll admit. Maybe I'll buy this level of intelligence could have come up with ways to fake video footage well enough to stand up to the classified authentication methods we used, even though they're considered foolproof. But not *half* of a continuous shot. Not without leaving some evidence. And the footage I showed you was one continuous shot. You've vouched for its authenticity yourself."

Kira frowned. This was true, and certainly didn't help her argument. "Maybe it's the one authentic piece of evidence mixed in for good measure." She leaned forward and stared intently at the colonel. "But I'm telling you the message didn't come from your friend."

"If it didn't," challenged Jake, "tell me why anyone would go to the trouble. Why would anyone introduce me into the game?"

"So whoever is behind this can sit back and have you do all the work to root me out. To root *Icarus* out. Then they're free to do whatever they want. They can bide their time, build up power and resources, until you've knocked off the competition. Until you've eliminated the only people who can possibly stand in their way. Once we're gone you go back to blissful ignorance, thinking enhanced intelligence is a thing of the past."

Kira realized this was the reason whoever was behind this had gone out of their way to discredit her longevity treatment. After even her brother had failed to pry or trick it from her, they must have decided not to make an attempt. But they had learned that the lure of the fountain of youth was so powerful it could corrupt anyone, and they didn't want to give Jake and his group any reason to keep her alive.

"You're being used, Colonel," she said. "They've taken a page out of my brother's playbook. He framed me and used the military also. The difference is, he unleashed them to keep me running and to set me and David up for his perfect storm. Whoever is pulling the strings this time wants me eliminated."

"What are you talking about?" said Jake in confusion. "You *killed* your brother. Even before Desh was sent to find you."

Kira frowned. "If only," she said. "My brother didn't die in the fire. He was *behind* it all. I'm not surprised that whoever sent you the information didn't mention this little fact."

She went on to tell him about Putnam and Alan and everything that had happened.

"Very inventive," said Jake when she had finished. "Even you have to realize how farfetched all of that sounds."

"I do. That doesn't mean it isn't true. Besides, how could I come up with a story this complicated without tripping up even once? Because the truth is much easier to keep track of than a lie."

"If you were anyone else this might be convincing. But you're inventive enough to spin a web of bullshit on the fly without contradicting yourself."

"Colonel, you and I are on the same side. All I ask is that you at least consider the possibility that the information you have is false. Review it again with a more skeptical eye. And do the same with any new information you get. If you're right, no amount of reexamination will change the fact that I'm an enemy of civilization. But if *I'm* right, you'll discover you're pointed in the wrong direction. That the true enemy is waiting patiently for you to do their dirty work. What do you have to lose?"

Jake considered. "Despite your legendary persuasive abilities, I'm still convinced you are who I think you are. But I won't close my mind completely to other possibilities."

"*Thank you*," said Kira emphatically. "Again, we really are on the same side. I'd love to prove that to you. I know you're on other projects, trying to keep the world safe from WMD. If you're ever in a bind, hitting a brick wall on an important op, and think an enhanced mind could help break it open, I'm willing to help. You know how to reach me."

Jake tilted his head. "I know we've been having a pleasant little discussion here," he said. "And you've made some interesting points. But I still plan to lock you away for the rest of your life. Nothing has changed. So yes, I do know how to reach you."

Kira couldn't believe her own stupidity. What could possibly have possessed her to make a statement like this? To suggest so clearly she thought her stay was only temporary. She was very lucky she hadn't put him on guard. She could have found herself surrounded by twenty men and encased in cement if he chose to exercise his usual paranoia. At *exactly* the wrong time.

She quickly changed the subject, asking Jake about the base, the responsibilities of his group, and anything else she could think of to stall for time. She estimated she only needed to engage him in conversation for another ten minutes, but it turned out she was wrong. She only needed seven.

Kira's neurons reordered themselves in the mother of all chain reactions.

Her mind surged.

As familiar as the effect was, it never ceased to take her breath away.

She immediately turned her attention to analyzing various escape plans. She hadn't bothered putting any effort into this beforehand, unsure of what situation she'd find herself in, what location, how heavily guarded, or what state of physical incapacitation. But she hadn't been worried. She knew once her mind had jumped by orders of magnitude, she could figure it out on the fly.

A simple analysis made it clear that she should kill the colonel in front of her. It would make her escape easier. And he was talented, as far as normals went, and would be relentless in coming after her and the group. But she had to factor in the wishes of her pathetic alter ego, who controlled their body for all but a vanishingly small proportion of the time.

And moronic Kira thought Jake was a good man who was simply misinformed. Who fucking cared? Her analysis should only take into account the level of danger he posed, not whether he was good or bad, honorable or dishonorable, or just unlucky enough to be in the wrong place at the wrong time.

Moronic Kira was pathetic and weak, and her superior self had come to loath this weakness. Kira's brother had been right. She was nauseatingly self righteous, and managed to do everything the hard way, never willing to capitalize on the full potential of her invention. Always so worried that someone might get hurt, or she wouldn't get her good Samaritan badge.

Nonetheless, she would honor Kira's wishes in this case, and escape without killing anyone—if she could. Her first order of business was to incapacitate Jake and use his computer to plan her escape. Then she would take care of the guards patrolling outside his office.

She caused adrenaline to pour into her bloodstream to give her an added boost of strength to go along with her amplified reaction time.

Then, for the first time, she let the full power of her intellect shine through her eyes, and transfixed the colonel with a contemptuous, penetrating stare. She drew back her shoulders, tilted her head back haughtily, and her body language sent a shouted message of inhuman competence—and inhuman arrogance. The change in her bearing was unmistakable and intimidating on a visceral level.

The colonel gasped at the inner fire blazing in Kira Miller's eyes and became a mouse, momentarily mesmerized by a cobra.

Recovering from his initial shock, he shoved back his chair and rose, drawing his sidearm as he did so. But during his brief hesitation Kira had snatched the heavy stapler from off his desk, and in a blur of motion she tomahawked it two-handed at his head, before he could get off a shot. He slumped to the floor, dazed.

She moved around his desk and was on him in seconds, prying the gun from his hand and shoving it against his forehead.

She then turned a small fraction of herself into a dimwitted avatar, so she could communicate slowly enough to be understood. "Pounding your desk doesn't impress me!" she shouted, in case any of the guards beyond the closed door had heard the commotion and needed reassurance that it was benign. "*And don't you dare touch me like that again,*" she added for good measure. That should give the guards something to think about.

Jake's eyes were only half open and he was just clinging to consciousness. "But how?" he whispered. "We checked every inch of you for a hidden gellcap."

"You pathetic idiot!" she whispered with a sneer. "So worried about high-tech inventions that you forgot about a technology that's been around for decades. I took a controlled release capsule, *dumbshit.* Timed to release its contents in eight hours. I swallowed it before entering the ravine." She shook her head in contempt. "I hid a gellcap in my stomach, *you fucking moron.*"

With that she lowered her gun and maneuvered behind him. Despite having to keep her hands together, she was able to lock one slender arm under his chin in a chokehold, and slowly increased pressure to his neck until he bridged the short gap that separated him from unconsciousness.

25

Earth was home to almost two hundred sovereign countries, including dictatorships, democratic republics, theocracies, and constitutional monarchies, among others. And in every one of these countries, within every government, a frenzy of activity was taking place.

No one knew exactly what the alien craft would do once it arrived at its destination. But it was clear that whichever country controlled it might well control the secrets of the universe. It could contain a computer with blueprints for technology thousands of years more advanced than human technology. Even if it only—*only*—yielded the secret of zero point energy, the advantages this would give the country who discovered it were immeasurable.

So if it did come down to earth, where would it land? If its landing were random, it would most likely end up in the sea, which covered more than two-thirds of the planet's surface. If it came down on land, the largest countries by land mass were Russia, Canada, the United States, China, Brazil, and Australia.

But even the largest countries were well aware that the chance of it landing inside of their borders was small. For all anyone knew, it might set down in one of the smallest countries, like Tuvalu, Macau, or Monaco. The cosmos had a way of playing absurd statistical tricks on mankind. And if it happened to land in the world's smallest country, Vatican City—which comprised less than a square kilometer of the earth's surface—what would that mean? Or the Western Wall in Jerusalem? Or the Bhodi Tree in Bodh Gaya, India? Would this validate the religious beliefs embodied by these locations?

The level and intensity of communication between allies and enemies alike was unprecedented. Each government jockeyed for position. None held back a single card in whatever hand history had dealt them. Seen by an omniscient observer, the maneuverings would look like a two hundred piece game of chess, played in fifteen dimensions. Only more complicated.

Endless simulations were run. If the ship landed within the borders of a major military power, all other major powers would almost certainly ally in an attempt to take it away. If it landed in a small, helpless country, the world would be thrown into chaos as all other nations battled to take it by forging complex alliances, or using their own economic, political, or military power—like two hundred starving hyenas fighting over the scraps of a wildebeest.

In the end the complexity of trillions of possibilities quickly boiled down to an elegant simplicity. Regardless of where it landed, and what alliances were struck, the ending would be the same: chaos and disaster.

There was only one simulation that worked. If all the countries of the world agreed beforehand to cooperate. If every government—Islamic fundamentalist, socialist, and democratic republic alike—agreed that wherever the alien ship landed, it would be the property of the world, examined by representatives of each of the world's countries.

Different countries arrived at this conclusion at different speeds, but they all got there eventually. As more and more governments signed on, even the most independent, reluctant regimes had no choice but to do so as well. No nation could stand alone against the world. Or take the chance of not being a part of first contact with an envoy from an advanced alien species.

26

Kira found a paperclip in the top drawer of Jake's desk and unwound it. With her hands so close together, cutting through the hardened plastic around her wrists was nearly impossible, even if she found a knife or scissors, but Desh had taught her how to remove these restraints with a paperclip or pin. Some magicians had incorporated this more modern mode of handcuffing into their acts, since freeing oneself from metal handcuffs had been done so many times it was no longer interesting. Success required a high level of skill and precision, but Desh had drilled her on the technique until she could perform it even with her normal intelligence.

Plastic handcuffs were simple in design. They were slipped around a prisoner's wrists and ratcheted tight by threading the ends of the plastic straps through a centered retaining block. But the ratchet system housed in the sugar-cube sized plastic block could be disabled by shoving a paperclip inside in a precise way, between the roller lock and the teeth on the straps. Once this was done, the straps would slide out, almost as easily as they had slid in.

Kira calmly freed herself and dropped the intact plastic handcuffs on the floor. She lifted the photograph Jake had not wanted seen, although she was nearly certain of who it depicted. As expected, it turned out to be a young girl, probably ten or eleven years old. It didn't take an amplified intellect to figure this out. This was the daughter Jake spoke of to Kolke. The colonel didn't wear a wedding ring, and his divorce had probably occurred years earlier. He was in a line of work that made marriage very difficult, and any man who had five offices spread out across the country was never home. The failure of his marriage had been all but preordained.

Kira sat in Jake's chair facing his laptop, and her fingers flew over the keypad and touch screen at a furious pace. She digested entire screens of information as fast as they appeared before jumping to the next. In minutes she had hacked into the base's personnel files, which weren't all that secure, and found what she needed.

Her escape plan set, it was time to leave. She just had to decide how to accomplish the simple task of getting by the three highly trained men outside. She could lure them into Jake's office and shoot them, but this would likely result in their deaths. And if all three didn't enter, the last could close the door and call in reinforcements and she would lose the element of surprise.

If she exited, however, all three guns would be trained on her before she finished opening the door. She calculated she would still have a ninety-four percent chance of taking all three men out before one could get off a shot, but these odds weren't high enough.

The zipper of the jumpsuit she was wearing ran from just below her chin to just below her navel. She zipped it down all the way, pulled the jumpsuit open, and then, gripping the fabric with both hands, forced a jagged tear lower still, so that her vagina was now fully exposed along with her breasts.

She lowered herself to the floor near the door and calmly forced her tear ducts to release their contents from the corners of her eyes. She banged on the door, about six inches off the ground, with both fists together.

"*Help me,*" she yelled hysterically. "*Oh, God, please help me.*"

The door was thrown open almost immediately. The moment it was she rolled out into the hall, keeping her hands behind her, and lay sprawled on her back as if she were injured, tears streaming down her face. "Your boss is an *animal*," she whispered through sobs. "He tried to . . . to rape me."

The three guards all had their guns drawn and pointed at her, but her tears, her torn jumpsuit, and her nakedness had the desired effect. They had been trained to react decisively to almost any situation, but this was an exception. She counted on their chivalrous instincts to lead them astray, and they didn't disappoint. They each lowered their weapon to assess this unthinkable turn of events, and determine the extent of injuries that had been inflicted on this beautiful naked woman, dangerous though she might be.

Two of the guards leaned through the opening in the door to see how the girl had managed to fend off the colonel as he had tried to assault her.

This was all Kira needed. She swept the legs out from under one of the guards so viciously, and with such precision, that he had no time to cushion his fall. His head hit the ground with a loud crack and he lost consciousness. She sprang up from the floor acrobatically and drove the heel of her palm into the neck of a second man, knocking him out cold. As he slumped to the floor she kicked the gun from the third guard's hand and faced him.

Just before he assumed a fighting posture, his eyes darted down to her bare breasts for just an instant. The single-mindedness of the male brain, even during a crisis, was surprising even to the *enhanced* version of Kira Miller.

He attempted several blows that would have knocked out a moose had they landed, but none came close. Kira read his body language precisely and knew where his attacks were coming from, and going to, as soon as *he* did. She waited until he tried to land several more blows, with both his feet and hands, and then calmly drove a knife-hand into his neck while he was lunging at her, knowing he would miss and wouldn't recover fast enough to block her. Sure enough, her strike landed with stunning force and accuracy, and he fell to his knees. Before he recovered his senses, she threw an arm around him in a choke hold and coaxed him gently to sleep.

She stepped out of the jumpsuit and began stripping the smallest of the guards, who was still quite a bit larger than she was. The clothing was ridiculously baggy but better than a torn jumpsuit, and would make a soldier hesitate before firing, if only for a moment. One of the men had a small night vision scope in his belt, which she confiscated, along with a gun and a number of spare clips. She returned to the office and retrieved Jake's laptop and cell phone.

While she had been unconscious, day had turned into night, and she slipped out of the building and ran to open ground, where she shot out two lamps that were providing the only illumination for the area. She only had minutes before reinforcements would be arriving. She sprinted west and shot out several more lights in a straight line toward the nearest gate. She paused to toss the colonel's phone into a thicket of trees, where it would serve as a decoy and draw a crowd, and then circled back to where she had started.

The men coming after her would quickly discover she had taken the night vision scope, and given her attack on lamps, would assume she planned to cling to darkness. But she had no intention of relying on night vision to gain an advantage. Their night vision equipment was superior to hers, so she would do the opposite. She would stay in lighted areas to the east while they were running around with their goggles down searching the darkness to the west.

She was almost half a mile to the east when reinforcements appeared, fanning out from Jake's building westward. She continued sprinting at a pace she could have only maintained for a minute or two if not for her ability to optimize oxygen delivery to her muscles.

She had covered several more miles and was sprinting across a deserted parking lot when a shot rang out behind her. Apparently, not *everyone* was looking to the west.

Shit! she thought. Even *she* wasn't immune from bad luck. She had already determined this was the riskiest stretch of ground she had yet covered, since she was somewhat visible, despite the lot not being lighted, and there was absolutely no cover to be had.

"Halt!" shouted a deep voice behind her, and she calculated from its direction and distance that even with her amplified reflexes and reaction time, she needed to follow this order. She stopped abruptly and turned around. A lone commando was holding an assault rifle on her unwaveringly, fifteen feet away. "Hands up!" he barked.

She lifted her arms straight up, gripping the colonel's laptop in one hand. When her hands reached as high as they would go she released the computer, which fell to the ground and smashed into the concrete near her feet.

The commando followed the dropped computer for only a few seconds, but this was enough. Having precalculated the effect of her diversion, Kira was a blur of motion from the instant she released the laptop. Before he could return his attention to her, she had removed her gun and shot the weapon from his hand, and then, already racing toward him, put a bullet through the meaty part of his leg, making sure on behalf of her pathetic alter ego that the wound was one from which he would fully recover.

She closed the distance between them in seconds, not wanting to give him a chance to alert others to her whereabouts. She reached him just as he finished drawing a second gun and kicked it from his hand before he could squeeze off a shot. He tried to fight her off, but he would have been no match for her even with a fully functioning leg, and like the others who had faced her previously, he, too, was soon unconscious.

And Kira Miller continued on into the night.

27

The colonel walked along the east perimeter of Peterson Air Force Base and frowned deeply as he spotted several helicopters in the distance, returning to base after yet another unsuccessful search-and-destroy mission. His forehead was bandaged, and he had a nasty headache that had lasted a full twenty-four hours and showed little sign of subsiding.

"At this point, we're probably just wasting our time," said John Kolke walking along beside him.

Jake nodded. "Four more hours, and I'll call off the search. At least from the air." He shook his head in disgust. "By now she could have reached anywhere in the world." He stopped walking and stared up at the razor-wire fence, wondering if the girl had pole vaulted over—or perhaps levitated.

"I have to admit," said Kolke, "I always thought you were giving this woman too much credit. She couldn't possibly be as good as you thought. But I was wrong. I still can't quite believe what she was able to do. In addition to you, she took out four of our best men without even breaking a sweat, and then managed to run a gauntlet and somehow escape. I spoke with Lieutenant Doherty, the guard outside of your office who fought her hand-to-hand—at least *tried* to. He told me he never came *close* to landing a blow."

"If only I would have been conscious," said Jake, knowing there were a number of 'if only' scenarios he'd be beating himself up over for some time to come. "We'd have probably stopped her. Or had her at the fence line. The second it was clear she was heading for the west perimeter, I would have sent all of our forces *east*."

"I'm not sure that would have mattered. Yes we concentrated our forces and technology on the west perimeter, but it's not as though the east was unprotected or unwatched. You can't just waltz out of a base when it's on high alert, no matter which perimeter you choose."

A burst of rage surged through the black-ops colonel, but this only served to heighten the pain in his head to excruciating levels. He forced his emotions to settle down and the pain subsided to merely throbbing.

Now they were almost back to square one, he thought in disgust, but this time he kept his anger in check. No Rosenblatt, no Desh, and no Miller. And she had all but telegraphed her escape. She had offered her help and told him he knew how to reach her, as though she wasn't even a prisoner. Her audacity was mindboggling. She had practically dared him to take greater precautions, and he, like a fool, had ignored his instincts.

But why had she spared his life? And the lives of everyone else she had encountered? They had been hers for the taking. By not killing them, she had slowed her own escape and increased the chances she would be caught.

Jake had turned into a ruthless monster when he had been under the influence. The tiny voice that was his true self had tried to rein in his altered self, but had been ignored. The force of personality it must have taken for Kira Miller to stop her enhanced self from killing anyone during her escape must have been off the charts. Jake was certain he could not have done it.

Did this mean that she wasn't the monster he was led to believe? Was her story true after all?

He frowned, and shook his head, almost imperceptibly. More likely, this was exactly what she *wanted* him to think. She was a monster fooling the villagers into thinking she was docile, to put future hunting parties off guard.

Kolke gestured in the direction of their offices. "Should we head back?" he asked, interrupting the colonel's musings.

Jake took one last look at the perimeter fence in both directions for as far as he could see, as if somehow a clue to how she had managed it would emerge where none had before. "Yes. Let's go," he said as he began walking. "We have a lot of work to do."

28

David Desh and Matt Griffin pulled up to the guard gate in a van, the technology on their key rings ensuring any camera that picked them up wouldn't get a clean enough image to satisfy the needs of facial recognition software. Desh had altered his appearance enough that even if the guard had a picture and description, he was sure to let him pass. And Griffin was still off the grid as far as the military was concerned, which was good, since no wig or application of makeup could hide this bearded bear of a man.

"Bill Sampson," said Desh to the guard. "Crazy Eddie's Carpeting. We're here to install carpeting for a . . ."

Beside him Matt Griffin consulted a tablet computer he was holding. "Captain Hernandez," he offered.

"Right, Captain Hernandez," repeated Desh. "I have the work order right here. I'm told you've been notified to expect us."

"Why isn't there any writing on the van?" asked the guard suspiciously. "Shouldn't it say *Crazy Eddie's Carpeting?*"

Desh smiled. "We're independent installers," he replied smoothly. "Eddie sells it, we install it."

"Mind if I look inside?" the guard asked politely. But Desh knew it wasn't a question.

"Sure thing," replied Desh.

The guard opened the sliding door. There was nothing inside except a long wooden box along one wall, about the size of a coffin. He lifted the lid, which was on hinges, and peered inside. The container was completely filled with a tightly rolled section of thin carpeting."

"What's with the box?"

"Makes it easier to carry the carpet," explained Desh. "I've got a bad back."

"Doesn't look like a lot of carpet," noted the guard.

"It isn't. We're just doing a few closets. Shouldn't take us more than an hour or so."

Satisfied with Desh's answers, the guard tore off a sheet from a pad of paper, with each page depicting a map of the base. "You're here," he said, drawing an X on the pad. He ran his pen straight, then right, and then left. "On-base housing is here," he added, marking another X. "Do you have the captain's address?" he asked, handing Desh the map.

Desh nodded and the guard waved him through.

Once they were out of sight of the gate Griffin's fingers moved over the tablet. *We're in*, he wrote. *Be ready for pickup in approximately six minutes.*

He hit *send* and the message appeared seconds later on the computer of a Major Hank McDonough, received by an e-mail address unknown to him.

Kira Miller sat in Major McDonough's comfy mesh chair and breathed a sigh of relief. Not that she had expected them to have any trouble. Griffin had seen to it that the forged work order to install carpet for the actual Captain Hernandez was sent to the guard station computers. Still, you never knew.

I'll be waiting, she sent back. *With bells on.*

Actually, her three nights and two days as an uninvited house guest of the major and his family, who were happily on leave in Cancun the entire week, had been just what the doctor ordered. When she had used Jake's computer during her escape to tap into the base's personnel records, she had learned that nineteen families were on leave that week. And her enhanced self had chosen well. Her temporary hideout had been perfect. The major's wife was very nearly her size, and had tasteful clothing that was quite comfortable. And they had a well stocked cupboard, which was more important than ever after she had come down from her gellcap induced adventure. She had been pushed to her limits—this time *physically* as well as mentally—and her hunger had seemed unquenchable

The major had a smooth Internet hookup, and she had been able to spend hours reading scientific literature; planting information she wanted to be accessible by her amped mind in the future. She was careful not to do anything that could tip off the neighbors that the major's house harbored a squatter, which including going outside, getting too near a window, or turning on a light at night—all of which had done wonders for her—ensuring she did little else but read and relax. For the first time since she could remember, she was able to catch up on her sleep. She felt like a new woman.

But, alas, it was time to go. The hunt for her had cooled off enough and she had too much to accomplish to waste another second convalescing here. But she would miss this place. She hadn't been in a homelike atmosphere for some time, and sipping cocoa and reading in a comfortable bathrobe—even if it wasn't hers, was a welcome respite from a life that had grown ever more complicated and intense.

She had to remember to have Griffin anonymously pick up the tab for the McDonough's weeklong stay in Cancun. It was the least she could do—especially since she'd practically cleaned out their cupboard the very first night. Good thing the refrigerator and freezer were well stocked as well.

Any trouble finding the magician's prop? she e-mailed the two men in the van.

Given the heightened alert the base was still under after her supposed escape two days earlier, she knew the guards manning the gate would conduct a thorough search of the van on the way *out* as well as in. But lithe magician's assistants had been crammed into small, secret compartments in coffin-shaped boxes for decades. This was a simple illusion requiring a simple prop. And Desh and Griffin didn't even need to saw the box in thirds while she was inside and pull the pieces apart. They just needed to ditch the carpeting somewhere it wouldn't be found, wait an hour or so, and then leave.

No trouble at all, came the reply. *When money isn't an object, all things are possible.*

There was a pause, and then another message appeared on Major McDonough's computer. *David says to tell you we're one minute out, he loves you, and if you risk yourself like this again, he promises to kill you.*

Kira laughed. She still couldn't help but love David Desh. Now she just had to be sure she really *knew* him. And decide if she could trust him.

Part of her was tingling in anticipation of seeing him again. Of melting into his arms.

But another part was wary.

She and her husband needed to have a little talk.

PART TWO

"I am become death, the destroyer of worlds."

—J. Robert Oppenheimer, father of the atomic bomb
upon seeing the first test detonation
(quoting from Hindu scripture)

29

Once the countries of the world agreed to cooperate, they needed to decide where they would gather. Olympic villages were considered from the past several Olympics, but no matter which country was proposed to host operations, scores of other countries were vehemently opposed.

It was quickly agreed that this project would be done under the charter of the United Nations, since all but a few of the world's countries were members.

The United States argued that because it gave the most money to the United Nations, and the organization was headquartered in New York, the operation should be conducted on U.S. soil, perhaps near Area 51. This was a location the U.S. used to test advanced aircraft and weaponry and could be easily converted for the current purpose. Besides, since Area 51 had been rumored for decades to be the site at which the U.S. studied alien spacecraft, it seemed fitting to finally make the rumor true. A number of countries agreed to this proposal, but China and Russia were so adamantly opposed, and were able to get enough of their allies to rail against it as well, that the proposal fell though.

Finally, after hundreds of proposals got nowhere, one emerged that evolved into something the countries of the world reluctantly agreed upon. The alien craft would be studied in international waters, so it wasn't on *any* nation's home turf. And the effort would be located as distant as possible from the worlds' major military powers. This ended up being in the South Atlantic, closest to Africa and South America, and nearly equidistant from North America, Europe, and Asia.

To provide the proper platform, the U.N. commandeered *The Spectacle of the Sea*, built in Finland, which was the latest leader in a race that had gone on for decades among luxury cruise lines to build ever more gargantuan ships. *Spectacle* could house twelve thousand passengers and crew. It was over five football fields in length and one in width. It was twenty-eight stories tall. It was an exercise in decadence and the amazing potential of human enterprise and engineering, costing well over two billion dollars to build.

The ship had several full sized basketball and volleyball courts on its upper deck, and a half mile running track. It boasted a grassy park, a football field in length, which sported a variety of different trees and other vegetation, as well as streams packed with freshwater fish. During cruises, over seventy-five tons of ice were produced to satisfy the needs of the ship's twenty-seven cafes and restaurants and forty-six bars. Forty-two tanks stored the nearly one million gallons of freshwater used by passengers each day. *The Spectacle of the Sea* was home to eight swimming pools, two nightclubs, several huge auditoriums and three theaters.

It would barely be big enough.

Scientific equipment of every kind would be flown in. Pools would be drained and seats removed from theaters. Parks, restaurants, ballrooms, and spas would be pressed into service housing equipment, or would be converted into other needed facilities.

A large portion of the upper deck would become a makeshift airport for jets and helicopters alike, turning the ship into the world's largest aircraft carrier. All air and sea approaches to the ship would be patrolled by a U.N. peacekeeping force, and only those craft that had been cleared by U.N. representatives at various staging areas on the West Coast of Africa, which meant their passengers and crew were on the approved list and they had been thoroughly screened for weapons, would be allowed through the gauntlet and onto the ship.

The effort would be managed by the winners of the last twenty-one Nobel Prizes in physics, chemistry, and medicine, awarded over the past seven years. These twenty-one could elect internal leadership as they saw fit, in much the same way that juries elected jury foremen. This central committee of Nobel Laureates would select up to two thousand additional scientists to join the cruise, without concern for nationality. The governments of each of the nearly two hundred countries represented would be allowed forty delegates in addition to these scientists—with no questions asked, although arms would not be allowed on board—and each would be assigned their own block of quarters, Olympic-village style. Along with these two thousand scientists and eight thousand delegates, two thousand members of the ship's standard crew and staff would round out the on board population.

Every stateroom on board was already equipped with at least a thirty-inch screen for entertainment and for passengers to plan and book on-land excursions. Each screen would be tied into a ship-wide network, so that all delegates would be able to receive important feeds and schedules.

Getting this immense floating platform ready would require a heroic effort, but no one suggested it shouldn't be done. Yes, the effort could be a bust. The alien craft could change course. It could hover above the Earth for a few minutes and then sail into the Sun. Perhaps it would reveal its secrets immediately, bringing the enlightenment and making the U.N. effort unnecessary.

If the craft didn't land, or wasn't retrievable, returning the cruise ship to its original condition, and reimbursing the company for its use, would set the governments of the world back about a hundred million dollars. On a global scale, this was rounding error, even if the world was still suffering from one of the harshest economic climates in recent memory.

A number of names had been suggested for the ship, since *Spectacle of the Sea* was somehow not a fitting moniker for the ark that would host an unprecedented worldwide collaboration to study an object that would forever change history. *United Earth, Pax Humanity, The Spirit of Mankind,* and *The Tower of Babel* were all considered. But in the end the biggest vote-getter was the *Copernicus,* after the man who many believed had ushered in modern science, creating the Copernican revolution with his heretical theory that the Earth was not the center of the universe. Not only was Earth *not* the center of the universe, in one fell swoop the incoming alien craft had made it clear it wasn't even the center of *life* in the universe, or even *intelligent* life.

The *Copernicus* would fly the flag of the United Nations, a body that had become hopelessly corrupt in many ways, serving as a public forum for countries with hateful and intolerant ideologies. A once august body that now allowed countries with the worst human rights records in the world to head human rights commissions, attacking political enemies with human rights records far better than their own. But even the most ardent critics of the U.N. were hopeful that this effort could at least redeem the concept of cooperation among nations.

So plans were made and delegates selected. The *Spectacle of the Sea,* now the *Copernicus,* would be stationed in international waters, just off the coast of Angola, but close enough to Namibia, Botswana, and South Africa that ports and aircraft from these countries could be used to shuttle delegates to the ship.

The massive sea vessel crawled through the waves toward its destination at just over twenty miles an hour, not wanting to be late for a rendezvous with a craft that had traveled trillions of miles for unguessable purposes.

The alien object might change course, or it might not be retrievable.

But if it was, the world would be ready.

30

Colonel Morris Jacobson took one last look at the waters of the Potomac and turned back toward the street, where a stretch black limo, its windows tinted, was pulling up beside him. He checked his watch. Punctual as always.

The door swung open and he slid inside the cocoon of luxury. His boss, Andrew Dutton, was inside, sipping a glass of scotch. Dutton's official title within the Department of Defense was *Senior Civilian Advisor on Special Operations Forces, Counterterrorism, Irregular Warfare, and Counternarcotics*. But unofficially, off the radar, he was much, much more. There were those in the government with fancier titles, both civilian and military, and who reported, at least on paper, to higher levels, but none had more power than Dutton nor readier access to the ear of the president.

Jake extended his hand to shake, but Dutton ignored him, offering only an expression of contempt in return. "Let's not waste time beating around the bush, Colonel," said Dutton by way of greeting. "I read your report. What the fuck is going on? You lose her before I even know you *have* her! What kind of bullshit is that?"

Jake met his boss's steady gaze. "I admit it wasn't my finest hour. But you of all people know I work independently and call my own plays. You, yourself, insisted on this level of autonomy. Once you and I agree on the direction of the end zone, I'm responsible for driving the team down the field."

"If I hear one more fucking football metaphor in this town I swear to God I'm going to puke."

"The point stands," said Jake.

"Then let me make myself crystal clear," snapped Dutton. "From here on out, if you know anything useful about this Icarus—*anything*—I want to know about it without delay. And if you have Kira Miller in your sights—I want to know about it *yesterday*. Is that understood?"

"Understood."

"And I'd like to see the footage you have of her." He shook his head in disgust. "You know, during the brief time you were able to hold on to her."

"There is no footage."

"*You didn't film her?*" yelled Dutton in disbelief.

"I'm afraid not," lied Jake, inwardly cursing himself for revealing to Kira that he had taken a gellcap, and describing his actions while under its influence. This was now on the video, and was not something he wanted known, *especially* not by Andrew Dutton.

"I've always thought you were very good at what you do," said Dutton. "But I may have to modify that assessment. How could you be so fucking incompetent as to not have a camera on her?"

Jake held his ground. "Because it was a brief meeting, *not* an interrogation. Once the interrogation started we'd have all the footage you could ever want. But I wanted a few minutes alone with her beforehand. Just to size her up. Get a feel for her. See what she looked like in person."

"See what *she* looked like. Or her tits?"

"She was fully dressed the entire time I was with her."

"That's not what it looked like to the men outside your office door. And according to them, the girl claimed you tried to get a *feel for her* all right—with your pecker."

"She made that up to help her escape, and you know it!" snapped Jake. "I didn't touch her! One of the guards she attacked is a third level black belt in two different martial arts, and he couldn't lay a *hand* on her. I couldn't have raped her if I wanted to. It'd be easier trying to rape a wood chipper."

"I don't know," said Dutton. "Maybe that's why you didn't want any filming. Without video, how do we know what really happened in there? Maybe you were forcing yourself on her when her super IQ kicked in and you lost control of the situation. You admit yourself she was just normal, helpless Kira Miller before she surprised the shit out of you."

"There's nothing normal or helpless about Kira Miller, believe me. Even when she's not amped up."

"Maybe you ripped her clothes open and uncuffed her so you could have better, um . . . access."

"What are you saying? That you believe the word of a psychopath over mine? One trying to distract my men to help her escape at the time?"

"No. I'm saying you didn't film your meeting! And your very own report says her cuffs were found near your desk, completely intact. Removed from her. She couldn't have done it herself."

"The report also said there was clear evidence of scratches on the ratcheting mechanism, and we found an unwound paperclip nearby. She picked them."

"You can pick plastic handcuffs with a paperclip?"

"If you know what you're doing, yes."

"Then why are they considered the ultimate restraint?"

"Not many people have the knowledge or skill to pull it off." He shook his head angrily. "But enough of this. I told you I didn't touch her. I *won't* say it again, and I won't defend myself further. I'm offended by your accusations. If you have even the slightest doubt that I'm telling you the truth, I'll tender my resignation right now."

Dutton stared at him for a long moment. "I believe you, Colonel," he snarled. "If I didn't, I'd have relieved you of duty already." He swirled his drink and studied the dark amber liquid before bringing it to his lips once again.

He lowered the glass. "But I grilled you just now for a reason," he said. "Because you fucked up big time. And you know it. How about taping your sessions with prisoners from now on? You have a session with perhaps the most important prisoner you've ever had, and you let her get away. *Without any record she was even there.* If it weren't for the quality of your service, I'd not only take your resignation, I'd *insist* on it. I'm still spitting blood over this one." He paused. "But I'm going to give you a second chance." He leaned in closer to the colonel and glared at him. "Believe me, you won't get a third."

For just an instant, Jake contemplated telling his boss to shove the job up his ass, but he contained himself. The irony was that he didn't *want* another chance. He was beginning to hate this job. He'd be thrilled to let someone else do it. But since they wouldn't have the benefit of experiencing an enhanced IQ the way he had, they would have no idea what they were really up against. Unfortunately, he was uniquely qualified to respond to the threat posed by Kira Miller and Icarus.

"Do you have any other leads?" asked Dutton, his voice now less confrontational.

"Some. Which we're working through. But I'm not all that hopeful."

"So you're back to where you started before you found that physicist, Rosenfield?"

"Rosenblatt," corrected Jake. "Yes. Pretty much."

"That's just fucking great," growled Dutton in disgust. "Well, I've got more bad news when it comes to what you're now calling the Icarus op," he said. "We're throttling back for now. I have a new job that takes precedence. Still keep ten percent of your attention and resources focused on Icarus, and another fifteen percent on your other ops."

Jake looked on in disbelief. "What could be important enough to displace what I'm doing now?"

"The alien craft heading our way," replied Dutton simply.

Jake did a double take. "What could that possibly have to do with *me?*"

"They're setting up a cruise ship off the coast of Angola to study it," explained Dutton, who then went on to describe how this would be handled; information that, while currently privileged, would be communicated across the globe in less than twenty-four hours. "I want you and a few handpicked men on that cruise ship. As security. I may join you as well, but that's still being decided. I also want your team back in the States to profile all delegates, scientists, and crew who come on board. When it comes to anything having to do with the alien craft, you're now the intelligence arm of this country."

"Why me?" protested Jake. "My charter is to stop WMD. Not to babysit scientists and dignitaries."

"Because you're a ghost. You aren't on the radar of any country—including our own."

"I will be after this assignment."

Dutton shrugged. "Can't be helped. But at least while you're on that ship, to intelligence agencies around the world, you'll be an enigma wrapped in a black-ops mystery."

"Aren't there others equally off the radar who could do this?" argued Jake. "Again, I'm WMD, which has nothing to do with this alien craft."

"We can't be sure of that."

Jake shook his head. "Any civilization this advanced will have had to conquer their self-destructive and aggressive nature," he said. "If they stop by for a visit, they're bound to be peaceful."

"Really?" said Dutton, shaking his head in disgust. "And what makes you the expert on alien civilizations? Who the fuck knows what might motivate them." He paused. "Look, this isn't up for discussion. I have you cleared all the way to the Oval Office. You need to get started immediately. I'll feed you the list of delegates the moment a country finalizes their list, and the exact layout of the ship. I want you and Major Kolke on board. And I want you to handpick five others. No weapons will be allowed, so I want your top people in hand-to-hand combat, who excel at improvisation."

"Are you expecting trouble from the delegates?" asked Jake.

Dutton swirled his drink. "Colonel, I'm always expecting trouble," he replied with a dark scowl. "And I'm rarely disappointed."

31

Kira, Desh, and Griffin returned to their Denver headquarters. Jim Connelly was away, providing new identities for Rosenblatt's family and hexad, and helping them get established in their new surroundings and life.

Kira was grateful to be able to slip into some of her own clothing for a change, and added back to her pocket the key ring she had removed before driving out to surrender herself to Jake. She spent a few minutes attending to some pressing administrative duties and checking the computer logs for both Denver and Kentucky, making sure she had a full accounting of the actions and schedules for each hexad.

With this completed, she and Desh drove to their favorite Thai restaurant for dinner. They had been in communication via computer while she was holed up in Peterson, and she had already been thoroughly chastised by her husband for taking the risk that she had. Given that it had turned out so well, she knew he wouldn't bring this up again.

The restaurant was dark and cozy, and the food outstanding. She ordered a glass of wine and took a small but satisfying sip.

"Believe it or not," said Desh as their Mee Krob appetizer was placed on the table, "we haven't talked about the alien ship yet. We may be the only people on earth who haven't."

"Well, we *have* been busy conducting prisoner exchanges," pointed out Kira with a smile. "Not to mention escaping from military bases."

"That old excuse," said Desh with a grin of his own. "If I've heard that once I've heard it a *million* times." He took a sip of his own glass of wine. "So what *do* you make of our alien friends?" he asked, serious once more.

Kira shrugged. "I don't know. The fact that they've conquered zero point energy is stunning. But I find it depressing that as advanced as they are, they're still bound by the speed of light. Maybe there really isn't any clever way around it." She paused. "I saw that several hexads have been enhanced since the news broke. What do *they* make of it?"

"There's not nearly a consensus, even among enhanced minds. There are as many theories as there are Icarus members. They haven't come up with anything much different than the general population."

Kira nodded, but she was obviously distracted. "Look, David," she said, before he could continue. "I need to change the subject. I told you about my impressions of Jake and how I escaped, but I didn't tell you everything."

Desh considered his wife carefully. "Go on."

"There's a person or a group out there with access to my enhancement treatment. I'm sure of it."

Desh's eyes narrowed. "How do you know that?"

"Jake admitted to me he'd been enhanced," she replied. "And he didn't get a gellcap from me, that's for sure." She quickly recounted her discussion with the colonel.

"So Eric Frey is alive after all?" said Desh when she was finished.

Kira nodded. "Yes. Under a false identity, no doubt. It's the only possibility I can see."

Frey had been a molecular biologist at USAMRIID, the U.S. Army Medical Research Institute of Infectious Diseases. Putnam had been blackmailing him to recreate Kira's work and produce gellcaps for her brother. Putnam had evidence that Frey was a pedophile and more, evidence Putnam insisted would be released automatically if he turned up dead, giving Frey and others he was blackmailing a stake in his continued health. True to Putnam's word, the day after his death, evidence against Frey was sent to the authorities, which was how Desh had learned about him to begin with. He and Kira hadn't known his name at the time, just that he was a molecular biologist at USAMRIID. So when the story broke that a talented scientist was charged with pedophilia, and then committed suicide rather than face the charges and the shame, it all fit together perfectly. Too perfectly.

"I should have made certain he was really dead," said Desh. "You'd think I'd know better than that by now."

"We all had the same data, and we all were convinced that this loose end had been severed. We had no reason to suspect Frey had duplicated my therapy and managed to keep it secret. He definitely had my brother fooled. If we thought for a second he had his own supply of gellcaps, we'd have suspected his suicide was staged immediately."

Desh frowned and shook his head dejectedly. "So déjà vu all over again," he mumbled. "Only this time, Frey is pulling the strings instead of your brother."

"This probably explains the attack last year when we were visiting Ross. Frey must have found us, attacked, and then lost us again."

"Probably," agreed Desh, carrying rice and shrimp to his mouth with a pair of black lacquered chopsticks.

"There's no telling how extensive his organization is by now."

Desh swallowed. "Not," he said. "That would be my guess. Which is one reason he decided to extend his reach by deploying Jake and his team against us. Strangely enough, when it comes to adding personnel, the good guys have the advantage over the bad guys."

"What do you mean?"

"Backstabbing sociopaths tend not to be very trusting. Especially when dealing with other backstabbing sociopaths—which is who would be attracted to Frey's organization. Think of how nervous we are, and we're the good guys. In an organization built for selfish purposes rather than altruistic ones, all of the power and access to gellcaps would have to be concentrated at the very top.

Alan never allowed Putnam to be enhanced. He allowed Frey to be only because he needed more gellcaps."

"Good point," said Kira. "And true to form, Frey double-crossed them both and ended up on top."

Desh nodded. "But we're better off this time than we were when Alan was pulling the strings," he added. "At least we have a handle on who we're up against. No matter how good he is, I should be able to track him down. I'll get started on that right away."

"As if you don't have enough to do," said Kira.

"It *has* been a busy few weeks." He gazed at his wife with an amused expression "It seems that people are either in love with you . . . or want you dead."

"Look . . . David," said Kira haltingly, her expression making it clear she was about to change the subject to one she found uncomfortable. "There is something else."

Desh's stomach clenched, as if he were a boxer bracing for a body blow. "So the Frey thing wasn't enough bad news for one meal?"

"David, do you remember when we escaped from Putnam's safe house?"

"Do I remember?" said Desh in disbelief. "How could I forget? It was the first time I was ever enhanced. Not to mention our lives were on the line. And it was the first time I realized I was in love with you."

"Do you remember you left me for a few minutes when we were upstairs? To check on the guards you'd knocked out in the basement? You told me you wanted to see if they had any ID."

His eyes narrowed in thought, looking for all the world as though he were struggling to understand where his wife was going with this. "Yeah," he said slowly. "I remember that too."

"So what happened when you got down into the basement?"

Desh tilted his head as if he hadn't heard correctly. "What do you mean? I checked them all to see if they were carrying IDs or anything else that would give us a lead. Then I returned upstairs."

"That's all that happened?"

"Yeah, that's all. Why? What is this about?"

Kira described the video Jake had shown her, with him as the star, which presented a very different take on the events in the safe house basement. At first, Desh listened with a look of horror and shock, but his expression soon changed to one of relief. "Kira, the footage was faked," he said matter-of-factly. "None of that happened. It's part of the frame."

Kira studied her husband for several long seconds. "I thought so too," she said. "At first." She shook her head. "But it wasn't. Jake convinced me of that. So I need you to tell me about this, David," she continued, her voice failing to hide the hurt she felt. "It's not pretty, but after all we've been through together, I need to know the truth."

"Kira, this didn't happen. I'd tell you if it did."

Tears welled up in her eyes. "David, I love you. And enhancement brings out demons. There's no shame that you couldn't control them. But I need to know. And I need to be able to trust you."

Desh shook his head helplessly. "I told you exactly what happened," he said with a pained expression on his face. "I checked their pockets and returned upstairs." He paused, and she realized he had never looked more frazzled or vulnerable. "Kira, you mean the world to me. You *know* that. We trust each other with our lives every day. I'd never lie to you. I'd sooner lie to *myself*," he added earnestly.

Kira didn't respond, but saw her husband's eyes widen slowly and a thoughtful expression come over his face. "Which is something we should consider," he said softly.

"What do you mean?"

"What if I *did* lie to myself? If the video *is* real, the only explanation is that the enhanced version of me is keeping this memory from normal me. It makes a kind of brutally efficient sense, when you think about it. We had a lot on our minds at the time—to say the least. When I returned to normal, if I knew I had slaughtered helpless men, that I hadn't been able to control my baser instincts while enhanced, it would have preyed on my mind. At a time I needed total focus the most. My alter ego must have calculated this would slow me down, and that he couldn't let this happen."

"You sound like you're talking about two different people."

Desh nodded grimly. "Aren't I?" he said. "You've been there. You know the enhanced version of you holds normal you in disdain; that you're the painfully stupid half of a split personality."

Kira considered. He was right, of course. "This is true. But my smarter half knows she can only come out and play for very brief periods. Her welfare is tied up with my own. And I have to take a conscious action, swallowing a pill, to invoke her. So I can trust her, because she knows I have ultimate control." She paused. "But there is no evidence from anyone that their enhanced selves have kept things from their normal selves."

"Maybe not yet," said Desh. "But we know it's well within the capabilities of an enhanced mind," he pointed out. "You purposely suppressed your memory of your longevity breakthrough."

There was no question he had a point. But this raised even more troubling possibilities. "So what other activities have you engaged in and forgotten?" she said worriedly. "Which other of your memories might be false?"

"Obviously a question I can't answer. But every other time I took a gellcap I was in the enhancement room. Not many degrees of freedom there, by design. Constrained in this way, you can't really take actions that you'd *need* to forget. This would most likely be relevant only when you're a free-range sociopath." He raised his eyebrows. "Like you just were."

Kira's eyes left her husband's as she replayed events in her mind. "My memory tells me I was careful to leave everyone alive. Not that my alter ego wouldn't have happily killed them all if I would have let her. But when we get back home, let's investigate this further, just to be sure. If it turns out I killed those men and gave myself false memories, we'll have to re-evaluate everything we're doing."

Desh poked at the remains of his meal, too preoccupied to finish. "We know we're playing with fire when we use your treatment," he said. "But the idea that I can't trust my own memory scares the shit out of me."

"Not just you. It forces us to question everything we *think* we know."

They both fell silent and worked on their meals, which were now on the cold side.

"Wait a minute," said Desh suddenly, and his already somber expression became even bleaker. "This forces us to consider your second level of enhancement in a different light. Can we even trust this? What if this level isn't the sociopathy-free nirvana we think it is? Maybe it brings on an even more severe negative change in personality than the first level. Maybe the Kira at that level knew that you would never attempt to go there again—invoke her again—unless she planted false memories that would appeal to you."

Kira reeled as if she had been hit in the stomach. *David could be right.* Everything to which she was dedicating herself could be a sham. She suddenly felt weak.

She searched her memory once again of her brief stay at an unimaginably high plane of intelligence. She remembered the pure, overwhelming joy she had felt just after coming out of it—before her body broke down and she was rushed to the hospital. She was sure this level brought out the best in human nature and not the worst. She wasn't just sure intellectually, but emotionally as well.

She had never been more certain of anything in her life.

But couldn't a transcendent intellect create these powerful feelings within her, even if they were false?

She shook her head. This thinking led to madness. If you could never trust your memories, where did that leave you? If what you were striving for was based on false pretenses . . . it was unthinkable. As Desh had pointed out, most of the time their enhanced selves were trapped in a small room, furiously writing down epiphany after epiphany, so ˈ their normal selves never had any indication they might be deceived. Until now.

Kira's eyes moistened.

"Kira? Are you okay?" asked Desh, reaching out and taking her hands in his.

Kira shook her head. "I feel like giving up," she said softly. "It's just too hard. Too many obstacles. They never end. The universe is against us. The speed of light is impossible for even an advanced alien species to crack. The military is after us again, with a group capable of using my therapy pulling the strings. After all of our efforts to disappear. And now this. It's hard to believe this will end in any way other than disaster."

"Things seemed just as bad when we first met, and we made it through. Against ridiculous odds. And it wasn't just luck. We made our own luck. We'll do it again."

"I don't think so," said Kira, as the moisture in her eyes grew. "Not this time. I think we've used up all of our miracles."

"You have every right to feel that way. You've been through the trials of Job. And it's cruel and unfair. You're one of the greatest scientists in history—maybe *the* greatest—and one day you'll be celebrated like Einstein or Galileo. But you know they didn't have it easy all the time either. Einstein faced anti-Semitism in Germany and couldn't get a job in his field, even after he published his revolutionary papers. Galileo was excommunicated from the church and put under house arrest until his death."

He paused, and then smiled sheepishly. "I have to admit, none of them had to go up against scores of special forces operatives. But you know, different times, different crosses to bear."

Kira smiled and used her napkin to dab away the few tears that had fallen. "You're right," she said, strength returning to her voice. "I was just feeling sorry for myself. Sorry for being so weak."

Desh laughed out loud. "*Weak?* Your will is stronger than any man or woman I've ever known. And that's why we'll succeed, despite everything thrown against us. I'm sure of it. When Jake first told me you were trading yourself for us, I was terrified. I thought I'd never see you again." He shook his head. "I was a fool. Hard to believe that I could still underestimate you." He paused. "I won't make that mistake ever again," he vowed.

"And I feel very sorry for anyone who does," he added with absolute conviction.

32

David Desh gazed at his wife sleeping soundly beside him and once again reflected on just how exceptional she was. She was a sleeping goddess, a Helen of Troy who would have a greater impact on the world because of her brains than Helen had because of her beauty. And while she was undeniably appealing physically, this was true of any number of women. The truth was that a person's personality and intelligence affected how others perceived their looks. A beautiful woman with an ugly personality wasn't quite so beautiful anymore. But a beautiful woman with *Kira's* personality was beyond breathtaking.

In other rooms, Griffin and Connelly were sleeping as well, although certainly not as majestically.

Desh himself had slept poorly. The entire night was spent searching his memory, as if by repeatedly going over the same neuronal real estate he would somehow find the memory of his throat-slitting actions like a roach hidden under the floorboards. But as hard as he strained, he kept coming to the same conclusion: he had done nothing more than search the men for ID.

But then his mental unrest took a troubling turn. He thought about his interactions with Kira. Of discrepancies between her words and actions he had noticed over the past few years. Times when she had said she was one place but he had seen evidence she had been somewhere else. When he noticed a slight change in the location of her laptop and she had later lamented that she'd been unable to do any work on the computer all day. Minor discrepancies to which he had previously paid no attention. Kira was overworked and overwhelmed. Who could blame her if, like Einstein and other great scientists before her, she could be a little scatterbrained on occasion.

But now it was possible to see these discrepancies in a more troubling light.

He slipped from beneath the covers silently and pulled on a blue silk robe, cinching it at the waist, and quietly exited the bedroom. It wasn't rare for one or the other of them, having trouble sleeping, to steal away for several hours during the night to continue to nibble at their never diminishing mountain of work.

Only this time would be different. This time he wasn't being whisper quiet so as not to wake his beloved Kira. This time he was leaving to *spy* on her. And himself.

What had happened, or what had not happened, in the basement of a safe-house years ago was driving him mad. Had he really killed three men in cold blood? Or had Kira made this up for reasons of her own? But for *what* reasons? And had the video been faked, despite Kira's certainty to the contrary?

And if it *was* real, was it possible that some of the evidence Jake had against Kira, which they had yet to see, was real as well?

Desh had to know. He would investigate himself, and while he was at it, her as well.

He removed her laptop from its charging station and crept soundlessly through the halls until he reached the enhancement room, relieved not to have run into Connelly or Griffin in the wee hours of the night, which would have forced him to abort the exercise. He entered the enhancement room, set the timer on its vault-like door for eighty minutes, and closed himself inside.

He slid his left thumb over his keychain and a gellcap fell into his other hand, the replacement for the one he had dropped in the woods. Kira had the keys to the pills, and this was the only way to become enhanced without her being aware of it. Which would mean he wouldn't have an emergency dose if he needed it. But this couldn't be helped.

Fireworks erupted in his mind.

Like a neuronal big bang, his consciousness expanded to fill a universe that hadn't existed the moment before. A feeling that was now quite familiar to him, but was always exhilarating. He knew instantly. The video footage Kira had seen was accurate. All of it.

Desh could see himself killing the men in the safe-house basement in his mind's eye like it was happening that moment. He felt the handle of the knife as its sharp blade sliced through each man's carotid artery with surgical precision. He knew his slower self would find the memory grisly, and would find the utter helplessness of these men horrifying. But he knew it was neither. Killing them had increased his and Kira's chances of success and survival, nothing more.

But there was no longer any reason not to let his dimwitted self have access to these memories, given the circumstances. Suspecting he had a false memory was driving this other Desh mad, and maintaining this fiction would help neither of them any longer.

He searched his mind in an instant and knew he harbored no other secrets from himself. Other than this one false memory of the events in the basement, he had played it straight with his dimwitted alter ego.

His normal self would remember his enhanced self had not been hiding anything else, but of course, that version of him could never know for certain if this was just another implanted memory. Not even he, with all of his brilliance, had an answer for this conundrum.

He manipulated Kira's computer, digesting entire screens of information in a literal blink of the eye. He caused the computer to spit up page after page of time-stamped logs, indicating to the tenth of a second every session Kira had ever had on the computer. He crosschecked this against his memories, which he could pinpoint precisely in time to match the records of the computer.

A pattern emerged. For several hours each week, Kira Miller was engaged in computer work that she either didn't know about, or was concealing from him. He found hidden files, imbedded in innocent programs, which were set to automatically transfer to yet another file—this one not only well concealed but tightly protected.

And even he couldn't break in.

There was no encryption that could be written by a normal, no matter how expert, that he couldn't break through in minutes in his current state. Which meant this one was built by another enhanced mind. It was the only possibility. A mind even more capable than his own.

Laptops were prohibited from the enhancement room. Only the main Icarus computer could be accessed from here to ensure online activity was properly monitored and controlled to prevent the sort of mischief Jake had taken part in. But Kira had obviously disregarded this rule, had encrypted this large file on her laptop while enhanced. She was the keeper of the pills, and accounted for them, so she could use them off the record any time she wanted.

Desh continued searching, probing; trying to piece together and read whatever tea leaves he could find, no matter how ephemeral. He made attempt after attempt, beating his genius against the computer's will like a diamond sledgehammer.

Finally, a measure of success. Hints of files that had been erased, but which he could reconstruct just enough of to make them somewhat meaningful. A little more than two and a half years ago Kira had done considerable research on world affairs, wars, infighting, political systems, dictatorships, and nuclear capabilities of countries around the world. She had actively searched for the Achilles' heels of world governments, gaps in their defenses, pressure points. She had studied the effects of various stimuli; military, political, and economic, on world order, paying particularly close attention to those that would cause widespread devastation. This work was barely concealed at all.

A few months later she had broken into classified government computers that held detailed information on the construction of weapons of mass destruction, both nuclear and biological. But this work, which had occupied her for considerable time, was far better encrypted, so much so that even with a mind of incalculable power, he was only able to nibble around the edges.

Then, abruptly, she must have instituted an even tighter layer of security, and he wasn't able to catch even a whiff of the skunk she had trapped inside her files. He was completely shut out from that day forward.

What did this all mean? Had she thrown in the towel? Had she given up on faster-than-light travel, on infinity, and decided to take matters into her own hands and thin the human herd— for its own good? To reduce the population so her longevity discovery could be revealed?

Good for you, Kira, he thought. Finally making the tough choices without artificial ethics and morals—throwbacks to early human development that were now as unnecessary as a pair of tonsils—getting in the way.

Or was her intent something else entirely? He had only seen the tip of the tip of the iceberg, and since this was being orchestrated by the enhanced version of Kira Miller, it could be one hell of an iceberg.

Regardless, he needed to find out. And his dumber half could assist in this effort.

But better to keep this from Kira herself. Whether she knew about it or not, anything he did to tip her off would tip off her enhanced self as well.

And if that were to happen, then his investigation would be over before it started.

And as arrogant as he was in his current state, as supremely brilliant, an enhanced Kira Miller was the one entity against whom he knew he would be overmatched.

33

Desh knocked on the door of the yellow one-story home that was straight out of a Norman Rockwell painting. Small but impeccably well kept, with a bright white picket fence in front that was as quaint as it was cliché.

An older man opened the door. He had white hair and was obviously retired, but he had a vigor to him that suggested his retirement had been recent and he continued to stay active.

"Dr. Arnold Cohen?" said Desh.

"Yes," replied the man at the door. "And you must be Detective Nelson."

"That's right," said Desh, "David Nelson." He held up a fake badge, which was a flawless forgery, but which he might as well have pulled from a cereal box for all the scrutiny Cohen gave it.

Desh gestured to Jim Connelly beside him. "And this is my associate, Lieutenant Jim Tyler. Thanks for agreeing to meet with us."

Since Desh had made the initial contact, they had decided he would do most of the talking while Connelly would take notes.

Cohen shook their hands, invited them in, and sat them at his kitchen table. "Can I offer you anything to drink? My wife just made up a batch of iced tea before she left for her book club."

Both men politely declined. "As I mentioned over the phone," said Desh, "this has to do with an investigation we're conducting. Unfortunately, I'm not at liberty to disclose the nature of the investigation. But I appreciate your cooperation."

Cohen nodded. "Glad to help in any way I can."

Desh had begun trying to learn who Eric Frey had become, what new Phoenix had arisen from the old psychopath's ashes, right after his dinner with Kira a week before. He had immediately discovered that two weeks after Frey's supposed suicide, the detective on the case had turned up dead. The papers quoted police sources who speculated his death was related to several murder cases he had been working on, but Desh knew better. The detective must have discovered evidence that Frey wasn't as dead as he had been led to believe, and had paid for it with his life. Learning of this had only served to rub salt in Desh's wound. If he had done even the smallest amount of follow-up, the situation would have been obvious, and Frey would have been removed from the board long ago.

Desh had compiled a list of Frey's friends—of which there were basically none—and people who knew him well. Almost all would be contacted and interviewed over the phone, but Vernal, Utah was close enough to reach by car, and nothing could take the place of a face-to-face interview. Besides, Griffin was on a plane, so this would give Kira some alone time, which was good for relationships no matter how loving the couple.

And it was especially good for him right now. He was finding it hard to maintain the fiction with Kira that nothing had changed between them. He could chalk it up to stress, but he had to find a way to shake off the misgivings he now had. It was possible that the intent of Kira's alter ego was relatively harmless, and he was misreading things. And he was certain that the woman he loved was still the woman he loved, unaware of what her altered self was doing. Even so, there were subtle differences in their relationship that she would pick up on if he wasn't careful. He loved her, but feared and distrusted what might be lurking inside. While making love to a woman who'd been bitten by a werewolf, it was almost impossible not to cast an anxious glance up at the moon on occasion—afraid to be caught off guard when it became full.

"So you're here to learn more about Eric Frey, correct?" said Dr. Cohen.

"That's right," replied Desh. "I understand that you worked with Dr. Frey fairly extensively at USAMRIID for a number of years."

"I did."

"What was he like at work?"

Cohen hesitated. "Can I speak freely?"

Desh smiled warmly. "That's what we're here for," he assured him. "Whatever you say will be kept in strict confidence."

"Well, I hate to disparage the dead, um, you know . . . who can't exactly defend themselves . . . but in my opinion, Frey was a psychopathic asshole. And that was on his good days."

"Go on," said Desh.

"He was pure poison. But he was *talented* poison, I'll give him that. And he was a political maestro. He would backstab, cheat, suck-up, badmouth colleagues, take credit for the work of others—you name it. Anything to further his career. He could lie with more conviction, and less sense of shame, than I could tell the truth. And he could be charming when he wanted to be. He'd be smiling at you while he slipped the knife in your back, and he was so good at it you had to be stabbed five or six times before it really sunk in that it wasn't accidental."

"You're obviously aware that he was a serial pedophile," said Desh. "And he was thought to be involved in other illegal activities as well."

Cohen nodded.

"Did you suspect anything when you were working with him?"

Cohen shrank back in disgust. "If I had *any* idea of how big a monster this guy really was, I would have turned him in in an instant. Pedophilia is the most horrible crime there is, in my opinion. But you know how a lot of guys, they turn out to be pedophiles or serial killers and the cops interview the neighbors, and they say, wow, who'd have ever thought it? Seemed like such a nice guy. Well, with this guy, you *would* have thought it. I had no idea he preyed on kids, but after it came out, it didn't surprise me at all." he shook his head. "I'll tell you what *does* surprise me, though. That he committed suicide. That I would have *never* guessed."

Perfect, thought Desh. Rub it in some more, why don't you. "Why is that?" he asked.

"Suicide indicates remorse, and after several years working with this nut job, this wasn't in his lexicon. Pedophiles aren't treated well in prison, as you know. I understand that. But I'd have expected him to flee to an island somewhere and prey on kids there."

"This is helpful," said Desh. "We're trying to build as complete a profile of him as we can. So anything and everything you can tell us about him would be huge. Favorite sports teams? Did he smoke? Any unusual foods he liked? Was he into opera? Nascar? Did he collect wooden ducks? Favorite restaurants? Type of books he read?" He paused. "Nothing is too trivial."

"I'll tell you everything I can remember, and point you to some other people you should speak with. But I don't get it. I mean the guy's dead. How will a complete profile on him help you in your investigation? "

"You'd be surprised," said Desh with just a hint of a smile.

***

Kira Miller sat at her desk in front of a computer, once again attending to administrative duties, the only person present in the large headquarters facility that principally provided housing for the core council. She had booked hexads at the facility, and in the enhancement room, for several months in advance—with the next group due on site in two days—but she had a few slots that had been booked by members of Rosenblatt's hexad that she needed to reassign until they were ready to resume their activities.

Given the loss of the decoy building, the flurry of activity the alien craft had set in motion, and the new threats against Icarus that had grown like weeds in recent weeks, recruitment, which had been slow previously, was now stopped in its tracks.

She turned her thoughts to Anton van Hutten. He was the first member of what would be a new hexad, but they weren't about to wait until the full unit had been recruited. He was a star, their great hope to finally conquer faster-than-light travel. In the short time since his first enhancement, he had already been back twice, and was scheduled for two more visits next week. She just hoped he wasn't tapped to be part of *Copernicus*, which had been on the news nonstop since this world cooperative effort was first announced.

Kira heard a faint shuffling behind her and twisted around in shock to see what it was. "Anton?" she said in confusion, recognizing the cherubic-faced physicist immediately. "I was just thinking of you," she added.

"Hi Kira," he said as he continued to walk toward her.

Van Hutten had been here only yesterday, but he wasn't scheduled again until next week. Had one of the core council changed the schedule and failed to notify her? Highly unlikely. And even if they had, who had brought him here?

Something was horribly wrong.

As she struggled to understand what was happening, van Hutten pulled a stun gun from his pocket and pointed it at her.

Her eyes widened. "How did you find the facility?" she asked, instinctively stalling, trying to establish a connection, trying to get him talking.

"I hid a tiny GPS locater here the last time I visited. Your cloak and dagger attempts to keep this location secret only work until one of us actively tries to find it. Then it's easy."

Kira tensed, ready to spring from her chair and dive on van Hutten the moment he let down his guard. "But why? What is this all abo—"

Twin electrodes shot like harpoons from van Hutten's weapon and attached to her shirt, stopping her in mid-sentence. She convulsed and slid to the ground, unconscious.

When she regained her senses five minutes later she was lying on her back on the floor, and there was no sign of her attacker. Her mouth was covered in duct tape and her arms were crossed tightly against her chest.

And she couldn't move them at all. *Was she paralyzed?*

A moment later she realized what had happened. Van Hutten had placed her in a straitjacket. The heavy white garment constricted her arms tightly and the straps were buckled around her back, with a strap between her legs. Van Hutten had cut out the section of elastic in the front of her panties with a scissors, removing the vital signs monitor, bug, and transmitter.

And he had used several long plastic zip-strips to tie her to her heavy desk. What was going on?

Van Hutten's resume was well known. He didn't have any military training. He was a highly regarded physicist, not a spy or a double agent. Yet he had carried out his attack with precision and had used nylon ties favored by police forces and the military.

Then again, thought Kira, anyone with a brain and an Internet connection could become marginally proficient at just about anything these days.

But *why* was he doing this? Had he gone mad?

Van Hutten returned, pulling a large red wagon, the kind a five-year-old child might play with. Inside the wagon sat several containers, about the size of the clear plastic jugs used in office water coolers, filled with a dense liquid that reeked of petroleum and polystyrene. He had a pump mechanism and sprayed the liquid liberally around the room, before moving into the next, his pace brisk.

Kira fought to get free, but it was hopeless. And the more she struggled the greater the amount of noxious fumes she breathed in. Van Hutten was going to torch the place, that was certain. But would he leave her inside when he did?

How could they have been so wrong about Anton van Hutten? He tested as a good man with a stable personality.

Kira had never felt so violated. This building was their sanctuary. They had state-of-the art electronic security protecting it, but if anyone within Icarus was to turn traitor, which apparently had happened, their security wouldn't be difficult to defeat. A traitor could figure it out while enhanced and encode instructions to themselves as part of their notes.

They had made the classic mistake, the mistake of Julius Caesar, who was unmatched as a general, survived many a battle against mighty armies, but who was brought down from within by someone he had trusted.

Van Hutten finally returned, fifteen minutes later. He cut her loose from the desk and pointed the stun gun at her. "You need to come with me," he said gently, his tone and expression conveying nothing but sadness and regret.

He marched her to the back of a van that was similar to the one they used to shuttle visitors back and forth to the airport, containing no windows, and secured her inside. The van smelled of the chemical mix van Hutten was using as a fire accelerant.

"I can't tell you how sorry I am about this," he said with all the sincerity in the world. And then he slid the door closed and began driving, pausing only long enough to throw a makeshift torch out of the window and onto a shallow puddle of the liquid he had brought.

***

"Frey was big into saltwater fishing," said Cohen. "Even bragged about an annual trip he took to Costa Rica to spearfish, using scuba equipment and a spear gun."

Desh glanced at Connelly. He wasn't surprised that Frey would get more satisfaction from being able to personally control a spear and watch it plunge into his prey than from having fish bite a stationary hook out of his sight.

"And he had his own boat," continued Cohen. "For the more traditional fishing, which he did all the time. He docked it in Baltimore."

"What size boat?" asked Desh.

"Not huge, but high quality. I heard once it cost him almost a hundred thousand dollars. Supposedly very fast."

"Do you know how often he used it?" asked Desh, as his cell phone vibrated in his pocket. Two vibrations, followed by a brief pause, followed by two vibrations again. This was the code they had programmed their central computer to use when a member of Icarus was in trouble. Connelly was just pulling his own phone out with a worried look on his face.

"I'm not sure exactly," replied Cohen, "but I'd say about—"

"Hold that thought," interrupted Desh. "Can I use your bathroom?"

"Certainly," said Cohen, eyeing Desh with a note of disapproval, as if wondering how bad his bathroom emergency had to be that he couldn't let him finish his sentence. "It's around the corner to the right."

Desh removed his phone as he entered the bathroom and scrolled to the proper screen. It was a vital signs alert. Kira had been rendered unconscious. According to the algorithm, she had been shot with a stun gun. Either that or struck by lightning; a possibility that Desh dismissed immediately. And her bug wasn't transmitting.

Desh scrolled to another screen. After he had discovered Kira's clandestine activities, he had installed cameras to spy on her. The footage was stored temporarily on a secure Internet site, which he could access from his phone. But he was interested only in what was being transmitted at this moment. He tapped into the transmission and checked three different views.

His breath caught in his throat.

Kira was unconscious, and someone was strapping her into a straightjacket.

It was Anton van Hutten.

Desh didn't wait to see more. He rushed from the bathroom.

Had the physicist gone mad?

Desh glanced meaningfully at Connelly and turned quickly to their host. "Thanks for your time, Dr. Cohen," he said. "But an urgent matter has come up that I need to attend to." Desh walked briskly to the front door and threw it open. "I'll give you a call as soon as possible," he finished as he and Connelly rushed to their car.

***

Jake was meeting in his office with his second in command when a light flickered on his office phone. Line four. This was a line he reserved for his *Steve Henry* alias, a key false identity. He rarely used it for outgoing calls, and he couldn't remember the last time he had an *incoming* call on this line.

"I need to get this," he said to Kolke, pressing a button that would put the call on the speaker. "Steve Henry," he said.

"Steve, this is Gill Fisher, Denver fire chief. We spoke a few weeks ago."

Jake eyed Kolke questioningly. Kolke spread his hands and shrugged. He had no idea what this could be about either.

"What can I do for you Chief Fisher?"

"Something's come up that I thought you might want to know about. It's the damndest thing. We're currently battling a fire at a facility that's the spitting image of the one that was cratered a few weeks ago. The one you asked me to treat with maximum discretion. If I didn't know better, I'd think it was the same building. And it's a nasty one. Like a grease fire, but worse. Almost like homemade Greek fire."

"So you're saying it's arson?"

"No question about it. And there's a warehouse about eighty yards to the east that's burning the same way. Since they aren't connected, this is even more evidence for arson."

Kolke and Jake eyed each other in dismay. *Icarus had duplicate facilities.* A nearly identical main building could have been a coincidence—an unlikely one, yes, but still a possibility. But the presence of a warehouse at the same distance as the other set-up made it a certainty. Not only had Miller and Desh escaped, *Jake and his men hadn't even bombed the right facility.* They had been operating under the assumption that Miller and Desh were reeling, without a headquarters and on the run. But they had been played for fools once again.

"Would this arson take special skills?" asked Jake. "Any way to get a sense of who might be behind it?"

"I'm afraid not. You can find the recipes for almost anything on the Internet. But you have to really want something to burn to spend time experimenting to get the right blend of ingredients. Most of this homemade napalm is just Styrofoam soaked in gasoline. And while that is a total bitch to deal with, this is worse. With this kind of fire—water just makes it worse. We're doing what we can, but these buildings are a lost cause. Just thought you might want to know."

"You were right, Chief. Thanks. I owe you one." He jotted down the address of the fire and hung up.

Jake turned to his second in command. "Major, find out if there were any street cameras with eyes on that facility, or if you can get satellite footage. Hurry," he added, although the urgency of the situation was clearly not lost on the major.

Kolke rushed out of the office. He returned ten minutes later with the footage Jake was after. He put it on the computer screen. "No satellite," said Kolke, "but we did get a clean image of this guy going in and out of the facility numerous times, with a kids' red wagon filled with large containers of liquid. And we got video of a van speeding out from the facility just as the fire started."

"Did you get the license plate?"

Kolke shook his head. "I'm afraid not."

Jake paused the video and studied the man pulling the wagon. His round face was flush and he looked fatigued, as though he had run a marathon, when all he had really done was pull a wagon at a brisk pace. Not exactly special forces material, thought Jake. The colonel turned to Kolke. "Recognize this guy by any chance?"

The major shook his head.

"Yeah. Me neither."

Jake had no idea what was going on, but whatever it was could well be the break he needed to end Icarus once and for all—assuming the man in the video hadn't already accomplished this goal.

"Send this guy's image to the supercomputer people," instructed Jake, "and have them begin facial recognition searches through all criminal and public image databases." He leaned in toward the screen and studied the man's face once again. "Let's find out who this mystery arsonist is," he said softly. "And then let's figure out where he's going."

34

The ride had been smooth but was now bumpy, as if they had entered a dirt or gravel road. After five minutes of this, the van stopped and the door slid open. Kira found herself in an expansive woods, in front of a large, two-story cottage that abutted a wide stream.

As van Hutten coaxed her inside at the end of a stun gun, she did her best to take in the surroundings. As far as she could tell, the cottage was completely isolated.

Van Hutten tied her to a heavy wooden chair against one wall, still restrained in the straightjacket, and tore the tape from her mouth. He backed away and sat on a small couch facing her, near a central red-brick fireplace.

"Anton, what is this about?" she asked, her voice strained. She couldn't even begin to hazard a guess.

"I can't tell you how sorry I am about this," said van Hutten. "But it's something I felt I had to do. For what it's worth, I think you're a wonderful human being who couldn't be more well meaning."

"Then why are you doing this? I don't understand. You were eager to join our efforts after that first day. Euphoric. You couldn't have faked that."

"This is true," replied van Hutten. He lowered his eyes. "But things have changed. I've had a taste of this sociopathy you mentioned. The first time I was enhanced I didn't experience it. But by the third time my thoughts were turning selfish; ruthless. Evil wouldn't be a bad way to describe it."

"We did warn you about that."

"I know, but there were several other factors that finally tipped the scales. That led to this. The second time I visited with you, you described the vision you had while you were at the second, higher level of enhancement. This was very troubling to me."

"Which part?"

"All of it," he replied simply. He paused and gazed through a distant window that looked out on the serene stream that ran by the house. He turned back to his prisoner. "Did you know I was a spiritual man?"

Kira nodded. "Yes. We studied you for a long time. A spiritual man, and a truly good one. That's why we were so excited about having you join us."

"Do you think it's odd for someone who's a scientist and hard core fan of science fiction to believe in God at the same time?"

"Not at all. Many scientists hold these views. Including a number of other cosmologists."

He frowned and shook his head. "It troubled me how much the higher IQ version of me disdains the very idea of God." He paused. "Are you aware that our universe is fine-tuned for life?"

Kira nodded. "Yes. I understand that we're in the Goldilocks zone. Not too cold, not too hot . . . just right."

"Exactly. If any one of a number of fundamental physical constants were altered, even a hair, life wouldn't be possible. If a proton were just one percent heavier, it would decay into a neutron, and atoms would fly apart. If the weak force were slightly stronger than it is, or weaker than it is, higher elements necessary for life would have never been created in the cores of stars. And so on."

"I've heard the odds against all of these constants being precisely what they need to be are trillions to one against."

"That's right. And I tend to see God in these constants."

Kira considered. He didn't seem irrational so far. So how should she play this? Should she avoid challenging him at all costs? Avoid risking upsetting someone who didn't appear unstable, but whose actions couldn't be interpreted in any other way? Or did her life depend on *challenging* him?

She didn't have enough information to make a rational decision. She knew that all she could do was trust her gut instincts.

"You are aware of the counterarguments, correct?" said Kira conversationally, trying not to appear to be challenging him too much.

Van Hutten didn't seem put off by her question, which was a good sign. "Yes," he replied. "That if our universe wasn't suitable for life, we wouldn't be around to observe it, so what other result could we possibly get? And chaotic inflation theory. That ours is just one of an infinite number of universes springing from the quantum foam and inflating in their own big bangs. Each of which could have different fundamental physical constants. In an infinite number of universes, there are bound to be *a few* suitable for life. Evolution has even been applied to inflationary theory. Some of my colleagues have suggested that physical constants suitable for life are also those that lead to a greater number of baby universes being created. So universes that are randomly born with constants that don't allow life to emerge, also don't reproduce. While universes with more um . . . pro-life physical constants, come to dominate." He paused. "There are other counterarguments as well, but suffice it to say I'm aware of them all."

"But you don't believe any of them?"

"These are brilliant theories put forth by brilliant physicists. But look at the lengths scientists will go to cling to their belief that life is nothing more than a happy accident. The idea that the perfect tuning of physical constants implies the existence of God is completely unacceptable to many of them. Many scientists will believe *anything* before they'll believe this. No matter how convoluted. An infinite number of universes? With countless new ones constantly forming like bubbles in a bath? Sure, *this* is rational and reasonable. God? Don't be ridiculous."

Kira nodded. She had yet to disagree with a single thing van Hutten had said. And it wasn't just the concept of infinite universes that were incomprehensible and completely unreasonable; or even a *single* universe. A single star, all by itself, was an impossibility great enough to blow the mind of any human. The Sun, a relatively small star in the scheme of things, was a raging fireball so massive a *million Earths* could fit inside, maintained a core temperature of twenty-seven million degrees Fahrenheit, and was capable of burning for *billions* of years. How could any belief be more ridiculous and improbable than the existence of even one such inferno?

"Okay, so you believe in God," said Kira. "I won't try to argue you out of it. I, personally, haven't settled on a final position, but I agree that the God hypothesis is just as likely to be true as any other; just as likely to be an explanation for the inconceivable. But you still haven't told me what's going on here. Or what troubled you about my vision at the second level of enhancement."

A quizzical smile came over the physicist's face. "Isn't it obvious? Your ultimate goal is for humanity, along with any other intelligent life in the universe, to *become* God. A tiny bit . . ." He paused. "I hate to use the word *blasphemous,* since it sounds too fundamentalist for my taste, so let's just say *presumptuous.* A tiny bit presumptuous, don't you think?"

"Maybe," she allowed. "But you know the laws of physics work equally well if time runs forwards *or* backwards. And Einstein's equations allow for time travel, in theory. What if we need to evolve into God so he can create the universe billions of years in our past?"

Van Hutten shook his head. "I don't believe that. Not if this evolving into God takes us across the path of immortality you laid out, which will result in us losing our humanity along the way. I remember our discussion about this vividly. Even you have to admit that the idea of dropping our brains into artificial bodies is abhorrent. I saw your expression during our first meeting. You defended the concept, but you were more aware of the thorny theological questions than any of us. What is man? Would we lose our soul?" He paused. "I found it a horrific concept. And now that I've experienced the more evil nature of this incredible intelligence you've unleashed, I'm even more troubled. I can't believe the path to heaven and enlightenment leads through hell and sociopathy. The negative effects of your treatment must be God's way of sending a message."

Kira didn't respond right away. She lowered her head in thought for several seconds and then locked her eyes on van Hutten's. "Look . . . Anton, I don't have all the answers," she acknowledged softly. "And I agree with most of what you say. The path to immortality, at least the way my feeble mind lays it out, is very disturbing in many ways. But I'm convinced this is only because we're too limited right now. We'll keep learning and growing. We'll find better answers; a way to do it right."

"I admire your optimism, I really do." He paused for several seconds. "But what you're trying to do almost exactly mimics the tragic story of Adam and Eve. And I see it ending the same way."

Kira tilted her head in confusion. "I'm afraid you've lost me," she said.

"Look," explained van Hutten. "I believe in God, but I don't believe in organized religion. Even so, the classic story of Adam and Eve is fascinating to think about in the context of what you're attempting. In this context, you're Eve."

"I'm *Eve?*" repeated Kira in disbelief. "Now you've really lost me."

"According to the story, there were two trees in Eden that were noteworthy. The Tree of Knowledge of Good and Evil, and the Tree of Life. The Tree of Knowledge represented omniscience. And the Tree of Life represented immortality. Many scholars think these were really two aspects of the same tree. Mankind was allowed to strive and make progress, but was forbidden from taking a one-apple leap to omniscience and immortality. You're reaching for the same apple that Eve ate."

Kira was intrigued despite herself. She had never thought of it in quite this way before.

"I don't believe in the accuracy of the bible," admitted van Hutten. "But I do believe that all efforts to reach immortality and godhood, made by Adam and Eve or by Icarus, are misguided and doomed to failure." He adjusted his glasses and added, "The story of Adam and Eve has nothing to do with my final reasoning, by the way. I just find it fascinating."

"It *is* interesting. But nothing you've said can possibly justify what you're doing right now."

"I agree. But I'm not done. Along with being disturbed by your vision of immortality and the sociopathic pull of your therapy, your superenhanced alter ego had a second, even more troubling vision. That all life should be merged into a universe-spanning intellect. Analogous to trillions of single celled organisms giving up their independence and identities to merge to form a human being. To form something far greater than themselves. Have I got that right?"

"Essentially."

"Are you familiar with the Borg from Star Trek?"

Kira frowned. She had streamed the entire seven seasons of the *Next Generation* when she was a little girl, and had watched every last one. Borg was short for *cyborg*, half organic, half machine beings, organized into a massive collective. Far more technologically advanced than the humanity of this fictional future age, and ruthlessly dedicated to absorbing all intelligent life in the universe into itself. Their defining phrase being, *resistance is futile.*

Kira's lip curled up in disgust. Her vision of immortality, in which people would become almost entirely machine—despite having neuronal circuitry that was an exact duplicate of their organic brains—combined with her vision of a collective intellect, *could* be construed as being Borg-like.

"I can see from the look on your face you can tell where I'm going with this," said van Hutten.

"Yes. And I agree that the Borg were horrific. The idea of giving up your identity in this way seems horrible beyond imagining. But maybe there is a way to be part of a collective while also maintaining individuality. And the Borg were purposely portrayed badly. They were the show's greatest villains." She shook her head. "*My* vision couldn't be more different. Unlike the Borg, I would never force this on anyone. Each individual would be free to pursue their own vision of happiness and fulfillment. No one would be coerced."

"*Really?*" said van Hutten, almost in amusement. "Did you ever think you would coerce anyone to become enhanced? Like you did with me?"

Kira frowned deeply—her expression giving van Hutten his answer.

The physicist pressed forward. "What if you knew being part of this collective consciousness—on its way to godhead—was the best thing for everyone? You know, like giving penicillin to a dying primitive. Think about individual single celled organisms. Would they choose to band together to form a human? Maybe not. They might want to cling to their identities. But once human, they would understand, right? You'd be justified in forcing that understanding on them, right?"

Kira felt herself reeling, as though his words and concepts were physical blows. "You're a brilliant debater, and you make some good points. Maybe the difference between us is that you believe in God, but don't have faith. Not in what Icarus is trying to accomplish. I may not be sure about God, but I have faith. Faith that we'll come to the point where we'll know the right path. And whatever it is, even if it's the opposite of my vision, it will be obvious at the time."

This gave van Hutten pause. "You may be right," he allowed. "But I have to go with my gut on this one." He sighed. "But just for the sake of argument, let's take away my misgivings. Let's pretend you *are* right. Now imagine what would happen if you came out of the closet tomorrow. You announce everything you've done, everything you're aiming for. Some will see this as a dream. Religious people will see trying to become God or usurp God as the ultimate blasphemy. Others will see what you're doing as blasphemy of a different sort; a secular blasphemy. Tampering with the human mind. Tampering with what it means to be human. And people want their children to be like them. If a father is circumcised he wants his son to be, regardless of the religious or health issues involved."

He paused to let Kira digest what he had said.

"So suppose you could make the increase in intelligence permanent," he continued. "Suppose even without the negative effects on personality. Yes, people want the best for their children, but would they want children who are by every measure a different species? Children who would be to their parents what a human is to a block of wood?"

Kira stared at him intently, but chose not to respond.

"And people will see a universe-spanning intellect as too foreign," continued van Hutten. "As a threat. They'll do anything within their power to stop you."

Kira drew in a deep breath. "As I've said, I don't have all the answers. And the questions are mind-bogglingly complex. But does that mean we just give up? Posing these questions to me is like asking an amoeba to explain relativity. When the amoeba becomes Einstein, then this question can be answered. I'm counting on humanity to make the best decisions we can given everything we know. Hopefully a transcendent intellect will bring with it the wisdom to grapple with these issues, and make correct choices. And I continue to maintain that those who don't want to go forward can choose to stay behind." She shook her head in disbelief. "But I still don't understand. You chose to torch the Icarus building and kidnap me because of wild fantasies I have about the future of humanity? Fantasies that won't be realized until far in the future, if ever?"

"Your goals are *not* wild, far future fantasies," insisted van Hutten. "And you know it. If you could attain star travel, you would double the span of human life right now. This generation could well stay alive long enough for enhanced minds to create the sort of immortality you envision. This very generation could live to see you implement your grandiose scheme, even if it takes millions of years."

Kira remained silent. She had hoped that this argument would sway him, but she wasn't surprised he had seen through it as easily as he had. He was absolutely right. That was one reason the stakes were as high as they were.

"But I'm not finished," explained van Hutten. "There was something else that drove me to this point. That gave me the deciding push." He paused, as though considering where to begin.

"Go on," said Kira.

"Have you considered this alien object—this ship?"

"Of course," replied Kira. Wow, she thought. This was out of left field. "What about it?" she asked warily.

"Have you considered that it might be coming this way because of *you*? That the enhanced minds you've made possible are attracting it here like moths to a flame?"

35

Kolke handed the colonel a color eight-by-ten glossy, fresh from the printer. "His name is Anton van Hutten. He's a physicist at Stanford."

"You've got to be kidding me. Any military training in his background?"

Kolke laughed. "He was never even in the Boy Scouts. Chess team, debate team. Record is clean as a whistle. No traffic violations. Not even a record of old parking tickets. Single. Gives far higher than average to charity. Volunteers five hours a week teaching the illiterate to read."

"What a monster," said Jake, rolling his eyes. He stared at the photo in his hand. Van Hutten looked like a kindly man who might soon be a grandfather. "Well, he's got balls, I'll give him that. We can't as much as scratch Icarus and he burns it to the ground. Go figure." He dropped the photo on the desk in front of him. "So what kind of reputation does this guy have?"

"You won't believe it," said Kolke. "Rosenblatt's reputation is top flight, but this guy's is even better. I've only begun researching him, but the rumor is that he'll win a Noble Prize in a few years."

Jake grinned. This was getting more and more surreal. What would he win his Nobel for, his fine work with fire accelerants? "Nice work, Major," he said. "We need to have a talk with this Anton van Hutten. Any idea where he might be?"

Kolke nodded, and a sly smile appeared on his face. "As a matter of fact, yes. Yes I do."

36

Kira stared at van Hutten as if he were mad—which he probably was, despite his ability to sound rational up until this point. Of all the ideas van Hutten had just floated, the idea that the alien craft was earthbound because of her discovery was the most absurd. "What are you talking about?" she said, unable to keep the disdain out of her voice.

Van Hutten was as calm, unperturbed, and apparently rational as ever. "What if there's a galactic civilization," he replied, "but you have to be able to sit at the grown up table to join. Maybe these ships, or probes, or whatever they turn out to be, are all over the galaxy, cruising along at very limited speed, and monitoring the stellar neighborhood. Maybe they have an intelligence cut-off. When they detect intelligence above a certain level, they change course, pick up speed, and head for it."

"How could they possibly detect what is going on inside my head from several light years away?"

"I assume you're familiar with quantum entanglement. Everything in the universe is connected in some way with every other thing. Drove Einstein crazy. And quantum physics suggests that the universe is shaped by consciousness rather than the other way around. Another point that can make even the most rational physicist spiritual. The state of the universe only comes into being when it's observed. Einstein himself tried for decades to poke holes in this interpretation of experimental data and couldn't do it, although his efforts were brilliant and helped strengthen the field. There are those who theorize consciousness makes use of these quantum effects. So who's to say that your intelligence enhancement doesn't stand out like a neon sign against the quantum background of the cosmos—for those who know how to look for it?"

Kira was speechless. She had been sure he would have no answer, but she knew enough quantum theory to know that what he said was not beyond the realm of possibility. Van Hutten had been uncannily accurate over his career as a scientist, even when making predictions most thought ridiculous.

"It's something worth considering, isn't it?" he said knowingly. "No inhabitant of this planet has ever had an IQ above about two hundred and fifty—until you and your therapy came along to make this number look pitiful. And we've never had a visitation by aliens. At least not one the world can be absolutely certain of. So what are the odds of both events happening within a few years of each other? Could be a total coincidence. But maybe not."

"And if it isn't a coincidence?"

"Then they'll want to meet a representative of the group responsible for the high IQ signal. And we'll make a bad first impression. The increased bandwidth your therapy creates brings out the ugliest side of our nature. And given human nature, that's pretty damn ugly. It's bound to make the galactics nervous."

"So this is what got you so spooked?"

"Yes. Added to my other misgivings, this was the straw that broke the camel's back. Plus, there's another interpretation to this." He paused. "Are you familiar with the story of the righteous man and the flood?"

Kira tilted her head in thought. She had read voraciously on every subject under the sun, and retained most of it, even when she was normal, but this wasn't ringing any bells. "If it isn't about Noah, then no."

"Not about Noah. Here's how it goes. A righteous man who has been pious all of his life is on the roof of his house during the mother of all floods. The water just keeps rising. A motorboat drives by and stops in front of his house. "Hop in," says the man in the boat. The righteous man shakes his head and says, 'Don't worry about me. God will save me.' A few hours later, with the water now just a few feet from his level on the roof, another boat passes. 'Quick, jump in,' a woman on the boat says. The righteous man smiles serenely. 'Thanks, but the Lord will save me. I'm sure of it.' Finally the water has reached his waist and a helicopter overhead lowers a rope ladder down to him. He ignores it and says a prayer to the Lord, whom he knows will reward a true believer." Van Hutten paused for effect. "Five minutes later he drowns."

The physicist seemed delighted by the confused expression on Kira's face. "So the spirit of this righteous man floats to the pearly gates," continued van Hutten, "and he sees God. 'Lord,' he says. 'I've been a righteous, pious man my entire life. I'm just curious as to why you didn't save me from the flood. I thought surely you would.'" In reply, God shakes his mighty head and says, 'Are you kidding? I sent you two boats and a helicopter. What more do you want from me?'"

Kira smiled broadly. "A great tale," she admitted. Her expression turned thoughtful. "So you're turning this story around one hundred and eighty degrees, aren't you? You're suggesting God sent this alien ship as an extension of his *ill* will. Just as surely as he sent your righteous man two boats as an extension of his *good* will."

Van Hutten's eyes lit up. "It really is a pleasure speaking to someone who can connect the dots as fast as you," he said in admiration. "I can't tell you how much I wish we weren't at odds on this."

"Yeah, me too," mumbled Kira under her breath.

"You're right, of course. This is another alternative, unlikely though it may be. There's always the slight possibility that we're reaching for the forbidden fruit and God wants to slap our hand. Well, maybe by stopping you and destroying your entire supply of gellcaps, I'll deflect some of this ill will we've invoked."

"So do I become an offering to God?" asked Kira. "To appease the almighty." After she said this a smile came over her face.

"What's amusing about *that*?" asked van Hutten.

"You know I'm not a virgin, right?"

Van Hutten laughed. "No, you're not an offering. Virginal or otherwise. And just to be clear, I believe that my first theory about your IQ enhancement attracting the aliens here is more likely to be the correct one. But maybe if no one on earth enhances themselves again, the alien ship will change course. Whether it was sent by God or not."

Kira stared at van Hutten intently. Part of her desperately wanted to write him off as a crackpot, but part of her knew his speculations could not be dismissed out of hand.

"I think the world of you," added van Hutten. "We just have two different views of the future of humanity, and the wisdom of your ultimate vision. I've brought up God throughout because I find these conjectures fascinating, but I'd take the same course even if I weren't the least bit spiritual. And none of these misgivings, by themselves, would trouble me enough to take this step. Even all of them combined were barely enough to tip the scale." He gazed at her earnestly. "I really am sorry about this, and I wouldn't think of ever hurting you."

"Just of destroying all my gellcaps and keeping me from making more."

Van Hutten nodded. "I know there's a good chance I'm wrong," he admitted. "But the consequences if I'm right are too great. After we find out what the alien object is all about, this will be another data point, and I'll have to perform another analysis."

"And if the alien ship does veer off? Will this convince you that preventing Icarus from eating sociopathy-laced apples from the Tree of Knowledge was the right decision?"

"I don't know. Let's just see what happens. In the meanwhile, I'll keep you in this cabin for a few days in as much comfort as I can while I try to figure out longer term accommodations. I know I'm the last person anyone from Icarus will suspect is involved in this. But David and Jim are very good, and I'm sure they'd find you here if we overstayed our welcome."

"Any ideas about these longer term accommodations?"

"No good ones yet. But I'm working on it. I'll try to find the most comfortable imprisonment possible while we wait for the alien ship to arrive." He frowned. "I'm sure you're uncomfortable, and I'm sorry about that. It doesn't take much to get your friends on the core council to start talking about you. Your courage and resourcefulness are legendary, which is why that straightjacket is a precaution I felt I had to take."

Kira sighed. "Look, Anton, you've made some compelling points here," she acknowledged. "But all of it is conjecture. You of all people should know we can't turn our backs on progress, regardless of the issues it might create. Industrialization led to a horrible air pollution problem in our major cities. But we found ways to clear up the air while keeping the rewards of industrialization. The progress of a species and a civilization aren't linear." She paused. "And what if you're dead wrong. What if God not only applauds our attempts to improve ourselves, but helped me achieve my breakthrough? The fact that our brains are such that they allow for this kind of massive leap in intelligence is *astonishing*. The fact that I found a way to bring this out without killing myself, dodging countless landmines that I now know were there, is even more so. I see the hand of God in my therapy, not in an unknown alien object."

Van Hutten nodded. "If not for the negative personality changes that come along for the ride, I would agree with you. What you've done is breathtaking."

"What about this second level of enhancement?" pressed Kira. "It brings out your better nature rather than your worse."

"Maybe. But you're the only person alive who's experienced it. Once. The negative personality changes didn't hit me until the second or third enhancement. And we can't corroborate your account. For all we know this level is pure, distilled evil, and your normal self has been deceived. Have you considered that?"

Kira frowned. No one on the team had ever questioned her account until just recently, when she and David had been forced to face this as a possibility, as painful as it was. But van Hutten had seized upon it immediately. His mind was every bit as impressive as they had hoped, misguided though he now was.

She locked onto the physicist's eyes. "I can't defeat your conjecture with debate," she said. "But I know in my heart that you've got this all wrong. You're making a terrible mistake."

Van Hutten sighed. "I hope you're right. I really do."

His expression was tortured for just a moment as he said this, and Kira had no doubt that he was sincere. "You know, Anton, we've been worried about making a mistake of our own," she said wearily. "About recruiting someone with latent megalomania who would undo our efforts for selfish purposes. And yet you, the man who's come the closest to destroying us, tested as the most decent of us all. Compassionate. Kind hearted. Empathetic." She shook her head slightly and a wry smile crept over her face. "If there is a God, he certainly has a sense of humor."

37

Jim Connelly watched for cops while Desh accelerated to over a hundred miles per hour, blowing by highway traffic as though it were standing still.

Connelly knew nothing about the cameras Desh had installed to spy on his own wife, so Desh had to lie and say he spotted van Hutten's reflection in the mirrored glass of their headquarters building through their security cameras. While Connelly hadn't seen this, he had no reason to doubt the sighting made by his friend and colleague.

They were headed almost due east, back to Colorado. Wherever van Hutten was going, he wouldn't be *flying* there—not with Kira in a straightjacket. And while Colorado bordered seven other states, any of which could be the physicist's destination, their best bet was to get back to Colorado as quickly as possible until they could get a better handle on his location.

Desh tried to focus on driving and fight off panic. Despite what he had uncovered about Kira—or more accurately, about her enhanced alter ego—he still loved her deeply, and fear and worry were drilling into his head, making clear thinking impossible. Images of her kept flashing into his mind. Kira in a straightjacket, hanging from a meat hook. Kira being tortured, her face a bloody mask as razors sliced through soft skin. Kira being dumped in a lake, water filling her aching lungs as she fought to the end to remove her restraints.

Desh shook his head vigorously. He had to get himself under control. If not, he'd be no good to her.

He cursed himself for not hiring additional muscle the instant he was free from Jake. When they had thought they were off the grid for good, he and Connelly were security and muscle enough. In all the time the group had been around, with the exception of the attack that had killed Ross Metzger, they had had no need for police or military style activity. And no one was ever kidnapped or hunted or in danger. The good old days. A few weeks ago.

But now the shit had hit the fan—repeatedly. He and Connelly needed good men who could respond. If van Hutten was acting alone—for reasons Desh couldn't begin to fathom—and provided they could find him, then he and Connelly would be able to extract her themselves. Assuming she was still alive.

But how likely was it that van Hutten was working alone? Not very. He was a world-class physicist, not a soldier. Someone had to be pulling his strings. But even so, how they had gotten him to betray Icarus was anyone's guess.

Connelly's phone began to vibrate. He glanced at it. "It's Matt," he announced. They had left an urgent message for Griffin to call back the second he landed. Connelly threw the call on speakerphone.

"I got your message," said the voice of Matt Griffin. "What's up?"

Desh and Connelly quickly filled him in on recent events.

"You *sure* it was Anton?" asked Griffin. "I'd believe almost anyone before him."

"It was Anton," confirmed Desh yet again. "Matt, we need something to go on. *Anything*. We need your brand of magic, and every second counts."

"I'm passing a McDonald's," noted Griffin. "I'll grab a table and tap into the airport's Wi-Fi. I'll get back to you as soon as I can."

Ten minutes later he called back. "I've got it!" he declared triumphantly. "Van Hutten rented an isolated cottage just outside of Rocky Mountain National Park three days ago. For two weeks. And his lack of neighbors wasn't accidental. He found the rental online searching for 'Rocky Mountain homes for rent, isolated," and 'Rocky Mountain homes for rent, secluded.'"

"That has to be it," said Desh excitedly, and both he and Connelly traded expressions of relief. They weren't home free, but their odds had just taken a dramatic turn for the better.

"Great work, as always, Matt," added Connelly.

Griffin read them the address while Connelly entered it into the car's GPS guidance system.

"We're driving there now," said Desh, "but we have no idea what we're up against. Grab a supersized meal or two, Matt, on me, and see if you can find out what the hell has gotten into van Hutten. And if we're likely to run into just one crazed physicist in the cabin or an army."

"I'll get right on it," said Griffin. "I accessed all of his accounts when we were vetting him as a possible recruit, so I'll have a big head start. If there are any clues to his behavior, I'll find them."

"Thanks, Matt."

"No no, thank *you*," said Griffin in amusement. "It isn't every day someone offers to buy me *McDonald's*," he finished, ending the connection.

Desh pushed the car to one hundred and ten. Van Hutten's cabin was closer to Denver than to them, but not by much. They were very lucky to be this close, Desh knew. But the acid in his stomach didn't go away. Because the universe had a way of evening out luck. And you just never knew when yours was about to run out.

38

"I have to use the bathroom," said Kira.

Van Hutten nodded. "It occurred to me that this might happen eventually. I'm afraid I'll have to ask you to hold it for an hour or two. Hopefully less."

"Why? What happens then?"

"I have a room set aside for your use with its own bathroom. I need to finish installing a door handle I can lock from the outside. When I do, we can get rid of that straightjacket at least. I'll still have to keep you strapped to a leash—one situated so you won't be able to reach the outer door—but it will be long enough for you to use the bathroom."

"Sounds like heaven," said Kira, rolling her eyes.

"I'll make sure you have a comfortable bed and couch within reach. I'll supply you with whatever food and drink you want, along with books, a computer not tied to the Internet, that sort of thing. I'll work on other ways to give you as much freedom as possible without risking your escape. If I didn't have so much respect for your abilities, I wouldn't have to be this paranoid."

"Yeah," muttered Kira. "I get that a lot."

"I'll go and finish your room now. I'd planned to have it ready for your, um . . . visit. But I was listening in at your headquarters. And when I learned you'd be alone for the day, I had to act."

"Listening in?"

"Yes. I needed you to be alone. After all," he added with an impish grin, "if I had to engage in hand-to-hand combat, I didn't want to risk hurting David or Jim."

"Very thoughtful of you," said Kira. "So how did you bug us? New technology of yours?"

"No. Why reinvent the wheel? I just activated the microelectronics from the waistband of one of my Icarus-issued briefs."

"Glad we could help," said Kira wryly.

She didn't really have to use a bathroom, but Desh had trained her to attempt escape sooner rather than later in this type of situation, before the enemy was dug in and had perfected security procedures. "Can I have some water, at least?"

"Absolutely," said van Hutten amicably. He rushed off and returned a moment later with a cold plastic bottle. He unscrewed the cap and put it to her lips.

Kira bolted up from underneath him—taking the chair she was tied to along for the ride—and angled forward, driving the top part of her head into his lower jaw. Van Hutten screamed in surprise and agony and staggered backwards.

The heavy chair now protruded from Kira's backside like a wooden anchor. She turned and tried to whip the legs into van Hutten, but given she could barely remain standing, the move was awkward and landing a blow in this manner was hopeless.

Van Hutten was recovering his senses after her first blow, and Kira knew that if she didn't connect with him in the next few seconds her small window of opportunity would be closed forever.

Out of sheer desperation, she turned her back to him and launched herself backwards, without regard for how she would land or the damage to her body this move would cause. This time the legs and bottom of the chair hit him squarely in the chest and head, and he was driven to the wood floor, dazed.

Kira's reckless move took its toll on her as well. Bleeding from several shallow wounds and as dazed as her target, she forced herself back to life, drawing on her tremendous will, which had been further hardened by the many attacks she had sustained over the past four years. She fell to her side, taking the chair with her like a turtle with its shell, and twisted awkwardly until van Hutten was lined up, at which point she kicked him savagely in the face, driving him into unconsciousness.

Kira Miller gathered herself and tried to ignore the pain she was in. She took several deep breaths and willed herself to rise. Using reserves of strength even she hadn't suspected she possessed, she slammed the chair into the brick fireplace wall over and over again, until it broke into small enough pieces that she was able to finally wriggled free, ignoring the stabs from several sharp splintered pieces of the chair that would have penetrated deep into her torso had she not been protected by the tough fabric of the straightjacket.

After several minutes of intense concentration, Kira finally managed to open the door, using her forehead, chin, and mouth, and escaped into the woods. Without the use of her arms for balance, maintaining even the slowest jog across the uneven terrain required all of her athleticism.

She focused her considerable attention on putting as much distance between herself and the cottage as she could, making sure she kept her balance. If she tripped even once, without being able to break her fall, the consequences would not be pretty.

39

Desh and Connelly approached the door to the cottage from opposite sides, slithering through the underbrush in military crawls, guns extended. Their practiced eyes could see evidence that the woods had been disturbed in any number of directions leading to the house. They neither saw nor heard anyone.

Griffin had found nothing that hinted at van Hutten's motives, but he did learn the man had purchased a used van two days previously. This van was now in sight of Connelly, parked alongside the cottage on a thin gravel road, its hood propped open. Connelly slid up the side of the car and looked inside the open hood. Belts, hoses, and other engine parts had been torn out almost randomly. It wasn't artful, but it effectively transformed the vehicle from a means of transportation into a lawn ornament.

Desh had progressed to the point where he could see the door had been kicked in, and he and Connelly came to the same conclusion at almost the same time: they were too late. But too late for what?

The two men continued on to the cottage, staying out of sight of windows, and rose on either side of the front entrance, where the door had been almost entirely ripped from its hinges. They strained, but couldn't hear any noise coming from inside. Desh peered around the corner and then yanked his head back, not knowing what to expect.

No shots were fired in his direction and he had detected no motion whatsoever.

Desh motioned to Connelly and they both bolted through the opening, guns drawn.

The room was deserted, but several windows had been breached and glass was scattered like so much glittery gravel below them. To the right, near a brick fireplace, were the remains of what had once been a chair, but was now just a scattered pile of kindling.

They spread out and canvassed the room, moving as though expecting a trap to be sprung from any direction. Desh crept silently up to a couch and used his foot to drive it backwards.

He heard a groan of pain from behind the couch and had his gun on its source almost instantly.

"*Anton?*" he whispered to the man sprawled out on the floor in front of him, hogtied with plastic handcuffs. He had tape over his mouth and looked as if he had been used as a piñata.

Van Hutten nodded and then moaned in pain once again from even this tiny exertion.

Eliminated as a possible threat, Desh ignored him. Instead, he and Connelly systematically canvassed each room like the commandoes they were, making sure there were no surprises lying in wait.

Once they had assured themselves the house was clear, they returned to van Hutten. Desh rolled him onto his back and ripped the tape from his mouth. "What happened?" he demanded, keeping his voice to a whisper.

"I only wanted to stop the gellcaps, slow her down," babbled van Hutten. "I didn't wish her any harm."

"*What happened?*" repeated Desh with such intensity his whisper seemed like a shout. "*Where is she?*"

Van Hutten shook his head, wincing in pain as he did so. "I don't know. She—"

Desh slammed a large hand over the physicist's mouth. "Whisper, or I'll see to it that you never talk again," he threatened.

"I don't know," repeated van Hutten when Desh had removed his hand, this time with barely enough volume to be heard. "She escaped."

"How long ago?" whispered Desh.

"I'm not sure. I was just coming to when six men . . . six commandos . . . swarmed in here. They wanted Kira. I told them she'd escaped, and they tied me up and set off after her on foot."

"When was this?" asked Desh.

"Five, ten minutes ago."

Connelly knelt down closer to the physicist. "Did you capture Kira alone, or are there other players we should know about?" he asked.

"Alone," mouthed van Hutten.

Desh considered. They had seen no evidence that the men who had raided the house had been opposed in any way. Perhaps the physicist *had* been acting alone.

Desh and Connelly traded glances that said, *time to go.* Desh replaced the tape over van Hutten's mouth. "Wait here," he said to the cherubic physicist. "When we get back, you've got some explaining to do."

40

Kira saw movement off in the distance and instinctively ducked behind a tree. The absolute whiteness of her straightjacket—and the fact that she was wearing a *straightjacket*—stood out like a burning flare.

A young couple was hiking through the woods, both wearing heavy canvas backpacks. Kira breathed a sigh of relief. Finally. This was her chance. But if she didn't play this right, she might spook them. A battered girl in a straitjacket in the middle of the woods? What's not to trust? she thought, allowing herself a brief smile at the ridiculousness of her situation.

She took a deep breath. "Hello," she called out, still out of sight. "I could really use some help."

She emerged from behind the tree and approached them. They stopped immediately and began inching backwards.

"Hi. Can you help me get this off?" she said matter-of-factly, hoping that keeping her voice even and showing relatively little emotion was the proper pose to strike.

They glanced at her and then each other, unsure of what to do or say, or if they could believe what their eyes were showing them. "Is that a *straightjacket* you're wearing?" said the male half of the couple suspiciously.

Yeah, it's the latest fashion rage on the East Coast, thought Kira flippantly, but aloud she said. "Okay, yeah, it's a little weird. I know that. I came up here last night with a new boyfriend," she continued, making the instant decision to put on the persona of a coarse, not-too-bright party girl. "He rented a place a half mile from here. We ended up getting shitfaced last night, and, well . . . you know . . .

he kinda wanted me to wear this—so I did. I guess he's into some weird sex shit. I mean, I know this is some wild, bizarre shit," she said, gesturing toward the straightjacket with her chin, "but I mean, couples handcuff each other to beds and all, right? And like I said, I was totally shitfaced at the time." She paused. "Anyway, we ended up getting into a big fight, and the fucker just took off. He just left me in this damn thing. What an asshole!"

The girl eyed her suspiciously. "You look like you've been through a war."

"Yeah. That's what the fight was about. I thought the asshole was just into bondage games, but he's heavy into this S&M shit. That's not my thing. But he didn't do all this," she added, gesturing with her head toward her injuries. "I fell down a few times trying to find someone like you to undo this." She smiled sheepishly. "I guess that's why hikers don't wear these things, huh?" She turned her back to them. "I think you just have to undo these straps," she said.

The two hikers came closer and inspected the straps. "You look worse than I thought," said the guy, and Kira was encouraged to hear concern rather than suspicion in his voice. "You going to be okay?" he asked as he began unbuckling the restraints. "You need me to call 911 or anything?"

"Nah," said Kira. "It looks worse than it is. I'll be fine. Not that I don't feel like a total moron for letting this guy talk me into this."

The buckles undone, the two hikers helped pull the jacket over her head. Kira blew out a relieved breath when it was finally on the ground. "Thanks," she said gratefully. She turned to the female half of the duo. "Do you mind if I use your phone to make a quick call?" she asked. "I have a friend who lives about thirty minutes away. I wanna ask him for a ride."

"Yeah, go ahead."

Kira took the phone, reveling in the use of her arms and hands once again. She walked a few steps from the hikers and turned away. "David, hi, it's me," she said when Desh answered, keeping her voice low.

"*Kira!*" he shouted in a whisper, the relief in his voice palpable. "Are you okay?"

She realized that he must have learned of the fire by now, and probably thought she'd been in it. "Yes. But believe it or not, I'm on the outskirts of the Rocky Mountain National Park."

"I know," said Desh, which was the very last thing she expected to hear. "Jim and I are here too," he continued hurriedly. "We know about van Hutten. Six commandoes raided his cottage about twenty minutes ago, with more probably on the way."

Kira adjusted to the new information and circumstances immediately, crouching down to make herself less visible, her heart picking up speed. Talk about out of the frying pan and into the fire. "Who are they?"

"My guess is Jake sent them," replied Desh. "But we aren't certain. Which direction did you run from the house?"

"East."

"Shit. We went west." There was a pause. "Circle back to the cottage. We have a car about a quarter mile from it. This is a national park, so Jake's men can't make themselves *too* obvious. But be quick. And be careful."

41

Jim Connelly climbed through the attic window of van Hutten's rented cottage and onto the roof, sliding toward the edge on his belly. In most situations like this, binoculars would have come in handy, but not in this one. He needed as panoramic a view as he could get, especially given the woods made this exercise far more difficult. He was looking for movement, nothing more, and evolution had made human eyesight exquisitely sensitive to picking this out against a still background. Even if the figures were tiny in the distance, he could guess their identities. Moving fluidly and blending into their surroundings: commando. Moving stiffly and making no attempt to conceal themselves: tourist. Girl alone: almost certainly Kira Miller.

"See her?" said Desh into his phone, fifty yards away to the east.

Connelly continued scanning the area. "No. But you have a hostile at three o-clock. And he's moving with purpose. If he keeps his bearing he'll pass twenty yards due north of you in about forty-five seconds."

"Copy that," said Desh, plotting an intercept course and moving as stealthily through the woods as he always did.

As the commando passed in front of him, Desh dove out of nowhere, timing his assault perfectly, and drove the man to the forest floor. The commando had been so intent on tracking Kira, and so confident he and his associates owned the woods, that he was taken entirely off guard. Desh kicked his gun away and drove an elbow into his face. After delivering three more blows in rapid succession, the man fell to the forest floor, helpless.

"Who are you?" said Desh, pointing his gun at the man's head.

"Fuck you," said the commando calmly, giving Desh the voice sample he needed. Desh delivered another blow to his neck and the man was out cold.

Desh lifted his cell phone to his mouth. "One down," he whispered to Jim Connelly. "Any Kira sightings yet?" he added anxiously.

"No. But I've got another hostile thirty yards due west of you on a southeasterly vector."

"Got it. Get off the roof and meet me behind van Hutten's van. I'll take this second guy out and send the others to the southwest." Their car was parked to the *northeast,* so if he could send their pursuit in the exact opposite direction, they should be able to escape.

"Roger that," said Connelly.

Desh removed the earpiece and attached microphone from the man lying unconscious before him and worked his way farther north. He intercepted the second man the same way he had the first, and although this soldier was able to block a few of Desh's blows and even land one of his own, the end result was the same.

Two down, thought Desh.

He crouched down and focused on the *Fuck You* the first commando had been kind enough to utter. His voice was deeper than Desh's, and it had a gravelly, resonating quality. Desh lowered his voice and practiced a few times. Hopefully, it would be close enough. Desh lifted the microphone he had removed from the second commando to his mouth. "This is . . ." he began, and then mumbled incomprehensibly, counting on the man's colleagues to think his call sign had been the victim of poor reception, which wasn't unknown in the Rockies. The ease with which he had surprised these two men showed they weren't expecting company. They saw themselves as the hunters, not the hunted, regardless of the warnings they may have been given about Kira's skills. "I've spotted the girl southwest of the house, moving fast," he continued in his deeper voice, making sure the words were clear once again. "She's . . ." He garbled more words and then tossed the headset away. He paused for a moment to consider his next move when Kira Miller emerged from behind a tree.

She saw the unconscious body next to Desh and rushed to his side, just as he was shoving the commando's gun into his pants. "Where's Jim?" she whispered when she was beside him.

"Back at the cottage," replied Desh, so quietly she wasn't sure if she heard him or had just read his lips. He began moving and motioned for her to follow.

In minutes they had rejoined their colleague. Like Desh, Connelly wasted no time on greetings. "What about van Hutten?" he whispered to Kira.

"Leave him," she mouthed back. "He can't tell Jake anything new. He's brilliant, and a good man."

"Then what's with the arson and kidnapping?" whispered Desh.

"Long story," replied Kira as they headed northeast, to the car Desh and Connelly had parked a quarter of a mile away. Desh led, with Kira behind him, and Connelly taking up the rear.

Once they began moving, no one spoke, or even attempted to mouth any words. They were nearing the finish line, and if they could manage not to give away their position for just a little longer, they were home free.

After a few minutes double timing it through the woods, they could see their destination off in the distance, a light gray Ford parked under a tree.

Desh heard the faintest rustle behind them and off to the side.

He spun around, pulling his gun with the speed and reflexes of a world-class athlete—but not fast enough. Seeing him move, the commando behind them emerged from the cover of a tree and sent a bullet racing toward Kira Miller's heart.

Jim Connelly dove in front of her, pushing her aside. The slug meant for her exploded through his neck, taking out his jugular and killing him instantly.

Before the commando could get off a second shot, Desh drilled a hole neatly between his eyes, and the woods were still once again.

Desh surveyed his surroundings but detected no one else. The gunman had been alone, but that wouldn't be true for long. He yanked the car keys from Connelly's pocket and handed them to Kira. She was in shock and seemed completely paralyzed. "Go!" he shouted, but his words didn't register. "*Go!*" he screamed again in her ear. "*You're driving. The others will have heard the shots!*"

Kira broke from her fog and ran to the car. She threw herself into the front seat and shoved the key in the ignition. As the car's engine came to life she turned to see what had become of Desh. He was rushing to the car with Connelly's body draped over his shoulders, the ex-colonel's neck torn open and still leaking the last of his blood onto the forest floor.

"Pop the trunk," yelled Desh as he neared.

Desh laid his friend in the trunk and slid into the passenger's seat. The car began moving before he had closed the door.

"*Shit, shit, shit,*" said Kira as she picked up speed, tears beginning to roll down her cheeks. "I can't believe he's dead. It should have been me."

Desh was reeling every bit as much as she was, but once again they couldn't afford to mourn. Not yet. Not only had a man he respected more than any other just lost his life, but Desh had taken a life as well. A man who had thought he was fighting on the side of right. In the heat of the moment, acting on rage and instinct alone, Desh had shot to kill.

He forced these thoughts from his mind as they turned onto a main road.

Desh considered ditching the car but thought better of it. Jake's men would arrive at the site of the gunshots on foot, with no way to follow. And the car he and Connelly had driven here was off the radar.

Kira seemed on the verge of an emotional collapse, so he kept her talking, getting her to explain van Hutten's motives. The physicist had thought his fire had destroyed their entire supply of gellcaps. Since the gellcaps couldn't withstand high heat, even if the safe they were in wasn't consumed by the fire, he was correct to believe they were destroyed.

But he didn't know they had another facility. Like Jake before him, he had dealt them a serious blow, but still not a fatal one. "How's our inventory of gellcaps in Kentucky?" asked Desh.

"Good. We should have plenty to hold us until I can produce more. I made sure each site had enough to carry us through if we lost one of the headquarters. But we'll have to suspend the west hexads indefinitely."

Desh nodded grimly. They had been on the defensive and had been taking a beating. They needed to get to the RV, clean up, bury their friend, and join Matt Griffin, who was manning Icarus's Kentucky headquarters this week— now Icarus's *sole* headquarters.

David Desh felt the loss of Jim Connelly as deeply as he had the loss of his own father. At least his friend had died a hero. But even as he thought this he realized it might not be true. He had to admit to himself that his wife was now as alien to him as the object hurtling through space. Had his friend sacrificed himself to save a woman who could well be the most important human ever born?

Or had he died to save something else entirely?

42

The small alien ship slipped inside the orbit of Pluto and continued on, inexorably, toward its target. Although decelerating, it was still moving hundreds of times faster than any terrestrial object had ever managed, and it quickly passed inside the orbits of the gas giants of Neptune, Uranus, Saturn, and Jupiter. Now travelling at pedestrian speeds its mass and length had long since been stable to within the limits of terrestrial detection. It was a perfect sphere, approximately nine feet in diameter, still emitting Casimir radiation, although at these speeds it was now only siphoning off a drop of the ocean of zero point energy available to it.

All attempts made by humanity to communicate with the craft in a variety of possible ways were ignored.

Inside the orbit of Mars, the ship began breaking even harder, as every one of the nearly eight billion inhabitants of Earth held their breath.

Would it stop? Fly by? Crash? Would flying pigs emerge?

These questions were moments away from being answered as the ship neared ever closer, tracked by every hobbyist and professional astronomer in the world and thrown up on countless televisions and computer monitors. At this point, Jupiter and Saturn could have jumped to light speed and collided, and not a single telescope would have recorded this event, being otherwise preoccupied.

The ship slid smoothly into low orbit around the third planet from the Sun. Then, undetected by the vast array of instruments trained on the ship, thousands upon thousands of tiny transparent spheres, just a hair larger than microscopic in size, were ejected from tiny pores in its hull with enough force to rain down uniformly across the planet below.

The ship crisscrossed the globe and injected its invisible payload for several hours, and then assumed a perfect geostationary orbit above the Earth's equator, matching its orbital speed to that of the Earth's rotation so that it maintained a fixed position above the planet.

Its orbit established, it ejected a metal sphere the size of a large beach ball directly at the Sun, and an instant later the Casimir radiation issuing from the object ceased entirely.

Thousands of different scenarios had been modeled by the people of earth, and this one, in which the ship just parked itself in a stable orbit, had long been considered one of the more likely possibilities. The U.N. had contracted with a private company, *Space Unlimited*, to retrieve the alien craft should this occur, and a terrestrial retrieval ship was launched within hours of the alien ship having established a stable orbit.

All attempts at communication continued to be ignored, but *Space Unlimited's* ship was not fired upon or hindered in any way. The alien craft was checked for life and for any form of computer or robotic intelligence, but none were found.

The alien craft was then plucked from its orbit and placed in the cargo hold of the *Space Unlimited* ship, and although no life had been detected, microscopic or otherwise, it was put through a thorough decontamination process—just to be sure. Finally, less than a day after its arrival, the alien craft was brought to the surface and transported to thousands of eager scientists waiting on board a luxury cruise ship flying a U.N. flag, now called *Copernicus*, waiting in the South Atlantic.

43

Desh and Kira joined Matt Griffin at their Kentucky headquarters and there began licking wounds and discussing plans to rebuild. The setbacks had been fast and furious over the past month. When they had been on the verge of recruiting van Hutten things had finally seemed to be heading in the right direction. But now they felt like Sisyphus, condemned to push a backbreaking boulder uphill, only to have it roll back down whenever it neared the top. Sisyphus had been condemned by Zeus to repeat this futile endeavor for all eternity, but for the Icarus team, just recovering the ground the boulder had lost a single time was a daunting prospect.

The three remaining members of a core council that once had numbered five held a private funeral for Colonel Jim Connelly, a truly great man whose loss cast a further pall on an already battered and discouraged group.

While they kept their heads down for a short time, not wanting to attract any more attention until their trail had grown ice cold, much of the craziness that had gripped the world at the approach of the alien craft was subsiding, and the world was returning to a new normal.

The alien ship had come. Neither God nor the devil had emerged from it. The world had not been destroyed or dramatically altered in any way. No sermons on the mount were issued from the spherical ship. No technology discovered that would transform society. Scientists aboard what had become the most famous ship in the world, the *Copernicus*, had yet to find anything, unable to discover how to even activate the zero point energy drive that had propelled the ship. After finding no electronics or computer guidance and control systems, or the alien equivalent, scientists became convinced that the vital brain of the ship had been ejected into the Sun to ensure alien secrets would be kept.

The ship was scoured inside and out using x-rays, radio waves, nuclear magnetic resonance—basically every wave across the wide electromagnetic spectrum—yet no messages, no hieroglyphics, no images—absolutely nothing—was discovered, not even microscopic scratches. And then everything else under the sun was tried, down to checking for invisible ink, with the same result. What they had was an empty hull of a ship, with a dead and incomprehensible engine, and no brain.

Desh, Griffin, and Kira had waited with baited breath for days, wondering if something would pop out of the vessel, jack-in-the-box style, and demand Kira Miller's head, or complain that the planet was filled with morons rather than the towering IQs that had beckoned it across spacetime. But this had not happened, which was a relief, especially to Kira, since van Hutten had her half convinced that his analysis was correct.

They continued to check satellite coverage and look for electronic eyes that might be pointing in their general vicinity, as well as check other early warning systems they had in place, but they found no reason to believe they weren't safe and hidden, at least for the moment.

While Jake was their biggest threat, they would never be able to breathe easily until the puppet master behind him was found and stopped. So Desh threw himself into tracking down the man who had once been called Eric Frey, enlisting the help of Matt Griffin. He loved working with the affable giant, which brought back memories of the last time they worked together on a manhunt. That time they had been trying to find the enigmatic Kira Miller, a woman who had once again become far more enigmatic than Desh wanted to admit, even to himself.

Kira gave Desh and Griffin a description of the sort of biotech equipment Frey would need to reproduce her therapy, including names of private companies that sold DNA synthesizers, and other companies from which he would almost surely order some of the more common cloned genes he would need. Griffin spent five minutes while enhanced and compiled a list of the approximately eight thousand customers who had ordered necessary ingredients.

From there it was just a matter of whittling the list down. Desh interviewed several of Frey's colleagues by phone to supplement his discussion with Arnold Cohen, and assembled a profile of the man. He was almost sure to own a boat, and subscribe to two or three saltwater and deep sea fishing magazines. Griffin had hacked into police records and had learned that Frey had befriended numerous young boys and had taken them on his boat, a few accusing him of molestation—certainly representing the tip of the iceberg—although all charges were ultimately dropped. A boat was ideal for this type of predatory behavior since there would be nowhere for a victim to run or hide; no one who could possibly interrupt; and no one to hear any screams.

Isolated in international waters, Frey could apply a carrot or a stick, intimidate and cajole, and use the entire arsenal of tactics employed by those who preyed on helpless children throughout the ages, including threatening their lives if they ever told anyone what had transpired.

Of the eight thousand or so customers who had purchased necessary biotech equipment in the right time frame, only about two hundred and thirty were boat owners. From there, knowing the types of clothes Frey had liked to buy, wine he liked to drink, performances he liked to attend, books he liked to read, and so on, they were able to narrow the list in short order. An enhanced Griffin checked out the few remaining names and identified Frey immediately: he was now Adam Leonard Archibald.

A month after Frey had supposedly died at his own hand, Archibald had bought a small, but well equipped, San Diego biotech company with cash. Since this purchase, the company had made several breakthroughs, and was now contemplating an IPO that would value it at twenty times what Archibald had paid.

And while the enhanced version of Frey could plant data in computers in ways that were untraceable by the best human experts, the enhanced version of Griffin was able to unravel his efforts in no time. The real Adam Archibald had passed away eight years earlier. Frey had taken his name and social security number, and had rewritten history in computers around the world, creating college degrees, work experience, and even dental records that could stand up to the highest level of scrutiny. He had grown a beard, had surgery so he wouldn't need his glasses, and added a toupee of thick brown hair where balding brown had been before. But while these physical changes were enough to fool an ex-colleague if he passed them on the street, his wide nose, weak chin, and shallow face were a dead match for Eric Frey—as were his habits.

Desh had flown to San Diego, Kira's old haunt, to spy on this Archibald to learn as much as possible about him and attempt to discover who he was working with. But after five days, Desh had been shut out. Archibald/Frey had developed electronic technologies that nullified the bugs and homing devices Desh planted, which wasn't possible since they made use of technology undetectable by anyone on earth, a further confirmation that Archibald was indeed Eric Frey.

Desh could continue surveillance and hope he got a lucky break that would provide a handle on Frey's network. But he had to weigh the probability of success against the probability that Frey would learn Desh was on to him and go to ground. In the end, the decision was obvious.

It was time to act.

44

Desh waited patiently inside the shower of the guest stateroom of Frey's multimillion-dollar yacht, the *Codon*. The craft was spectacular. Frey had moved up in the world since he had purchased his last boat, but access to Kira's gellcaps could do that for you.

The *Codon* was a sixty-foot triple-decker that, despite its size, had sleek, aerodynamic curves that screamed speed and agility: a racing boat scaled up ten-fold. The cabins were elegant and decadent, resembling nothing more than the sleeping quarters of European royalty. Desh was sickened by the thought of what was certain to have taken place on this magnificent ship. If anything, Frey's dramatic increase in wealth would make him even more of a predator than he had been in his previous life.

Desh had arrived early enough to avoid being seen by the few marina residents who called their boats home. After silently inspecting every square centimeter of the upper decks of the *Codon*, and disabling a red and black jet ski, he had picked a lock and hurried below, out of sight from any awakening eyes. He had gone over the rest of the boat just as carefully as he had the outside decks, finding nothing that had caused him any concern. No alarms. No surveillance equipment. And no means of leaving the ship other than swimming.

Now Desh was sitting as comfortably as he possibly could on the floor of a shower, reading one of the eBooks he had downloaded to his phone the night before. He finished the first book and had started on the second when he heard noise from above

Frey had finally arrived for his scheduled outing. If Desh's intelligence was correct, the man who had become Adam Archibald would be alone on this excursion.

Before long the boat began to move slowly as it cleared the dock and harbor. After five minutes, Frey opened the throttle and the huge ship darted forward. Desh waited another ten minutes and exited the shower. He pulled a military style stun gun from his pocket and walked soundlessly across the cabin.

Desh's face twisted in confusion. *Why did he feel so weak?* He stumbled, shaking his head as if to clear cobwebs. He righted himself and tried to take another step, but he couldn't get himself to move. His arm returned to his side as if it had a mind of its own, and his hand became so weak the gun slipped from his fingers. Seconds later he slid to the floor as well, and blackness rushed up to greet him.

***

Desh returned to consciousness without any sense of how much time had passed. He was clothed and unbound, but his pockets had been emptied and his stun gun and Glock were gone. He reached for the handle of the cabin door, but it was locked.

"Why don't you sit down and let's have a talk," said a clear voice from a hidden speaker. A voice belonging to Eric Frey.

Desh's eyes darted around the room, his mind calculating. He kicked the stateroom door with as much force as he could and felt a pain surge through his leg as the door held, clearly reinforced in some manner.

"You can't leave unless I let you," said Frey. "And the next dose of gas I send into that room will be just as odorless and colorless as the first. But this one will be *lethal*. So I'll be expecting your cooperation from now on," he added pointedly.

"How long was I out?"

"Only ten minutes," replied Frey. "I'm not a patient man."

"Oh yeah, *that's your fatal flaw.*"

Frey ignored him. "Sit down in the chair by the bed and turn on the monitor in front of you."

Desh did as instructed and a video image of Frey appeared, wearing blue swim trunks and a white, button down shirt, opened to reveal a tanned but pudgy body. He was on the bridge, but nowhere near the helm, which he must have put on autopilot. In a small corner of the large monitor, Desh could see an image of himself, which was no doubt being transmitted to Frey's own screen.

Frey leaned in close to the camera with a self-satisfied smirk. "I knew from Alan that his sister didn't like to use her own invention," he said. "And she's managed to surround herself with others who share the same view. Incredible. How noble and yet how fucking stupid. You're good, David Desh, but if you thought you could eliminate me on my home turf without being amped, you've got your head up your ass."

"I wasn't going to eliminate you," said Desh. "Just stun you."

"What if I was amped?—what you call enhanced."

"Even with perfect control of your body, you can't stop electricity," replied Desh. "The gun would have worked. I've used myself as a guinea pig to make sure."

"Good to know," said Frey. He shook his head derisively. "So what took you so long? When I got wind you were talking to my old colleagues, I expected you sooner."

"Sorry to disappoint you," said Desh. "How did you know I was on board?"

"I have hidden cameras in the staterooms. Especially in the guest shower," he added with a twisted, lecherous grin, and Desh had an overwhelming urge to jump through the screen and beat him to death with his bare fists. "Cameras modulated to avoid detection from traditional detectors or any you've come up with," continued Frey. "As you no doubt have realized, while amped, I've gone to considerable effort perfecting surveillance electronics, capable of both defeating yours and making mine undetectable."

Frey raised his eyebrows. "And if you haven't guessed already," he continued with a smug expression, "the fancy electronics you have in your waistband are useless on the *Codon.*" He paused and then shook his head in disgust. "I have to say, I'd have more respect for you if your plan was to kill me."

"Yeah. And your respect means the *world* to me," snapped Desh sarcastically. "If it makes you feel any better," he added with bitter intensity, "I plan to kill you the next chance I get."

Frey ignored him. "So . . . what? You were going to interrogate me? Try to learn the extent of my organization?"

"You know what they say: it's not the cockroaches you can see when the light goes on. It's the ones hidden under the floorboards you have to be sure to exterminate."

"Be as big of an asshole as you like, Desh. You're going to be a prisoner for some time, and I have a long memory." He tilted back in his seat and put his feet up on something off camera. "When I learned you were talking to my ex-colleagues, I knew it wouldn't be long until you came after me. *Finally.* My plan was to be patient, and I have been, but I'm not getting any younger," he added pointedly.

"So why am I still alive?" asked Desh.

"So I can trade you for the secret of longevity."

Desh frowned. Kira's life would have been so much easier if she had never developed this treatment in the first place. "She can't give it to you if she wanted to. I'm sure you're aware of the lengths John Putnam and Alan Miller went to get her to reveal it. But it's hidden, even from her."

Frey laughed. "We both know that's not true anymore. I wasn't there in person, of course, but I was listening in when Alan pulled off his perfect storm. When he tricked her to voluntarily unlock the memory cage in which she had trapped this secret. I have no doubt it's *still* unlocked."

"I'm afraid you've miscalculated."

"Jesus, Desh. I'm not even amped and I can tell you're lying. I'll check this later, when my IQ is boosted, but I'm sure I'm right. You have to work on that poker face."

"So you're responsible for getting this Colonel Jacobson involved, correct?" said Desh, changing the subject.

"You already know that. It's a transparent attempt to get me talking. To gather what you military guys call *intel.*"

Desh ignored him. Just because Frey had guessed his intent didn't mean it still wouldn't work. People liked to talk—and to boast. Especially when they had the upper hand and felt invulnerable. "But why involve the military?" asked Desh. "If you want Kira's treatment, you need her alive. So why unleash this colonel, who's hell bent on killing her?"

"I tried to find her myself, but I didn't get very far. I finally hit pay dirt when I set up a system to look for work too advanced to be done by normals. Where do you think the colonel got the idea? I have a man inside his camp I had feed it to him, or he would never have figured it out. Anyway, I got lucky and found Ross Metzger, whose computer contained work so advanced, I wasn't able to make any sense out of it, even when amped. I kept watch, and when I learned Kira was visiting, I set up a raid to capture her."

Desh pursed his lips. He had thought the raid was too flawless to be set up by a normal, and he had been right. At the time, Kira had accounted for every last gellcap, so he thought he must have been wrong. If only he had taken this thinking further, questioned his certainty that no one else could duplicate her treatment, he might have realized Frey was still alive long ago.

"Did you try to perfect the cold fusion reactor while enhanced?" asked Desh.

Frey laughed. "There was nothing to perfect. The device did absolutely nothing."

Desh's eye narrowed. The device wasn't ready for prime time since it barely put more energy out than was put in, but it did more than *nothing*. "You reassembled it wrong," said Desh with a patronizing air.

"We reassembled it *perfectly*. And it doesn't do shit."

Desh didn't know what to make of this. He couldn't see what Frey had to gain by lying about the generator. The most likely explanation was that he had just reassembled it incorrectly, after all, but Frey's insistence otherwise was something he needed to tuck in the back of his mind.

"That facility was my only lead at the time," continued Frey. "When you torched the place, and when my high-priced soldiers failed to catch you, I tried to regain the thread. But with no luck. So I decided to unleash the colonel and his vast network. So I'd have plenty of free time to build wealth, power, resources, organization—you get the picture. By bringing in the military, I expanded my reach a hundred fold."

"Making sure to discredit longevity when you did."

"Right. It's a bit too alluring. Didn't want any competition from Jake or his men. This way I kept him focused on the goal. But I wasn't worried he'd succeed in killing Kira. She and you are too good for that. But I figure if he got anywhere, if he harried you, you'd start making mistakes and I could capitalize. I couldn't believe he managed to acquire Kira, but then the fuckhead lost her the moment he had her."

Frey shrugged. "But no matter," he said evenly. "It all worked out for the best. He did his job. He beat the bushes. And during the brief time he had Kira he managed to give her the clues she needed to finally figure out I was alive."

"You wanted her to know?"

"That's right. It was my plan B. If it hadn't happened naturally, I was about to force it. If I couldn't find you, I'd bring you to *me*. Like Alan said, you guys are so fucking predictable. You'll always do the noble, heroic thing. And I figured if you did come after me, you'd come here, to my yacht. It's perfect for an ambush." He grinned once again. "It's perfect for um . . . *entertaining* as well. Although you're several decades too old for my taste."

"You are one sick fuck," spat Desh in disgust.

Frey's smile faded. "Again, I may be a sick fuck, but I have a long memory. I'll make a trade with Kira for her longevity therapy. And I'll keep my part of the bargain and return you to her. But nothing says you have to be returned healthy," he finished with a malevolent scowl.

45

For a week, scientists, bureaucrats, soldiers, and those whose responsibilities for their individual governments could only be guessed at had occupied the *Copernicus*, and the eyes of the world were upon them.

The small floating city maintained its position off the coast of Angola, and the brilliant men and women who now called her home—the greatest collection of scientific talent ever assembled in a single place, dedicated to a single task—scratched their collective heads.

Why had the alien ship come? What was its purpose? There was no message inside, no robots to establish communications. No plaque with images of alien beings, or prime numbers, or pi. No recording of alien top forty hits, no Rosetta stone to teach primitive Earthlings an alien language.

Perhaps it had made its journey just to dispel humanity's ethnocentric notion that it was the be-all and end-all of life in the universe. Maybe aliens had detected humanity's efforts to find them, through the SETI program and others, and while unwilling to reveal anything of themselves or their technology, had sent the ship to answer a question that earth had undergone considerable effort to ask. Or perhaps it was a test of species maturity. Solve the riddle of zero point energy, or find a way to evoke a hidden, quantum message, and earn the right to join the galactics.

But if revealing the ship's secrets was a test, humanity was failing miserably. The scientists on board might as well have taken a pleasure cruise, complete with frequent onshore excursions, for all the good being on the ship did them.

The alien object had been a bust. Yes, it could have failed to take orbit above the Earth and moved on, in which case there would be speculation for decades and centuries to come as to its design, what it all meant, and the purpose of the flyby. But given the ship had actually been retrieved, the results could not have been more disappointing. The hull was unique and had impressive properties, but it was made from a composite of materials, all of which could be found on earth.

Whatever electronics had guided it to its destination had been jettisoned into the Sun. The ZPE drive had been disengaged, and none of the world's top scientists could get it on again, nor with it off, make any progress understanding how it might work.

Minute parts of the ZPE drive were removed, recorded, submitted to endless spectroscopic and other analyses, and carefully returned. Research proposals were submitted to the management team of Nobelists for approval.

But mostly the scientists speculated, and twiddled their thumbs. At some point soon the nearly two hundred participating countries would decide the project had been a failure and send their teams home, but this wouldn't happen while there was even the slightest hope of deciphering the ZPE drive. So a ship full of disappointed scientists found their counterparts from other countries and worked on terrestrial projects of their own, determined that a collection of brainpower this great not be wasted.

But on the seventh day, as biblical as this may have been, no one rested.

Because on the seventh day, all hell broke loose.

And the privileged community on *Copernicus* barely had a head start before this new and rapidly moving phenomenon would explode onto the rest of the world.

Reports began coming in of the discovery of what some, at first, thought was a new microbe; albeit a large one. But one look under a microscope dispelled that idea instantly. Not only wasn't it a microbe, it wasn't a form of life at all. It was part organic and part machine. A Borg on a microscopic level. A nanite.

These nanites were being discovered in locations around the world. And they were being fruitful and multiplying. In only a few days they would be so plentiful as to be observed, not just by biologists with powerful microscopes wondering what had contaminated their cell cultures, but by any kid with a twenty dollar microscope and a sample of air, or water, or dirt.

Nanotechnology had been all the rage now for decades. Scientists had long known of the possibilities, and potential, of manipulating matter on an atomic scale, and nanotechnology departments had become a mainstay of universities around the globe. And while considerable progress had been made, the alien nanites were far more advanced than anything humanity was capable of, although they appeared deceptively simple in construction.

As early as 1959, Richard Feynman had asked the question, what if items could be manufactured—*assembled*—from the bottom up, using *atoms* for building blocks? And in 1986, Eric Drexler had built on this to ask, what if an assembler could be designed at the nanoscale level that could not only assemble any blueprint given to it, but that could even make copies of *itself*? These were breathtaking visions.

And there was proof that this could be done. Endless proof. In an eagle, or an armadillo, or an oak tree, or a single blade of grass. All multicellular life on earth had been assembled in precisely this manner.

The complex entity called a human was composed of trillions of cells, and each of these trillions of cells had arisen from a single fertilized egg. This single fertilized cell, drawing half of its genes from a male donor and half from a female, was the ultimate nanite, converting bits of raw material taken in (food) into copies of itself, and doing so exponentially. And exponential growth was truly awesome in its capacity. A single cell became two, and two became four, and four became eight, and so on. But while this growth didn't look like much in the first ten or fifteen doublings, if left unchecked, in only forty doublings this single cell would become over a trillion cells. *From one to a trillion in only forty doublings.*

But as impressive as this rate of growth was, a trillion *identical* cells would be useless; a pile of protoplasm that couldn't walk, or watch a sunset, or write a sonnet. What was truly awe-inspiring was that a single progenitor cell had the programming necessary to make an entire human. At some point early in the process, using methods that science still didn't fully understand, the cells would begin to differentiate—to specialize. Some in the early ball of identical cells, following a complex program in their DNA, knew to become heart cells. And some eye cells. And some brain cells. And so on. And each group of cells knew where to position themselves, and how to properly integrate themselves into the whole. All the instructions, the entire blueprint, was there in that first microscopic, fertilized cell.

An absolute miracle of nanite construction, each and every time it occurred.

And if organic material, made up of lipids and protein and DNA, could pull off a miracle, why couldn't a manmade assembler do the same? Not for constructs as complex as a human, or even an ant, but at least for relatively uncomplicated construction; for far less demanding tasks.

This was the vision, and scientists had pursued it ever since. As early as 1989, a physicist managed to move individual atoms for the first time, and in less than two months was able to arrange thirty-five xenon atoms to spell out the letters *IBM*. Scientists had gone on to construct motors the size of a single molecule and found clever ways for their tiny machines to self-assemble.

The alien nanites were built precisely along the lines human scientists had long envisioned, just thirty to a hundred years more advanced than was currently possible. They were simple, which made them versatile, able to convert minute quantities of raw material into more of themselves.

Bacteria had long proven the effectiveness of simplicity of design combined with an unequaled ability to reproduce and spread. The human body harbored ten times more bacteria than it had cells of its own. In fact, more than thirty times as many bacteria could be found in an ounce of fecal matter than there were humans in the world. Bacteria inhabited almost every square inch of ground on the planet, and could be found forty miles above the surface and twenty miles below. They existed in frigid arctic climates and in boiling hot springs. On the surface of oceans and below the waves. They could thrive in oil, pesticides, and toxic waste. Bacteria teamed throughout the globe in incomprehensible numbers, and there was nowhere they couldn't penetrate.

The alien nanites appeared to be just as unstoppable. They could chew through plastic and steel, one molecule at a time, so no barrier stopped them for long. Scientists isolated them and put them in environments containing various raw materials. At the average rate of duplication, and given the power of exponential growth, the weight of the nanites would exceed the weight of the Earth in less than two weeks.

But of course this wouldn't happen. The nanites couldn't grow unrestrained forever. They would run out of raw material. And they must have a purpose.

But what?

Huge numbers of them were injected into experimental animals with no effect. They were found on human skin and in human feces, also with no discernable effect. They appeared to be as harmless to terrestrial biology as the trillions of bacteria that called the human gut their home.

All of *Copernicus* was briefed on these emerging findings at the same time, in dozens of languages on thousands of monitors.

The race to understand the end game of the alien nanites was on. The news couldn't be contained for much longer. The *Copernicus* needed to get ahead of this story, needed to find a way to fend off the panic that would inevitably come. For the alien ship hadn't just travelled uncountable trillions of miles to assume a dead orbit and become nothing more than a fancy decoration. It had somehow disgorged a plague upon the world. The nanites could well be for the good—perhaps eventually serving as tiny MDs, entering human bloodstreams and patrolling to destroy cancer and other maladies and repair damage— but their presence, and their reproductive abilities, were terrifying.

Their purpose could also be malicious, a conclusion that the majority of the world's population would jump to immediately. And the nanites would soon reach a point at which they were so plentiful, even if they continued to be harmless, panic would reach critical mass.

So hasty plans were made to rush nanotechnologists, roboticists, computer scientists, and software engineers to the *Copernicus*, and nonessential personnel were identified who would be sent home to make room. But given the ubiquity of the nanites, this time the *Copernicus* was not the only game in town. Each government mounted its own homegrown effort as an adjunct to the collaborative effort that would be undertaken at sea.

Within days the nanites would be so easy to find, grade schoolers would be part of the effort to unlock their mysteries.

46

Eric Frey, also known as Adam Archibald, removed a gellcap from a steel container and brought it close to the camera so Desh could get a clear view. "Time to begin part two of this interrogation," he said with a smug look on his face. He popped the pill in his mouth and swallowed. "For this part, I need to know with absolute certainty if you're telling me the truth or not."

Frey waited calmly for the effect to hit. Four minutes later it did. Desh could tell immediately from the haughty expression on Frey's face and the gleam in his eyes. Desh knew Frey would have to create an avatar, a tiny portion of his mental capabilities set aside to emulate a normal, or else communication would be impossible, since Frey was now operating on a level Desh couldn't begin to understand or keep up with.

Desh fought to maintain a poker face, but was cursing inside. *Shit.* Frey had gotten lucky. He had chosen the exact right time to enhance himself. He glanced over at a clock by the bedside for just an instant, without realizing it, but this was enough.

"You're expecting company," said Frey. It wasn't a question. "You're pissed that I took a gellcap just minutes before they're due to arrive. You still think you've got the upper hand, but you're worried the pill might give me too much of a chance." He shot Desh a withering stare. "You're right to be worried."

"What are you talking about?" said Desh, unable to help himself from lying, even knowing that attempts at deception would be useless.

Frey disappeared from view and returned thirty seconds later with a pair of binoculars. He took over from the autopilot and the yacht made a wide arc that ended with it pointing back toward the San Diego shoreline, much too far away to be visible. He opened the throttle all the way and the craft sliced through the waves at its full speed of almost forty-five miles per hour. Then Frey re-engaged the autopilot.

Finally, he returned his attention to his prisoner. "I'll be damned," he said. "What happened to David Desh, Lone Ranger? You actually did something unexpected; something *not* retarded. Incredible. So you *can* teach an old Desh new tricks." He leaned forward intently and his eyes bored into Desh's with the full intensity of his expanded intellect, which was intimidating on a primal level. "From the air or sea?" snapped Frey.

Desh sat perfectly still and said nothing.

"I see. Air only. Mercs?"

"The best," replied Desh, knowing his silence wouldn't keep the information from Frey and hoping to shake his confidence.

Frey just laughed and began scanning the skies with the binoculars.

The ex-USAMRIID scientist had been right about him, Desh knew. He *was* predictable, and he *had* been stupid for a long time. As soon as Jake had appeared on the radar he should have begun to beef up his forces. With the loss of Connelly, and given everything else that had rained down on their heads, an army of one wasn't about to cut it. And Desh knew when going after someone who was ruthless, slippery, and capable of being enhanced, the tables could be turned in a hurry. So he had organized a team of mercs while in San Diego. And they were as good as it got. Having access to unlimited funds made recruitment easy. Pay three or four times the going rate and things happened quickly. He had instructed them to come after him forty-five minutes after the *Codon* had left the dock, if they hadn't heard from him by then.

"How many, and what are their orders?"

"Six," replied Desh with as much bravado as he could manage. "In two large civilian helos. And they have explosives and firepower enough to destroy you and this craft, regardless of how smart you are now."

While Desh was speaking, Frey spotted the helos far off in the distance, too far away for the blades to be heard over the sound of the open ocean. The sky was a pure crystal blue and visibility was as good as it could be, not a rare occurrence for San Diego.

Frey rushed below deck and threw open the door to the guest room, not even bothering to point a weapon in Desh's direction. Ordinarily, even with a weapon trained on him by someone like Frey, Desh would have had the upper hand, but he knew that attacking Frey in his enhanced state was useless.

"Here are your choices," said Desh, forcing himself to stay calm, which was nearly impossible. Facing Frey while he was enhanced was like facing an oncoming hurricane, a force of nature that possessed a power so ferocious it could not be overcome. "You can let me go and surrender. In which case my men will let you live to fight another day. You'll be captured, but you'll be unharmed."

"Or I can kill you," said Frey impatiently, "and try to fight or escape."

"You can, but if I'm dead my men have orders to destroy this yacht and kill you from as far away as possible."

"And if I don't surrender, even if you are still alive, they have orders to do the same," said Frey, reading Desh's next sentence as surely as if it had been spoken. "You told them you were expendable." Frey titled his head and studied Desh. "I see. But they get a massive bonus if you live through this. Smart. You didn't want them to get itchy trigger fingers. If they got the same money whether you died or not, they'd just blow us up and be done with it."

"I'm prepared to die," growled Desh firmly. "Are you?"

Frey laughed. "*I'm prepared to die*," he mocked in an exaggerated, cartoon voice. "*I'm prepared to die.* Are you fucking *kidding* me? Where does the world *grow* people like you?" he barked in contempt. "Thank God misplaced nobility and monumental stupidity isn't contagious."

Desh ignored the insult. He had heard worse from his closest colleagues while they were under the influence of one of Kira's gellcaps. "My team has arrived," he told Frey. "You have two minutes to make a decision. If you haven't released me and surrendered by then, we're both dead."

Frey returned Desh's phone to him. "Call them," he said calmly. "Tell them to hold their fire. I'm surrendering." He shrugged. "As you guessed when planning this, I'm not prepared to die. And while I calculate I'd be able to kill you and your scary mercs four out of five times, I'm not willing to take a chance."

Desh touched the screen and the phone dialed. "When we get on deck," he said, "you'll have to return my stun gun and let me use it on you. Then I'll immobilize you and wait until you return to normal before we proceed."

Frey nodded.

"Hold your fire," barked Desh into the phone. "We're coming out. I repeat, hold your fire."

"Roger that," came the response, loudly enough to be heard by both men.

The two men emerged on deck. The helos kept a respectful distance, following Desh's instructions. Desh had insisted that if he needed their intervention, regardless of how frail and harmless Frey might appear, to consider him to be the most formidable opponent they had ever faced.

The ocean air whipped around both men, and Desh couldn't help but feel somewhat exhilarated by the speed of the large craft as it cut through the Pacific. "Okay," said Desh. "Give me my stun gun."

Frey pulled out an H&K .45 and shot Desh point blank in the torso.

The move had been impossibly fast. Then, in another flash of movement, before Desh could even fall to the deck, Frey executed a perfect kick that sent him flying over the edge of the yacht and into the sea below.

"Sorry, changed my mind," said Frey calmly, rushing below deck once again as the *Codon* raced on.

47

"Hello, Kira. Thanks for taking my call," said Colonel Morris Jacobson from inside a cramped but luxurious cabin on board the *Copernicus*. He had contacted her hours earlier to schedule the call, using the IP address he had used to contact her previously. Kira had left this IP address open, but had made sure it was untraceable by linking it to thousands of other IP locations that constantly shifted like the inside of a kaleidoscope, all but one a dummy.

Kira was seated in front of a large monitor which displayed the colonel's face, with Matt Griffin beside her, intending to be a silent observer.

"I know what you look like now," continued Jake. "So any reason not to put yourself on screen this time?"

"Yeah," spat Kira bitterly. "My reason is that you want me to."

It was true the colonel had been given false information, but he was also responsible for Jim Connelly's death, something for which she could never forgive him. And the bullet Connelly had taken was meant for her. "You ordered your men in the Rockies to shoot to kill, you bastard!"

"How can you act surprised?" said Jake calmly. "You know I see you as enemy number one. When I bombed what I *thought* was your headquarters, I was shooting to kill. So this is hardly a new strategy. The one time you had me promise to take you prisoner and not try to kill you, you, yourself, taught me this was a mistake. That you're too competent and dangerous to capture."

"You killed a great man," she said, her voice a feral growl.

"I really am sorry about that. The evidence I have suggests you're the one plotting power-grabs and massacres on a global scale, and that your followers are just innocent people sucked in by your lies and charisma. Adoring followers willing to drink poisoned Kool-Aid at your command."

"What do you want?" snapped Kira.

"I'm calling to ask for your help."

Kira glanced up at the bearded mountain standing next to her in disbelief. "Of course you are," she spat. "How can I help?" she added sarcastically. "Wait a minute. Let me guess. You want me to blow my brains out. Or shove a bomb up my own ass maybe."

Jake made a visible effort to remain calm. "Look, in my office, you suggested we were on the same side, and offered your help if I ever needed it. So you're admitting that was just bullshit?"

"No. That was a real offer. But that was before you killed my friend."

"Again, I bombed your headquarters to slag, intending to kill you and several others. My intentions were never a mystery. You knew that when you offered to help me."

"What happened with van Hutten?" asked Kira, changing the subject.

"I interrogated him, of course. Like Rosenblatt before him, he believes you couldn't be more compassionate. Although he also believes you're dangerous and misguided."

"Did he convince you the aliens would ask to see me?"

Jake smiled. "Almost. He's got some pretty wild ideas, but he's nearly as persuasive as you are. But you have him fooled. He doesn't believe for a second you're meeting with terrorists and plotting a massive power grab. He thinks you want to turn us all into the Borg from Star Trek."

"I know what he thinks!" snapped Kira with a scowl. "Do you still have him in custody?"

"No. After he torched your facility and kidnapped you, he's not exactly an Icarus member in good standing—so he's of no further use to me. We let him go. He's a future Nobel

Laureate, after all. We made him sign stiff confidentiality agreements preventing him from telling anyone about you or Icarus, for reasons of national security. But he's free. We warned him you might retaliate for what he did but he didn't seem the least bit nervous." He leaned in closer to the camera. "Should he be?"

"Of course he should," she said flippantly. "I'm the evil Kira Miller."

"You're also brilliant and know if you try anything, you risk giving me a lead."

"And you're a lot less intelligent than I once thought," she said scornfully. "I could have killed him in the Rockies if I wanted him dead," she pointed out. She gazed at the screen with contempt. "So what do you want? You have to be desperate to come to me for help. And crazy if you think I'll help you after the Rockies."

"I *am* desperate," he admitted. "Have you heard about a microbe that's contaminated some Petri dishes here and there?"

Kira shook her head. "No. I've been *busy*," she said pointedly. "Can't pay attention to everything."

"Well, within twenty-four hours, *everyone* will be paying attention to this. More attention even than they paid to the alien craft."

Kira's face wrinkled in apprehension. "Bioterror?"

"Half bio, half not. But terror, definitely. Enough to get me to call you. They're nanites. Alien nanites."

Kira and Griffin exchanged stunned glances. "I thought the alien ship was pronounced totally clean before it was brought down."

"It was," said Jake. "It must have rained them down on us when it first got here. The nanites weren't just random stowaways on the alien ship that survived decontamination. Infecting us was the entire purpose of the visit."

Jake went on to give Kira—and without knowing it, Griffin—as complete a briefing as he had been given. "We obviously need to know what these things are up to," explained Jake when he was finished. "So far they're harmless. Maybe they'll stay that way. Or maybe they're about to become the most destructive force we've ever seen." He paused. "We need your intelligence enhancement therapy."

"You can't have it."

"I didn't say that right. We need someone from your group who has experience being under the influence of your pills."

"Who would you want, and what would you want them to do?"

"We want your top computer expert. Nanites are tiny machines. Machines that require programming. We need to figure out what that programming is. We both know any human with an IQ in the hundreds rather than in the thousands isn't going to have a chance figuring this out. I doubt even an enhanced expert programmer could, but at least we'll have a chance."

Kira eyed Matt for several long seconds. Finally, he nodded decisively.

"And his role?" asked Kira.

"He'd head up the American team that's been assembled to study this. No one would know about enhancement. We'd just pawn him off as an off-the-charts talent; a singular genius who was previously undiscovered. Like that Indian mathematician who went to Cambridge." Jake paused. "He'd have immunity of course."

"So you're proposing a truce. A cease fire. We work together until this threat is resolved."

"Exactly. If your man isn't successful, I'm guessing there's a good chance we're all dead anyway. If he is, we let him blend back into the woodwork."

"And then continue trying to hunt us down like vermin."

"Unless you can prove to me that you're innocent with as much tight evidence as I have that you're a monster."

"But once you've seen and worked with our computer expert, he isn't anonymous anymore. What if he's the type who stands out? That'll make your job easier once he's helped you, won't it?"

"It can't be helped. We both have to choose the lesser of two evils. You don't want to expose yourself to me and give up your top man. I don't want to have to work with someone I'm dedicated to bringing down. And you know how I feel about what your treatment does to people. I still worry the cure might be worse than the disease."

Griffin got Kira's attention and mouthed, *I'm going to jump in*. Kira nodded.

"Hello, Colonel," began Griffin. "I'm the local computer expert. I just happened to be listening in on the entire conversation."

Surprise registered on Jake's face, but only for a moment. "Glad to hear it," he said smoothly. "We don't have any time to waste, and this saves me from having to repeat myself." He paused. "What should I call you?"

"Matt's as good a name as any," replied Griffin.

"So will you help us?" asked Jake eagerly.

"Can I assume the *Copernicus* is mounting an international effort to study these bugs?"

"That's right."

"Then I'll help you," said Griffin. "But only if I can head up the *international* effort."

Jake looked confused. "Why?" he asked. "The American effort will provide unlimited resources to you and your team. Given that finding nanites to study isn't exactly difficult, each country is fielding their own teams. And they're each putting their best people on their national efforts. The scientists being sent to *Copernicus*, although still brilliant, are the reserves. That's just the way countries think. Selfishly."

"Well it's not the way *I* think. If I make a discovery, I don't want it bottled up. I want it shared with the world."

"I can promise you that anything you learn will be shared with the world. What reason could we possibly have not to?"

"Who knows?" replied Griffin. "Reason and government rarely go hand in hand. But let me be clear: this is non-negotiable. I have to be a part of *Copernicus*. And not just because I've never been on a luxury cruise ship before," he added with a half smile. "I have to be certain my findings will be shared. And being on a U.N. ship will make me feel more comfortable that you'll keep your promise."

"I'll keep it," insisted Jake.

"Can you vouch for the people you work with?" asked Griffin.

"Right now, I'm the only one who even knows I'm contacting you. If you agree, only my boss and my second in command will know anything about it."

"I stand by my demand. *Copernicus* or bust."

A deep frown came over Jake's face. "Impossible," he said firmly. "I can make you head of the American effort. I don't have the authority or power to make you head of the international effort."

"Come on, Colonel. I'm sure America still has plenty enough influence to make this happen. Eight of the twenty-one Nobelists are American. So is Madison Russo, who discovered the alien probe. So are a disproportionate number of scientists on that ship."

"True, but I still can't just demand that you be put in charge. You're a complete unknown."

"I've seen the news reports," said Griffin. "Everyone keeps bragging about how *Copernicus* is a perfect meritocracy. No politics, just great minds working together. Well, use your influence with the Nobelists and others to run a worldwide contest to determine who leads the team. Two competitors from each country, chosen by their governments. Each devises software challenges for the others: puzzles and traps and mazes. The one who solves the most in an hour becomes the leader."

Jake paused for a long moment and then a smile slowly came over his face. "I'll say this for you, Kira, your people are impressive, even without your treatment. It's a good idea. I could get this to happen. Who could argue it isn't the fair way to choose the best for something this important? And when Matt runs rings around them all, he'll instantly earn the credibility he'll need for them to follow him. Far more so than if I had the ability to make him head of the project by decree, which I don't."

"Then I'm in," said Griffin.

"*Thank you*," replied Jake, visibly relieved. "How fast can you get to Peterson Air Force Base in Colorado Springs?"

Griffin glanced at Kira. Any geographic information he revealed would aid Jake later on, but there might not *be* a later on if they didn't get a handle on the alien bugs. She nodded. "Wright-Patterson in Dayton would be closer," he said.

"Fine. I'll have a jet waiting to fly you to Saldanha, South Africa the second you arrive. I'll try to have the software competition scheduled for soon after you land, so no time is wasted. And we'll be fueled up and ready to land you on *Copernicus* the minute you finish."

Kira frowned. "I want David Desh to be allowed on board as well. Same deal. He walks when this is over."

Griffin brightened immediately, obviously delighted by the idea.

"Why?" said Jake.

"Because I believe this is as important as you do. And I'd feel better if he was there. To help Matt and to keep you honest."

Jake considered for several long seconds. "Okay," he said finally. "Can Desh make it to Wright-Patt with Matt?"

"I'm afraid not," said Kira, checking her watch. Where was he? He should have checked in an hour ago. "Have a jet ready to go at Camp Pendleton in San Diego, and I'll send him to the guard gate. Make sure he gets VIP treatment."

Jake nodded.

"And call back in exactly thirty minutes. I'll have a few more questions, and we can discuss logistics."

"Fine. Anything else?"

"Yeah," said Griffin. "Think about by how much you want me to win the competition."

"Are you kidding?" said Jake. "Blow them all away. This is no time to be shy. Shock and Awe is what we're going for."

"Shock and Awe," repeated Griffin with a wry smile. "Good. That happens to be my specialty."

48

As the *Codon* raced out of sight, saltwater bit at David Desh's wound, and the blood rushing from his body created a red bloom around him; a clarion call to any shark within miles of his location.

Struggling to keep his head above water, Desh had no way to staunch the flow. He concentrated on maintaining a dead man's float, but wounded as he was, even this was difficult, and he feared it wouldn't be long until he'd be sinking to the bottom like a brick. A swell hit him in the face and he inhaled water, coughing as he did so, sending a paroxysm of pain throughout his upper body.

Both helicopters rushed to his location, and in less than a minute a small raft had been pushed from one, self-inflating as rapidly as a car airbag as it fell. Several of the mercs dropped from one of the low flying craft into the ocean, pulling Desh to the raft. When he was successfully on board, they turned him on his back. One of the men in the other helo dropped a medical kit down, which was caught by one of the mercs, and they immediately went to work dressing and bandaging Desh's wound.

Desh gritted his teeth and tried to ignore the pain. He forced himself to think. *Why hadn't Frey killed him?* He could have easily put a bullet in Desh's head. For some reason Frey wanted him wounded, but alive.

Of course, thought Desh. Frey wanted a diversion. A head start.

If the mercs killed Frey they'd get a massive bonus. But doing so and keeping Desh alive at the same time was even *more* rewarding. So both helos had stuck around to be certain he'd pull through. Which must have been exactly what Frey had wanted. The mercs would have no fear that Frey would get away while they were rescuing Desh. Where would he go? It was open ocean for miles and miles and there was no hiding a beauty like the *Codon*.

"Go after him. Now," croaked Desh as loudly as he could, but it came out as little more than a whisper, and couldn't be heard over the noise of the helos and the Pacific. He began to shiver as the men wrapped jackets around him and secured him in a gurney that had been lowered from one of the helicopters.

As soon as Desh was lifted into the aircraft he motioned feebly for a set of headphones.

"What time is it?" he said into the microphone when the headphones had been placed over his head.

The mercs looked confused by this question, but one of the men told him.

Desh nodded. Frey had now been enhanced for almost twenty-five minutes. "Go after him," he whispered. "But keep your distance. Just keep him in sight. Exactly forty minutes from now, board the ship and take him out."

"Why wait?" asked one of the mercs. "Let's *end* this asshole."

Trying to board the *Codon* while Frey was still enhanced would be suicide, regardless of the number of men or their skills. But once Frey snapped back to normal he'd be unable to take another gellcap for at least a few hours. The brain had a remarkable plasticity, but making it toggle from amped to normal to amped again in rapid succession was too much to ask of it.

"Forty minutes," insisted Desh as forcefully as he could manage. "Not a minute less. Cheat on this and he'll kill us all. Guaranteed." And with that, Desh's eyes slid shut and he drifted into a troubled unconsciousness.

***

Desh awoke five hours later with an IV in his arm and the hole in his side stitched closed. One of the mercenaries had kept watch over him while he was out, an Israeli named Ari Regev, who had been a member of the Mossad.

Desh turned his head toward the Israeli. "What happened?" he asked, feeling much better than he had expected.

"After you passed out," said Regev, his Israeli accent unmistakable, "I flew you directly here. To a medic friend of mine who doesn't ask questions. We figured one helo could easily do the job."

"And the target?"

The olive-skinned mercenary frowned. "While I was bringing you here, the team boarded his boat, which was still traveling at full speed. They waited forty minutes like you asked." He shook his head. "They went through every inch, but didn't find anything alive, not even a jook." He waved his hand, searching for the English equivalent. "Um . . . cockroach."

"Impossible. He was too far out to swim it. Not this guy."

"I agree. From the air, he looked like he'd have trouble making it across a swimming pool. But the chopper executed a search pattern and didn't spot any swimmers."

"So how? I disabled his jet ski. Could he have met up with another boat?"

Regev shook his head. "No, nothing around for miles. He scubad out."

"Impossible. No scuba gear in his boat."

"When the team couldn't find a swimmer, they tore the ship apart. Literally. That bonus you offered had everyone *very* motivated. They found a hidden compartment, with molded containers in the shape of two oxygen tanks, fins, and two powered propulsion units. One set was still there— the other gone."

"Shit!" said Desh, picturing Frey in scuba gear, calmly holding on to a propulsion unit as it pulled him rapidly toward shore, at a depth that would make him invisible from the air. "Now that bastard will go to ground. He wanted me to find him this time. Next time won't be so easy."

"Look on the bright side," suggested Regev.

"The bright side?" repeated Desh, raising his eyebrows.

"Yes. You should be dead. The path of that bullet was just right. You took a very clean hit that missed anything vital. We pumped some blood back in, sealed you up, and you'll be good as new in no time. You're a very lucky man, my friend."

"It wasn't luck. He needed me alive and flailing on the waves. If I was clearly dead, you'd have bombed the shit out of him before he could don his scuba gear."

The Israeli shook his head. "I saw how quickly he fired. Without aiming. It was a random shot. It was just dumb luck that he missed anything vital."

"If you say so," whispered Desh wearily.

49

Desh had Regev assure the rest of the team they would get their full bonuses for a job well done, despite the outcome. He had made the mistakes, not them. Besides, he wanted to use this group again, and if you had unlimited funds, overpaying was a good way to ensure loyalty.

After Regev left, he put in a call to Kira, using a secure Skype function on his specially-made phone, which hadn't been affected at all by its immersion in the Pacific. He quickly described his encounter with Eric Frey. She listened with great interest and then filled Desh in on her conversation with Jake, letting her husband know that Matt Griffin was in a military supplied jet en route to South Africa.

"After the initial conversation," said Kira, "I told Jake to call me back in a half hour. Then I took a gellcap and locked myself in the enhancement room so I could be a lie detector. The colonel was telling the truth about everything. He didn't exaggerate the nanite threat at all."

"Too bad," said Desh. "Because that is some scary shit."

"Tell me about it. I thought it might have been a ruse, but no such luck. And he's telling the truth about the truce as well. He'll honor it. And he'll let Matt go his merry way when he's done." She paused. "I gave Matt more gellcaps than he could ever use. Given how ugly he gets, that's a big risk. But Jake is right. Desperate circumstances call for desperate measures. We have to know what these nanites are doing here. And even enhanced Matt will realize it's in his best interest to figure it out."

"How many people aboard *Copernicus* will know about Matt and the gellcaps?"

"Jake and two others."

"You vetted Jake when he couldn't lie to you. But what about these other two? You sure they'll be able to withstand the temptation of knowing there's a supply of gellcaps within easy reach?"

"I let Jake know the pills will be in a specially made stainless steel bottle that will only open for Matt. Only his thumbprint on the top of the canister, and his fingerprints around the side, at an exact pressure unique to Matt, will do the trick. Anyone else tries to open it and the pills will be destroyed. And if Matt is coerced, the canister will detect an increase in his pulse and destroy the contents as well."

Desh whistled. "That's quite the upgrade from the single-pill key ring container. When did you have the time to design that?"

"I didn't," replied Kira with a wide grin, her blue eyes sparkling with an incandescent radiance that only she could generate. "It's a total bluff. You can save a lot of time that way."

Desh laughed. "Very true."

"And I'd bet my life they'll buy it, too."

"No doubt about it," agreed Desh, but a moment later the smile vanished from his face. "That will prevent the theft of Matt's pills. But what about releasing him when it's over? Given what you've said, we can trust Jake. But again, the other two he's told." He paused. "Not so much."

"Unfortunately true," admitted Kira.

"I think this may have been a mistake," said Desh. "Matt could have studied these nanites from headquarters. We've got all the equipment we need. He could communicate anything he learned to Jake on the *Copernicus*. Our government wouldn't keep it a secret. Not for something like this."

"We can't be certain of that. And this way, Matt will have a team of nanotechnologists and software geniuses to draw on."

"Who won't even begin to understand what he's doing," countered Desh. He shrugged. "I think it was a mistake, but the stakes are very high, as usual." He frowned deeply, "Probably even *higher* than usual. I get that. And it's too late now anyway."

Kira gritted her teeth. "Um . . . there is one other thing. I thought you'd support this idea so I kind of . . . volunteered you. Jake agreed to the same deal for you as well. Sorry for not checking first. But there was no time. And I thought for sure you'd want to chaperone Matt."

Desh nodded. "I do. I might not have made this decision—although it would have been close—but you and Matt agreed. Given that, making sure I could be there with him was the right choice—just in case one of Jake's confidants isn't as trustworthy as he is." He shrugged. "Why not? In for a penny, in for a pound."

"Since when did you start quoting British proverbs?"

Desh smiled. "I like to hold a little back," he replied. "So I can surprise you now and then."

"Good. Surprise can be good for a marriage," she said, smiling for the first time in a long while.

Desh fought to keep his face placid, but this remark brought him back to reality. For just a moment he had let himself forget—let himself believe he was talking to the Kira he thought he knew. Surprises could be *bad* for a marriage as well. He wondered how many more were in store for him. And yet part of him clung stubbornly to the belief that there was a valid explanation for Kira's actions. There had to be. He loved her too much for there *not* to be.

"Here's the million dollar question," continued Kira. "Given your condition, are you sure you're up for this?" she asked, the deep concern in her voice unmistakable.

Desh nodded stoically. He *had* to be up for it. With Connelly gone, he was the only option. "I'll be good as new in no time."

Kira sighed. "I'm going to hold you to that," she said, forcing a smile. "But make sure you get a gellcap from Matt the second you see him. And take it right away."

Desh nodded. An enhanced mind could actively direct the body's healing processes, putting into motion a highly accelerated recovery.

Kira let him know a jet was waiting for him at Camp Pendleton whenever he felt up to it. "By the way, no luggage allowed. The colonel will change you out of your clothes before you arrive and provide additional clothing for you once you're on board. No keys, no cell phone—no underwear," she added pointedly. "Matt will be able to keep his pill bottle, but that's all. Apparently, Jake doesn't like bugs. What happens on *Copernicus stays* on *Copernicus*."

"Not surprising," said Desh. "I'm going to call Jake as soon as we're done. I assume he gave you his number?"

"He did." She paused. "I know you have the sturdiest phone money can buy, but I'm still impressed it survived your ordeal."

"Are you kidding?" said Desh with a broad grin. "When the world comes to an end, all that will survive will be the cockroach and my phone."

"An end of the world joke would have been a lot funnier yesterday," noted Kira grimly.

50

Desh's call to Jake was answered almost immediately. "I found Eric Frey," said Desh after he had identified himself. "The man who set us up. The one from USAMRIID Kira told you about."

"Go on," said Jake noncommittally.

"I confirmed he has his own supply of gellcaps. In fact, he took one while I was with him. That's where you got your sample from. He knew all about your activities. He said he had a man inside your camp."

Desh went on to detail how he had found Frey, who had assumed the identity of Adam Archibald, an identity he was surely sloughing off like snake skin even as they spoke. He then described how Archibald/Frey had escaped.

Jake considered. "Do you have any evidence other than your word? Anything you can tell me to convince me you're not just making this up?"

"Just pay attention to news out of San Diego tomorrow. You'll hear that this Archibald is missing and they found his yacht abandoned and trashed. I'll be at Pendleton soon. But I want a slightly slower jet than you had planned. Slightly larger and more comfortable also. So I can recuperate. And make sure you have a fully equipped medic on the flight."

"Roger that," said Jake. "See you in the South Atlantic."

***

Ari Regev's medic friend had agreed to load Desh up with a last dose of antibiotics and pain killers and drop him by the Pendleton gate. But first Desh wanted to check on the bugs he had planted to keep tabs on his wife. He forced himself to fight off his guilt, to push through the intense love he had for Kira Miller, and to remember that if her alter ego had taken over, all bets were off.

The video footage was on his computer, and he accessed it with his indestructible phone. He fast forwarded through the footage, most of which didn't even have Kira on it. His mind had started to wander when he caught something that caused him to stop the video.

He wasn't sure what he had seen, but his instincts told him to take a closer look. It had happened so fast that if he had blinked at the wrong moment he would have missed it.

He hit rewind and then ran the footage forward again.

The room spun around him as though he were hopelessly drunk, and his temples began to throb.

Ross Metzger was on the screen. On Kira's computer monitor.

Alive after all.

Desh had suspected the breach of the physics facility was too flawless, and was either an inside job or had been planned by someone who had been enhanced.

But maybe it had been both.

Desh had ruled out the possibility that Metzger had faked his death because Kira kept close watch on the gellcaps, and without one of these—which Kira insisted he did not have—he couldn't have done it. It had never occurred to Desh that the woman of his dreams, the woman he was passionately in love with, had simply lied to him.

But it was occurring to him now.

He played the footage from his hidden camera, which showed Kira receiving a video call from the not so deceased special forces pilot. After greetings had been exchanged, Metzger said, "I know we've both been crazy busy, but I thought a face-to-face call was long overdue."

"You were right. But unfortunately, you caught me at a bad time. I have some things I need to take care of. I need to call you back later."

"I'll be here," he said.

"Good. But from now on, don't contact me. After Denver was destroyed there's more activity here than usual," She paused and looked upset. "And I think David is beginning to suspect something is up."

Metzger's eyes narrowed. "Why do you think that?"

"No concrete evidence. Just intuition. David's been acting funny toward me. It's subtle, but I'm picking it up. And he's the last person we should ever underestimate. So send me a scrambled text when you want to have a face to face, and I'll contact you. No use tempting fate."

"You've been very careful, Kira. You're probably just imagining things."

"Could be," said Kira. "But let's not take that chance."

And with that, the connection ended.

51

The story of the alien nanites spread around a horrified globe in hours. Every man, woman, and child was stunned to their cores. What did this mean? Would the nanites emerge as a powerful force for good, improving the human condition? Or were they a harbinger of doom? Was the end of the world only days or hours away?

Representatives of the *Copernicus*, still the most respected global authority on all things alien, held press conferences, and individual nations did the same. Scientific and governmental authorities everywhere tried to calm nerves and avert panic. Each described experiments showing the nanites were harmless—that a person could ingest them all day, could *bathe* in them, without any adverse effects—and insisted that that they would reach a population equilibrium as did all organisms. They called on microbiologists to hit the airwaves, reminding people that humanity had always shared the planet with microbes, which were the dominant form of life on Earth in terms of biomass, and had been for ages, despite being invisible. That harmless microbes populated human bodies by the trillions and were breathed in with every lungful of air ever taken, yet were almost universally ignored. Scientists were quick to point out that if the aliens wished humanity ill, they could have programmed the nanites to digest human flesh as efficiently as they were able to digest metal and rock.

These efforts succeeded in steadying nerves to some degree, and raw, mindless panic was largely averted—at least for a while. But this panic wouldn't be contained for long.

The study of the alien nanites went on around the world and around the clock. And in contrast to the study of the alien ship and ZPE drive, rapid progress was made in understanding the construction and reproductive strategies of the nanites. But this was a far cry from understanding their purpose or finding a way to stop their spread. Encyclopedias could be filled with what scientists had learned about the rhinovirus, which caused the common cold, but mankind was still helpless to prevent this ancient scourge.

Software was the key. Sentient beings had programmed the nanites for some purpose, and there were only two ways to learn what this purpose was. Wait until whatever was going to happen happened. Or find a way to get a peek at the instruction manual.

Because of the high visibility of the U.N. effort, the work of the *Copernicus Nanite Team* became more closely watched than any national or individual effort, although the identities of the scientists involved were carefully guarded. It was not only the most important team on the *Copernicus*, it was likely to be the most important team ever assembled on the planet. And Matt Griffin was at its helm.

And he was hard to miss.

Jake had worked through the American Nobelists to arrange for a contest to be set up almost exactly as he and Griffin had discussed. Thirty software experts, who were engaged in their own nation's programs and weren't eligible for the *Copernicus* effort, had each compiled a puzzle, a computer problem that was diabolically difficult but solvable in a reasonably short period of time by someone with the proper genius and experience. About four hundred experts, two nominated by each government, participated in the hour-long contest. The winner would lead the *Copernicus* team, and would be able to organize the other four hundred participants in any way he or she wished, and call on any of them as needed.

Fully fifteen percent of the entrants didn't solve a single puzzle in the time allotted. Seven contestants solved four puzzles, and one solved five. Matt Griffin solved fourteen. He could have solved every one of them within the hour, but fourteen would already raise enough suspicions.

Even at fourteen, the other contestants cried foul. Solving five or six was at least *conceivable*—but what Griffin had accomplished was not. He must have found a way to cheat somehow. So immediately after boarding the ship, Griffin held an hour-long meeting inside the ship's central park, which was open to the sky and bordered on all sides by five stories of rooms, like a football-field-sized atrium in a Las Vegas resort. During this meeting, in the presence of hundreds of members of his team, Griffin fielded additional software challenges from the top five runners-up, his computer monitor tied into a fifteen-foot-high screen behind him. He solved problems in ways that hadn't even occurred to their designers, and with such speed and elegance that not a single member of the crowd saw his abilities as anything short of miraculous.

At the end of his first day leading the *Copernicus Nanite Team* he was legendary. For his brilliance, yes, but also for his erratic personality. One minute he was arrogant and caustic. He was demanding, rude, and insulting. He seemed to take a perverse pleasure in humiliating the geniuses around him. The next minute he was gregarious, yet discouragingly unhelpful, claiming to be too busy to solve problems easier than those he had previously solved in an instant.

And as near as anyone could figure out, the only time he stopped eating—*ever*—was when he was talking. Yes, he was big man, but his appetite seemed unquenchable.

Where had this guy been? Most decided he was working with the U.S. government on cyberterror, cyber war, and intelligence gathering. Intelligence agencies across the world were called on the carpet for not knowing of the existence of this bearded phenom. Nations realized in an instant that systems they had thought were impenetrable were as flimsy as tissue paper where this Matt character was concerned. He could hack their computers and lay bare their most guarded secrets whenever he wanted.

The members of Griffin's team couldn't begin to understand his intuitive leaps—but his ideas never failed to work as promised. And while he drove his subordinates to exhaustion, none could say he spared himself this same outcome.

But he was still required to report back to his U.S. backers, so as exhausted as he was, he found himself slumped against a bed in a luxurious but tight stateroom facing a wall-to-ceiling window that overlooked the South Atlantic. His view was currently being blocked, however, by Major John Kolke, Colonel Morriss Jacobson, Andrew Dutton, and his friend and acting chaperone, David Desh.

Desh had joined Griffin only six hours after the hacker's arrival, not having to take a sojourn in South Africa to win a software contest. One gellcap later, Desh was healing beautifully, although it would take weeks for him to fully return to normal.

At least normal physically. Emotionally, he was a train wreck. And for good reason. He had repeatedly made costly mistakes. His close friend was dead. The Icarus project continued to take body-blow after body-blow, and his vision of creating a better future was getting more and more unlikely to come to pass. And worst of all, the woman he loved and respected, instead of being a trusted emotional anchor, had become unpredictable, and possibly treacherous.

All of this was enough to test the emotional balance of the strongest psyche, but the list didn't stop there. He was injured, an alien plague had been discovered, which had him on edge along with everyone else in existence, and he was forced to interact with Colonel "Jake" Jacobson, the man responsible for killing Jim Connelly. Worse, he found himself *liking* him. Not really surprising, but very disconcerting, and another blow to his emotional stability. Jake and he spoke the same language, possessed the same skills, had had many of the same experiences, and even the same goals. He had heard more than one tale of old-time cold-warriors from Russia and America, who had spent their careers as adversaries, becoming fast friends once detente had hit due to the undeniable connection they shared.

Desh couldn't have felt the loss of Jim Connelly more profoundly. And he hated himself for not hating Jake more. At the same time, he hated himself for not loving Kira Miller *less*.

In short, Desh knew he was a giant fucking mess, although he suspected a psychologist might use a slightly different term for his condition.

Desh was here as an observer, so he had tried to keep as low a profile as possible, pretending to be a fly on the wall. Dutton cleared his throat and Desh knew the meeting was about to begin.

"We'll try to keep this brief," began Jake's civilian boss, staring at Matt Griffin. "But we need to know where you are. And if you're getting anywhere. We'd also like to request that you try to tone yourself down when you're enhanced. To put it bluntly, you're considered the most vile asshole who ever lived around here."

Griffin swallowed a chocolate chip muffin and reached for another from a bag Desh always managed to keep filled. He winced. "I'm doing the best I can," he said miserably. "I'm just glad my alter ego hasn't killed anyone—or worse. I'm managing to control him, but only a little. And then only because this problem is one of the few he's encountered in a long time that is truly challenging."

Dutton sighed and decided to move on. "You've had two days now," he said. "I know you've been making progress, but where are we?"

"I've been splitting my time between two initiatives," reported Griffin. "The first is learning what our nanite friends are programmed to do. And the second is discovering a way to broadcast a self-destruct command."

"You think these things have a self destruct switch?" asked Kolke.

Griffin nodded. "I'm nearly certain they do. But it doesn't matter. If they don't, I'll find a way to design one myself." He paused. "As to learning what these bugs do directly, that's not going to happen. These are alien devices with alien logic and alien programming."

"Yet I'm told you've made great strides in *unpacking* the software," said Jake. "Is that the right word?"

Griffin nodded and tore the cap off another muffin.

"Your team is the only one making any progress from among the thousands around the world," said Dutton. "It's gotten to the point where all other teams are basically waiting to see what you'll come up with next. You tell them to do something, and it works—it moves the ball forward. But no one on any team, including your own, has been able to figure out *why* it works, which is driving them crazy. They expect not to understand the alien instructions. But they expect to understand what *you're* doing. They ask you how you knew to take the approach you did, and you basically tell them to fuck off."

Griffin sighed. "I tell them that because I have no clue myself. You've never been enhanced, but the gulf between me and my alter ego—call him Super-Matt," he added with a grin, "is like that between a bird and a human. I'll be honest with you, what we're trying to do should be flat out impossible. Yet my alter ego is getting very close to breakthroughs on both fronts. If I could explain why what I'm doing works, I would."

"Don't worry about it," said Jake. "If everyone is frustrated because they have no clue what you're doing, that's too damn bad." He paused and gestured toward Griffin. "So please continue. Where are we? You said you couldn't learn directly what these nanites are up to. Does that mean you have a plan to learn *indirectly*?"

"Very good," said Griffin. "Yes. You can think of these nanites as computer worms, in a way. A worm burrows into your computer software and multiplies and spreads. But the most malicious ones have time clocks. They spread for weeks or months beneath the radar, not causing any problems, until they've invaded millions of computers. And then, at a certain date and time, they mount a coordinated attack. They carry out programmed instructions, or access certain websites to get instructions from their masters, who can use them to take over huge networks of computers for nefarious ends." He shoved a muffin into his mouth as the others in the tiny cabin considered his words.

"Did you just use the word *nefarious?*" said Kolke with a crooked smile.

Desh grinned. Matt Griffin's word choices often brought smiles to people's faces.

Griffin swallowed another huge chunk of muffin and ignored the major's comment. "So when you find a worm that is multiplying but otherwise not doing anything," he continued, "a common trick is to speed up time. Accelerate your computer clock. Make computer time run a thousand-fold faster than real time. If the worm and its brethren have been programmed to lay dormant until March 5th, you make them think its March 5th, and you see what happens. This won't tell you how to stop it from happening. But at least you'll know what's coming without having to wait until D-Day, when it's too late."

Jake scratched his head. "But how would you do that with the nanites?"

"Again, I have only the faintest idea. But my alter ego seems to think it's doable. With the help of the team, he's discovered a way to tie into the nanite's sensory systems. The Europeans spent almost a billion dollars recently building a computer model of the entire world. It's been nicknamed the Matrix, for obvious reasons."

"We're familiar with it," said Dutton. "We have one also, but we don't advertise it."

"Good," said Griffin. "So basically we would tie a nanite into it, so it thinks this simulation is the real world. Then we set its clock back to just after arrival here. Then we speed up the simulation a thousand fold and watch the nanite replicate, spread—basically do its thing. We'll see its programming play out, and we'll track its brethren. When we've reached our current point in time, we should see the same density of nanites in the virtual world as we do in the real. Then we accelerate forward from there and see what they do. Do they just keep dividing until they run out of raw material? Do all the nanites form letters as high as skyscrapers saying, *freaked you out, didn't we, dumb Earthlings*? Do they phone home? What?"

"And you've discussed this with other experts on your team?" said Dutton

Griffin nodded.

"And they think it will work?"

Griffin grinned. "No freaking way. They think it's impossible. Beyond impossible. Except they've been getting used to me *doing* the impossible, so they aren't so sure. And Super-Matt has already done the programming. So it's all ready. We just need access to the Matrix."

"I'll get you access to the U.S. version," said Dutton. "I'll have it ready for you within the hour."

Griffin shook his head. "Let's go with four hours from now. The last time I took a gellcap I calculated that three hours from now was the earliest I could go under again and survive. There are limits to how often you can do this, and I've been testing them. As it is, it's going to take me a month to recover."

"Okay, four hours from now," agreed Dutton. "How fast until you get results?"

"How fast is the computer that runs your Matrix program? On the fastest desktop," explained Griffin, "we're probably looking at years."

Dutton and Jake glanced at each other questioningly. Neither had any idea.

Kolke shook his head in amusement. "Twenty petaflops," he said matter-of-factly.

Griffin whistled. "*Now* we're talking." He paused in thought for several long seconds. "At that speed, I'd say we can get our answers in less than an hour. Maybe less than thirty minutes. But we need to boot everyone else off the system so we get the entire bandwidth. We'll need to run the nanite through the simulation thousands of times or more to be sure we capture its programming holistically. I'll run it with just my top lieutenants with me to analyze the results, which I can present across all shipboard channels. Let's alert everyone on the *Copernicus* to stand by for new information in five and a half hours."

"I admire your optimism," said Dutton. "But you still don't know if you can really do this."

"True, but I never bet against Super-Matt," said Griffin with a smile. "If he thinks we've laid enough groundwork, made enough breakthroughs, to give these nanites the Matrix experience, who am I to argue against him."

"And has Super-Matt calculated the odds that the purpose of these nanites is positive rather than negative?" asked Jake.

"He has no idea," said Griffin. "Personally, I'm hoping the nanites assemble into a quantum computer containing all the secrets of the cosmos."

Jake nodded, and he forced out an anxious smile. "Wouldn't that be nice," he said with a sigh. "I guess there's only one way to find out," he added grimly.

52

David Desh and Morris Jacobson stood alertly outside the cabin door while the bearded giant within slumbered, trying to recover from the repeated abuses to which he had submitted his body and brain. Four other American men patrolled the corridors leading to this particular cabin, bodyguards for the most important person on earth who was about to undertake the most important task ever attempted—when he awoke from his catnap. And Andrew Dutton was arranging for Griffin's sole use of a classified computer programmed with the most complete model of the real world ever built.

Desh had spent most of his time with the colonel since he had boarded. Jake's job was to watch Desh and Icarus's prized software genius, Matt Griffin. Desh's job was to watch Matt as well, helping him in any way he could and making sure that he was safe from anyone with malicious intent, both inside or outside of Jake's group of men. So in the final analysis, since both men's job was to watch Matt, *and* each other, they spent most of their time together by unspoken agreement.

Desh had only spoken with Kira twice, using a borrowed cell phone, but each conversation had been brief and in his view, stilted. He needed to get to the bottom of what was going on back home: what she was involved with and how Ross Metzger fit in. Not knowing was eating at his psyche like a marauding colony of army ants, but there was too much happening for him to make any progress on that front, so his fears festered like an open sore.

Jake nodded at him. "I've had some of my people back in the States check out your story, like you asked."

Desh raised his eyebrows. "And?"

"And it checks out. Adam Archibald disappeared, like you predicted, although given the condition of his yacht, he's assumed drowned."

"Go on."

"After considerable digging, my people have verified that Archibald is the reincarnation of Eric Frey, a genetic engineer from USAMRIID wanted for a lot of bad shit." He shook his head. "They told me the identity switch was flawless. If they weren't already tipped off that Archibald was really Eric Frey, they'd have never made the connection."

"Ready to believe we aren't the villains you think we are yet?"

Jake smiled. "Let's just say my mind continues to be open to additional evidence. Your problem is that you and Kira are so creative and clever. And deceptive."

Desh considered. "I get that," he admitted. "You can never be certain you aren't being played when dealing with someone of Kira's capabilities." He frowned. He knew the feeling well. "But I have every confidence if you keep digging you'll find a truth that can't be faked."

"I hope you're right," said Jake simply.

"So back to Frey," said Desh. "Can I assume you're having people outside of your normal sphere take the next step?"

"The next step?"

"Come on, Colonel."

Jake smiled sheepishly. "You're right. Not sharing information gets so ingrained it becomes reflexive. Yes. I'm having someone I trust outside of my organization look for any communication or connection between Frey and any of my people. But since *you* gave me the heads up on this one, even if we find a connection we can't know if it's real."

Desh sighed. "I know," he muttered in frustration. "But keep digging. You'll get to the bottom of it. At some point, you get to information that's beyond even Kira's ability to plant."

"I hope you're right," said Jake for a second time. "I really do."

53

Every monitor on the ship was tuned to Matt Griffin, broadcasting alone from his stateroom in front of a stationary camera. More than ten thousand *Copernicus* passengers looked on. Many in their own cabins, or gathered in dining rooms, nightclubs, restaurants, auditoriums, or theaters. Hundreds of passengers sat in the atrium-like park, gazing at the fifteen-foot screen Griffin had used when he had first came on board. Others watched on laptop and tablet computers from deck chairs overlooking the South Atlantic. But all had their eyes glued to the screen, wherever they happened to be.

Griffin looked haggard, as though he had aged a decade in the few days he had been on board. His continuous snack-food gluttony while on board had become almost as legendary as his genius, and rumors abounded that he either had the mother of all tapeworms, or else he was actually an alien himself.

A medic had attached him to a small, battery powered IV pump several hours earlier, since his enhanced mind had burned through glucose like rocket fuel, and he needed to become enhanced one last time, long before it was healthy to do so. The camera was in tight on his face so his left arm, with plastic tubing extending from a vein in his hand, was hidden from view.

"Time is short," he began, his voice weak and his body language screaming total exhaustion. He had purposely scheduled the broadcast for after he had returned to normal, so the message wouldn't be delivered by the arrogant, caustic version of himself. "So I'll get right to it. Several members of the *Copernicus Nanite Team* just completed an analysis of data generated by tying nanites into a computer simulation—fooling them into revealing their future plans. I won't go into technical details. Suffice it to say it was a success.

Griffin took a deep breath. "I wish I had better news, but I don't. In a nutshell, the nanites have been programmed to replicate and spread until every square foot on the planet contains at least a few. A saturation level. I'm also afraid to say that they can detect uranium and plutonium from many miles away and migrate to it preferentially." He paused for effect. "At a predetermined time, they will detonate enough nuclear bombs to end the vast majority of human life on this planet."

Griffin paused, imagining the gasps from thousands of viewers and their horror stricken faces. He gave them only ten or fifteen seconds to digest this news and then forged ahead. "Members of my team are sending every official on this ship a copy of the software code and protocols used to tie the nanites into the simulation, which enabled us to reach this conclusion. I ask the representatives of the world's governments assembled here to send these instructions back home, where your own people can run simulations, so there can be no doubt as to the veracity of our findings. All of you have access to nanites, of course. We used a very sophisticated model of the world, but you should get the same results on any supercomputer with even a modest simulation. I would also ask that any governments with access to free uranium or plutonium verify the nanites preference for these materials, as well.

"At time zero the nanites communicate and decide which warheads to blow, among thousands of different possible combinations. The goal seems to be to ensure worldwide radiation coverage and global initiation of nuclear winter using the fewest number of detonations.

"For any unfamiliar with the concept of nuclear winter, basically this is when so much smoke and soot are released into the atmosphere as a result of multiple nuclear blasts, that the sun is blotted out for extended periods of time, leading to catastrophic cooling."

Griffin knew that in every corner of the great cruise ship, the esteemed passengers were being shaken to their cores, and he was glad he had decided to make the announcement alone so he could do it quickly and not have to pause as the audience reacted. "After detonating the bombs," he continued, "the surviving nanites—those not directly in the blast zones—reproduce to saturation levels once again. And then they phone home—well, not exactly home, but I'll go into that in a moment. We have no idea what message they are trying to send, but something like, 'mission accomplished,' wouldn't be much of a surprise.

"After this the nanites differentiate. Some are designed to clean up radiation, and they multiply to fantastic levels to do so. Some are designed to seed the atmosphere—changing its composition, reducing the nitrogen and oxygen content and increasing argon, helium, and nitrous oxide to such an extent that the atmosphere becomes poisonous to the plant and animal life currently on Earth."

Griffin paused, knowing this was another stunning revelation, but also that by now the news couldn't get much worse, no matter what he said, and his audience was likely getting numb from repeated bombshells. "The nanites broadcast to space two more times, twenty-one and twenty-five years after the explosions. Conducting a sort of triangulation on their broadcasts, however, indicates they are transmitting to a large armada, traveling directly toward Earth, at near light-speed, in the same way as did their probe. While the armada is limited to light speed, judging from the timing and positioning of broadcasts, the broadcasts themselves are sent at speeds far beyond light, probably taking advantage of quantum entanglement in some way. The nanites act as though their messages reach the ships instantaneously, and I have no reason to doubt this."

Griffin paused. "The bottom line is that the aliens sent their probe to terraform our planet—or rather to do the opposite, transform it into one conducive to *their* biology. To de-roach the hotel and make sure a chocolate mint is waiting on the pillow for their occupying force. They were clearly aware of the content of our atmosphere and the existence of our nuclear weapons. The chronology of events the aliens are apparently hoping will come to pass is as follows: the probe they send arrives and disgorges nanites. The nanites infect and detonate our nukes. The nanites then clean up the radiation and modify our atmosphere to fit their needs, which we calculate they will accomplish in approximately twenty-five years. Approximately nine years later—thirty-four years from now—the alien armada arrives to colonize a planet sanitized of life, and tuned to their biology."

Matt Griffin took a deep breath. "After running thousands of simulations, we have pinpointed time zero with great precision," he reported grimly. He glanced at his watch, swallowed hard, and then turned back to the camera. "The nanites are set to trigger Armageddon in a little over five hours from now."

54

Kira had cancelled all activities. The Icarus team was effectively in limbo, but this didn't matter. The entire world was doing little more than holding its breath at this point, waiting for someone in authority to tell them what was going on, what it all meant, what these alien machines were doing here.

The cold war had been psychologically taxing to people around the world. The terror war being waged by jihadists against all of modern civilization had also dramatically elevated the level of global stress. But nothing could compare to the fear, paranoia, and psychic fragility provoked by the alien nanites.

Kira had been through some pretty crazy and consequential months before, but never like this one. Nor had anyone, for that matter.

She had been entirely alone at headquarters before. Being the sole inhabitant of a building so extensive tended to magnify the feeling of isolation. But if she stayed in her and David's quarters, she couldn't tell she was anywhere other than a high-end apartment, other than the absence of a yard or deck, and she could ignore the unseen presence of conference rooms and labs just beyond the confines of her humble abode.

A mental image of David Desh and Matt Griffin jumped into her mind. David, rugged and insightful, decisive and competent. Matt, lovable and unpredictable. Never using a small word when a bigger one was available. What were they doing at this instant? She hadn't heard from either one in almost twenty-four hours.

She wondered if Matt Griffin was making any progress with the nanites, and then returned to the work she was doing, hoping this would take her mind off events that she couldn't possibly control.

55

Every person aboard the *Copernicus* was gripped by a horror and fear that was indescribable. Not just the horror and fear at the prospect of their own imminent deaths, which would have been daunting enough, but by the broad, encompassing horror at the prospect of species extinction. At the passing, not only of themselves, but of their entire world.

Around the ship, passengers reacted in different ways. Some became numb and psychologically debilitated. Some meditated, some wept, and some vomited. Some attempted to get drunk as quickly as possible. The majority banded together in large groups, trying to draw comfort from the presence of others.

And hours away from Armageddon, the potential savior of the world, Matt Griffin, was sound asleep in his quarters, hooked up to an IV dispensing yet another bag of glucose and other nutrition directly into his bloodstream.

Three men were stationed just outside his room, and six more covered all points of access from the corridors. Ironically, Jake had heightened security around Matt Griffin when he needed it the least. He was the only hope to fend off doomsday. The fate of the world was riding on his mountainous shoulders, and disturbing him in any way, let alone killing or kidnapping him, was equivalent to suicide for the perpetrator—and for the planet.

Desh rapped on the door to the stateroom three doors over from Griffin's. The colonel swung the door open and motioned him inside. Dutton was the only other inhabitant of the room.

"You asked to see me?" said Desh, his stare fixed firmly on the powerful civilian who was calling the shots.

"That's right," replied Dutton. "How is Matt doing?"

"Sound asleep last I checked."

Dutton frowned. "I know he's exhausted, but shouldn't he be working? He's our only hope."

"*He* isn't," corrected Desh. "You could give Matt a million years and he'd never figure out how to disable the nanites. Sleep is the biggest contribution normal Matt can make to this project. His altered self is our hope, and he can't be recommissioned for a few hours yet. As it is, even then Matt will be taking a big risk."

"You really think he can pull it off?" asked Dutton nervously. Desh could hardly blame him. It was a chilling feeling to know that nuclear Armageddon was just hours away and it all hinged on the suppositions of one slumbering hacker.

Desh shrugged. "You heard the same thing we all did," he said. After Matt had all but delivered humanity's epitaph to everyone on board, he had done his best to reassure his listeners that he was nearly certain he could perfect a self-destruct code in time to stop the threat. "Matt told me in private before he went to sleep that he thinks his alter ego will only need about ten minutes to crack the final piece of the code." He paused. "Personally, I think our chances are better than fifty-fifty."

"Good to know," said Jake wryly. "Heads it's doomsday, tails it isn't."

"So what's happening at your end?" asked Desh.

"It's been a real shitstorm as you can imagine," said Jake.

"Ninety percent of the countries have confirmed Matt's analysis on their own now," said Dutton. "Those with ready access to free uranium or plutonium have verified that the damn bugs migrate toward the shit right away, just like Matt predicted."

"So the world's governments are convinced the threat is real?"

Dutton laughed. "Yeah. they're convinced all right. And they're shitting in their pants. And why not? So is everyone here."

"Did they all agree to keep it under wraps?"

Jake nodded. "After Matt said in his address that he was confident he could disarm the things with an hour or two to spare, what would be the point of disclosing it? Not even the most open governments in the world would do that. If the world ends, it doesn't matter. And if Matt succeeds, they'll have thrown their citizens into mass panic for nothing."

"Not time enough to really disclose the situation anyway," added Dutton. "Those in the know are probably at home fucking their wives one last time."

"What are you talking about?" protested Desh. "Aren't they all making sure they disarm their nukes?"

"Too late," said Jake. "If this had been discovered earlier, it could have been done. As it is, it's Matt or it's Armageddon."

"If he does perfect his self destruct sequence?" said Desh. "Will an hour or two before time zero be enough?"

"Should be plenty," replied Jake. "Matt said he's certain that if he does find it, it'll be relatively simple, and transmittable by a variety of means. Every radio station, cell phone tower, Wi-Fi provider, and communications satellite on earth will be standing by to transmit."

Desh shook his head. "You'd better be making sure that someone on every last submarine and in every last nuclear silo will transmit the signal as well. Up close and personal."

Jake nodded. "All governments, including no doubt, any terrorists organizations harboring nukes, have gotten this message."

Dutton walked to a minifridge and pulled out a soda. "We still have a lot to accomplish, so why don't we get to the reason I asked you here."

Desh raised his eyebrows. "Which is?"

"We need to ready an evac for you and Matt for the second he comes up with a self-destruct code." Dutton frowned deeply, and it was clear he was adding, *if he comes up with a code*, in his head.

"Say again?" said Desh in confusion.

"The moment this crisis is averted, Matt becomes the most wanted man on earth."

"What are you talking about?" challenged Desh. "He becomes the most idolized *hero* on earth."

"Yeah. That too. Idolized by the people of the world. *Feared* by their governments."

Desh considered. "He was just a little too impressive, wasn't he?"

"You think?" replied Dutton, rolling his eyes. "If I knew they had a Griffin equivalent in China, and suspected he worked for the government, I'd be shitting bricks also. Unofficially, we'd put out a hit on him so fast your head would spin. What do you think China, and Russia, and Iran, and Syria, and a handful of others are planning right now?"

Desh shot the civilian a look of disgust. "So it's, *thanks for saving our bacon, but you're too off-the-charts talented to be allowed to live?*"

"Basically," replied Dutton. "I think we can protect him, especially on a neutral, weaponless cruise liner. But why take chances?"

"I'm not buying it," said Desh. "Have you not been paying attention? If we survive the next few hours—an enormous *if*—the world will never be the same. We've got some other species out there to worry about now."

Jake nodded. "That's where I came down also. When the survival of the world is at stake, no one is going to take out the only man who has any insight into alien technology and alien programming. No matter which government he's working for."

Desh thought about this. Would Matt Griffin become the property of the world, perhaps working for the United Nations? But even as he thought it he knew this was out of the question. Because Matt couldn't hide for long that he was only brilliant on rare occasions. If he worked publically, he would risk outing Kira's treatment and Icarus, which was still unacceptable. Matt could still research alien technology, but he'd have to do it from off the grid once again, which would be far more challenging. But those were problems for another day, Desh knew. If there *was* another day.

"You both may be right, and I'm wrong," admitted Dutton. "I hope you are. And maybe all nations on earth will share your exact, rational viewpoint. But old habits die hard. Why take the chance? Let's get Matt off this boat before anybody realizes he's gone. Let's get both of you back stateside and release you back into the wild like we promised. What's the penalty for being on the safe side?"

"Agreed," said Desh after a few seconds of further thought. "But Jake needs to be our escort on the evac. That's the deal."

"Why?"

"He's the only one we trust."

"How touching," said Dutton with a sneer. "Even though he killed one of you? And has tried to kill you all?"

This was a direct hit on an open sore, but Desh forced himself to not let it show. "Right," he said evenly.

"Whatever you say," said Dutton.

"And one more thing," added Desh. "We have to be absolutely sure Matt's code really does disable the nanites before we go anywhere."

"No shit," snapped Dutton with contempt.

56

Matt Griffin was slumped in a wheelchair, still connected to a small peristaltic infusion pump that pushed nutrition from a transparent bag into his bloodstream. Four members of the American contingent made sure the path ahead of him was clear, one pushed him along, while four others, including David Desh, surrounded the chair as it moved, ensuring the most recognizable man on the ship wouldn't be recognized.

They made it to the makeshift flight deck ten minutes later, just in time for the pill Griffin had swallowed on the way to take effect. A powerful computer, which Griffin had said was sufficient for his needs, awaited him on a desk placed near a large, opulent Sikorsky helicopter, about the size of a Blackhawk, colored white with red accents. It was one of hundreds of helicopters parked in just this single section of upper deck, which before being converted to a heliport had been two beach volleyball courts, a full sized basketball court, and an eighteen-hole miniature golf course. Runways for planes had been built on the opposite end of a deck that was five hundred and twenty yards long. Typically, there was at least *some* activity here, but now it was deserted. What was the point of going anywhere? There was no outrunning the destruction the nanites were about to unleash, and the *Copernicus* was as beautiful a setting as any to await death and contemplate the nature of the afterlife.

Dutton dismissed everyone but Desh, Kolke, and Jake: the only three men on board who knew about the gellcaps. They stood beside the helicopter, eyes outward to make sure they were not interrupted.

Desh wheeled Griffin to the desk they had set up beside the Sikorski so he could reach the wireless keyboard and mouse. The hacker immediately scrolled through screen after screen filled with incomprehensible symbols—which he must have converted from inputs he had coaxed from the nanites—faster than a normal human could even follow, let alone read and digest. But Griffin just stared, unblinking, at the monitor; drinking from a fire hose without missing a drop. After a few minutes his fingers began to fly over the keyboard, and he toggled between several screens at a blazing pace.

Desh checked the watch Jake had issued to him, along with clothing, before he had come on board. "Ninety-seven minutes and counting," he said grimly to the colonel standing beside him.

Jake nodded woodenly but said nothing in reply. There was nothing to say.

Six minutes ticked by. The slowest minutes Desh had ever experienced. And the fastest.

"*I've got it!*" shouted Griffin triumphantly, startling all three men. "*You fucking little bastards,*" he growled. "*You can kiss my fat ass.*"

"What?" said Dutton, his face wrinkled in confusion. The words had been shouted so quickly they were incomprehensible.

Griffin, as exhausted as he was, still glared at Dutton with superhuman intensity and superhuman disdain. "*Sending,*" he said pointedly, and hit a single button on the keyboard.

Dutton's eyes widened hopefully. He may not have understood Matt before, but the word *sending* had a nice ring to it. "Liz," he said into a phone, "Matt has transmitted the self-destruct sequence. You should be receiving it on your computer now."

There was a brief pause. "Got it," said an American molecular biologist from her stateroom twelve levels below. "I'm transmitting it now from my computer as a radio signal."

The moment this was complete she peered through the eyepiece of an expensive microscope at dozens of nanites she had placed on a slide.

Her breath caught in her throat.

They were coming apart.

The nanites separated into five discrete pieces and lay dormant, unmoving. While she watched, the intricate biological portions of the bugs dissolved, like sugar after water had been applied.

The self-destruct sequence had worked.

Screaming, whooping, and other unmistakable sounds of celebration came over Dutton's phone loudly enough to be heard by everyone nearby. Griffin's face remained impassive, but Desh closed his eyes, tilted his head back, and blew out a huge mouthful of air in relief. The tight faces of Jake and Dutton relaxed for the first time since Griffin's discovery of the nanites' true mission, and tired smiles appeared on all three faces.

The molecular biologist finally stopped shouting and described to Dutton what she had seen under the scope. Even before her description was completed she had forwarded the code to every computer on the *Copernicus*. Within minutes it would be distributed to governments back home, and then uploaded to satellites, cell phone towers, radio stations, and nuclear bunkers around the world.

Jake extended his hand toward Matt Griffin. "You *magnificent* bastard," he said in awe. "*You did it!*"

Griffin ignored the outstretched hand. "Of course I did," he said haughtily, as though Jake's enthusiasm was insulting because it suggested he had previously had doubts.

Dutton stayed behind while the four others boarded the Sikorski, an exclusive model used by titans of industry that was much like a limousine inside. While Kolke, who had been an experienced pilot in a past life, started up the engine, Desh helped Griffin take a seat in one of the leather captain's chairs and hung his IV.

"I'm inducing sleep now," declared Griffin the moment he was situated, and seconds later he was unconscious.

Desh was fascinated. Griffin would still be in an enhanced state for almost forty minutes, but his superior mind must have calculated that while he couldn't snap himself back to normalcy to spare his overtaxed system, he could at least put his brain in idle.

Desh checked his watch once again. If everything worked as hoped, they should be able to avert the crisis with ten or twenty minutes to spare. But worst case, if they missed a few nukes, at least the destruction and mass death would be *local*—the world would still survive. Still, Desh knew he would feel a whole lot better in seventy-two minutes. And better still in seventy-two *hours.*

Jake and Desh donned headphones as the helicopter lifted off and banked to the east. Desh took one last look at the magnificent *Copernicus*, lighted up like a massive firefly against a blanket of endless darkness, a fitting testament to mankind's creative genius. Like everything else about the past month, the situation was surreal. If someone would have told him a month earlier that Matt Griffin would save the world from alien nanites—from the deck of the world's largest luxury cruise liner—and that rather than being heralded as a savior, he would be whisked away as though fleeing the scene of a crime, Desh would have laughed his ass off—just before having whoever had spouted such nonsense institutionalized.

The Sikorski continued on a southeasterly heading toward South Africa; the ride smooth as silk. The interior of the craft sported lacquered wood cabinetry, mirrors, and inlaid video screens, along with a fully stocked bar, and was largely empty since it had a passenger capacity of ten.

The men gazed out of the windows in silence as the clock counted down to zero, alone with their thoughts. Griffin was still out cold, having doubtlessly made the transition back to normalcy some minutes before.

With five minutes left until time zero, Jake rose from his chair, walked the short distance to the bar, and poured two glasses of champagne into delicate crystal goblets. He returned to his seat and handed a glass to Desh.

Desh took the glass and nodded. Just when he thought things could not get more surreal, here he was in a decadent helicopter, flying over the South Atlantic with a sworn enemy and an unconscious friend, seconds away from the end of the world, holding a glass of champagne like it was New Year's Eve.

Desh placed the glass on the armrest beside him, glanced at his watch, and once again peered out the window. Would the sky suddenly turn crimson? Would the fire of man-made suns turn night into day, and Earth into a lifeless hell? How many seconds would they have before a nuclear shock wave shattered the Sikorski like a rose dipped in liquid nitrogen?

Griffin's code should work. But *should* and *would* were too different things.

"We're through!" declared Jake excitedly beside him. They had hit time zero while Desh had been lost in thought.

Desh nodded, not allowing himself to be excited. Not just yet. "Let's wait for the celebration," he said. "Until you get your report."

They had to wait five additional minutes until the report came in over Jake's headphones. He lifted his glass of champagne and faced Desh. "No explosions reported anywhere. Looks like your friend's code worked like a charm."

Desh grinned from ear to ear and clinked glasses with the colonel. *Griffin had done it*, thought Desh as he drank. If not for Kira, the world would have ended. Her treatment to boost the human IQ had staved off total disaster. But at what cost to *her*?

Jake listened to his headphones on a private channel and then switched over to a channel that Jake and Kolke could hear. "I've been told that reports are coming in from around the world—from basically everyone studying nanites—that they've disintegrated," he said triumphantly. "The full story of the Armageddon we just dodged, and how we dodged it, is now being released around the globe," he continued. "Also, the *Copernicus* is setting up a press conference. They were frantically searching for Matt to headline, so Dutton had to disclose that he was no longer on board."

"How was *that* received?" asked Desh.

"Not well," replied Jake. He frowned and turned to face Griffin. "I just wish the big guy was awake so we could lift him on our shoulders." He made a face. "Metaphorically speaking, of course. When he's not the world's biggest asshole, he's a heck of a sweet guy."

Desh laughed. He wanted to ask if that meant Jake would stop trying to kill him, but he didn't want to spoil the festive mood.

They landed forty minutes later at another hastily constructed heliport near the coast of South Africa, and were finally forced to awaken Matt, as well as remove his IV, since the bag was nearly drained. They showered him with congratulations, but he was too exhausted to even smile, barely able to lift himself out of his seat to exit the helicopter.

The staging area handled all helo traffic to and from the *Copernicus.* A U.N. security force patrolled the perimeter and ensured that no weapons were smuggled aboard the international ship.

A Humvee pulled up as they exited the Sikorski and drove them to the American quarters, consisting of several hangers, temporary barracks, and a hastily constructed office building that had been designated as headquarters.

As they emerged from the car, now beyond the U.N. perimeter and on what was considered American soil for the duration of the *Copernicus* mission, four soldiers surrounded them, each aiming a semi-automatic pistol at the group.

"You're under arrest!" barked one of the men, a lieutenant.

"*At ease, Lieutenant,*" snapped Jake, a hint of barely contained rage in his tone. "These men are my guests. I gave explicit orders that a jet was to be readied to take us all stateside."

None of the men moved in the slightest.

"Lower your weapons!" shouted Jake. "That's a direct order!"

The lieutenant shook his head. "You are no longer in command," he said. He turned to face John Kolke. "What are your orders, Colonel?"

"*Colonel?*" snapped Jake incredulously.

"That's right," confirmed Kolke. "I've been given a field promotion." His lip curled up into a snarl. "And you're under arrest for crimes against your country *you son of a bitch.*"

57

Desh was exhausted, but his body and mind snapped to full alert, not that this would do him any good. Jake had intended to keep his word, as Kira knew he would. But as they had feared, those around him had no intention of doing so, although it was surprising they had enough power to throw Jake under the bus. Desh glanced at his bearded friend, but he was as emotionless as a zombie, his body still in a low energy state as it fought to regain equilibrium.

"What crimes?" demanded Jake, his eyes burning like twin lasers.

"Don't worry," replied Kolke as he joined the soldiers, obtaining a spare weapon from one of them. "I'll list the crimes and show you the evidence against you soon enough."

"And you've *seen* this evidence?" asked Jake skeptically.

"That's right," said Kolke. He gestured to the men who surrounded them. "We all have. It's as tight as a drum."

"It's a frame and you know it!" spat Jake.

"Not *this* evidence," insisted Kolke. "But enough of this. You'll have your day in court."

At Kolke's order, plastic handcuffs were ratcheted around the wrists of all three prisoners. Kolke gestured to Desh and Griffin. "Bring them to the C-20 and have the pilot take off as soon as possible. As for the colonel, I'm taking him into the headquarters building for immediate interrogation."

"We were told he's to be sent to the States in a separate jet," said the lieutenant.

"Keep it ready," said Kolke. "This won't take long. But there's some key intel I need from him immediately."

"How many of us would you like to accompany you, sir?" asked the lieutenant.

"None, Lieutenant." He raised his gun and pointed it at Jake's chest. "I've got this. And I need to be alone. If he doesn't talk willingly, things may get a little . . . messy."

Desh and Griffin were driven to the airfield several miles away and marched into the C-20 waiting for them there, a military version of the Gulfstream corporate jet. Once inside, additional restraints were added, and Desh knew they had no chance of escape during the flight—not with elite soldiers on board to mind them. Desh could only hope that once they landed, whoever they were up against would let down their guard long enough for him to make an escape attempt. But the odds of this were long.

Eric Frey had told him he had someone planted inside Jake's camp, and it looked like this someone was John Kolke—or at least the recently promoted colonel was working closely with whoever it was.

But regardless, the stench of Eric Frey was all over this. He had no doubt that the captain of the recently deceased *Codon* would be paying a visit soon after they landed. Desh's last encounter with the man had been a disaster. But he was certain his next encounter would be even worse.

58

John Kolke entered the office behind Jake and ordered him, still at gunpoint, to take a seat. He closed the door and took a seat himself behind a large desk, facing his ex-commander.

Kolke lowered the gun. "I'm really sorry about this, Colonel," he said earnestly. "But I do have a plan."

Jake's eyes narrowed. "Does that mean you're still with me?" he asked in surprise.

Kolke nodded. "Dutton has unimpeachable evidence against you. Evidence of treason, payoffs, millions of dollars in accounts in the Caymans, and more. Much more. It's a spectacular frame." He allowed himself a shallow smile. "Hell, I was half expecting to see evidence that you were responsible for 9/11."

"If the evidence is so good, why don't you believe it?" asked Jake.

"I don't care if God himself came down and told me you were a traitor, I wouldn't buy it. I've worked with you too closely not to have gained a sense of your soul. I've seen what this job has done to you. I've seen you make hard choices when a lesser man would have made easy ones. I've seen the agony you feel when you cause others unnecessary pain. You wouldn't work against this country."

"Thanks, John. Your faith in me means more than you'll ever know."

Kolke gave Jake an almost imperceptible nod to acknowledge these words and then continued. "Dutton says he's long suspected you. He shared his evidence with me and the men here at the staging area, so we could move on you the moment you left the *Copernicus*."

"And you decided to play along."

"Right. I figured it was the only way I could help you. If he suspected I didn't buy the evidence against you, he'd have rolled over me as well."

"I'm sure you're right."

"That bastard was *relentless* making sure this happened. He told me he'd pulled strings to have me promoted to colonel—just to ensure my loyalty, I'm guessing. But the thing is, he arranged all of this *after* the nanites came on the scene. Before Matt figured out exactly what they were up to, true, but at a time everyone was pretty sure we were in deep shit. Can you imagine? The world is coming to an end and all he's worried about is taking you off the board."

Jake thought about this for several seconds. "No. Taking me off the board isn't what he wants. I was just in the way. He's after Icarus. But he knows I'd have honored my commitment to Matt and David, and let them go—which he has no intention of doing."

"So he's willing to destroy you," said Kolke in disgust, "and break a promise to the man who just stopped doomsday?"

"Yes. And I won't be given my day in court, either. Believe me, he'll see to it that a rogue black-ops agent like me is taken care of quietly and discretely." He paused and stared intently at Kolke. "So what now?"

Kolke pulled a pair of plastic handcuffs from his pocket. "I've prepared these. I've sawed the teeth off the strips, so it'll look like you're bound, but you can free your hands whenever you want. You'll have the element of surprise, and I'm well aware of your reputation in hand-to-hand. Can I assume you'll be able to overpower a lone escort, no matter how well armed?"

Jake nodded. "That shouldn't be a problem."

"Good. Escaping from me would arouse Dutton's suspicions. So I'll call the lieutenant in here to take you to your plane. If you can overpower him quickly enough that he doesn't even realize you escaped your cuffs, so much the better. But whatever you do, be sure to take the cuffs *with* you. If anyone gets a look at them, they'll know I was behind the escape."

Jake nodded grimly.

"Once you've escaped, I'm afraid you're on your own in South Africa for awhile. But just until I can find a way to clear your name. I'll pretend to be loyal to Dutton and get to the bottom of this as fast as I can."

He removed Jake's cuffs and replaced them with the ones he had doctored. When he finished, he put his hand warmly on Jake's shoulder. "Good luck, Colonel. I'll get you out of this. I promise."

"You're a good man, John," came the heartfelt reply. "I will never forget this."

Jake's mind raced as Kolke called for the lieutenant. Escaping should be doable, although the next five or ten hours were not going to be fun. But then what?

What did this all mean?

For one thing, it called into question everything he thought he knew about Kira Miller. If he could be framed so skillfully, then perhaps she had been also, just as she claimed.

And Desh had warned him there was an insider in his camp. It could be that Dutton was just power hungry, or even thought he was being patriotic by hanging on to Desh and Griffin. But given that Dutton had no qualms at all about framing Jake, and probably having him killed, it was far more likely that Dutton was the inside man, taking orders from a deceased USAMRIID scientist named Eric Frey.

Maybe Kira Miller was just who she claimed to be.

What if he and Icarus were on the same side, after all?

59

The story broke around the globe within an hour of the disaster being averted. First, the nanites had disintegrated while literally millions of people were examining them under scopes. And then the full story came out. Rumors and whispered suspicions had already been leaking like water through a cracked concrete dam, but when this dam burst the force behind it was *unthinkable*.

The aliens had designed the nanites to migrate preferentially to uranium and plutonium. Their goal had been to set off a nuclear Armageddon and reshape the planet's atmosphere to their needs. And they had been minutes away from success. Only the efforts of a supremely gifted man on the *Copernicus*, an American known simply as Matt, had thwarted this terrible plan.

The news of the failed attack was met with stunned shock and horror. It was met with curses and prayers and words of outrage; uttered in Chinese, Hindu, Bengali, Spanish, Punjabi, Vietnamese, and Hebrew. In Russian, Javanese, Turkish, Pashto, German, Korean, and Telugu. Within twelve hours almost eight billion people, speaking thousands of languages, knew that the Earth had been under attack; that Homo Sapiens had been targeted for extinction; not out of hatred or malice or misunderstanding—but as an *afterthought*. As part of an ice cold calculation made by beings uncountable trillions of miles distant.

Shock, horror, and relief were quickly followed by fear. These aliens were far ahead of humanity technologically. And they were on their way. The Earth wasn't a mighty planet hanging majestically in space—it was the mother of all sitting ducks.

And while fear remained the prevailing emotion in many; in many others fear had quickly turned to anger— and to resolve.

Who did these aliens think they were? They didn't *know* us. They sent their little bugs as impersonally as could be to pave the way for their arrival. And they knew the Earth was filled with sentient beings, because they fully expected nuclear warheads to be available to infiltrate. They just didn't care.

Yes, Earth had been lucky to survive the initial surprise attack, but now it was *personal.*

Humanity might go down, but it would not go down easily. So much of the planet's resources were squandered by governments with only their own interests at heart, by countries jockeying for position on the world stage like so many chess pieces, and by war and preparations for war.

This would have to stop.

Humanity had been in a boat rowing in thousands of different directions, pausing only long enough to shoot holes in the boat on a continuous basis—and yet had *still* moved the boat forward a remarkable distance. But things would be different now. When the aliens arrived in thirty-four years they would find out what *eight billion* humans could do when they were all rowing in the same direction. And when they were fighting for their lives. Humanity could be weak and pigheaded and barbaric; a tribal species quick to take offense, war on neighbors, and succumb to violence and self-destructive behavior.

But it was a species you did *not* want to piss off.

Thirty-four years wasn't long to prepare, and the aliens had a clear head start. But much could be done in thirty-four years. In the thirty years preceding the turn of the century, technology had advanced in ways that were nothing short of stunning. From bulky black and white televisions to huge, sleek monitors with vibrant colors, so thin they could be hung on walls like paintings. From card catalogs in libraries using the Dewy Decimal System to a repository of billions and billions of pages of text, audio, and video, extensively cross-referenced and instantly searchable. From primitive telephones that had to be tethered to walls to cell phones bouncing signals off satellites and across towers to seamlessly connect callers thousands of miles apart; phones possessing far more processing power than computers that had filled entire buildings thirty years before.

No one knew just how much further humanity could propel itself in the next thirty years, but with everyone working in cooperation, it would be even more unimaginable than had been the progress of the previous thirty.

Human beings could be lazy and petty and shortsighted. But they were nothing if not goal oriented. And now the entire species shared a goal. And a purpose.

And they had become very, very motivated.

60

Desh and Griffin landed at MacDill Air Force Base in Florida. Griffin had slept for most of the trip, and Desh had convinced their captors to feed the nearly comatose hacker continuously during his brief periods of consciousness. Given that Griffin had just saved the world, the elite soldiers sharing the ride with them were eager to help him in any way they could—short of releasing him. After they landed, the prisoners were whisked to a safe house at an unknown location by a mercenary posing as a civilian, under Dutton's orders.

Once inside the safe house, the two men were placed on a black leather couch, their hands cuffed behind their backs, while four mercenaries kept a close watch.

Matt Griffin was sound asleep yet again when Eric Frey walked through the door several hours later, along with Andrew Dutton, fresh from the *Copernicus.*

Frey motioned to two of the mercs, who promptly pulled Desh off the couch and into a standing position. The pudgy scientist had kept his toupee but had shaved his beard, so he now looked like a cross between himself and the fictitious Adam Archibald. He walked over to Desh with a self-satisfied grin on his face. "David Desh," he said. "Good to see you again. I have to say, I was a little pissed off that you escaped from the *Codon.*"

Desh kept his face passive and didn't respond.

"You know you cost me an identity," he said, and without warning punched Desh as hard as he could in the exact place Desh had been shot. Desh's face recoiled in pain and it was all he could do not to scream out. "*Not to mention*

a very nice yacht," finished Frey, seething, as though Desh
had tortured a loved one.

"I don't know," spat Desh through clenched teeth. "I
thought it was a little *garish.*"

Frey delivered another blow to the same spot, and this
time tears came to Desh's eyes.

"I'd heard your gunshot wound was progressing nicely,"
said Frey. "But still not fully healed, I see."

Desh gritted his teeth while he waited for the waves of
pain to recede. *Not a good idea,* he thought. It was stupid to
wave a red cape in front of a bull for no reason. If he was
going to risk this kind of retaliation, at least it should be
for a purpose—like trying to stir the pot. He straightened
to his full height again and shot Andrew Dutton a look of
contempt. "So how do you feel about being the lapdog of
this pudgy asshole?" he said. "That's got to be humiliating.
I bet it gets under your skin, doesn't it?"

Desh braced himself for another blow, but instead Frey
just gave him a look of mild amusement. "It's not going
to work, Desh," he said calmly. "Andrew knows where his
bread is buttered. I created his identity and arranged for
him to assume the role he's in now. His title is little more
than a cover. He wields more military and black-ops power
than any other civilian in Washington. And I finance a
lifestyle far above his pay grade. He knows if he sticks with
me he'll have more power than he's ever dreamed of." He
smiled icily. "He also knows I've taken out an insurance
policy. If anything happens to me, a hit is put out on him,
financed by a considerable sum of money that becomes
available for this purpose upon my death. I learned from
Putnam and Alan Miller that when working with people of,
um . . . questionable . . . morals, you can't be too careful.
You need to have leverage."

"So what shoe did you scrape Dutton off of?"

Frey laughed. "I don't think I'm going to tell you right
now. But suffice it to say, he's one of *my* kind of people. In
fact, he makes me look like *Santa Claus.*"

Desh's upper lip curled up in revulsion. Given how much Frey liked having kids on his lap, the thought of him as Santa Claus was highly disturbing.

Frey nodded toward Matt Griffin on the couch. "While your friend is sleeping—which is rude if you ask me—I need you to call Kira Miller for me. When she answers, tell her you want to have a video call with her and have her go to a desktop computer to receive it."

"We have a secure version of Skype on our phones," noted Desh.

"First off, since you've forgotten, you didn't bring your phone with you to *Copernicus*. So you'll be using mine. And second, I want to have a steady, crisp image of her from a high-end webcam. She's a beautiful girl. I want to be sure to see every last line in her face."

Desh's jaw tightened. "What makes you think I'll lift a finger to do what you ask?"

"Do you always have to be so cliché?" said Frey in contempt. "Really?" He paused. "Okay, I'll play along. I won't waste time threatening you. The cliché says that noble dumbasses like you will sacrifice themselves for the cause. But it also says you won't sacrifice *others*. Make the call, or I blow away Matt's kneecap." Frey glanced over at the large hacker and shrugged. "I don't know, something like that just might be enough to wake him."

Desh stared deeply into Frey's eyes and detected not the slightest hint of compassion or any evidence he was bluffing. Reluctantly, Desh nodded his agreement.

One of the mercs cut him loose while his three companions stood back, their automatic weapons trained on his chest. When his hands were free, Frey tossed him a phone. "Here. And don't get any cute ideas. If you don't convince her you're your own man, Matt here will never walk again." To underscore his point he took out his gun, chambered a round, and held the barrel just a few inches from Griffin's left knee. "Make your performance convincing," he warned.

Kira's phone didn't identify the incoming caller, so she answered uncertainly, but when she heard Desh's voice she became ecstatic. "*David!*" she squealed happily. "*Thank God.* I heard about what happened on *Copernicus*—about Matt stopping doomsday—but why didn't you call? I've been worried to death."

"Everything's fine," Desh assured her, not allowing his voice to betray the strain he was under. "The world really dodged a bullet this time. I'll tell you all about it, but first I'd like to show you something. And I want you to see it on a big screen. How far away are you from the computer in the conference room?"

"Three or four minutes."

"Great, I'll be waiting for you online when you get there," he said, and then ended the connection.

"Well done," said Frey, reholstering his gun and retrieving his phone. "Matt gets to keep his kneecap for a while longer." He removed a gellcap from his pocket and swallowed it. "I want to be at my best for my conversation with the esteemed Kira Miller," he explained to Desh.

Frey had the mercenaries bind Desh once again, this time leashing him to a heavy desk, and then dismissed all but Dutton, who leveled a gun at Desh and kept watch.

Five minutes after Desh had given Frey the IP address for the computer connection, Kira Miller's face appeared as large as life on a high-definition screen affixed at head height on the wall behind them.

When Eric Frey appeared on *her* screen she shrank back for just an instant.

"Expecting someone else?" asked Frey with a smirk. His eyes were blazing and it was obvious he was now enhanced.

After her initial surprise, Kira's features became calm and impassive. "So, if it isn't the smarter version of Eric Frey. And you have David. Can I assume you have Matt as well?"

"Interesting," said Frey, his voice showing genuine surprise. "You aren't concerned at all. You're still missing the fucking point, aren't you?"

"Not at all," said Kira smoothly. "You had a man on *Copernicus.* You managed to capture David and Matt despite the promises made by your puppet, the colonel. And now you want to trade them for my longevity therapy."

Frey's eyes widened. "I'll be damned," he said. "You don't *care* what happens to Desh. You'd prefer I didn't kill Matt here, but it wouldn't trouble you a bit. You may be colder even than I am. What a glorious bitch you are."

Desh held his breath for several long seconds, waiting for Kira's strenuous denial of Frey's accusations. *But none came.* Which meant that what Frey said was *true.* Enhanced, he could not be deceived. Even if she was a split personality, she was telling the truth as that part of her personality knew it, or Frey would have called her on it.

Frey shot Desh a broad, cruel smile, knowing exactly what was going through his mind and that it was causing more pain than the two physical blows he had landed earlier.

Frey turned back to the monitor and to Kira Miller. "You were *hoping* I would contact you," he continued, reading her like a book, his eyes still blazing with an inner fire. "Because you want to team up with me." He paused. "You know I can read your body language with perfect accuracy, so when I ask a question, you already answer it. But for the benefit of Mr. Dutton and your boy toy," he added, throwing Desh a self-satisfied smirk, "why don't you spell it out? The pained, betrayed look on your beau's face is priceless. Hearing about your betrayals in your own voice is like repeated daggers to his throat. Only he survives each time so the next one can have its full effect."

"Nice thought picture," said Kira dryly. "Okay, I'll pretend you're normal and spell it out. I was a split personality for many months while I grappled with myself. My enhanced personality and my normal personality waged quite a battle. In the end my enhanced personality won, assuming control even when I'm normal. So now I'm an integrated personality—with *her* personality traits. *Thank fucking God*," she added passionately. "No more pathetic, misguided attempts at altruism. No more stubbornly ignoring my own best interests. Normal Kira's personality is enough to make a *saint* vomit. Gods should act like Gods, not mice."

Desh's stomach clenched. His worst fears had been realized. He had been utterly betrayed by the women he loved. He had seen all the signs, but he hadn't let himself believe. Not really. Part of him had clung to the hope that she'd have a good explanation for her actions. Somehow. His deep love for Kira had corrupted the logic centers of his brain. But he couldn't fool himself anymore. Yes, the woman on the screen was no longer Kira Miller, but that didn't matter. He couldn't help but feel as if she had betrayed him nonetheless. That if her love for him was truly strong, she would have found a way to win the battle she had waged with herself.

"So here's the deal," continued Kira. "We work together. The world is big enough for the two of us. You get my longevity therapy and my organization. None of my recruits would have to know anything has changed. Think of them as a brain trust you can trust. They'll keep on spitting out breakthroughs." An amused smile crossed her face. "For the good of the world, of course. And you get me and my talents, the likes of which only come along once in a generation."

"You forgot to mention Matt," said Frey, delight in his voice. "I can see it in your face. He knows of your plan to join forces with me, and he's eager to see it happen. In fact, you and he made sure to plant him on the *Copernicus* because you hoped this would draw me out. You *hoped* I would snatch him and Desh and call to make a trade, so you could propose an alliance. Matt could have prevented doomsday in his pajamas from home."

Desh was numb. He had thought it strange that Kira had agreed to send Griffin to the *Copernicus*, but now it made an awful sense. His head was spinning from the shear enormity of Kira's betrayal, but he seized on a thought that allowed him to keep his emotional perspective: twenty-four hours earlier, all life on earth had narrowly avoided extinction. Even if *he* didn't see a tomorrow, eight billion others would. He clung to this thought as desperately as a man adrift at sea would cling to a floating bit of wreckage in a powerful storm.

Kira smiled. "Turns out Matt's enhanced personality finally won the day and corrupted him as well. Good thing. You know what they say about sinners having more fun. You go to heaven for the air conditioning. You go to hell for the *company*."

Dutton laughed, while Frey remained expressionless, having known what Kira would say long before she said it. "Matt is quite a sweetener to the deal. So what about Desh?"

Kira frowned.

"I see," said Frey immediately. "He's not immune from the personality corrupting effect of repeated IQ boosts, but his amped alter ego isn't strong enough to take over. Too bad." He paused. "But back to negotiations. In exchange for what you're offering, you want me to call off the hunt. Restore you to anonymity. Partner with you. Use my influence with the government and black-ops to help catapult us to power on a global level."

"Exactly," said Kira. "But these are just the broad terms. We can hash out how we'll work together later—when you return to normal." A smile crept slowly over her face. "I don't know much about negotiations, but I'm pretty sure negotiating with someone who's a hundred times smarter than you is a bad idea."

"Okay. We'll sort it all out as equals," agreed Frey.

"Good. As a show of good faith, why don't you bring David and Matt to my headquarters. I'll give you directions."

Desh had spent so much energy implementing their headquarters operations, complete with decoys and multiple locations, that it shocked him that Kira would give out the address so casually. But it shouldn't have. She could trust Frey implicitly now. He needed her to double his lifespan, ensuring he was around when immortality was finally solved.

But this was all insanity, Desh realized. Who cared? There would be *no* immortality. The aliens would be arriving in three short decades, and they would see to that.

Frey had been monitoring Desh from the corner of his eye and interpreted his body language in an instant. "Your boy David here is worried about the alien threat," he explained to Kira. "He's thinking we're fiddling while Rome burns."

"He always was a bit shortsighted," noted Kira. "Would you like me to spell it out for him?" she asked.

"Please," said Frey.

"The threat from the aliens is the primary reason Eric and I should join forces, David dear. Ironically, even though we're doing it for purely selfish reasons, our alliance will probably end up saving the species. Not that I don't already deserve the credit for saving us the first time, since I placed Matt on *Copernicus* and he used my therapy—but I do try to maintain my humility. If Eric and I work together, in just a few years we'll either be *on* the world throne or the power behind it. Left to its own pathetic devices, and due to a lack of a cohesive, decisive worldwide governing authority, humanity has no chance of withstanding an alien attack. Politics and endless stupidity would do us in. What we need are competent dictators to take the reins." She flashed an insincere smile. "Like me and Eric. And we'll have no false sentimentality. We'll be willing to do what needs to be done. Make the hard choices. Drive the species at the end of a whip to implement our strategies and inventions. With us at the helm, our chances of survival go up dramatically."

Desh was horrified, but everything she said rang true. Their chances of surviving the alien threat probably would be greater with her and Frey as dictators, wielding their supply of gellcaps.

"And worst case," continued Kira, "if we *are* unable to fend off the aliens, then at least we'll be able to solve the ZPE drive and run away, and live to see immortality another day."

"Very poetic," said Frey. "I think this is going to be the beginning of a beautiful relationship."

"As long as we work together," cautioned Kira. "If we don't stab each other in the back for petty power, we're unstoppable. Someday, thousands of years from now, we can split the universe between us." She raised her eyebrows. "Although if we do, I want the half with Saturn in it. I've always been partial to rings."

"I'm looking forward to further discussions," said Frey.

Kira gave the address of the Kentucky facility. Frey manipulated the computer with superhuman speed and an aerial view of the facility appeared in the corner of the monitor the moment she finished. "Your facility won't work," said Frey. "For our first meeting I want a neutral location."

Kira frowned. "Why? I know you trust me."

"I do. But your building is too big and too out in the open. And if we'll be negotiating how we work together, I want neutral turf for our first meeting."

Kira opened her mouth to speak, but before a single word could come out, Frey added icily, "Save your breath. I've already discounted all of your counterarguments."

Kira wore an expression of frustrated resignation. "Where then?" she asked

Frey consulted his now photographic memory. "There's a safe house about eighty miles south of you. A horse farm the FBI uses to hide key witnesses. It's isolated. If I don't call back, assume it's available and the meeting is on."

"How is that neutral territory?" complained Kira.

"I've never been there either," said Frey. "I'm in a safe house in Florida now. I'm not asking you to come *here*. We'll both have to travel." He gave her an approximate time for the meeting and told her he would call her with the address once he and Dutton, with Matt Griffin in tow, had arrived and made sure the site was open and ready for business.

"Bring David along as well," said Kira. "He was getting suspicious of me in the end. I need to interrogate him. I like to learn from my mistakes."

"Very admirable. But rumor has it that you don't make mistakes."

Kira smiled. "I try to keep them to a minimum."

"Good policy," said Frey. He raised his eyebrows. "And if Desh tries to be a hero and causes trouble before we get there?" he asked.

"Then kill him," replied Kira with a shrug.

***

Ten minutes later the fire left Frey's eyes and he began shoveling food into his mouth at a rapid pace. He turned to Dutton. "We'll take the team of mercs with us," he said as bits of food flew from his mouth. "And I'd like you to activate a few more."

"Worried she might be setting a trap?"

Frey laughed. "Not at all. You know I can't be deceived when I'm under the influence. You've tried. That's how I know your intentions toward me are, um . . . *honorable*," he added wryly. "Kira Miller is on our side. I guarantee it. She won't try anything."

"Then why the mercs?"

A malicious smile crept slowly over Frey's face. "I never said that *I* won't try anything," he replied in amusement.

61

The state of Kentucky was known for its extensive cave systems, navigable waterways, and bourbon, but it was nicknamed *The Bluegrass State* for a reason: this lush grass thrived in Kentucky's fertile soil and was ideal for supporting the breeding of Thoroughbred horses. The *Noble Equine* farm was similar to hundreds of other horse farms throughout the region, although it was far smaller than most. It was isolated and absolutely picturesque, with gleaming white fences, gently rolling hills, and a beautifully appointed farm house, with pointed spires reaching through the roof between six evenly spaced dormer windows.

The only real difference between the *Noble Equine* horse farm and others of its type was its total lack of horses, which tended to make its name a misnomer. It was on private property, off the beaten path, so no one was likely to ever discover its secret. If anyone did happen to get lost and drive by, they would assume the horses were in the barns rather than out to pasture.

Kira arrived alone, in a spacious van that was an almost identical twin to the one they had used in Denver. She parked in front of the stunning farmhouse and cautiously approached the door, which opened from the inside as she neared it. Eric Frey stepped across the threshold and offered his hand warmly. "Welcome, Kira," he said as she took it. He gestured inside. "Let's go make history."

As Kira stepped inside two commandoes raised automatic weapons and trained them on her chest. As she turned back to protest, Frey gave her a gentle shove and closed the door behind them.

She found herself in the living room of the farmhouse, which had hardwood flooring and little else save a small coffee table off to the side near a couch, and several large monitors hanging on the walls. Kira's eyes swept the room nervously. Sitting against one wall, their hands behind their backs, were David Desh and Matt Griffin. Andrew Dutton was off to one side, and six additional commandoes were spread evenly throughout the room.

"What's all this about?" demanded Kira, her voice strained.

"What do you think?" said Frey.

Kira shook her head. "You know you can trust me," she said in confusion. "You were enhanced when I agreed to partner with you—in good faith," she added pointedly.

Frey smiled. "Yes, I *do* know I can trust you. But do you know if you can trust *me?*"

Kira shook her head in horror. "But *why?* The world is plenty big enough for the both of us."

"Let's just say I don't work well with others," he replied dryly. "Never have."

Frey issued orders to two of the soldiers. One pulled Kira's hands behind her back and bound them tightly with plastic handcuffs while the other began to frisk her roughly. Dutton made sure she knew there were no pins or paperclips to be found anywhere within the premises, so she wouldn't be pulling a repeat of her escape from Colonel Jacobson.

"The good news for you," said Frey in amusement, "is that I'll let you keep your panties on. I'm not interested in adult women. And I've set up a field that will dampen the electronics you're carrying."

The man frisking her removed a cell phone and key ring—which housed her spare gellcap for emergencies, and handed them to Frey, who immediately passed them to Dutton to store in his pockets. The merc then removed a Sig Sauer 9mm and a military grade tranquilizer gun. Frey pocketed the handgun, but held the tranquilizer gun in front of his face and examined it with great interest. "I see you come to negotiations well prepared," he commented. "A little *too* well prepared for my tastes."

"*Fuck you,*" spat Kira.

"Again," said Frey smugly, "I'm not interested in adult women. But thanks for the offer." He paused in thought. "I know you were honestly prepared to work as partners, so why the weaponry?"

Kira said nothing.

"Makes sense," mused Frey, thinking aloud. "There was always the chance I'd double cross you, and then all bets would be off. And it pays to be prudent and paranoid. We both subscribe to that philosophy. Which reminds me," he said. He quickly ordered four of the six mercs to take up positions outside of the house.

"See what I mean," he continued after the commandoes had exited. "I know this many mercenaries is overkill, especially since I was certain you were kindly delivering yourself to me. But I always err on the side of paranoia. Like you. Besides, these assholes missed you at *Advanced Physics International,* and I wanted to give them all a chance to redeem themselves. There are two more I'd love to introduce you to, but they're busy keeping an eye on things about a hundred yards from here. Snipers. Just in case someone was following you—without your knowledge, of course."

Desh saw a flash of alarm in Kira's blue eyes, undetectable by anyone who didn't know her as well as he did, but very real nonetheless.

Frey dangled the tranquilizer gun by its trigger. "I can respect bringing the pistol for paranoia's sake. But why this one?" he asked, scratching his head. "Surely if the shit hit the fan, you weren't worried about sparing lives." He studied her carefully but she remained expressionless. Finally, he shrugged. "Oh well. It doesn't really matter. I'm planning to take a gellcap a little later and I'm sure it will all make perfect sense to me then."

"This is a big mistake," insisted Kira. "What about teaming up to prepare for the aliens? You know I wasn't bullshitting. The world—which includes *you*," she added pointedly, "will have the best chance to survive if we work together. Making full use of my collection of geniuses. Why would you give that up? Not to mention the secret to longevity? It makes no sense."

Frey smiled. "I won't be giving up a thing. We'll still work together. We do still need to make sure my extended life isn't cut short by these fucking aliens," he said. "And I'll still tap into your organization of sickeningly loyal geniuses. But you can't have two equal partners. You yourself said a single dictator running the world was far more efficient than leaving it to bickering governments. Same is true in any business endeavor. You never want two fifty-fifty partners. You have one in charge and you have subordinates. So I'm just setting the tone. You'll be a valued subordinate. Like Dutton here. I'll decide if and when you're enhanced, and how you'll help us. And I'll watch you to make sure I'm the one calling all the plays. I like to have leverage on people I work with, helps me sleep at night. When I have the proper leverage, you'll have some autonomy again. But not until."

"*You fucking bastard!*" snarled Kira, her face a mask of rage. "I can't believe you're doing this!"

"Come on, Kira. You and I are exactly alike. You yourself said that heaven was only good for the air-conditioning. Don't pretend you're motivated by anything other than total ruthlessness and self interest." He paused. "And I came up with a great idea for leverage. You want to hear it?"

Kira seethed but didn't take the bait.

"Remember when Putnam told you he had surgically implanted a powerful explosive in your skull, which he could detonate at will? Well that was just a hoax at the time. But it's a hell of a good idea."

"If you think you're going to get the secret of my longevity therapy under coercion, you're out of your mind. I was

346 *Douglas E. Richards*

going to give it to you freely. But if you don't reverse course on this, I'll see you rot in hell before you get anywhere *near* it." She paused and gathered herself, deciding to come at him from another angle. "Look, you're an intelligent, rational man. Can't you see the world is big enough for both of us? How can you not see that working together is in your own best interest?" she pleaded.

"There's an old story," interjected Matt Griffin from out of the blue, still sitting behind them against the wall. "About a scorpion and a frog."

Frey turned and glared at the bearded hacker. "Did I invite you to join in on this private conversation?" he barked angrily.

"I just saved your ass from nuclear Armageddon," replied Matt with uncharacteristic fervor, as though something had snapped inside of him. "So I invited *myself*." His expression softened as he fought to calm himself. "To continue," he went on as if he were never interrupted, "a scorpion asks a frog for a lift across a river. The frog refuses. 'The second I let you on my back, you'll sting me,' points out the frog. 'No I won't,' says the scorpion. 'Because if I sting you, you'll sink to the bottom, and *I'll* die as well.' The frog considers this and can't find any flaw in this logic, so he agrees, and allows the scorpion to climb on his back. Halfway across the river the scorpion stings the frog. As the poison is taking effect, with his last breath, the frog says, 'but why? Now *you're* going to die too.' The scorpion shakes his head sadly and replies, 'I *know*. But I couldn't help it. It's just my nature.'"

There was silence throughout the room as everyone digested Griffin's tale. "Okay," said Frey. "Good story. But now you're done talking."

"You should think long and hard about the moral of this story, Frey," insisted Griffin with an air of contempt. "Your instincts are self-destructive. So why don't you fight them? Why don't you pretend you're in this for your rational self interest instead of being a totally fucked up asshole."

Frey turned to Griffin and without saying a word fired a tranquilizer dart into his stomach. "Did you not hear me say you needed to stop talking?" said Frey as Griffin's eyelids slid shut and he slumped over, unconscious once again.

Kira shot Frey a withering stare.

"No reason to get upset," he said with mock innocence, handing the tranquilizer gun to Dutton. "I'm just trying to help out. I'm guessing he needs just a little more rest and recuperation. Don't you worry though, Kira. I have big plans for Matt here."

Desh contemplated escape, but with his hands tied—tightly—behind his back with plastic handcuffs he didn't have a chance. But as he had told Kira—when he thought she still *was* Kira—there was no honor among thieves. He would stay alert for a chance to create a wedge between Frey and Dutton. His initial attempt in Florida had failed, but there had to be some way to get them to follow their natural tendencies to stab each other in the back. He couldn't turn Dutton against Frey, but maybe he could do the opposite. It was a long shot, but the only chance he could see. Until an opening presented itself, he would stay perfectly still and off the radar; a forgotten presence. Griffin had shown that sticking your head up could have unfortunate consequences.

"Matt's story," continued Frey as if nothing had happened, "cute as it was, missed the point. You're no frog, Kira Miller. If anything, you're a bigger scorpion than I am. We're both wired the same way—at least now. If I didn't take the upper hand, you'd eventually try to take it yourself. It's inevitable. Putnam was trying to screw your brother. I was trying to screw them both. Round and round it goes, with the smartest and most ruthless ending up on top. And you're already too damn smart for your own good, even without your pills."

Kira was about to respond when there was commotion from just outside the door. The handle was turned roughly and the two snipers Frey had mentioned entered the room, supporting a limp male body between them. His head flopped down against his chest lifelessly, and blood seeped from a hole in his shoulder. As soon as they passed the threshold, the two mercs released the body unceremoniously and it fell to the floor like wet cement.

Desh's mouth fell open, but he was able to recover before anyone noticed his reaction. He recognized this newcomer immediately.

It was Ross Metzger.

Eric Frey didn't have to know what was happening to know there was more danger here than expected. He pulled a gellcap from his pocket and swallowed it. He was now minutes away from being the absolute master of any situation that might arise. "Report!" he shouted at the two snipers.

"This bastard took out Curt and his entire team," said the merc on the left. "Quietly, and without firing a single shot," he added. "They're all dead." He pushed Ross Metzger's body with his boot. "But so is he."

"This guy took out four armed and trained men, all by himself?" said Frey in disbelief, and in that instant Desh realized Ross Metzger must have been enhanced. Ross was good, but he wasn't *that* good. Desh remembered being a hostage years earlier, and facing certain death, when an enhanced Ross Metzger had came to his and Kira's rescue, killing Alan Miller in the process. It was a bit of Déjà vu. Only this time, Ross wasn't his ally. This time he was working with the poisoned Kira Miller for corrupt ends of their own.

The sniper nodded. "I saw him take out Dmitri through my scope. His speed seemed almost, I don't know . . . *superhuman*," he added, both fear and awe in his voice.

Frey gasped. He had finally realized that their mystery assailant was enhanced.

Which meant he could control his vital signs.

Frey began to raise his arm to fire a bullet into Metzger's head, but he could have been moving in slow motion for all the good it did him. Before his arm had moved a foot the bloody body on the floor twisted to the side and flung a stainless steel combat knife, which buried itself between Frey's eyes, killing him instantly.

Metzger yanked the legs out from under both snipers beside him before they even registered that he had thrown the knife, and broke the neck of the merc to his left with the sound of a branch snapping in two. He was an instant away from breaking the second soldier's neck when Andrew Dutton shot wildly at the blur on the ground using the tranquilizer gun Frey had handed him earlier. The dart hit Metzger in the leg, which wouldn't have stopped him if it had been a bullet, but Metzger's superhuman speed ended abruptly, like a video that had been in extreme fast forward being stopped on a dime—and he fell once again to the floor, blood still seeping from his shoulder.

"Get up!" shouted Dutton to the soldier lying near Metzger, whose life Dutton had just saved. Dutton rushed over to Kira Miller, grabbed a handful of her hair, and yanked her face toward his. "*Who is he?*" he demanded.

"I don't know," croaked Kira, wincing in pain. "He's not with me."

Dutton put a gun to her head and chambered a round. "*Who is he, and who else is coming? You have three seconds!*"

"Kill me and you'll never see my longevity treatment!" she blurted out breathlessly. "I wasn't planning a double-cross. Frey would have known. Think about it! I have no idea who he is. But if he has backup we're sitting ducks in here," she added.

Dutton turned toward the two mercs who had remained in the living room since Kira had entered. "You two are with me," he commanded. "We'll split up, recon the area, and meet outside this door in fifteen minutes. Look sharp." He turned to the sniper he had saved. "As for you," he added, "stay here and babysit these two."

Desh had remained hyper-alert since the moment Metzger had made his move, waiting for an opening. During the commotion he had managed to come to a standing position by the wall without being noticed. Desh could tell that the sniper Dutton had ordered to guard them was still a little shaken from the torque Metzger had applied to his head and neck faster, and with greater strength, than should have been possible. Desh's hands were still bound behind his back, but he readied himself for action and studied the man's eyes. As Dutton left with the two armed mercs in tow, and closed the door behind him, the sniper shifted his gaze to follow and lowered his arm for just a moment.

This momentary lapse of attention was all Desh needed. He exploded forward and closed the ten feet between himself and the guard. The sniper raised his arm to fire as Desh collided with him, head down, and kept his legs churning, like a fullback running through an attempted tackle, driving him into the opposite wall with bone jarring force and causing the gun to fly from his hand. The sniper recovered from the initial shock and reached in his belt for another weapon, but Kira swept his legs out from under him and he fell to the ground, where Desh kicked him in the face with enough force to break through concrete. The man's head snapped back and his eyes rolled into the back of his head.

Griffin and Metzger were still unconscious from the tranquilizer darts, and Frey and both snipers were dead. Only he and Kira remained standing.

Desh rushed over and dropped down onto Frey's lifeless torso, angling back until his bound hands came into contact with the hilt of Metzger's knife. He tugged at it until the blood-covered blade dislodged from between Frey's eyes, which required more strength than he had expected.

Desh tried to maneuver the blade to cut through the hardened plastic of his cuffs, but his hands were tied too closely together and he couldn't get the proper angle, or the leverage to do anything more than stab himself with the bloody knife repeatedly until fresh blood was leaking from cuts of his own.

"Give me the knife," said Kira. "I'll free you."

Desh shook his head. Even if she were an ally, the plastic was too tough and his hands were too close together. She'd have a better angle than he did, but with her hands tied behind her as well, he was sure she wouldn't have enough strength to saw through the hardened plastic. It didn't matter anyway, since they were decidedly *not* allies. "Yeah, I'm going to give you a knife and let you use it near my wrists," he said sarcastically. He had already done enough damage to himself.

"Then cut me loose and I'll free you," offered Kira anxiously.

Desh laughed at the absurdity of her request. "No chance. You'll just kill me and escape. Jake was right, you're the most dangerous psychopath on earth. That's not going to happen."

"David," she said calmly, and it was the voice of the old Kira, the Kira he loved, which made him hate the current version even more. "I'm on your side. I've always been on your side . . . on *our* side," she corrected. "I know I've been acting strange and I've deceived you, but it's not what you think."

"Save your breath!" snapped Desh in disgust. "You really think I'd buy any act you could come up with at this point? Really?"

"David, remember when you figured out that Alan was the one pulling the strings? And his exact plan? Remember? And you kept that from me. You weren't sure how I'd react, and too much was on the line to trust my acting abilities. Remember?" she repeated urgently. "I thought we were dead, that we had lost *everything*. You *let* me think that— but for noble reasons." She took a breath and hurried on. "Well this is similar; an audacious plan that Ross and Matt had to be in on. But you and Jim didn't. I couldn't afford to take any chances and tell you. Too much was on the line." Kira's eyes grew larger and she looked as pained and vulnerable as he could ever remember. "But I've never stopped loving you, David. With all of my heart." She shook her head. "And I never will."

God she was convincing, thought Desh. He *had* deceived her in a life and death situation—for good reason. So was this true? Was she just doing this to him in return? He wanted to believe her with every fiber of his being, but his rationality returned like a baseball bat to the head, and he cursed himself for allowing himself to hope, if only for an instant.

"*You really think I'm that stupid?*" he screamed bitterly. "I was there when you had your chat with Frey," he reminded her. "When he was enhanced. I heard *everything!* You told him to kill me if he wanted. You told him you wanted to team up with him. That your sociopathic alter ego had absorbed your personality. And it was all true! Every word! Or Frey would have known."

"Jake called me from South Africa while you were on your way to Florida," said Kira hurriedly. "Dutton framed him to get him out of the picture. But he escaped. And now he believes we were framed also. So he called to warn me that Dutton had you and Matt and was heading to the States." She paused. "I knew Frey would try to use you both as leverage. So I was *expecting* his call. And I had time to come up with a plan. I knew the only way to get him to trust me with his life was to convince him I was on *his* side. While he was enhanced and I wasn't."

She stared intently at Desh, her large blue eyes pleading with him to believe, willing him to trust her. "When the call came in from an unknown phone," she continued, "I knew it was Frey calling to hold you and Matt for ransom. And I was ready. I took a gellcap before I answered. It turned out to be you at first, but by the time I was talking to Frey, *I was enhanced.*"

Desh stumbled backwards. She sounded so *reasonable.* And she wasn't enhanced now. Being able to come up with a story this complex and believable on the fly was beyond even her—or was it?

"Instead of just diverting a fraction of my capabilities to create a slower version of myself for communication, I put *a hundred percent* of my capacity into creating a Kira avatar that would pass as normal me. I made sure my eyes didn't gleam with an inner, superhuman intelligence. That my body language, my posture, was that of normal Kira Miller. And that my word choices were hers in every way. There is only one way to lie to an enhanced mind: if *you're* enhanced also. Enabling you to control your every facial expression at the *cellular* level so your body language is precisely on track with your words."

"So it was all a set up?" said Desh, afraid to believe, only to be fooled again.

"*Yes!*" replied Kira emphatically. "I offered Frey everything he could want in a way that ensured he would trust me. Then when he and Dutton came to our headquarters, Ross and I could easily take them out and get you back. And finally—finally—explain to you what's really been going on. I didn't count on him wanting to meet here, and I especially didn't expect a double-cross when he had everything to gain from working with me. Even so, I had Ross as my ace in the hole." She shook her head. "The plan *still* should have worked. It was just bad luck it didn't. Having snipers hidden out of sight is a level of caution I could have never predicted."

This would explain the tranquilizer gun she had with her, that Frey himself didn't understand, since sociopaths weren't exactly dedicated to the use of non-lethal force. She had wanted to take Frey and Dutton alive so she could get as much intel as possible and unravel his organization. "Your plan hinged on Frey being enhanced when he called, so he would think he could read you. What if he hadn't been?"

"I would have *insisted* on it," she answered immediately, "at the start of the call. To prove my sincerity to him. Jake had given me plenty of warning, so I had multiple contingences planned out."

As Desh considered this last, Kira's iron grip on her emotions broke down once again and the look of pain and vulnerability returned. This time, tears flowed from her eyes as well. "I *love* you, David," she whispered. "I know what I've done to your mind. And how badly I've hurt you. I can't blame you for not believing me. But I swear to you, I'm not the sociopath I pretended to be with Frey. I'm the woman you fell in love with."

Desh gazed at her, his mind numb. Everything she said was so plausible. But was he being played for a fool yet again?

"Dutton and his men will be back any minute," she said. "You have to decide if you can trust me."

Desh looked into her beautiful eyes, still moist but no longer producing tears. Maybe she *was* that good. Maybe his heart was clouding his judgment even now. But if this were the case, then it would be better if she *did* kill him. Death would be a welcome release.

"Okay," said Desh, nodding. "Let's do this."

They hurriedly positioned themselves back to back and Desh began sawing at her cuffs with Metzger's combat knife. Her cuffs, unlike his, had been left with a two inch length of plastic between her hands. Sawing backwards in such an awkward position with little leverage required every ounce of his strength and focus, but after just a few minutes he succeeded in freeing her.

Desh held a mental breath. What would happen now?

True to her word, Kira immediately began sawing through his restraints, her hands in front of her and, unlike Desh, now able to use the strength in her arms as well as just her hands. In less than a minute the razor sharp combat knife, its flat surfaces covered in dried blood, finished severing the plastic.

Kira retrieved her Sig Sauer from Frey's body and Desh chose one of several automatic weapons now strewn throughout the living room. Together they dragged the sniper Desh had killed with his violent kick out of sight of the entrance, and took up positions on either side of the door, about twelve feet deep in the room. Still clutching their weapons, they put their hands behind their backs as though they were still bound and readied themselves.

Less than a minute later, Dutton threw open the door and entered, spotting Kira in front of him and to his left. "The attacker was acting alone," he told her. "But I'm taking over for Frey, which means I'll be needing those magic pills of yours." He leered at her suggestively. "And for the record, I *do* like adult women."

He was about to continue when it finally dawned on him that something was very wrong. The sniper he had left to mind the prisoners was nowhere in sight. His two companions had caught on just an instant earlier, but before they could react Kira and Desh cut all three men to ribbons.

Kira knew they couldn't afford to do anything less, but it was a bloody massacre, and she fell to her knees when it was done, fighting back vomit.

She visibly shook off the horror of having been an instrument of death, and her physical squeamishness, and moved over to Ross to inspect his wound. "Find a first-aid kit," she ordered, and Desh marveled at her ability to keep getting back in the saddle after every fall. She was truly remarkable.

He raced through the safe house and returned several minutes later with a military style first-aid kit. Kira washed Metzger's wound and went to work dressing it. He had lost considerable blood, but in the few minutes he had played possum, his enhanced mind had marshaled clotting and immune factors to the wound and directed these biochemical armies to initiate the healing process far more efficiently than his body would have done naturally. Kira was confident he would make it.

She was just finishing up when Matt Griffin opened his eyes. The dose of tranquilizer had been fairly modest, and hadn't been enough to keep a man of Griffin's weight out for long.

He shook himself awake and then looked around the room, taking in the gruesome bodies and massive carnage. Then he did it a second time, as though he wasn't quite sure his eyes weren't playing tricks on him. Only two figures moved. Kira, who was tending to Ross, and David Desh, who he spied through the open door, keeping watch outside.

Griffin breathed a heavy sigh of relief, and Kira's head shot around at the noise. She caught his eye and visibly relaxed.

"Kira, um . . . just out of curiosity," he said wryly, making a show of turning his head around the room to take in the corpses that surrounded him. "Did I *miss* anything while I was asleep, by any chance?"

62

After they had freed Griffin and he and Kira had embraced warmly, Desh removed Kira's keys from Dutton's bullet-riddled corpse and they loaded Ross Metzger carefully into the back of the Icarus van.

"Is David fully up to speed?" asked Griffin

Kira blew out a breath and shook her head no.

Griffin's eyes roamed between Desh and Kira and back again, as if trying to guess the possible state of their current relationship. "In that case," he said finally, "I'll drive." He held out his hand toward Desh, who was holding the keys. "You and Kira can ride in the back. You two need to have some quality alone time," he said. He raised his eyebrows. "Well, alone time if you don't count Ross."

Desh looked into Kira's eyes once again. Was there really an explanation that would exonerate her? It seemed almost impossible. He so wanted there to be, but he still couldn't rule out that her explanation of events would fall short. But there was only one way to find out. "Thanks, Matt," he said, putting the keys in the giant's hand. "Find the nearest woods and we'll decide if we want to switch vehicles. I'm sure Frey and Dutton wanted their ambush of Kira to be off the record, so no one should be watching. But be alert and keep your eyes peeled anyway," he instructed.

"Wow," said Griffin with a grin, "it's like we're one big happy family again."

"That remains to be seen," said Desh grimly.

Desh and Kira sat in leather captain's chairs opposite each other and belted in as Matt pulled away from the charnel house.

"Okay, Kira. If you can truly explain away everything I've learned, every act you've taken, you're an even greater magician than I thought."

Kira sighed. "I have a gellcap in the key ring upfront. You could take it before I start to be sure I'm telling the truth."

Desh considered. The fact she was offering this up was encouraging. "That's okay. Let's just have a normal conversation. Emphasis on *normal.*"

"If you have even the slightest doubt, I'm going to insist you take one."

Desh nodded.

"All of this started a little over two and a half years ago," began Kira. "A few months before I tried the second level of enhancement. World events were getting me more nervous even than usual."

"Yeah, world events will do that to you," noted Desh with a frown.

"As you know better than anyone, my analysis suggested that extended life would be a disaster. That society was already struggling from the burden of overpopulation and the weight of increases in human lifespan. When social security was created, life expectancy in America was *below* sixty-five, the age when benefits kicked in. Now it's around eighty. We've been putting more and more burden on the system for every year longer in life expectancy medical science is able to create. In 1940 there were six people working for each person at retirement age. Now there are only *three.* And retirement lasts longer and longer every decade. Society's back is breaking already, and my therapy would accelerate this dramatically, which would inevitably lead to wars and the end of civilization."

"I'm well aware of this analysis," said Desh impatiently. How could he not be? The entire vision of Icarus had been to create efficient star travel, so mankind could leave its cradle and have room to grow—and room for an increased duration of life.

"I know. Sorry. The thing is, even having decided not to release my longevity therapy, the world seemed to be going to hell. European economies began melting down faster than my enhanced self had predicted. And most of the world's other economies performed worse than expected as well. Terrorist states were acquiring or building nuclear weapons. Islamic fundamentalism was rising around the world, with democratic-seeming revolutions leading to even *more* intolerant rule in many cases. Given all of this, I became more worried than ever. I had thought we had enough time to solve faster-than-light travel before the powder keg went off. But what if I was wrong?"

"I assume you tried to get a handle on this while enhanced," said Desh.

Kira nodded. "Yes. But without success. The analysis for a seismic shift like increasing life expectancy by eighty years was fairly straightforward. This wasn't. Even for an enhanced mind. It was clear that the probability of imminent self-destruction of our species was high. But just how high, and how imminent, wasn't clear. And regardless, even assuming the end *was* near, my superhuman intellect couldn't see any way to stop it."

Desh listened thoughtfully as the van drove on, with Matt Griffin at the helm.

"But then the core council agreed I would attempt five minutes at the second level of enhancement. So I studied up on world affairs, geopolitical conflicts, weapons systems and strategies, the effects of various stimuli on world order, and pressure points that could trigger wars. The works. I wanted to have as much raw data as I could for my uh . . . super-enhanced self to draw from."

Desh nodded to himself as at least one piece of the puzzle slid into place. He had found remnants of this research hidden on her computer, and had naturally jumped to the wrong conclusions. Kira Miller had wanted to be prepared for her five minutes at a level of intelligence that was all but omniscient.

"And?" said Desh.

"And . . . my mind at this transcendent level was able to easily perform the analysis. The results were even more sobering than I thought. Basically, we were out of time already. World War III or the equivalent was inevitable, and irreversible. On the course we were on, even if we invented faster-than-light travel the next day, it would be too late. Although if we did, at least a few would escape to seed the species elsewhere. But that's *if* we could solve faster-than-light travel, something even my transcendent self knew would be a considerable challenge."

Kira paused to gather her thoughts.

"Go on," prompted Desh, who as usual when speaking with Kira, found himself intellectually stimulated and totally absorbed by the case she was presenting.

"Transcendent Kira realized that the only possible way to save us from ourselves was to accomplish two things. One, relieve the ever increasing global tensions between countries. And two, render every nuclear warhead on the face of the earth impotent."

Kira paused to let Desh reflect on the enormity of these two goals.

"So during the five minutes she existed," she continued, "transcendent Kira hatched a plan that was insanely ambitious, even for her. And she split normal me—and the person I became while enhanced—both into two personalities. One aware of the plan, who would implement and monitor it, making course corrections as they became necessary. And one who was clueless, left totally in the dark, so she would behave and react normally as events unfolded."

Desh stared into Kira's eyes and saw nothing but sincerity. And her assertions were almost too outrageous to be anything but true.

"You weren't the only one I was deceiving, David. I was deceiving myself just as much. The fewer people who knew, the less chance something would go wrong. If you don't know something, you can't spill it during an interrogation. Disclosure was on a need to know basis only. If it had been up to me, I would have told you everything from the beginning." She rolled her eyes. "Then again, I would have told *myself* everything also."

Desh nodded. Knowing that he hadn't been the only who wasn't trusted with this plan made him feel better about the situation, even though he knew it shouldn't.

"Basically, transcendent Kira realized the only way to stave off disaster was to present an external threat. A threat to the entire planet. One that would scare the world straight. Freak out people and governments enough that they would have to learn to work as a single species. They would still have their own languages and cultures, but everyone would be striving toward a common goal, focused on a common enemy, rather than trying to tear out each other's jugulars."

Desh's eyes narrowed. Was she implying what he thought she was? He couldn't see any other alternative. "So what are you saying?" he asked, his tone incredulous. "You can't mean that . . ." He paused and waved his hands, somehow unable to finish a thought that seemed so utterly preposterous. "So what are you saying?" he repeated.

"What I'm saying," responded Kira with a grin, amused by his struggles, "*is that there is no alien species.* I'm saying that transcendent Kira found a way to fabricate one from whole cloth." She paused and raised her eyebrows impishly. "What I'm saying, David, is that the entire alien visitation is a sham."

63

Desh sat in stunned silence for almost thirty seconds. Had Kira Miller really engineered the greatest hoax in human history? A hoax swallowed whole by eight billion people? It was remarkable. Stunning. Impossible.

"Just a teeny bit ambitious," said Kira with a smile, "wouldn't you say? Even for someone with godlike intellect."

"How?" said Desh simply.

"Second level Kira came up with the entire plan, of course, and imbedded key parts of it in the neuronal structure of both normal me and enhanced me. Like programming a computer."

"It can't be done," objected Desh. "Implanting the epiphanies we have while enhanced in our minds for playback when we return to normal is impossible."

"Impossible at the first level of enhancement, yes," conceded Kira. "But as you know, the second level is as far above the first as the first is above normal."

Desh smiled sheepishly. He *did* know that. He was being stupid. They weren't using the word *transcendent* for nothing. "Go on," he said.

"We always thought Ross took enhancement better than any of us, without negative personality changes. Transcendent Kira was certain he was someone who could be absolutely trusted, even while enhanced. And also that if he studied enough physics, he could pull off a few miracles—with her help. So I gave him a lifetime supply of gellcaps, which sped up his advances dramatically, since he wasn't a danger to society and didn't need any babysitters."

Desh nodded. "So once you recovered from your five minutes at this second level, you had Ross bone up on physics. But not to tackle cold fusion."

"Right. Ross knew the real score from the beginning, even if I didn't. The hidden half of my personality told him everything. He was responsible for implementing three breakthroughs that transcendent Kira scorched into my mind. Zero point energy was one of them, of course. Ross needed to pretend to be making progress with cold fusion to justify his physics work. And the last thing we could do was risk letting you or Jim—or me, for that matter—know he was working to implement the principles of ZPE my much smarter self had laid out, or we might have connected the dots when the alien ship was discovered. During this time, Ross was also making great progress building his own group to move the plan forward. Doling out gellcaps from the supply I had given him."

"Can I assume he was also responsible for developing the nanites?"

"Yes. Although I helped some with the biological portion, and others he recruited helped as well." She paused. "Actually, the nanites are far simpler than you would ever guess. A concerted effort would have allowed us to create them even at the first level of enhancement, without the help of transcendent Kira."

"But then Frey discovered Ross and attacked," said Desh. Kira nodded.

Desh raised his eyebrows as something else occurred to him. "Frey discovered Ross because of advanced science he found on his computer. Frey told me it was so advanced, it meant nothing to him, even when he was enhanced. And Frey was a Ph.D. scientist."

"It was the principles of ZPE that transcendent Kira had laid down. Believe me, none of us could understand them either, even while enhanced. But Ross and his group kept at it and at least came to understand these principles enough to use them to produce a working drive."

"So when Frey attacked, Ross decided to be opportunistic and use this as a way to fall off the Icarus radar screen."

"*Exactly*. He really was shot. He needed to take a gellcap to help him heal—he was lucky the shot didn't kill him. But once enhanced he realized it was a golden opportunity. If he cut his ties to Icarus, he could act totally independently, without having to pretend to be working on something else. The great majority of time I was just as clueless about any of this as you, including that night. When his pulse stopped, I thought he was just as dead as you did."

Desh remembered her reaction to Metzger's supposed death, and knew she was telling the truth. She had been devastated.

"So then he continued building his organization," said Desh. "Keeping in contact with you periodically."

"Exactly. He perfected the nanites shortly after this time."

Desh rubbed his chin in thought. "You needed the nanites to cement the threat posed by the fictitious aliens," he said. "To create the illusion that an armada was on the way, and establish a specific deadline. To get our species working together."

"Right. If the threat was too far removed, it wouldn't have the same impact, the same urgency. But too soon wasn't good either. Transcendent Kira decided on thirty-four years." She paused. "But the nanites played another role as well."

"Well, obviously they were also intended to pretend to blow every nuke on the planet. To freak us out even more. And to get the nations of the world to take their nukes off-line."

"No. We still can't count on the nations of the world disarming. Even now." She grinned broadly. "The other purpose of the nanites was to take the nukes off line *for them*."

"What?"

"We created the nanites to preferentially migrate to uranium and plutonium. To lend further credibility to the hoax, yes. But their real purpose wasn't to infiltrate nukes to *detonate* them. It was to *disable* them."

Desh's eyes widened.

"Designing nanites to detonate nukes, to make a collection of uranium go critical, is a tougher challenge than you might imagine," continued Kira. "I learned a lot about nuclear weapons while I was helping Ross develop the nanites."

Desh nodded. He had discovered this as well. Kira had broken into classified government computers and studied nuclear weapons. But she had studied biological ones also. Why had this been necessary? "You studied biological weapons as well, didn't you?" said Desh.

Kira nodded. "Impressive deduction," she said in admiration, having no idea that it was *not* deduction. "Why reinvent the wheel? We needed to optimize the spread of the nanites. And the government has performed extensive modeling and analysis of the spread of pathogens as part of their defense against bioweapons."

Desh couldn't help but smile stupidly. She was doing it. She was putting endless and seemingly unrelated puzzle pieces together into a seamless whole.

"Anyway," continued Kira, "as I said, designing nanites capable of detonating nuclear warheads would have been quite challenging. And designing nanites capable of cleaning up radiation and transforming the atmosphere even more so. But it turns out that designing them to render nuclear weapons impotent was fairly easy. A nuke requires uranium enriched to levels that are very difficult to achieve, using high science and endless ultracentrifugation. So if you introduce even small impurities into your enriched uranium, your nuke becomes a door stop."

Desh knew this was absolutely the case. "So was Matt in on the plan from the start as well?" he asked.

"That's right. He was a key player also. It may be difficult to detonate a nuke using nanites, but it's impossible to tap into alien nanites, running alien software, and get anywhere. But we played a magician's trick. Matt did so much that seemed impossible while on the *Copernicus*, by the time he finished his act, even the most jaded scientists would believe anything he did was possible. And Matt *wasn't* tapping into alien nanites to try to figure them out. He helped to build them in the first place. Using code that he developed while enhanced to *look* alien and to be incomprehensible to a normal mind. So he knew exactly how to get the nanites to disgorge the fake end-of-the-world scenario. Because *he* had implanted it. The timing between his discovery of the nanites' evil purpose and time zero was carefully planned. Much longer and the story would have leaked before they could be stopped, which would have been a disaster." She shook her head sadly. "Enough people died around the world from panic and riots during this fiasco as it was."

Desh was finding it hard to get his arms around the enormity of what Kira had done. "So just to be clear," he said, "are you telling me that every nuclear weapon on earth is now disabled?"

"Every one," she replied proudly. "Eventually, my hope is that the nations of the world will disarm them anyway. When the species has gained back some sanity." She paused. "In the meantime, of course, governments can't know they've been disarmed."

"Why not?"

"If a psychopathic killer has a gun, better to fool him into loading it with blanks than to steal it. If you steal the gun, he'll just get another one. With blanks, he's clueless until he's ready to massacre a campus. Then his gun doesn't work. But his attempt still manages to attract the police."

"You've been thinking about this metaphor for a while haven't you?"

"Maybe," allowed Kira with a smile. "We've set the fictitious arrival of the alien armada to give an entire generation of humanity a chance to see themselves as a single species," she explained. "Fighting a common enemy."

Desh frowned. "But you've also condemned an entire generation to fear the skies. To fear the approach of doomsday."

A guilty look crossed Kira's face. "I know. In my defense, the plan wasn't mine. Transcendent Kira made the calculation that the negative consequences couldn't be helped. That if this wasn't done, *not enough* people would fear the approach of doomsday—ensuring we brought it on ourselves within ten years."

Desh tilted his head in thought as the van accelerated briskly. Griffin was probably on the onramp to a highway, heading for the nearest woods. "You said that when you were at the second level, you implanted three scientific breakthroughs into your normal mind. One involved ZPE, and one involved nanites. Did I miss the third?"

Once again Kira gazed at him with unabashed admiration. "Nice to see you've been paying attention," she said playfully. "The third breakthrough was the principle behind a gravitational wave detector. Ross had a scientist on his team take the credit for this discovery, which, as you know, has revolutionized cosmology. He had to time its release just right. If this technology was available when he launched the fake alien ship, someone might have detected it on its outbound journey—which we couldn't have. So he programmed the craft to hang out in interstellar space while the technology was adopted, so that it would be detected on the way back. It was critical for the entire world to know the alien ship was on its way. So the existence of advanced aliens would be hammered into the world's consciousness like a spike. And with enough advanced warning so the nations of the world would band together to prepare. The *Copernicus* was perfect."

Desh smiled appreciatively. "Your alter ego thought of everything."

"Being nearly omniscient has its advantages," said Kira wryly. "But believe me, she didn't think of everything."

"Wait a minute," said Desh as a new thought occurred to him. "Does this mean that Madison Russo is on Ross's team?"

"Great deduction, but actually no. We had to be sure the alien ship was discovered, and we *did* choose out someone on Ross's team for that purpose." She shook her head. "But Madison Russo beat him to the punch by five or six hours. Surprised the hell out of us. And it was a setback, if only a minor one."

"Why?"

"We knew whoever discovered the ship would be a part of the international effort to study it, and we wanted a few more of our people on *Copernicus.*"

"A few *more?*"

"We had three others. The *Copernicus* tapped the best and the brightest. The same group of people Ross was tapping." She shook her head. "But we decided not to use them. It wasn't required, and again, everything was on a need to know basis." She paused. "We had only one chance to get this right."

"It seems to me the plan had a fatal flaw. You were lucky it all worked out, but what if you hadn't been able to place Matt as the head of the nanite team? What if Jake hadn't called you? Or hadn't conceded to Matt's demands to work on *Copernicus?*" Desh paused in thought and a troubled look came over his face. "Wait a minute. Does this mean you're responsible for Jake coming after us in the first place? Because you knew he'd end up being part of the international effort?"

She laughed. "Not even transcendent Kira is *that* good. No plan survives engagement with the enemy. That's why she set a hidden personality as a watchdog of the plan, knowing she'd have to face curveballs she couldn't foresee. Believe me, the plan proceeded anything but smoothly. There were a whole host of disasters transcendent Kira didn't foresee. Van Hutten came from totally out of left field. Frey was an unexpected nightmare. So were Jake and his organization." She lowered her eyes. "So was Jim Connelly's death," she added sadly.

Desh thought back to that moment in the woods, when Connelly had sacrificed himself for Kira, without hesitation. He had wondered then if his friend's sacrifice had been worth it, and now he knew that it had been.

"The hidden part of me recognized there was a chance Jake would be assigned to the international effort to study the alien object," continued Kira. "That's why I planted a seed with him to call me if he ran into something big he couldn't handle. At the time, I was a prisoner, and I was kicking myself, wondering why I had said it."

In retrospect, thought Desh, it wasn't entirely surprising that Jake was tapped to be part of *Copernicus*. He reported to Dutton, who was Frey's puppet. And Frey would want to be sure he was represented on the luxury cruise ship. He had no way to know what alien secrets might be found, so he would want his proxies to have a front row seat. Still, Kira couldn't possibly have counted on this complex web. "But it was just dumb luck that it all worked out," he pointed out. "Dumb luck that you had planted the seed. And dumb luck that Jake was tapped to join *Copernicus*?"

"Not at all. If Jake wasn't on *Copernicus*, we'd have had some of our people try to institute a contest to decide who ran the nanite team. If that failed, Matt could just contribute from Kentucky. Remember, anyone could study the nanites. They were everywhere. It wouldn't have taken long for Matt to make more progress than anyone else in the world and establish his credentials. He would have ended up on the *Copernicus* no matter what. It just would have taken longer. But that wouldn't have mattered. Because time zero wasn't real. He programmed time zero to be five or six hours from whenever he had the nanites reveal their true purpose. Which he wouldn't do until he had established himself on the *Copernicus*."

Desh thought back to his friend's activities on the massive cruise ship and shook his head in wonder. "Matt's performance was flawless," he said. "Truly genius. The big guy should win an Academy Award."

"I have no doubt," said Kira proudly. "Although he really was enhanced when you thought he was. That's one thing that can't be faked. And he needed to impress everyone enough to believe he was orders of magnitude beyond them. But he had the hardest job of all. You and I didn't know what was going on—well, half of me didn't. The two halves only became fully integrated again once the news hit that we had pulled it off. But Matt knew the truth from the beginning. And most of the time he had to keep us both in the dark. Although on the infrequent occasions when my other half took over, he was able to confide in me then."

Desh knew he now had the entire story. Not that there wasn't more to discuss. But it all fit so beautifully together. Kira's plan was like a work of art—an exquisitely designed watch.

Desh unbuckled from his seat as he contemplated the true enormity of what had been accomplished. A herd of elephants had just stepped off his chest and the relief was indescribable. He turned to the woman he loved—who he had been *right* to still love—and tears began to run down his face. The emotional pressure of the end of the world, which he, like the masses, had absolutely believed, combined with believing he had been betrayed by a woman he loved with every fiber of his being, finally ended.

He felt euphoric.

He leaned forward and held his wife for several minutes, and tears began streaming down her cheeks as well. Finally, the embrace ended, and they kissed each other passionately, tasting a hint of the salty tears that had run down their lips as they did. Finally, Matt Griffin unknowingly ended their embrace when he applied the van's brakes fairly suddenly, probably at a stoplight, and Desh was thrown to the right, almost tripping over the still unconscious Ross Metzger.

Desh took this as a signal to return to his seat and buckle in once again.

Kira let out a heavy sigh while he clicked the belt into place. "I'm so sorry I had to put you through this, David," she said. "But transcendent Kira made that choice. After that there was nothing I could do. She put the clueless half of me through a lot of turmoil as well."

Both of their tears had stopped flowing, but they were now on the giddy side. Desh gave her a lopsided smile. "So you only found out about all this yourself when you knew Matt had succeeded?"

"Yes. It was quite a shock, I can tell you. Memories that had been walled off, memories of actions I'd taken but didn't know about, came rushing back to me like a dam had burst. First I was stunned. Then I was actually pissed at myself for keeping it from me. And finally, I was euphoric. It had worked. Nuclear weapons had been disabled and global tensions were about to recede rather than advance. Hopefully becoming a thing of the past forever." She gazed lovingly into Desh's eyes once again and smiled. "But what made me the happiest was knowing I could finally tell you about the plan. As an integrated personality again. That we would be back together the way we had always been, before the plan put a strain on our relationship." Her jaw tightened. "But I never suspected Dutton would have the audacity to whisk you and Matt off *Copernicus* long before the dust had cleared."

Desh nodded. He had to admit that Dutton had done a good job of justifying the need for Matt to leave the ship immediately.

"When Jake called I was frantic," continued Kira. "It was supposed to be time to finally celebrate. Not to be fighting for our lives once again."

"Well, you came up with a brilliant strategy to get us back."

"Which couldn't have gone more wrong," noted Kira.

"You made the mistake of thinking that Eric Frey would be rational. Matt's story about the scorpion and the frog was exactly on target. But your plan to get us back was still brilliant. Like you said, it still would have worked, despite Frey's ambush, if he wouldn't have added hidden snipers to the mix. There's paranoia and then there's ridiculous."

"Well, given everything that blew up in our faces in the last month, figuratively and literally, there is a silver lining. Jake is now on our side. When we get back to headquarters, and Matt has recuperated a little longer, he can restore Jake's good name. Undo the evidence Dutton planted against him, and replace it with evidence against Dutton."

"When you say Jake's on our side, what does that mean? That he'll stop hunting us or actively *help* us?" At minimum, Desh was hopeful this would mean Seth Rosenblatt's family could return to their lives, along with the rest of his hexad.

"Actively help us. He practically *loves* you and Matt. I don't know what happened on the *Copernicus* but he raved about you both. I think he went from trying to kill the two of you to being willing to take a bullet for the two of you."

Desh paused to let this soak in. "Will you tell Jake the truth about the aliens?"

"No. No one can ever know. Ross, Matt, me, and you. That's it. At least for the next thirty or forty years. Hopefully someday the world will be more enlightened and we can think about revealing this as a hoax."

Desh's thoughts turned to Kira's encounter with van Hutten. "Anton kidnapped you because the alien ship was on its way. This was what finally tipped the scales for him. So when he had you in a straightjacket, weren't you tempted to tell him the truth?"

Kira shook her head. "I didn't know it myself at the time. My hidden personality monitoring the situation didn't see the need to fill me in. The plan was too important to jeopardize by disclosing to anyone who didn't need to know, including me. Even when my life might have been on the line."

Desh digested this sobering thought. "But what if you *had* been killed?"

"At that point the plan still would have succeeded. Matt and Ross would have seen to that."

Desh considered this. She was right. At that point she truly was expendable. Thank God it hadn't come to that. "And Jake is really willing to help us?"

"Wholeheartedly. He's well aware of the power of a boosted IQ, and sees us as the good guys for once. Not to mention, the best chance to prevent Armageddon, round two, in thirty-four years."

"Does he want to join the group?"

"No. We're far better off leaving him in place. He and his black-ops team will act as our clandestine security arm. And he'll make sure we get support from the highest levels of government. When he tells them that the great and powerful Matt, who now has a godlike reputation, is just an average one of us, they'll realize we're the best hope for Earth in the coming alien war."

"Right," said Desh with a broad grin. "The coming alien war."

"Instead of killing ourselves engaging in cloak and dagger activities to disguise what we're doing, we can be much more aboveboard. We can't be crazy about it, but we won't have to stress as much."

"But we've talked about having the government involved before," noted Desh. "And we've always decided this would be a bad idea."

"But now *everything* is different," explained Kira. "I'm letting Jake continue to think the longevity therapy doesn't exist. So no one will be after that. And with the alien threat looming, the government will leave us alone. We can come up with a story that we have to screen potential recruits for genetic compatibility with the therapy. That anyone not compatible will die if they're enhanced. So if someone in power tries to force himself on us, we can play that card."

Desh gazed at her in admiration. She had given this a lot of thought.

"And we'll have Jake's full support," she continued. "We'll be known at the highest levels of government as having saved the planet and working to do so again."

"Okay, I can see your point. This will definitely be a great help. But let me get back to the big picture for a moment. I agree that transcendent Kira's plan will get us all working together against a common threat. And that global tensions will be significantly reduced. And I get we won't have active nukes anymore. But doesn't it trouble you that the entire world will be working on even more powerful weapons? Weapons powerful enough to stop these fictitious aliens?"

"Transcendent Kira considered this carefully," she replied. "Yes, new weapons will be developed, but mankind will be on the same team. And strategists will realize immediately that weapons and defense aren't the answer, anyway. That speed and maneuverability *are*. A planet is the ultimate sitting duck, especially when you're trying to protect it from ships capable of moving at light speed, and able to arrive from any direction. The real answer is faster-than-light travel. We need to be able to meet the alien threat as far away from Earth as possible." She grinned. "Well, if the aliens actually existed, that is. We'd need to destroy them in interstellar space before they could get close to us. Strategists will realize that only faster-than-light ships—controlled by an artificial intelligence, and ramming the aliens, kamikaze style—will allow us to defeat the, um . . . fictitious enemy."

Desh whistled. "Wow, good thing for the aliens they don't really exist. I think you'd kick their asses." With a smile still on his face, he added, "And this dovetails perfectly with our goals. Yesterday, faster-that-light travel was Icarus's number one priority. Today, it's the number one priority of *all humanity*."

"Not bad icing on the cake, huh?" said Kira. "And remember, we already have the zero point energy drive.

We'll wait until we all think the world can handle it, and give Ross another decade or so to really understand it, and we can reveal it to the world. This will at least allow us to seed a few explorers to colonize other planets, ensuring our survival no matter what happens on earth."

"But won't these trips take thousands of years to complete?" asked Desh.

"From our perspective," replied Kira. "But because of relativity, they'll be far shorter for the passengers. Regardless, we still need faster-than-light travel to accomplish our ultimate goals. But if we're helped by the military rather than hindered by it, and can recruit with less fear of discovery, I'm convinced we'll get there."

Desh left his seat once again and he and his wife kissed hungrily, as if they had never kissed before. A foreshadowing of the hours of ravenous, frenzied lovemaking that would be their first order of business once they arrived at their destination and Ross was attended to.

They finally parted, and David Desh stared lovingly into the sparkling blue eyes of the woman he adored. He was now convinced that they would accomplish their goals, as well. As long as this remarkable woman was involved, all things were possible.

Kira had found a way to harness human passion for constructive, rather than destructive, purposes. To disarm the planet. To transform a warlike species, splintered into thousands of selfish tribes, into a single unit, eight billion strong. And in the process, she had saved humanity from itself; pulling it back from the edge of the abyss.

Desh grinned broadly. It was hard not to be optimistic. Kira Miller had reined in humanity's enormous capacity for self-destructive behavior.

Compared to this feat, faster-than-light travel seemed like *child's play*.

From the Author: Thanks for reading *AMPED!* If you enjoyed this book, I would love for you to consider reading my new novel, *The Cure*. And as always, if you enjoy any of my books, your help spreading the world is greatly appreciated. Finally, if you would like to stay current on my activities and work, please feel free to Friend me on Facebook at *Douglas E. Richards Author.*

Thanks again!

Doug

Novels Written by Douglas E. Richards

Adult

WIRED (SF/Technothriller)

AMPED (SF/Technothriller, Sequel to WIRED)

THE CURE (Standalone SF/Technothiller)

Middle Grade/YA (widely praised by kids and adults alike)

THE PROMETHEUS PROJECT SERIES (Science Fiction Thrillers)

Book 1: *TRAPPED*

Book 2: *CAPTURED*

Book 3: *STRANDED*

THE DEVIL'S SWORD (Mainstream Thriller)

ETHAN PRITCHER, BODY SWITCHER (Adventure)

OUT OF THIS WORLD (Sci-fi/Fantasy)